LIGHTS

Karen Swan is a *Sunday Times* Top Five bestselling writer. She is the author of twelve other novels, although she's been a writer all her life. She previously worked as an editor in the fashion industry but soon realized she was better suited as a novelist with a serious shopping habit. She is married with three children and lives in East Sussex.

Come to find her at www.karenswan.com, or Instagram @swannywrites, Twitter @KarenSwan1 and Facebook @KarenSwanAuthor.

Also by Karen Swan

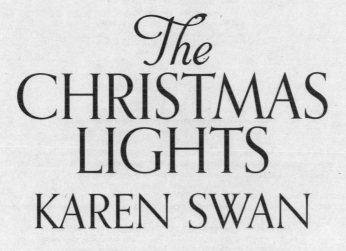

The CHRISTMAS LIGHTS

KAREN SWAN

PAN BOOKS

First published 2018 by Pan Books
an imprint of Pan Macmillan
20 New Wharf Road, London N1 9RR
Associated companies throughout the world
www.panmacmillan.com

ISBN (B) 978-1-5098-3808-0

Pan Macmillan does not have any control over, or any responsibility for,
any author or third-party websites referred to in or on this book.

3 5 7 9 8 6 4

A CIP catalogue record for this book is available from the British Library.

Typeset by Palimpsest Book Production Ltd, Falkirk, Stirlingshire
Printed and bound by CPI Group (UK) Ltd, Croydon, CR0 4YY

Visit **www.panmacmillan.com** to read more about all our books
and to buy them. You will also find features, author interviews and
news of any author events, and you can sign up for e-newsletters
so that you're always first to hear about our new releases.

For Cousin Alice and all you did for Mally.

Does the sun promise to shine?
No, but it will,
even behind the darkest clouds it will.
And no promise
will make it shine longer or brighter,
for that is its fate,
to burn until it can burn no more.
So, to love you is not my promise,
it is my fate,
to burn for you until I can burn no more.

Atticus (@atticuspoetry)
Instagram

Prologue

Lodal, Norway, 13 September 1936, 06.35

The horse stumbled over the rough ground, the air still thick with smoke as they breathlessly picked their way over the muddied rocks, their eyes continually drawn up to the desperate scene of devastation laid out before them.

Nothing was left. Every building had gone, even the grass had been ripped from the ground, trees lying on their sides, their exposed roots like claws. Furniture was smashed into kindling, a dead cow pinned under a boulder, its straight legs already stiffening as the sun climbed higher into the sky. A boat was improbably lodged in the branches of a distant tree, its prow tipping down. And the bodies – so many of them – lying inert and broken, still in their nightclothes.

A few survivors were staggering over the timber shards that had once been homes, their howls shattering the dawn silence as they tried to lift and clear the entire smashed village, searching for their children, their parents, their husbands and wives. Signy felt her heart breach her chest, knowing her own family was in there too, knowing they would have been in the front line, that they couldn't have survived – and yet her eyes scanning the detritus anyway, trying to find a marker that would indicate where their home had stood, showing her where they should start.

She heard a groan behind her and she turned. Margit was pushing, yanking, pulling the body off the saddle. The others tried to help but with a cry of rage that kept them back, she yanked it free. They watched as it slumped to the ground, broken and bloodied like everyone else. Margit stared at it for a moment, her chest heaving from the effort and emotion, before she picked up the horse's reins again and led them onwards into the destroyed village, not once looking back.

Chapter One

Upolu Island, Samoa, 4 December 2018

The sun was still a whisper in the sky, the heavy ocean at their backs rising and falling by degrees like a slumbering beast. The menacing swell that had both terrified and excited her last night as she watched the midnight storm, barefoot from her veranda, had subdued into sonorous rhythm again, becoming something more predictable, if still not tame.

The waves were no longer smashing against the rocks with furious violence but occasional splashes sprayed her legs and goosebumps bobbled over her bare skin as the ocean breeze came in regular breaths. With a shiver, she tied her long hair back in a ponytail and adjusted the strap on the mask. Sitting on the rock beside her, Zac was making the final checks on the camera, his muscles looking sculpted as if from marble in the weak grey, pre-dawn light. She could see his nervous excitement in the way he moved – sharp, alert, fine-tuned. He had slept well, as ever, undisturbed by the symphony of lightning flashes that had streaked and split the night sky, making it so hard for her to sleep.

A yawn escaped her. Now, though . . . what would she give to be back in their bed, the ceiling fan whirring above the teak four-poster, the mosquito nets a romantic cocoon that not so much kept the insects out, but the two of them in. The heaviness of sleep was still in her limbs, reluctant to be cast off, and she thought, right now, she would give all her worldly possessions – the whole rucksack of them – to swap this rockpool at her feet for another few hours in her cotton sheets.

That first step into its brisk embrace would be so hard, even though she knew the routine so well – a gasp, the clench of her muscles as the chill assailed her sleepy senses and then the release, the endorphin rush, and she would feel not only more awake than she did right now, but more alive. And that was the point, after all. It was always the point.

'Ready?' Zac asked, looking across at her, his mask and snorkel pushed back on his head, fins on, the waterproof camera poised on the selfie stick.

Bo smiled with more vim than she felt and nodded. 'Let's do this.' It was their catchphrase, the last thing they ever said to each other before they invariably held their breath and jumped, or leapt or ran or fell . . .

Gingerly, she rose to standing and adjusted the bottoms of her bikini – the red one; it always photographed better underwater – staring down into the sea. Only a light froth of smashed wave-tops laced the surface and she took several deep breaths, counting as she watched the waves ride in, finding the rhythm. She needed to jump at exactly the right point – too early and she would be hurled against the cliffs, too late and the ebb-water would be too shallow, dropping her onto the submerged rocks beneath.

With a deep breath, she leapt, arms outstretched, able to hear the click of the camera right up until the moment she hit the water and her own splash filled her ears, bubbles fizzing past her as she sank, her muscles gripped in sudden tension. And then she was rising again, the breath in her lungs a buoyancy aid that brought her bobbing to the surface, and as her face hit air again, she felt it – that moment of pure elation. Utter freedom. Total joy. Being alive.

Zac's splash came only a few moments after she surfaced – he wasn't one for hesitation – and together they kicked their fins with firm strokes, for there was (as they had been warned) a strong undertow, as they put on their masks.

'Readywhenyouare,' Zac said in an unintelligible babble, his snorkel already in. She nodded back, giving him the 'OK' hand signal they used on their scuba expeditions, and after several deep breaths she duck-dived down.

In an instant, the smash of breaking waves was replaced by a resonant wallow. It wasn't the sound of silence for there was too much activity and energy down there to allow that, but as she kicked and began to pass below the mighty cliffs, she felt the vulnerability and inconsequentiality of her life in this spectral watery dimension: one inhale and it would all be over; she was but forty seconds from death down here. That random group of air molecules that she had gulped in the moment before she dived was now solely responsible for preserving her life and, within it, all the memories and experiences of the life she had lived: the sound of her mother's laugh as she had run to her at the school gate; the heat of her father's huge hand enveloping hers on a frosty walk; the light in her brother's eyes as he'd cheated at cards and got away with it; the growing chill in his hands . . .

But the water slipped over her silkily and even with the undertow trying to pull her back out to the ocean, she was a strong swimmer and knew that any moment now the seal of water above her head would become a ceiling through which she could peer. They had researched this, they knew what to expect and what to do. They were adventurous but not reckless, that was what Zac always said. Sure enough, the domed underwater tunnel became suddenly angular, the water above her lidded and flat. With a hand raised cautiously above her head, she pushed through it and surfaced, blowing hard to clear the snorkel and taking several grateful breaths.

Zac was just behind her, the red light still flashing on the camera.

'Nice,' he said with an easy smile, looking around the long tunnel they now found themselves in. It was perhaps fifteen metres long, with roughly a thirty-centimetre drop from the rock ceiling to the water's surface. With their heads angled, they could breathe easily.

Bo kicked onto her back and floated, allowing the movement of the ocean to bob her about, using her arms and legs to push away from the sides.

'Hello,' Zac said, smiling as his echo reverberated up and down through the space like a pinball. . . . *ello . . . llo . . . lo . . . o . . .*

'I love you,' Bo called. *Love you . . . ve you . . . you . . .*

'Love you more!' Zac called back. . . . *ove you more . . . you more . . . more . . .*

'Yeah, you do,' she agreed with a grin, giving a sudden shriek as he swam over and tickled her underwater. She laughed, spinning and twisting on the spot.

'Always have. Always will.'

'Glad to hear it,' she grinned.

'You're supposed to say it back.'

'Am I?' she asked disingenuously, collapsing into laughter as he tickled her again, the sound of her laughter reverberating around them in amplification. 'Ah well. I wouldn't want you assuming anything.' She wrinkled her freckled, snub nose. 'Better to keep you on your toes.'

Zac watched her before he suddenly reached up, placing the flats of his palms on the ceiling, like he was Atlas lifting the world, his biceps flexed and gleaming as he used his fins to hold himself higher in the water. 'Marry me!' he called.

. . . arry me . . . rry me . . . me . . .

Bo's mouth dropped open. 'What?' she gasped. It was too quiet a sound to register an echo.

Zac grinned at her, his hands still above his head. 'I said . . . MARRY ME, BO LOXLEY!'

. . . arry me, Bo Loxley . . . me, Bo Loxley . . . Bo Loxley . . . Loxley . . . ley . . .

Bo gasped again, and then laughed, and then gasped again. Was he serious? Or just lost to the moment? Her legs were kicking furiously as she tried to tread water and comprehend what was happening. 'You want to *marry* me?' Still no echo, her voice was without shadow, making barely an impression in this watery channel.

'Of course I do,' he said, his eyes intense behind his mask, his voice suddenly thick with emotion. 'You're my soulmate. You and me, we were born to walk this earth together, baby. You're my family.'

'Oh, Zac.'

His eyes lit up, a half-cocked grin on his lips. '. . . So is that a yes?'

'Hell, yes it's a yes!' she cried, half laughing, half sobbing. 'YES!'

. . . Yes . . . Yes . . . es . . . es . . . sss . . .

'Wooooooohooooo!' he hollered, letting go of the ceiling at last and falling back into the water with a messy splash before swimming over to her again and grabbing her around the waist. He tried to kiss her but both their masks were too deep and even with their heads tilted at extreme angles, it was all

7

they could do to just about make very chaste lip contact. 'Let's get out of here. I need somewhere I can kiss you properly.'

'Yes,' she agreed, looking around them eagerly. At both ends of the tunnel, white light shone dimly, there was nothing to pick between either of them. 'Which way?'

'Uh . . .' Zac pivoted too. 'Hmm . . .'

In an instant, she felt the dark curtains of her old claustrophobia begin to drop. 'Zac . . .' Her voice felt breathy, the panic swooping down upon her like a black veil.

'It's okay, Bo. It's that way,' he said, pointing to the light behind her. 'We're swimming against the tide, remember?'

'Oh yes,' she said quietly, but the anxiety had already kicked in, her pulse spiking.

'You okay?' He was watching her.

'Of course. Let's do this.' She needed to get out of here. Now.

'Bo—'

. . . And putting her snorkel back in, she dived down again, feeling the pressure push against her ears almost immediately as she went slightly too deep, that hollow wallowy sound absorbing her as part of itself. Feeling the strength in her legs from the adrenaline burst, she kicked hard, her arms pushing against the water as though trying to part it. She travelled fast but within a few moments she knew she was swimming too hard for one breath – more effort meant more heartbeats, meant more oxygen. Up ahead, she could see the faint glow of light beginning to grow like a blooming white rose; pigment was beginning to intensify too, shades of aquamarine and celadon tinting the water as she headed for the light, a few small silver fish darting by the rocks, further away than they seemed.

Her lungs felt like they were inflating further with every

stroke, and she realized she should have travelled further along the tunnel on the surface before diving underwater again. Holding her breath for an extra fifteen metres was reckless. She glanced up but too late, she was beneath the cliffs once more; she couldn't surface here and the tunnel was too tight to turn, not to mention she would collide with Zac right behind her, the red light of the camera following her, always on her, like a shadow fish.

She swam on. The light, though closer, still seemed too far away, the instinct to let go of the breath now becoming a growing urge, the pressure in her lungs beginning to scream through her body as her arms and legs continued to propel her onwards. She was nearly there, five, maybe six, strokes away but she couldn't tell for certain, her vision was becoming spotted, her body fighting itself now. She couldn't hold on for much longer . . . She had to breathe—

Distantly, she felt an arm scoop round her like a belt, had the sensation of water moving over her more quickly and then, suddenly, air – like a slap upon her skin – making her gasp and choke.

'Bo?' Zac was holding her. She couldn't stop coughing. 'Bo, are you okay?' His voice was fractured, as though bits had been chiselled off it.

'What happened?' she managed, holding on to him, aware of a current pulling them back in the direction from which they'd come.

'You went limp, you were blacking out.'

'Oh.' Blankly, she could see now he was holding on to a rope. They had been told it had been put here precisely because of the strong undertow, pulling swimmers down and out towards the ocean tunnels. 'I'm sorry.'

'No. Don't be sorry.' He frowned, his handsome face

crumpled with worry and she could see for herself the fright she had given him. Holding her face in his hands, he kissed her tenderly. 'Why'd you go off so fast?'

What could she say? That she'd panicked? That it had taken only one moment of lowering her guard to spook her again? That it would never really be over, no matter how far she travelled or how brave she pretended to be? 'I just couldn't wait for that kiss you promised me,' she said instead.

In a single movement, Zac had both her and his masks off and he was kissing her properly this time, his body warm against hers even in the cool morning water. 'Tell me again you'll marry me.'

'I'll marry you, Zac Austen.'

His lips curved against hers in a smile as they kissed again, Zac holding the rope with one arm, his other looped around her waist. 'I had planned to ask you out here,' he said, indicating their new surroundings with a flick of his eyes. 'But I couldn't wait.' Together they both looked up and around them. The cave walls loomed up in a perfect circle thirty metres high, but where the ceiling should have been, there was a natural crater instead, the sky seemingly framed by the land. And even though they only had a small circle of it to view from here, it was a magnificent dawn, amber light flaming now like phoenix wings against the fast-receding indigo night.

'Holy shit,' Zac whispered, his Kiwi accent stronger than ever, as it always was when words weren't enough. 'It's even better than I thought it'd be.'

'Yeah,' Bo murmured, her body recovering from the fright and, grabbing the rope with one hand herself, allowing herself to float on her back again, the tow making her body drift. Giant green vines and creepers dangled along the walls and on one side a ramshackle no-rails ladder led down to a makeshift wooden platform. That was the entrance by which most tourists came and was precisely why she and Zac had come through the ocean tunnel. Those tourists were also the reason they had hauled themselves out of bed at the crack of sparrows, to have the place to themselves. Seclusion was their luxury.

Putting his mask back on, Zac plunged his head into the water again, looking down at the distant rocks and trying to identify the casually gliding fish. 'There's so many,' he said, surfacing briefly and looking like an excited child.

She smiled and watched as he disappeared completely below the surface, his arms like blades, the muscles in his back opening and closing with each stroke. He made swimming look effortless, as though he'd been raised as a pearl diver in Tahiti, and not an insurance salesman's son in Christchurch. The tide was going out but he reached the bottom easily, skimming along the pool bed on his stomach for a bit before turning over onto his back and waving up at her.

Even three metres down, he exuded the qualities that had drawn her to him like a magnetic charge: energy, positivity, boyish charm, adventurousness, curiosity, bloody gorgeous.

She waved back. That stunning, dynamic man was going to be her husband, her family, her home, and their life together would always be this: unpredictable, exciting and exotic.

Tragedy may have set her on this path but she was basking in rainbows now. Life was making it up to her. She was happy, she was loved. She was safe.

'I can't believe you didn't wait,' Lenny said, the beer bottle in his hand as he leant against the veranda, the Pacific Ocean a timpanic score over his shoulder. His lean frame, silhouetted against the sunset, looked like a gnarled and knotted piece of the driftwood that had been used to make the beach shack, his wavy, dark hair a good two inches longer since they'd been here so that it now rested on his shoulders, reinforcing his 'surf bum' vibe. But then, they had all grown feral-looking and thin here, their eyes bright against skin that was now as dark as tanned hides.

'Couldn't,' Zac grinned, tightening his arm around her shoulders and squeezing, making the hammock rock slightly. It was stretched out from the decking area jutting over the beach, or rather the water when the tide came in. 'It just burst out of me, there was no stopping it. I was lost to the moment, bro.' He reached over and kissed her again.

Bo beamed, resting her head on his shoulder and looking out to sea happily. They had swum and dived in the hidden lagoon until the first of the daytrippers turned up, Lenny recording it all – as ever – from his perch at the top of the cliffs. But then they had gone off plan, stealing a few private hours to celebrate by themselves by hiding out of shot and sneaking away from the lagoon. Bo didn't know how long it had taken for Lenny to realize they had left him there, but when he had returned to the beach he had knocked at their door intermittently for hours, she and Zac giggling under the bed sheets as they waited for his footsteps to retreat again. They didn't feel bad about it – Lenny wasn't usually at a loose end for long, women loved him.

'Well, it's great and all that shit – you're two crazy, free, very photogenic spirits. But you've left us with a problem now that there's no footage.' As their official photographer, Lenny's life was ruled by 'footage' and 'material' and his every waking thought was dominated by 'hits' and 'engagement rates'; he was the one taking the insouciant couple shots where she and Zac lay, legs entwined, gazing at a sunset or a rainbow, or of her piggybacking her fiancé on a mountain ridge or a pink sand beach.

'What do you mean?' Bo asked, lifting a bare leg and lazily wrapping it around Zac's. Her thighs were freckled from so long in the sun; they had been travelling through the South Pacific for four months now and northern hemisphere concepts of snow, coats and fires seemed almost cartoonishly ridiculous and unreal.

'Well, proposing in an underground ocean tunnel might be romantic but I don't suppose you thought to film it, did you?' he asked Zac.

Zac pulled an apologetic grimace. 'Sorry, dude, I turned it off automatically when we surfaced. Like I said, I didn't actually know I was going to do it there and then. I had planned to ask on the platform, like we'd discussed.'

Bo wriggled slightly to look at his face. He and Lenny had discussed it?

Lenny gave an irritated sigh, then shrugged. He was well used to Zac's spontaneity. 'It's fine, we'll just have to come up with something else, that's all. And fast, given that tomorrow's our last full day here.'

'What do you mean come up with something else?' Bo frowned.

'It's no biggie. Zac can just propose again, can't you, Zac?'

'Sure.'

'You mean, like a mock proposal?' she asked.

'Yeah, sort of. Zac can redo it the way he should have done – with *me* there getting it all on film – but you've got to look surprised.'

'So you want me to act? We're faking our engagement?' she asked incredulously.

'Hey, chill, it's not fake. You guys are doing all this anyway. It's just a matter of having something to show the followers.'

'But it's a *private* moment, Lenny. One of our only ones. I don't want to share it.'

'I don't see how you can't when you've got 9.4 million people emotionally investing in your life together.' Lenny shrugged. 'They're gonna feel pretty cheated if you just drop the E bomb on them but shut them out of all the excitement and drama.'

She looked up at Zac. 'You don't agree with this, do you?'

'Well no, but—'

'There's so little that's actually just ours. We share almost everything about our lives. I want to keep this as our private thing.'

'I totally agree, baby.' Zac kissed her again. 'It was our moment.'

Was it though? He had already discussed it with Lenny – set it up for the perfect shot, seemingly. 'I assumed you asked me down there because it was just about the only place we could go where Lenny wasn't,' she murmured, resting her head on Zac's chest and looking up at him.

'– I did,' Zac said.

'– Thanks!' Lenny huffed at the same time.

'You know I don't mean it like that, Len,' she said, looking over at him. 'But you've got to see it from our point of view; when are Zac and I ever truly alone? Sometimes a moment is ours, and it's not available to the rest of the world just because it'll get good hits.'

'Now that's just being naive,' Lenny said, swigging another gulp of beer. 'I get that you want to keep this private, Bo, but the reality is there's always a picture frame around your life. You don't get the population of a small country watching you by accident. It's design. It's why you hire me . . . Unless you're saying you don't need me?'

'Hey, hey, no. Bo didn't mean that,' Zac said quickly. 'We both know what you've done for the brand since coming on board. I guess . . .' He sighed. 'I guess I can see it from both points of view. Bo wants to keep our engagement private – as do I. But Lenny can see the followers are gonna be hacked off if we just present them with a fait accompli.' He narrowed his eyes thoughtfully, pulling his arms away from around Bo's shoulders and sitting himself in a crossed-leg position on the hammock. He ran a hand through his buzzcut, his dark eyes like hot coals as an idea came to him. 'But you know what, the more I think about it, the more I think Lenny's got the right idea.'

'Zac!'

'No, no, hear me out,' he said, holding his hands up. 'You want us to keep our moment sacred. Special, right? Well, if we mock up a fake proposal, we can do exactly that. Everyone will think they've shared it with us, but we – you and me, baby – we'll know the real truth: where it happened, when, how . . . No one else will know the details and, that way, it can remain ours, completely private.'

Bo stared at him. She supposed there was a twisted logic to it.

'Exactly!' Lenny said, looking pleased he had an ally, even though Zac always seemed to side with him in the end. 'And I can guarantee you'll get a massive spike in engagement on this. If we run the video as a story, we're looking at three million views, easy. And then we'll spool the shots out over the squares for several days and that should be, what – five million likes, I'm guessing?'

'Great,' Zac shrugged. 'So what's the plan?'

'Well, we can go back tomorrow morning and do it all over again—' Lenny suggested.

'No!' Bo said, a little too quickly. 'I don't . . .' She didn't want to go back in the tunnel again. 'I don't want it to be in the same place. If we're going to do this, then it has to be somewhere completely different. I don't want a single element of the fake engagement to overlap with the real thing.'

'Well that's easy enough,' Zac said with his easy smile and warm eyes. 'We can do it on the next stop, then. Norway's about as different to this as you can get.'

Bo considered for a moment. He was right – Samoa and Norway couldn't be more diametrically opposed to one another. Hot, cold. Beach, mountains. Summer, winter. Nothing about a second proposal there would seep into and stain their special moment together. And yet . . . She bit her lip. 'I know it makes sense in principle; it just still feels wrong somehow.'

'Hey, no. It's the perfect solution – we're giving the followers what they want, whilst keeping the real thing for ourselves. Private. Ours. You get me?'

She smiled, seeing the intimacy in his eyes. 'Yeah. I get you.'

One of their unspoken moments exploded between them, making the air crackle, and he crawled over the netting towards her again.

'No. Wait!' Lenny said quickly, knowing exactly what was going to happen. 'Before you . . . Listen, we've got to talk about tomorrow,' he said urgently. 'Seeing as it's our last day and we've got to get over to the sliding rocks in Papaseea first thing. I got a driver picking us up at four . . . Guys? *Guys?*'

Chapter Two

Alesund, Norway, three days later

'Holy *mother*,' Zac hissed, rubbing his arms around his shoulders in the freezing temperatures as they followed the receptionist up the steps to their suite – an upgrade Lenny had negotiated for them with one mention of their social media following. It had a fjord view, four-poster and a balcony, but the suites were also in a separate building from the rest of the hotel and, right now, even a two-minute walk through the polar chill in shorts and T-shirts was two minutes too long.

'You have come from far?' the receptionist asked, putting the key in the lock.

'The South Pacific,' Bo smiled tiredly.

'Oh my,' the woman replied in surprise. 'That is very far.'

'Yes. We've been travelling for over thirty hours now.'

The door opened and they walked into a blonde-wood entry hallway, an umbrella hanging from a hook on the wall, a vast armoire making barely an impression in the large space. A colourful woven mat stretched the length of the hall and a door to the left led to the bathroom. They followed the woman into the main room and Bo thought she might collapse in relief at the sight of the giant floor-to-ceiling cabin

17

bed: painted matt black and dressed with a fluffy white duvet, woollen blankets and a cloud of pillows, she had never seen such a welcome sight.

'Your bags were sent ahead,' the receptionist said, indicating the two suitcases on the luggage stands, and Bo gave a silent note of thanks to Lenny. For all their clashes about boundaries and what not to share, he always kept the wheels on their never-ending roadshow, making sure visas were in place, transfer transport arranged and that they were upgraded at every possible opportunity, as well as having the right clothes shipped to their new destinations. This was what they called their basic 'winter pack': jeans, underwear, base layers, T-shirts, jumpers and boots. Lenny had dropped off most of their summer kit – beach clothes and swimwear – to local charities as they made their way to the airport and sent the remainder back to their Left Luggage storage in London. She and Zac liked to travel light, both mentally and physically. They didn't own more than they could carry – not a home, not a car, not a dog – and whatever earnings were left over from funding their next adventure went straight into a joint account.

'I hope he remembered the crampons,' Zac said, walking over and unzipping their trusty giant yellow North Face bags. Bo smiled at the mere sight of them and his coiled ropes; they had become symbols of their wintry escapes.

'There was also a separate delivery for you,' the receptionist said, pointing to several taped boxes stacked beside the wardrobe.

'Great.' Bo knew it would be the merchandise from their new sponsors. Ridge Riders were a small Norwegian-based company looking to make the leap from being known as just a technical mountain kit brand – for skiing, hiking and climbing

– to the sexier athleisure market. They wanted to be Nike, North Face, Napapijri, and they were convinced that hooking up with Zac and Bo was the way to achieve it.

'If there's anything else . . . ?' the receptionist asked.

'No, thank you,' Bo said. 'This looks awesome.'

'Dinner is served till nine thirty. Please feel free to come to the drawing room for drinks beforehand.'

'Okay,' Bo nodded, looking longingly at the bed. They had travelled on four planes in the past thirty hours – flying from Samoa to Sydney, and then on to Oslo via Doha, before catching a local flight to Alesund – and she knew they would both be awake at two in the morning, regardless of the age-old advice to shift their routine to local hours and stay awake for as long as they could.

The door closed behind the receptionist with a soft click and Zac went over to one of the boxes, opening it with the edge of the bottle opener on the nearby media cabinet. 'How much are they paying us again?' he quipped, pulling out polythene-bagged heaps of labelled clothing and equipment in bright colours and waterproof fabrics that looked harsh to Bo's eye. After several months of drifting about in swimwear and sun-bleached cotton and linens, they looked artificial and the padded shapes comically outsize.

Bo watched as he shrugged on an orange soft-shell jacket over his T-shirt and zipped it up, her tanned and bare-chested free-diver transforming in an instant to a mountain tourer. But then he was all those things. All those men. 'It looks great,' she smiled.

'You'll look great in this,' he said, holding up an insulated butter-yellow hooded parka with furry trim. 'That'll shoot really well.'

'Mmm.' Bo collapsed on the bed and closed her eyes. She

didn't care about what would look good in a photograph right now.

'No, no, don't sleep,' he grinned, tossing the jacket on the suitcase and launching himself onto the bed, straddling her. 'You know full well we've got to stay awake until at least ten o'clock.'

'But I'm too tired,' she mumbled as he began nuzzling her neck.

'No you're not. I'm going to get the shower going for you. That'll wake you up. Then we'll explore the place and *then* we'll come back here and finish this . . .' He kissed her once on the tip of her nose and jumped off the bed again. Rolling her head to the side and watching his puppyish lope out of sight, she wondered where his endless energy came from. They lived the same days, doing the same things, and yet she was always dropping into bed by the end of the day whereas he could, it seemed, just push on through.

A knock at the door made her close her eyes in frustration. 'Come in, Lenny,' she called without even having to check. It would be him. It was always him. She and Zac were never just a couple, but a trio. He was there at every meal, on every walk, always in the next room, and his knock at the door was as identifiable to her as Zac's tread on the floorboards.

Lenny was their friend, naturally – it was inevitable, and frankly vital, when they spent so much time together – but as the third spoke in their wheel, his constant presence inevitably changed things. In the three years that he had been working for them, his role had tacitly evolved into something more managerial than the photographer they'd originally hired, a role that had become a necessity once their following had got to a certain size. What started as a personal lifestyle and travel mission for both her and Zac, had – once they had fallen in love and blended their brands – become a global juggernaut and they were now the beacons for honeymooners wanting the most romantic, secluded getaways; first-footers for the adrenaline-junkies searching for their next fix; models for the clothing and lifestyle brands that wanted to be associated with their free-spirited lives. Critical mass now meant they were paid to do all the things and visit all the places and wear all the clothes they would have wanted to anyway. In essence, they were being paid just to lead their lives and she knew they were incredibly privileged. She knew that. But recently she had begun to feel the balance had shifted and that the loss of privacy was becoming absolute. She kept trying to ring-fence areas of her and Zac's life that she didn't want to share but every day the public gaze somehow nudged a little closer to their feet.

But it wasn't Lenny's fault, she knew that. He was a good guy, just doing his job – a job that meant considerable sacrifice on his part as he had to subsume his own life to theirs. In spite of the generous salary they paid him and the global travel opportunities that were one of the main perks of the job, there was no way he could sustain a home life or a relationship when he spent eleven months of the year on the road with them. Not many people would be prepared to do that. And besides, she knew Zac was grateful for his company and equally gung-ho spirit when it came to setting up and shooting the extreme stunts he was known and famed for.

She opened her eyes to find Lenny standing by the side of the bed. He had changed out of the black Metallica tour T-shirt he had travelled in and was wearing the Pink Floyd Dark Side of the Moon one; Bo had joked that his collection of vintage rock tees justified an Instagram following of its own. 'Tired?'

'Yeah,' she sighed, curling herself up off the mattress and dropping her head in her hands. 'I just want to sleep but Zac's insisting we explore the place first.'

'He's right,' Lenny said, turning and walking over to the drinks tray set up on a cabinet. He tonged a couple of cubes of ice into a glass and poured her some sparkling water. 'Drink up. Rehydration will help.'

'Thanks.' His role was a fluid one: sometimes photographer, sometimes logistics and tour manager, other times mother. She took it from him and dutifully sipped, just as Zac walked back in, a towel around his hips, his tanned skin damp and warm.

'Len, how's your room?' he asked.

'Great. View of a tree.' Len had a deadpan delivery that would have made Eeyore proud.

Zac laughed. 'Helluva pretty tree, I bet though.'

'Yeah.'

'Babe, the water's hot,' Zac said to her.

'Thanks. I'm going to wash my hair,' she sighed, pulling out her long plait and shaking her hair free. She got up from the bed and walked into the bathroom, her hand trailing lightly over Zac's bare stomach as she passed. He grabbed her hand and kissed her wrist, before letting her go again with a wink.

'In which case, we'll see you in the main house, shall we?' he called after her. If there was one thing Zac was no good at, it was sitting around waiting. He always had to be doing something.

'Sure thing,' she mumbled, disappearing into the plumes of steam already escaping from the bathroom.

It was over an hour later before she was ready. Twenty minutes had been spent just standing under the running water, feeling her tired muscles begin to ease from the stiffness of the long-haul flight. Flatbeds were all very good in theory but she could still never sleep over the sound of the crew slamming doors and clattering about in the galley.

She stared at her reflection in the full-length mirror: long blonde hair half pulled back in a messy topknot, the rest hanging down her back in tousled waves; turquoise beaded hoop earrings from a street market in Bali; black skinny jeans ripped at the knee, old-school Vans and a chunky black cashmere Gucci rollneck she had treated herself to, en route at Doha airport. Her ultra-tanned skin looked incongruous against the all-black outfit, calling her out as an interloper, broadcasting that she was just passing through . . .

Shrugging on the new yellow jacket, she headed over to the main lodge. The air outside, on the brief walk over, had a purity and emptiness to it that registered like a slap. During their months in the Pacific, she had grown accustomed to the heavy, salty tang of the sea air, the constant hushing of the ocean an ever-present lullaby at her ear. But here, it was the very absence, the vacuum of both sound and smell, that set her senses ringing. She was acutely aware of the crunch of her own footsteps on the snow-dusted paths and she stopped for a moment to absorb the utter silence, twitching her nose like a hare as the cold stung at her cheeks. On the embankments, a heavy hoar frost was already stippling the grass so that tiny crystals glinted like diamonds in the early evening moonlight.

She passed by the windows of the hotel, the scenes held within their frames like little amber-veneered vignettes of lives being well lived as various groups of friends sat in fireside chairs, some playing backgammon, others drinking and reaching for cakes stacked on an ottoman. The buzz of conversation and staccatos of laughter escaped the building like the puffs of smoke from the chimney as doors opened and closed intermittently, couples heading back to their rooms or coming in for dinner. The Christmas season was already underway – white lights traced the roof apexes, candles flickered at every window and red-ribboned eucalyptus wreaths were nailed to the doors.

Bo entered, unable to resist a giant shiver as the warmth and glow of an open fire in the entrance hall enveloped her like a hug. The room smelled of pine and cinnamon cloves; two high-backed tartan chairs were occupied by an older couple reading the newspapers.

She walked through the dining room, where a long table had been set up down the centre of the room, seemingly for a large group, and into the drawing room she had passed outside only a moment before. One wall was flanked by library shelving, an enormous fireplace set opposite it on the other side. A group of slick-looking Oslo-ites was monopolizing the sofas in the centre of the room, laughing uproariously every few minutes. Zac and Lenny were sitting in a couple of club chairs by the far corner, both listening intently to a woman who was perched daintily beside them on a tartan ottoman.

Bo couldn't see her properly from behind, she had her back to the room, but her long glossy caramel hair glistened prettily in the firelight, and Bo could tell just from the guys' rapt expressions that she was attractive.

'Hey,' she said, coming to stand by Zac's chair and wondering where she could sit given that all the other chairs were taken.

'Hey!' Zac said, his eyes brightening as he saw her and pulled her down onto his lap. 'I was just about to come back and get you. Check you hadn't gone to bed after all.'

'No. I was just doing my hair.'

'Mmm,' he sighed, immediately burying his face in her mane – her freshly washed hair was his favourite smell; it didn't matter that he was mid-conversation with the woman, nor did he care who was watching; she had learnt long ago that it was impossible to embarrass him.

'Hi, I'm Bo,' she said politely to the woman who was looking on with a warm smile. As she had suspected, she was striking to look at but Bo couldn't decide whether she was simply pretty or in fact beautiful. Seemingly tall and athletic, she had a prominent bone structure that was almost masculine on the one hand – oval-shaped face, low hairline, sharp brows – and yet was offset by a pout mouth and lively, round hazel eyes.

'Bo, it is such a pleasure to meet you. I'm Anna Rem, marketing head at Ridge Riders,' she said, half rising from her perch to reach over a handshake. 'I've been counting down the days to this. We are so excited you've teamed up with us.'

'Oh, well that's lovely of you to say so,' Bo replied, slightly puzzled; she had no recollection of a meeting with Ridge Riders being booked in here. 'But the pleasure is all ours. We love your stuff.' As if to prove the point, she tugged the jacket closed.

'You look just stunning in that,' Anna sighed. 'We knew the colour would be perfect against your hair. You know our designers had you in mind when they first sketched it?'

'I *didn't* know that,' Bo smiled, feeling flattered as she shrugged it off and hung it from the hood on one of the 'wings' of the armchair.

'Oh yes. You two are our dream couple.' She looked across at Zac too. 'You embody everything our brand stands for: natural beauty, adventure, grit, strength, power, integrity.'

'Stop, you'll make Zac's head explode,' Bo quipped, trying to mask her embarrassment at such fawning. 'He's already quite pleased enough with himself as it is.'

'Ooh,' Lenny laughed, sucking his breath through his teeth and throwing Zac an amused look. His camera swung from his neck like a lanyard from one of his beloved concerts and Bo was quite convinced if he wasn't their photographer, he'd have been on the road with a band instead.

'So, are you staying here too?' Bo asked.

'No, our offices are based in Alesund, where you flew into earlier. I've only come over tonight to say welcome and to touch base with you, make sure everything's okay here?'

'Oh, absolutely, we've been through the clothes already and they're great. Everything fits,' Bo said. 'And this place is gorgeous. It's making me feel Christmassy already,' she said, looking across at the giant Norwegian spruce tree in the corner. 'It's hard to feel festive on a white sand beach.'

'Speak for yourself,' Zac tutted. 'I'm a Kiwi. Sunny Christmases are my shtick.'

'It's the one thing we shall never agree on,' she smiled at Anna. 'But this is a great start to our Norwegian adventure. I only wish we could stay here for more than a night.'

'Uh-uh-uh,' Zac said, bouncing her on his knee slightly. 'That's against the rules.'

'Rules that *we* put in place, Zac,' she said, tapping his nose playfully. 'We can bend them if we want. It wouldn't be a disaster to spend a couple of days recovering from the journey in comfort.'

'Rules?' Anna queried.

'We only stay in hotels for transfers, when we're on the road. And we never endorse them either,' Zac explained. 'The fans love that we integrate ourselves in the fabric of the places where we live. You can only ever be a tourist in a hotel and that's everything we're *not* about. Authenticity. That's our vibe. Going native.'

'Ah, of course – hence the shelf farm,' Anna smiled, agreeing eagerly. 'The fans will love it. Guaranteed.'

Bo suppressed a groan. They weren't so much going native as going wild – according to the photos she'd seen, the shelf farm was a tiny cluster of rickety wooden buildings clinging to a narrow ledge halfway up a fjord-side mountain. It had cold running water, walls, a roof and that was about it.

'I still don't think it's a cardinal sin to enjoy a couple of nights being looked after,' she muttered. 'That journey was brutal. I'd do anything for a massage.'

'Anything?' Zac asked, reaching up and kissing her on the cheek.

She rolled her eyes, swatting at him, but from the corner of her eye she could see Lenny was snapping away and that their work had begun – a few hours in and they were already upholding their end of the $200,000 deal: her sitting on Zac's lap, fireside, their jackets hanging from each wing of the chair . . . She could practically predict which filter he'd apply.

'It's funny seeing you both in proper clothes again,' Lenny said, stopping to look down at the screen and scrolling back through the shots.

'I know,' Bo said, looking down at Zac and taking in his grey-black jeans, boots, and a chunky knitted brown and cream Norwegian folk sweater – no doubt an ironic joke intended by Lenny but Zac still rocked it. 'I think we all stick out a bit with our tans though. There's such a thing as being *too* brown.'

'Not at all. It makes you look very glamorous,' Anna said.

Bo reached down to take Zac's drink off the coffee table.

'Mmm, what's this? It's good,' she said, sipping from the highball glass.

'Polar-bjork, gin and tonic water.'

'Polar-bjork?' she frowned. 'What's that?'

'Birch essence,' Anna supplied, reaching for the English translation easily.

'It's so good – really . . . aromatic,' she said, trying it again.

'I know, right?' Zac agreed. 'Even Lenny likes it.'

'Better than Aperol,' he shrugged. 'Still worse than beer.'

Anna laughed and Lenny looked pleased that his joke had found a receptive audience. His eyes lingered on her for a moment as though he too was trying to decide whether she was pretty or beautiful.

Bo relaxed back against Zac, swinging one leg idly. The large group on the sofas had quietened down a bit; in fact, most of them were on their phones. 'So – anyone ready for dinner? I'm starved.'

'Just about. We were hammering out the last details for tomorrow,' Zac said, squeezing her knee.

'Oh yeah?' Her spirits sagged again at the thought of more travelling. At moving on. She looked across at Lenny – their logistics coordinator – waiting for the itinerary.

'We're heading down the fjord tomorrow.' He glanced at Anna. 'Storfjorden – is that it? Am I saying it right?'

'Very good,' she nodded and Bo saw the spark flash between them.

'So we're going down the fjord road en route to Gerainger, which will be our new base. Now because we'll be driving, we won't get much actual fjord action; Anna was saying most of the roads go via mountain tunnels—'

'That is right. Between the mountains and the lakes, travel

around here is difficult. No railways can get here so the tunnels, bridges and ferries are all part of the road networks.'

'There'll still be some good viewpoints from the roads in some places though; Anna's been marking them for us on the map,' Lenny said. 'Plus the valleys on the other side of the fjords should be pretty dramatic in themselves, so if we get any height, they'll shoot well as backdrops. Just dress warm. We're gonna be in and out of the car all day—'

'Well that's not going to be a problem,' Bo said, smiling at Anna again. 'It's so good of you to have come over here like this. You've been so helpful. We'll make sure to get some really great footage for you.'

The deal was simple enough: $200,000 for a fortnight's collaboration – they would post at least one image per day on both her and Zac's Instagram grids, plus video footage in the stories and some joint images on their blog. It was to be subtle, nothing too overt or showy, but getting the logo in as often as was naturally possible was preferable.

'Well I can hopefully be of more help to you when I join you properly the day after tomorrow.'

Bo's eyebrows shot up. 'Huh?'

'At the farm. I'll be staying there with you.' She hesitated at the sight of Bo's expression. 'Didn't you know?'

Bo looked across at Zac. She had thought the company were simply sending over the product and leaving them to it; that was how they usually worked. They had always agreed that if these endorsements were to have any integrity, then independent curation was crucial. 'No—'

'Yeah you did,' Zac said, patting her thigh heartily. 'Remember Ridge Riders are picking up the tab at the farm? So in exchange for that, Anna's just going to hang out with us in the run-up to Christmas.'

Bo blinked. Christmas was a fortnight away. And this was the first she had heard of it. Zac and Lenny always negotiated the small print and T&Cs but why were they changing the usual arrangements? They could afford to rent the farm. Why give up editorial control for that?

'This two weeks coming up is our most crucial trading period so we really want to make sure we maximize our opportunities with you guys,' Anna said apologetically. 'But don't worry, I won't be directing you or anything like that. I'm just an observer more than anything. We already know you know how to communicate to your followers.'

'. . . Okay,' Bo said benignly. But she couldn't help but feel unsettled. Upset even. Now they would go from being a trio to a quartet? There would be yet another person watching them, shadowing them, sharing the experiences that were supposed to be exclusive to them as a couple? How ironic, she thought, that the business of showing their simple life together required a small team to convey it.

Anna shot an awkward look to Lenny, as though he was already an ally.

Bo looked away and was startled to find the group at the next table watching them, a couple of the girls photographing them on their phones. It made her flinch to realize the lenses were trained upon her like sniper eyes.

Realizing they'd been rumbled, the group quickly dropped their phones down, but it was too late. They had been listening, snooping, eavesdropping . . .

A dark-haired girl, seeing the shock on Bo's face, quickly got up and rushed over. 'We're so sorry. We didn't mean to intrude. But it's just . . . well, you guys *are* Zac and Bo, right?'

'Yeah, that's right,' Lenny grinned from the armchair. 'You follow Wanderlusters?'

'Are you kidding? Who *doesn't*?' the girl laughed, looking back at Bo with a look of unabashed admiration. 'We are totally obsessed with you guys. I just *live* for your stories. Oh my God, I can't believe you're here. That this is actually you.' For a moment, Bo thought the girl was going to pinch her just to check. 'I don't . . . I don't suppose you'd pose for a selfie with me, would you?'

There it was – the S-word. It was ironic, Bo always thought, that the very thing that had made her and Zac Insta-famous was the one thing she now sought desperately to avoid. She had learnt from experience – somewhere around the four million mark – that once one person had clocked them and asked for a picture, everyone else would do the same and things would quickly descend into chaos. Two years ago, when they had been in Tokyo to open a flagship store for a brand they had promoted, they had been spotted wandering off-duty in a back street. One fan had led to ten, to a hundred, until the police had had to close off the street to control the crowds. In the police car back to the hotel, Zac had thought it had been incredible; she'd been terrified.

She supposed the same couldn't be said of here though. It was quiet enough and no one else in the hotel seemed to recognize them; or if they did, they didn't care. 'Sure she will,' Zac agreed, jiggling Bo off his lap. 'Go on, babe.'

Bo smoothed her hair off her shoulders as the girl got her phone ready. She held the camera out in front of them but Bo reached up and automatically angled it to look down on them from above. 'More flattering,' she smiled, the girl looking at her as though she'd pronounced a great philosophical truth.

'And one with Zac?' the girl asked, as soon as the shutter clicked.

Bo took a breath and turned around to her fiancé. Wasn't it

ever thus? One photo became two, became all their friends wanting one too . . .

'Sure,' he beamed, jumping up to join them and throwing an easy arm over the girl's shoulder. If he was aware of how good he looked in that sweater he didn't show it, and the girl looked like she might faint with joy as he pressed his stubbled cheek to hers and said 'cheese'.

'Thanks,' the girl said.

'No problem,' Bo said, straightening up, wanting to get to their dinner table now. 'It's lovely meeting you. Have a great stay—'

'Hey, would you all like a photo?' Lenny asked, putting down his glass and reaching out towards the group for their phones.

Bo looked over at him in astonishment.

'Ohmigod, are you sure?' a couple of them chorused.

'Sure. I'm their official photographer, this is what I do. It's no bother, right, guys?'

Chapter Three

Lodal, June 1936

The track underfoot was soft from all the recent rain, deep puddles making the horses stumble occasionally and the butter churns clatter on their backs. Signy could feel the mud splatter along the hem of her dress as she darted on and off the path in a sort of dance, herding back the goats that strayed too far with a cry of *'hei'* and an outstretched lunge with her stick. But she felt as they did – yearning to roam, giddy with excitement; they had been released from the winter barns three weeks ago in order to become lightly reacquainted with the heady freedoms of outdoor grazing again, but this was the real point, what they'd all been waiting for. The *buføring*, when they brought the animals from the farm to the outfield pastures, was the mark of summer proper. It was to be her first season and she felt like she had been waiting for it her whole life. She ought to have gone the year before, having turned thirteen, but a broken leg incurred by jumping from one of the hayricks had put paid to that and she had had to look on as her sister Margit and their friends wound up the mountain paths without her in a cacophony of cowbells and clanging pots.

All her childhood she had listened, rapt, to the stories she heard from the older girls about their summers as *seterbudeias*, or milkmaids. The work was hard, there was no doubting it – long days spent tending and milking the herds, churning butter, making soured cream and cloudberry jam, grass-cutting and hay-tossing. But if hard labour was the price, freedom was the reward: nights spent under bright skies and evenings around fires; bathing in the stream; midday sleeping on the rocks; and there would be no grown-ups to boss her about. No Mamma to make her wash the stockings; no Pappa to send her to collect firewood. Yes, the farmhands would come by once a week to take the dairy produce they had made back to the farm where they would be stored in the *stabbur*, or storehouse, for winter; they would check the girls were okay, happy, well and in good health. They would bring news from the village and perhaps some treats too: flatbreads or fresh herrings. But apart from that, the summer would be theirs. Just her and her sister and their friends and the animals.

Their long, jangling procession was making steady progress, everyone moving with a kinetic energy as they reclaimed the mountain heights that had been closed off and impassable during the winter months. Patches of snow still clung to the highest peaks but they were ragged and torn now, like old, dirty skirts.

They had been walking for an hour already and she turned to look back, wanting to get a last glimpse of the village, a home she had never left before and now wouldn't see again till the leaves began to redden and curl and a blue chill crisped the air. But already there wasn't much to make out from this height. At 1,850 metres, the bushy *torvtak* roofs meant the cottages all but blended into their surroundings and it was only the grey wisps puffing from the chimney stacks and white sheets flapping on her mamma's clothes lines that caught the eye.

Feeling free, she tilted her face to the sky and stretched her arms out wide as a warm wind wrapped itself playfully around her, lifting even her boyish bob off her neck. This was it. She was finally on her way. After seemingly endless weeks of drizzle and the mists lying low in the valleys, the sky had tidied itself up at last, parcelling up the clouds to reveal the mountains' sharp angles once more. She caught sight of the pale speckled underbelly of a gyrfalcon wheeling high above them, hunting for lemmings, voles or shrews in the long grass.

'Signy, come! Stop stopping,' Margit called from her position at the head of the line. At seventeen, she was the joint-eldest girl but as the farmer's daughter too, that made her the most senior member of their group. Sofie didn't like it. Two inches taller and three weeks older than Margit, she felt that she should be the leader. That she was also commonly regarded as the village beauty reinforced her high opinion of herself; it somehow seemed to give her a status above her own low birth. Signy had noticed since early childhood that the first – and pretty much only – thing people said when talking about Sofie was her looks, be they gushing about her long raven hair or her pale blue eyes as though it somehow brought acclaim on them too. They never seemed to mention that she always forgot to close the goat pens or that she took more than her share of lunch. And besides, there was something in the set of her mouth that made Signy feel cold.

But Margit didn't see it. She and Sofie had grown up side by side, sharing chores on the farm, sitting together with their slates in the small schoolhouse, sharing secrets as they churned the butter or tossed the hay; and besides, Margit was always at pains to minimize anything that reinforced Sofie's lower status as the cotter's daughter. It was her sweet, generous sister who kept the peace, even today, when Margit should have been riding on horseback; it was an honour reserved for the chief *seterbudeia* but Margit had seen the twist in Sofie's lips as the rest of the townsfolk had waved and cheered them off – her, as the figurehead – and as soon as they had made the first turn out of sight, she had insisted Sofie take her place instead.

'But the gyr – do you see it?' Signy asked, pointing to the bird just as it suddenly dropped into a horizontal pursuit, speeding over the ground and gaining on the prey that would never be able to outrun it.

'I see it,' Margit smiled patiently. 'But I also see Stormy taking herself back to the valley.'

Signy turned sharply. Sure enough, Stormy, named after her grey-cloud colouring, had wandered off the track and was picking a nimble path down the steep-sided grassy slope. And as the lead nanny goat, where she went, the others would follow.

'*Aiee!*' Signy yelped, grabbing a rock and throwing it, the missile sailing just above the goat's curved horns and landing in the grass to her left. Stormy gave a forlorn, startled cry and immediately skittered her way back up onto the path again. 'Yes. You stay with me,' Signy said in the soothing voice she reserved for talking to the animals.

'Good shot!' a voice from behind her called. It was Kari, her wide mouth stretched in its usual delighted smile. She was walking at the back with her sisters Ashild and Brit. Their father Peder Jemtegard owned the farm next door; it wasn't as big as Signy's family's, was more exposed to the harsh north winds and the soil wasn't quite so fertile, but the two farmers were great friends and often helped each other out, especially during the harvest, working harmoniously side by side. Kari was the same age as Signy, albeit about to turn fifteen; she and her older sister Ashild had both been born in the same year which made them Irish twins apparently, but Signy didn't see how that could be: they didn't look anything alike and they were definitely Norwegian, for Signy's own mother had helped with the births. Brit was the eldest Jemtegard girl at sixteen and their brother Nils was the oldest of them all; at nearly eighteen he had gone ahead with the men and boys who were transporting the heavier items, melting the stubbornest snow patches with harvested soil, repairing the path where snow-melt might have degraded it, and clearing any obstructions left from the winter such as fallen trees. Signy hoped they would get the first fire going too so that they could sit around the flames in a circle and drink snarøl together.

With empty water buckets swinging at hip height from their shoulder harnesses, the three Jemtegard sisters would supposedly scoop up anything that was dropped by the rest of the party ahead of them, but Signy could hear from the ripples of laughter that splashed over her intermittently that they were far more focused on their conversation than on retrieving stray pots.

'Hey!' Signy cried over her shoulder, daring to take her attention off Stormy for only a fraction of a moment. 'Can't you walk any faster? I can't hear you all the way back there. What's making you laugh so much?'

'Your walk!' Ashild called cheekily, making the others start laughing again. She was the naughtiest of the trio, always in trouble with her mother for not putting the clothes through the mangle or dropping stitches or dipping her finger in the *risengrot* bowl and licking it.

'Hey! I can throw behind me too, so watch out!' Signy called over her shoulder, her eyes dead ahead.

'Yes?' Ashild teased. 'Try it then.'

Without hesitation, Signy picked up a small rock by her feet and, listening for just a moment to hear their voices and locate them more precisely, she tossed it up and over her shoulder. A second later, there was the loud, unmistakeable clatter of rock upon tin. She turned to find Ashild looking down into one of her water buckets in astonishment. 'I don't believe it.'

Kari and Brit cheered, laughing again at the sight of their sister's face.

'Hey, girls!' Margit called from the front. 'What are you doing back there? Who is watching the goats?'

Eeesht, the goats! With a wink, Signy turned again, reaching ahead with her stick to show the animals which way was forward. If only she could keep a thought in her head for more than a moment at a time!

They walked for another hour, the steep pass up the mountain gradually levelling out as they moved into the hinterland of a wide, circular valley. Summer, it seemed, had already set up shop here as the land spread out in vast hillocky swathes of green, the encircling mountaintops like a caldera trapping the heat. Signy was sure she could feel her skin browning in the sunlight already, and the yellow grasses of spring which had emerged from their long winter sleep beneath the snowpack less than six weeks ago were now a vivid intense green. Everything had woken up, it seemed: Clouded Apollo butterflies flitted in intricate games of chase, Common Swifts swooped to catch flies, red squirrels and pine martens scampered along the branches of the randomly dotted aspen and alder trees, and bright pink foxgloves swayed in clusters, like silken arrows. In the near distance, she saw a narrow carpet of dotted white flowers and she knew it was the heavy-headed lollipop buds of cottongrass tracing the banks of the stream that would be their water supply and bath for the next few months.

To her delight, a white twist of smoke was dancing into the air, heralding the menfolk's arrival too and they all upped their pace, eager to get to the farm and rest at last. The herd, sensing arrival, widened out, spreading from their line into an excited flock, bleating and bellowing their approach so that the men looked up.

Nils, sitting astride a roof of one of the buildings, waved to them and Signy waved back frantically. He was easy to spot even from a distance, his blonde hair marking him out like a white flag.

'*Hei!*' she cried, faltering slightly on the uneven ground. She wished she could break into a run but to do so would only scatter the herd and the last thing anyone wanted was yet more walking today. Still, she wasn't great at checking her impulses and she fell into a sort of jog that had Sofie tutting she would 'set off' the horses too if she didn't calm down.

Their summer farm was what was known as a *setergrender*, composed of a cluster of small huts, all of them built from solid, unplaned timbers that were almost black with age. They each had only one door, two windows and a stovepipe sticking through the traditional grassy *torvtak* roofs; the huts were grouped together in an avenue, with three on one side and four on the other, with a stables, haybarn and *stabbur* set across the back. The site had originally been chosen by her ancestors within this pasture not just for its level ground and proximity to the stream but also for the proliferation of rocks and smooth boulders that had been left on the ground there from the last ice age. Although the farm was nearly two hundred years old, Signy knew every building had been designed for its corners to stand on the bigger immovable boulders, with other rocks then brought in and cut into slabs that could fit along the perimeter base where required. This enabled the floor of the hut to be lifted off the damp ground, reducing the risk of rot, while the small rocks nestling in the grass outside, flanking the small avenue, doubled as stools for the girls.

Two downy birch trees were staggered either side of the path, their spreading canopies not quite close enough to touch. Signy had loved to play in them as a little girl, sitting on a branch out of the way of the busy adults and watching as her father walked over the grass-turf roofs, making repairs, just as Nils was doing now. But her father was not so agile any more. His bones hurt him most days and he walked slowly through the yard. He had ridden his horse here today, something her mamma had said would hurt his pride even more than walking would do to his joints, but as they neared, Signy could see him heaving a new, bigger whetstone into position with Ottar Doving, Sofie's father.

It had always seemed to Signy that Ottar was everything his daughter was not: humble, placid, kind. As Signy's father's cotter – or lease tenant – he always fulfilled the contractual obligations upon him with good grace and never the bitter resentment of his daughter. A tailor by trade, he nonetheless never seemed happier than when he worked his two weeks during the haymaking season, his one workday in the spring, the day of roadwork during *håbolla* (the quiet period between seeding and haymaking), and he always volunteered for the *buføring*. Sofie on the other hand would have far rather he concentrated on making dresses that flattered her, for she had confided to Margit that she was quite determined to win herself a wealthy husband. Not for her a life on the land, she wanted velvets and silks, a telephone and motor car.

'Pappa,' Signy cried as they arrived at the farm.

Haken Reiten turned and straightened up. 'My girls,' he replied happily, holding an arm out for Signy to run to, a frown flickering over his face as he saw that it was Sofie and not Margit on horseback. 'But what is this?'

Ottar, hearing his landlord's tone, turned too. 'Sofie?' he asked, shame in his voice.

Margit's mouth parted and her cheeks pinked as she saw her father's displeasure. He was a fair man but stern and he took etiquette seriously, maintaining that he and his forebears had worked hard to get to the position where such an honour was their right.

'Sofie stumbled and twisted her ankle,' Signy said quickly, not to protect the older girl, but Margit; she knew her sister could never lie to their father. 'Margit offered her place to prevent further injury.'

'Is that so, Sofie?' Ottar asked his daughter.

Sofie, who had been sitting imperiously on the horse, nodded as the rest of the men turned to stare. 'Yes. I'm sorry, Pappa. I couldn't place any weight on it.'

Haken held out his other arm and Margit walked into the crook of it, giving Signy a sheepish look. 'That's my Margit,' he said proudly. 'Always thinking of others. And you, Signy – did you keep control of the herd?'

'Well enough, Pappa. We have arrived with the number we left with.'

He chuckled. 'Very good. Then you have done well.' He

squeezed her around the shoulder. 'But the hard work starts here. You know that, huh?'

'Of course,' she said, resting her head on his shoulder, watching as Nils jumped down from his position on the *selet* roof and walked over to the horse.

'Here,' he said, holding out his arms. 'I shall help you down. Which ankle is it?'

'Oh, this one,' Sofie said, patting her right thigh and gratefully shooting him a dazzling smile.

'Then swing that leg over and slide down; I'll catch you.'

Sofie did as he instructed, slipping into his arms like a foot into a stocking. Seemingly, she weighed very little, for Nils didn't immediately return her to the ground, keeping her hovering for a moment, eye-to-eye, nose-to-nose, before he carefully set her down as though she was a china doll.

Sofie, remembering to pretend her right foot was injured, held it a few inches off the floor.

'Here, put your arm around my shoulders and we can get you over to that rock,' he said, helping her over, his other arm around her waist. Signy watched the way Sofie's black hair swung with every false hop, occasional winces and convincing little cries coming from her every few moments.

She shot an exasperated look across at Margit, but her sister was watching on with such a look of sympathy, Signy was convinced she seemed to have quite forgotten this was all an act.

'Is that better?' Nils asked.

'Much, thank you,' Sofie smiled from her perch on the rock.

'Shall I take a look at it for you?'

'Oh no, no, that won't be necess—' she said quickly, but his fingers were already pressing on the soft tissue of her ankle. She gave a short yelp and pulled away.

'It's tender.'

'Oh, it's just a light sprain. I'm sure I'll be fine by the morning,' she demurred, looking to the ground.

He frowned, looking concerned. 'Perhaps you should come back to the village with us.'

'And leave my friends here to do all the hard work without me? Absolutely not,' she said determinedly, prompting a proud smile from her father and the other men. There was no doubt about it, Sofie was an accomplished actress and Signy turned to see Kari, Ashild and Brit watching on with the same look of disbelief – Sofie had none of her father's work ethic and was always the first to down tools, or complain of a sore back, or pretend she'd lost something.

'Well, you should rest for the next two days at least,' Nils said, looking unhappy about it. 'Did you girls hear that?' he asked his sisters and Signy and Margit.

'Yes,' they chorused, rolling their eyes. 'No work for two days.'

'Good. You'll look after her, won't you, Margit?'

'Always.'

'But I'll ride back to check in a few days,' he said, turning his attention to Sofie again. 'If you're still limping or in discomfort, you shall have to come back to the village with me then.'

'As you like,' she smiled.

Nils smiled back. And Signy, still huddled in the crook of her father's arm, scowled.

Chapter Four

'Okay, guys, just take another step to the left. I can't quite see . . . yeah, that's it,' Lenny murmured. 'Okay. Now, Bo, can you sit just a little higher up? You look like a bag of potatoes.'

'Thanks!' she laughed. But she straightened her legs, hoisting herself further up Zac's back.

'And, Zac, tip your head back, mate. You're meant to look like her lover, not a packhorse.'

'Ooh, roasted,' Zac chuckled, tipping his head back. Bo pressed her cheek against him and they both gazed lovingly towards the camera. The piggyback was one of their signature images; they had been shot piggybacking on Philippine beaches, up the Spanish Steps, along the Great Wall, even on a rope swing over a lagoon in Borneo. Sometimes she would have her arms up in the air in a gesture of jubilation, triumph or joy but today, the cheek-to-cheek vibe worked better. It was cosier, more intimate. And right now, she wanted as much body heat as she could get.

'Howzat?' Zac asked after a moment.

Lenny lowered the camera and scrolled through the images as he walked over. 'Yeah, good. I think this one's the best.'

Zac put her back down again and they all put their heads together as he flicked one after the other.

'The yellow jacket looks great,' Zac murmured. 'I knew it would.'

'Yeah, especially against the snow and water,' Lenny mumbled back. 'I like that palette: white, navy and yellow. It feels Scandi.'

'Swedish, to be precise,' Zac said thoughtfully. 'Perhaps her jacket should have been red?'

Bo smiled. The boys always took the photography so seriously, considering the framing, the backdrop, the colours – or palette as they insisted on calling it – as though this was art and not a snapshot for a blog.

Snuggling closer into Zac's down jacket – in spite of their warm coats, they had mistakenly packed the gloves at the bottom of their rucksacks; it always took a while to readjust to all the layers the northern hemisphere required – she looked back at the view again; Geraingerfjord stood magnificently below her, its mirror-still indigo waters as dark as the cold eyes of a Great White. The cliffs rose so steeply they were only just off vertical, and even the heavy snow on the upper reaches was unable to cling on nearer the water line, exposing rock faces so black and bare, they were the very definition of bleak. To her left, the village of Gerainger sat at the tip of the fjord, nestled in a small basin where the two opposing mountainsides met in a dip, as though bowing to each other. An expanse of level grass area seemed to rise from the water, stretching back for a while before beginning to rise again, tall, narrow white houses dotted all along a winding road that disappeared between the steep cliffs once more.

To her right, the fjord angled away at a ninety-degree turn and three dramatic waterfalls cascaded over the slopes into the water below. She had expected they might eddy the water, given the size of them, but the fjord was so big and deep that there was not so much as a wrinkle on its surface, a small demonstration of its impermeability and might, its permanence.

And that was what had stunned her – the very scale of this place. In spite of the number of images she had seen before coming here, she still hadn't been prepared for it. They always researched their next location in great detail, wanting to know exactly what they would be giving their followers and whether or not they could justify the trip: two or three days of pictures wouldn't cut it. They weren't tourists, they were travellers. Nomads. Wherever they went, they went to *live* there, rarely staying anywhere for less than a month, and that meant getting down like a local. But the downside of all that research was that sometimes – increasingly often, in truth – she would have seen so much of a place beforehand that by the time they got there, she felt she'd already been and gone. It was getting harder to find the thrill of the new, the unknown, the exotic.

But this place had done it. It was the land of giants, the perfect conflation of air, land and sea. It felt like the crucible of the planet, where the world had begun and where time stopped – for what was the past or the future in a place like this? Nothing had changed here in millennia and nothing would.

It had knocked all three of them into silence – a first, surely – as they had crested the Eagle Pass road and caught their first glimpse of the fjord. The road – narrow, icy and punctuated by eleven hairpin bends – was the only way down to the village at this time of year. It was absolutely terrifying with Lenny at the wheel – although they all knew Zac would have been far, far worse, looking for his next adrenaline kick – but the ferry from the nearby village of Hellesylt stopped running in the autumn and the fleets of giant cruise boats that choked the fjord nine months of the year didn't visit during the winter due to the sea ice. And that was precisely the reason why she and Zac had chosen to come now; they wanted to be here when it was in its 'natural' state: no tourists, no ferries. They wanted it bleak, remote, imperious, untouched.

'Yeah, that's nailed it,' Zac said, pointing out one image in particular. 'Right, let's go, I'm freezing my balls off,' he said, heading back for the small silver hire car they had parked out of shot in a layby.

Blowing on their hands, they got back in, the heating on max, and continued on down. The icy road conditions improved as they drew closer to the water and within five minutes they were driving into the village. They hadn't passed another car for almost an hour through the valleys and it was no different here.

'Where the hell is everyone?' Lenny asked as they passed a small parking area outside the tourist centre, with no cars in it.

Close up, Bo could see that the open grassy area she had seen from the distance was in fact an empty caravan park and she suppressed a shiver, only too able to imagine how it must look in the summer – hundreds of white plastic blocks parked up on the edge of one of the most beautiful sites in the world. It was the invariable irony of tourism, all those people wanting to appreciate its beauty, never thinking that they themselves were becoming the very blight that ruined it.

'I can't wait to see the place we're staying,' she sighed, her chin cupped in her hand as she gazed out of the window. 'It looked so incredible in the pictures. Where is it exactly?' she asked as Lenny followed the road through the village, their little car climbing again in neat chicanes, the fjord at their backs now. She saw the steepled church and narrow, four-storey houses with illuminated stars and candles at the windows; a large river tumbling over rocks through the very centre of the town, a walkway and viewing platform built alongside it, no doubt as a safety precaution to stop the millions of tourists who visited from scrambling over them.

'We need to ask for a guy called Anders Jemtegard,' Lenny said, peering over the steering wheel as they passed by an enormous hotel on their left, a visitors' centre to their right. Ahead of them, the road appeared to travel straight on through the mountain pass, leaving the village behind.

'That's it?' Bo asked. 'No address?'

Taking her comment as a criticism, Lenny swore under his breath as he pulled into the visitors' centre car park and turned round again. 'The woman I booked it through said to ask for Anders Jemtegard when we got here. I assumed that would be sufficient if those were her instructions.'

Bo sat back in her seat, not wanting to start an argument – but were they supposed to go around the town just asking random strangers for the whereabouts of this man? That was assuming they could actually find any strangers in the first place. Beside her, Zac was on his phone, applying filters to the image he had decided upon. Could he get reception here, she wondered? Surely nothing but Valkyries could get past those mountains.

They drove back down into the town again and parked in the small turn-off they had passed on the way in.

'Well, there's the tourist centre – shall we ask them?' Bo said, zipping up her jacket and bracing herself to step outside again. It would have been hard enough dealing with these below-zero temperatures if they'd come from Europe, much less the South Pacific.

'We could, if it was open,' Lenny said, pointing to the dark building and the 'closed' sign on the door.

'Dammit,' she sighed. 'Well, can we get a coffee at least?' she asked as they clambered out, her gaze falling to the neighbouring building, a pretty single-storey cream-weatherboarded cafe with a scalloped tile roof and a Norwegian flag by the door. 'We haven't stopped since breakfast and we've been on the road for hours now.'

'Fine. I'll ask after this Anders guy and you can get the drinks,' Lenny said, pulling up the hood of his jacket and trudging off, bleeping the locks as he went. 'Make mine a double-shot caramel. I need the sugar hit.'

'If we can, bro,' Zac shrugged, one hand patting Bo's backside as they walked towards the cafe. 'We might just be lucky to get milk with it.'

Bo walked in and breathed a sigh of relief at what she found there: black log walls, a lofty white ceiling and trendy rattan lights. Civilization! This place catered to the international tourist crowd after all; they could be sure of a decent coffee here.

They met up with Lenny again a few minutes later, the steaming cups in their hands better than any gloves. The tip of his nose was glowing red and his eyes were watering from the cold. 'Okay, so the guy at the bakery there' – Zac pointed to another charming log building, this one black, across the road; it had gables in the pitched roof and wall-to-wall windows. 'He says Anders' place is the white house down there on the right, past the Ole cafe.'

'Let's go then. I want to settle in. I'm done with all this wandering about,' Bo said, zipping her yellow jacket all the way up to her chin so that the fur trim of the hood encircled her face completely. What she wouldn't give right now for a massage at the hotel and another night's sleep on their pil-lowy beds. The jetlag was kicking in and it was *evil*.

With their hoods up and hands clasped around their steaming drinks, they walked down the narrow footpath that led into the village, down and away from the road. A run of tiny, weather-beaten huts bordered the fjord on their right-hand side; some of them were in better condition than others, a couple of them looked almost derelict.

'Reckon they must have been boathouses originally?' Zac mused as they passed. They were all closed for the season and seemed to cater specifically to the tourist trade now, selling jewellery, Norwegian jumpers and locally made chocolate, offering bike hire and incongruously – now, at least – an ice-cream parlour.

Cafe Ole was impossible to miss a little further down the lane. It was a large creamy weatherboarded building on their left with an amusing sign written in English in the window: '*The more you weigh, the harder you are to kidnap. Stay safe – eat cake.*'

Bo laughed. 'Well I like them! I hope they're not going to be closed all winter too.'

'Me too. Jeez, and we thought Samoa was quiet,' Zac mur-mured as they carried on walking in the silence, no sign of another human being around.

Fifty metres further down, just as a vast and ugly 1960s hotel hoved into view and made Bo shudder again, they came upon a small white weatherboarded house on the corner. Its gable end faced onto the lane, making it at first glance appear smaller than it actually was, but as they walked around, they could see it stretched back towards the water. On its left-hand side – thankfully all but blocking the view between it and the hotel – there was an enormous boulder, almost as high as the two-storey house.

'Well, this must be the place,' Zac said, pushing the gate open with a squeak and walking down the path. The 'front' door was situated halfway down, a mailbox to the side of it, and Bo saw that the pretty windowbox was filled with tools, rather than geraniums. Zac rang the bell, both Bo and Lenny hanging back a little so as not to crowd the step. There was a light on in the far room that faced onto the fjord but no one came.

Zac rang again. 'Come on, mate,' he muttered, blowing on his fingers.

Again nothing.

Zac turned back to Lenny in annoyance. 'What exactly did the guy in the bakery say again?'

'That he lives in the white house beside the rock, just past the cafe. He never said anything about whether or not he was in.'

'He didn't say anything about him being *away*, did he?' Bo asked quickly.

Lenny shook his head.

'Well he's clearly not here now,' Zac muttered, looking irritated. He was never very good at being in limbo; whenever they relocated, he liked to transfer quickly and seamlessly to their next chapter. And although last night's hotel had been outstanding – notwithstanding the mobbing in the drawing room – they'd spent over three hours in the car this morning. They hadn't left until ten, which was when it had been light enough to set off; there had been no point leaving earlier as then they couldn't have taken shots along the way, but the receptionist at the hotel had told them it would start getting dark again from two and Bo could already feel the light beginning to dim – and tempers beginning to fray.

'Shall we go back to the cafe and wait?' she suggested,

taking his hand in hers to keep him calm. 'I liked it in there. They do pizza too. I could eat. I'm pretty hungry.'

'You're alw—' Zac began, just as the door opened suddenly. He turned back, pulling his hand away, to find a tall, rangy man filling the doorway. His dirty-blonde hair was long and shaggy, golden stubble on his cheeks and jaw, but he had eyes of such piercing blue intensity, Bo felt her lungs deflate a little. Give that man a horned helmet and a longboat, she thought to herself, flinching under his glacial gaze as their eyes met momentarily.

'. . . Ja?' the man asked warily, eyeing the three of them with a hostile look. Bo wondered how many people – tourists – he had to endure walking right past his windows, taking photographs, possibly even knocking at his door too. From his expression, she thought it must be too many.

'Hi, I'm Zac Austen. You must be Anders Jemtegard?'

Another short silence, suspicious stare. 'Yes,' he replied in English.

Zac's smile brightened with relief, his teeth looking comically white against his nut-brown skin. 'Great! We're here to pick up the keys for the farm.'

There was a longer silence this time, and Bo wondered how good the man's English was. Perhaps he was having difficulty understanding what her fiancé was saying? 'The farm?'

Zac grinned. 'Ah, right, there's a challenge. Okay, I think it's pronounced . . . Sy-oil-ip-ay?' Anders continued staring at him, no hint of a smile on his face as Zac gave a hapless shrug. 'Apologies. My Norwegian is non-existent.'

'Sjøløipet,' he said finally, pronouncing it Sholopet, 'is my grandmother's farm.'

'Your grandmother?' Lenny asked, stepping forward now.

'Now is her name Signy? 'Cause she's the person I've been dealing with. We've arranged a month let.'

'A month . . . ?' Anders' suspicious frown morphed into an outright scowl. 'Wait there.' And he slammed the door in their faces.

'Jeez, good to meet you too, dude,' Zac muttered, stepping back off the step and leaning against the boulder. 'Would it kill the guy to smile?'

Bo just shrugged, as though apologizing for this stranger's lack of manners. 'That's not good. He didn't look like he knew anything about it,' she said quizzically to Lenny.

It was Lenny's turn to shrug. 'What can I tell you? The woman's the one I had dealings with. How they communicate in their family is up to them.'

'But you booked through Airbnb, right?'

'Yep. Exclusive use.'

'I wonder why she didn't arrange to give us the keys herself then, if it was going to be such a hassle for him? Or she could have at least left them in a key box like most other places.'

Lenny shrugged and sighed. 'People.' This was his catchphrase, the sign-off he used whenever he couldn't explain other people's behaviour.

They looked back at the firmly closed door and waited. Minutes passed. Then more minutes.

'Fuck's sake,' Zac said, beginning to get irritated again. 'Is he even coming back or just going to leave us hanging here to freeze to death?'

'Zac, just—'

But Zac had already raised his arm to knock on the door again, just as it opened once more. Anders had changed and was wearing orange and navy waterproof trousers, a matching jacket and short rubber boots.

'Follow me,' he said with a jerk of his head, walking further down the side path towards the water.

Zac and Bo both looked back at Lenny in confusion. Should they?

'Well *I* don't know!' he protested.

With a roll of his eyes, Zac followed the terse Norwegian, Bo and Lenny skittering after them. They turned the corner, to find a small terraced area at the back fenced off from the fjord by white picketing, a small matching white-weatherboarded boathouse to the left side. Slab steps led down from the terrace to a makeshift stone jetty, which Anders was walking down, towards a moored orange rib. The exposed shore was stony, deep beds of kelp bearding the water's edge.

'Really?' Bo asked as she watched him hop aboard. They were going on the water, right now? It had looked cold enough from the vantage point on the Eagle Pass road, but up close, it looked even worse: viscous and frigid as the ice began to creep from the land out to the sea.

'Let's just get there. We can ask questions later,' Zac said, opening the gate and following down the slipway too.

Anders was waiting for them, impatience radiating from him, even though he wasn't twitching so much as a fibre and Bo took his hand gratefully as he wordlessly helped her step onto the boat.

'Is it far?' she asked him, her voice sounding muffled in the enormous furry hood which all but obscured her face, as Lenny jumped in last, making them rock.

'Not in this,' Anders replied, casting her only the most cursory glance as he threw out the mooring rope and got the engine going.

They sat on the hard plastic seats – hand-holds moulded into the tops of the chairs – and Zac squeezed her knee as they began to pull away from the little house, his mood improving already now that they were on their way again.

She looked around them as they moved into deeper water. By the water's edge, it was so clear she could see straight to the bottom – a glass bottle, a tyre that had been sunk as a buoy anchor, some bright orange starfish . . . But rapidly the colour of the water intensified, the pale, almost sandy tint of turquoise becoming teal and then that rich indigo she'd seen from the heights. From the water side, it was clear that the huts along the lane they'd just walked down were indeed old boathouses, enormous boulders laid out on the sloping shore in guiding rows below each one, with slim birch branches laid crossways to lift and roll the boats off the ground.

'Hold tight,' Anders said, glancing at them all to make sure they were holding on. Bo – even though her hands were freezing – tightened her grip, bracing for the acceleration. He eased forward on the gears, and within seconds they were moving so fast across the surface of the water, Bo was sure they must be skimming it. The air – now a wind in their faces – was so cold it made her gasp and she was grateful all over again for the storm hood of her jacket. Her eyes instantly began to stream and she heard Zac and Lenny whoop with joy, prompting their driver to glance round in puzzlement, his stern gaze meeting hers for a moment before he turned back again.

Now that they were out on the water, the true majesty of the fjord began to impose itself. The cliffs were like walls around them, unyielding and immovable, the stone streaked with ice like frozen tear tracks, as though the mountains themselves were weeping. If the terrain wasn't extreme enough, the arctic climate was and Bo thought she had never been anywhere so hostile, nor so beautiful. She didn't even need to shift her gaze to see up – the water reflected the scenery so perfectly, she could have put her make-up on with it.

She blinked in wonder as within minutes they turned the corner and passed the waterfalls she had seen from the road – one seemed to be made up of seven different tributaries, each one converging at the same point on the cliff before cascading into the fjord below.

'The Seven Sisters!' Zac called back to her, pointing it out lest she might have missed it.

She gave a thumbs-up sign. It had been one of the things they were most excited to see and seeing it up close sent a shiver up her spine. Photographs couldn't – hadn't – done it justice. They would need to get a shot there, somehow, for sure. But Anders didn't take the rib closer to it as they passed; this wasn't a sightseeing trip but a taxi, and he ploughed a straight, efficient channel through the very centre of the waterway.

Far ahead, she could see the fjord turned again in an S bend, just as another waterfall came into view, almost opposite the Seven Sisters. It was bottle-shaped with a narrow neck and flared base and she knew from their research it was called The Suitor. How long ago it seemed now, that they'd been lying on the hammock in Samoa, the ocean beyond their toes, looking at the very images of this, and now, now they were here in the full stinging biting cold of it.

She had assumed their driver would continue straight past this waterfall too but to her surprise, he was turning towards it – or at least, for a shallow bay that slunk around the corner just along from it, Gerainger now on the other side of this headland. He cut the throttle a little and circled in, bringing them closer. Lenny was already taking photos – 'recce shots', as he called them.

'We are here,' Anders said, beginning to let the boat drift in, straight towards the cliff-face. He jerked his chin and indicated to a set of iron rungs concreted into the stone.

'*That's* the landing point?' Bo asked.

He nodded.

She suppressed a shudder of fear. But Zac threw his head back again and laughed, baring his tanned neck and bright white teeth and looking like an exotic puma in this northern territory. 'Yes! I fucking love it! Let's do this!'

Lodal, June 1936

The flames licked at the air, warming it up and colouring it pink. The sun had dropped below the ridge line at last, but it was still bobbing above the horizon like a balloon unable to sink. It was the end of their first full day alone and they were all sitting around the open fire outside the cabins, their blankets wrapped over their shoulders as they rubbed their hands together every so often to keep warm. Only early summer, the evenings were still fresh and behind them in the pens and stables, the animals were settling down for the night in a decrescendo of grunts, bleats and the patting of hooves in the straw beds. But the novelty of the space, the fresh air and the freedom, was infectious and although she was stiff and tired after a day spent scrubbing the dairy equipment, milking the goats and picking berries, Signy knew she couldn't sleep yet.

She was sitting closer to the fire than any of them, her cheeks hot to the touch as she listened, enraptured, to the story being told in a hushed voice.

'. . . king had a daughter and he would *only* give her away to the person who could ride up the mountain, for there was a *towering* glass at the top, as *smooth* as ice,' Brit said in a dramatic voice, her eyes wide. 'The princess would sit at the very top of the mountain with three golden apples in her lap, and whoever could *ride up* and take the golden apples would have her *hand* in marriage and half the kingdom—'

Signy gasped excitedly. This had always been her favourite folk tale, not because of the princess being wooed, but at the thought of those golden apples – perfectly round, perfectly shiny . . .

'Now the princess was so beautiful, that everyone who saw her fell in love with her – whether they wanted to or not – and so, as you may imagine, all the princes and knights wanted to win her . . .'

Ashild and Margit sighed; Kari and Signy exchanged wry looks. But Sofie was impassive, looking into the fire with a regal poise, as though this story was *her* fairy tale, foreshadowing *her* destiny. It made Signy start to see the look of quiet determination on her face as she listened to Brit's words.

Signy watched her for the rest of the story, seeing how Sofie glowed ever more radiantly at the story of all the men of the kingdom vying to win the princess's hand and she felt her own good mood desert her. How easily Sofie had toyed with Nils. She could have any man she wanted. She didn't love Nils, Signy knew it in her bones, but she might just snatch him so that no one else could have him. He was a farmer's son and, whilst not wealthy, Sofie would know a security with him that her own father had never been able to guarantee: they would have their own homestead with animals and a store full of food. It was as much as she could reasonably hope for, even if she wished for much more.

'I just love that story,' Margit sighed, stretching her legs out, the flames throwing a flattering light on her gentle face and bringing out the richness of her long russet hair.

'Me too,' Ashild agreed. 'I wish Karl would run up a mountain to win me,' she said with an eye-roll and pointedly looking across the valley to the near horizon where the ground suddenly dropped away, swooping back down to the village. 'It's not like there's any ice stopping him,' she groaned.

'Ah, poor Ashi,' Margit chuckled, throwing an arm around her and drawing her closer on the timber log that served as their campfire perch. It had been common knowledge that Ashild had the most enormous crush on Karl Schumann, one of the carpenter's sons, ever since he had caught her in his arms as she fell off a wall she had been running along on the way back from church last Easter. That he had simply been passing at the right time was a fluke in Signy's opinion, but Ashi had taken it as proof of heroism and trailed after him ever since. Unfortunately, Karl himself had taken the incident as evidence of her already renowned clumsiness, something which looked especially bad against the contrived grace of Sofie as she drifted through the village in a froth of pretty dresses. 'He is a fool not to see what is in front of his very eyes. One day . . . one day soon he will wake up and see what has been in front of him all along.'

'You think?' Ashild quipped, tossing a knowing glance in Sofie's direction. Sofie was still staring wistfully into the fire, as though carried away on a dream, but Signy wasn't falling for it; she fully suspected Sofie was listening closely to every word that passed.

'Who knows, maybe he will wake up in time for the Midsummer's Day picnic,' Margit said optimistically. 'Absence makes the heart grow fonder.'

'Or it makes the heart forgetful. He probably cannot even remember my name,' Ashild sighed.

Signy inwardly agreed with her; he probably couldn't. Karl was not a bad boy; he was tall and strong and inoffensive to look at, but he had about as much wit and conversation as the cows. 'You can do better than him anyway,' Signy piped up.

The older girls looked over in astonishment at her forthright certainty and she suddenly felt like a child at the adults' table.

'Can she?' Sofie asked her, pinning her with sudden focus.

Signy swallowed. Making eye contact with Sofie was like looking into a whirlpool – mesmerizing but dizzying. Had she been wrong? Was Karl the best Ashi could hope for?

'And what about you? Is there anybody you love?' Sofie's stress on the word 'you' framed the statement as a rhetorical question; she always seemed to know exactly where Signy's pinch spots were.

'Don't be stupid,' Signy muttered, staring into the fire.

Sofie's eyebrow twitched at her tone; it wasn't sufficiently deferential for her liking. Though she may not be her better, she was certainly her elder and out here – here alone – that counted. 'Well, what about Nils? We all know you're sweet on him, even if he doesn't,' she said. 'But he might look upon you differently if one of us was to tell him for y—'

'Don't you dare!' Signy cried.

'But we wouldn't mind, Signy, it's no problem.'

'I said no!'

'Hush,' Margit said from across the way, calming them down with her soothing smile. 'Sofie's only teasing you; *of course* no one would tell him.'

'Of course I wouldn't,' Sofie said, covering the lie with a smile.

The Christmas Lights

'If nothing else, it would embarrass him terribly,' Margit continued. 'Why, he's a man now and you're still a child.'

'Yes. Exactly,' Signy muttered, hooking her hair behind her ear and staring at the floor. Only, she wasn't a child now. Her chest ached all the time with her breasts swelling into little buds, and the curse afflicted her every month too. She was just like them, only smaller and thinner.

'Talking of Nils – did I hear him say that Rag is back from his training?' Sofie asked the group.

'He is. At least for a short while,' Brit said. 'He's completed the infantry training and I think it's the mountain training next.'

'So then, he'll be around for the Midsummer's picnic?' Kari asked, with a small thrill in her voice. Rag Omenas was the *lensmann*'s – or sheriff's – son; and if his father was the most powerful person in the district, he was the most handsome, with a planed jaw and apple cheeks, white-blonde, thick side-swept hair and grey-green eyes. The womenfolk of the village had been bereft when he had left a few months earlier – having turned eighteen – for his national service training. Well, all the women bar Signy – she hadn't been sad to see him go; her opinion of him had been low ever since she'd glimpsed him kick a stray dog as he walked ahead of her one evening and she abhorred anyone who was cruel to animals; animals were her world. But no one else had seen it and he, as the heir apparent in the village, enjoyed a special sort of exalted status. The men liked his raw athleticism and mannish charisma and all the womenfolk harboured a crush on him. Even Signy could admit he was powerfully attractive. But it was a fact, not a compliment.

'Yes, I think so,' Brit agreed, before looking over at Margit

61

and nudging her with her elbow. 'Which will be good for *you*. I bet he's even more beautiful in a soldier's uniform.'

The others laughed delightedly, a swell of excitement rolling over them at the prospect of Rag's return; the village had been far too quiet and dull since his departure. There was a dance in his eyes that made all the girls' hearts skip when he looked at them. (All but Signy's, anyway.)

'Oh, but I'm not . . .' Margit's voice trailed off as she looked away bashfully, her cheeks colouring up. As the elder daughter of the village's richest farmer, a match with Rag was all but expected; they had known each other their whole lives and been in the same class in the village school, but since turning teenagers, as though knowing their fates, they had barely spoken to each other – easy-going Margit suddenly tongue-tied in his presence.

'Well it's not like he'll be wearing his uniform to the picnic, Brit,' Sofie said testily.

'I know that,' Brit said. 'I didn't mean—'

'And he may not even come anyway. There's no point in getting excited over nothing. Midsummer's isn't for another three weeks,' Sofie said, dousing their girlish high spirits with a bucketful of cold pragmatism.

'That's true,' Margit agreed.

There was a tight pause suddenly, the crackle and pop of the fire filling the silence.

'Well I hope he does come,' Kari said defiantly. 'At the very least it would mean there's another boy to dance with; last year, I had to dance with Ashi.'

'And what was so bad about that?' her big sister asked indignantly. 'I wasn't so bad.'

'My bruised toes would disagree!'

They all laughed. Poor Ashi, she really wasn't the lightest

on her feet; perhaps Karl's fears weren't *entirely* misplaced. But Sofie didn't join in the laughter and as Signy turned her gaze back to her, she saw that she was smiling into the fire again, her expression far away. Signy pulled her blanket tighter over her shoulders, feeling a chill ripple down her hot skin as she understood that Sofie didn't want to be a farmer's wife, churning the butter and feeding the pigs; she wanted someone more and she felt her beauty entitled her to it.

Suddenly, the thought of Sofie taking Nils as her husband wasn't the most horrifying thing she could imagine. Because if not him . . . Her eyes slid over to her big sister; she was rubbing Kari's hands with her own to warm her up, unaware that beside her Sofie was staring into the flames as though images were dancing there just for her, and they were showing her exactly what she wanted to see: a beautiful princess and a valiant prince who was coming to claim her hand. At last.

Chapter Five

Zac and Lenny disembarked first in a display of bravado and manners, 'testing' the hand and footholds for her, even though Anders had assured them with three words and a dour look that they were secure. Bo sensed he was a man of his word. She sat on the rib, looking up as they scrambled like mountain goats up the thirty or so rungs to an incredibly shallow ledge that, from this vantage, didn't look deep enough to accommodate Zac's size-ten feet. Nonetheless, it appeared a railing had been secured into the cliff face up there and that by holding on, they could pigeon-step their way a short distance along to where the ledge became deeper.

'All good, babe!' Zac waved down at her. 'You're gonna love it up here!'

Bo cast Anders a nervous smile. 'Well, I guess it's my turn then.'

Anders, who had tethered the boat to a ring also set into the rock but was still holding on to it to keep the boat extra stable, looked back at her. 'Can you swim?'

Oh God. As if that helped! 'Yes,' she nodded.

'But you don't like heights?'

'Mmm, not so much,' she said, giving an embarrassed smile as she scanned the sheer escarpment again.

'So then why are you staying in a shelf farm?' he asked,

incredulousness the first emotion she had seen him display yet.

'Well, that's sort of the point,' she said quietly, biting her lip. 'Facing our fears.'

He frowned. 'You are on a therapy course?'

'No!' she laughed, feeling some of the tension at least dissipate. 'We have a blog. We try to be . . . free. Unencumbered by possessions or commitments. Or fears.'

The way he looked at her left her in no doubt as to his thoughts on that matter. 'You'll be fine,' he said finally, holding out his right hand to help steady her as she stood. 'I'll be behind you. If you fall, you fall on me.'

It was a surprisingly reassuring thought.

'Right then.' Putting on her best brave face, she raised a hand to the first steel rung. It was so cold it made her bones ache instantly and her hand flew off it, as though it had scalded her instead. With nothing else to hold on to, the boat rocking lightly beneath her, she grabbed Anders' outstretched arm where he was holding the boat to the rocks. 'Whoa,' she said in a shaky voice.

'It is very cold, yes,' he said calmly behind her, his other arm on her back and stabilizing her. 'You don't have gloves?'

'Not on me,' she murmured, feeling foolish; exactly what good were they sitting at the bottom of a backpack?

'You are sure you want to do this?' he asked her, watching the fear play patterns over her face.

Categorically not. 'Yes. Absolutely.' And before he could give her a way out, she took a deep breath and tried again. She was jittery with nerves, the familiar old panic zooming around her, awake again, and she winced as the bone-aching temperature shot through her once more, but it had the desired effect of making her move quickly – holding on to the rungs was unbearable, and she realized that was perhaps why the boys had climbed so fast too. She didn't give herself time to think about the even colder icy water immediately below her; if she lost her grip, there would be nothing to grab or hold to stop an immediate plunge downwards. It would be like the Cresta Run but feet-first. Before she knew it, she was tip-toeing across the ledge and towards Zac's outstretched arm.

'Well done, babe!' he said, one arm hooked over the railing as he held out his other arm to hoist her up. He planted a kiss on her lips. 'You did that so well. Full disclosure – I was worried you might get freaked.'

'No,' she fibbed. 'I was fine. Anders was very kind, kept me calm.'

'Thanks, man,' Zac said as their driver appeared, as cool as if he was climbing a loft ladder.

'Hold the rope with both hands here,' Anders said instead. 'Go forwards.'

Not daring a glimpse down, keeping her chin firmly – and probably quite comically – pointed up, Bo followed the men off the stony ledge and breathed a visible sigh of relief as they quickly came to grass and the treeline. The grass was still exposed this close to the water – snow and ice only clung to the upper reaches of the mountains – and although incredibly steep, they didn't need a ropeway or rungs here.

'Uh – so where now?' Lenny asked, looking around the dense woods and not seeing any visible path.

'This way,' Anders said, tucking behind them and stepping over the roots of an aspen tree. They followed after, ducking and dodging pinged-back branches. In some places, steps had been cut into the rocky ground, in others, there were steel or rope handrails for where the pitch increased again. Either way, it was relentless. The going was tough, a full-on scramble up the mountain-face, sometimes using roots and boulders as footholds, and branches as hand grips. Within minutes, the three of them were puffing and panting like sledge dogs but Anders walked upright and with almost a bounce in his step, waiting for them patiently but never himself looking worried or tired by the route.

Occasionally Bo looked up, regretting it each time as she was met with views of overhanging rocks, or grassy slopes that she wouldn't have dared ski down; she couldn't understand how the trees could take root here. Even Zac was breathless and she realized they had allowed themselves to lose some of their fitness in Samoa, too tempted by lazy days lying on the white sandy beaches, swimming in lagoons and swinging in the hammock.

With no one capable of speech, Anders kept looking back every so often to check they were all still together, still okay. But just when she was thinking she was going to have to call for a prolonged stop, they suddenly crested a ridge and the land cut back by a hundred yards or so. Bo wanted to cry with relief as she saw the ramshackle timber huts she and Zac had pored over from their bed in Samoa. There were three that she could see: two principal long, low cabins and a blockier, two-storey old barn or storehouse to the side. Each of the buildings was set upon a stone base, their backs so close to the slopes as to have been cut into the mountain itself, which Bo knew was to protect from avalanches.

'I just love those lids, man,' Lenny grinned, nodding at the deep turf roofs, their long grasses swaying and bending in the gentle breeze.

'They are called *torvtak*,' Anders said. 'Turf laid over birch strips. The root system of the grasses keeps it warm and waterproof.'

'How far up are we here?' Bo asked nervously, beginning to turn around again, to see from where they'd come.

'Two hundred and fifty metres.'

That was all? And it had taken them half an hour at least, to climb it.

'Whoa!' she said in surprise, as she looked back across the fjord. Directly opposite from where they stood was the Seven Sisters waterfall, as though it had been positioned there precisely for the enjoyment of the farmers who had lived here.

'Jeez!' Zac said, turning too.

'Holy shit!' Lenny cried.

The three of them stared, open-mouthed, at the view in complete silence. There were no words. There simply weren't and Bo wasn't sure there would be sufficient pictures either. Nothing could capture the majesty of this place. It was, in the truest sense, epic. To their right, Gerainger lay hidden behind the bend they had just travelled. To their left, another bend and several miles beyond it, the village of Hellesylt. It was rapidly getting dark now, and it was as though a fine black net was being cast over the sky, forcing the landscape into a negative of itself: toplighting the blue-white snow on the mountaintops, blackening the water.

'These views are among the best I've ever seen – and I'm a climber, man,' Zac said to Anders earnestly. 'I've gone way higher than this and not had such a buzz.'

'It is good,' Anders replied in a neutral tone and Bo smiled, knowing Zac would be disappointed he hadn't taken the bait and asked Zac about which other peaks he had climbed.

'Hey, you guys . . .' Lenny said, in that voice Bo knew meant he was pointing a camera at them.

Automatically, pushing her hood off, she threw her arms out wide and tossed her head back, letting her hair fly freely behind her, laughing as though giving thanks to the gods. Slowly she turned, hearing the camera clicks – this pose was always a favourite with the fans.

When she stopped, Anders was staring at her as though she was mad and she felt herself blush under his withering scrutiny; she knew it looked ridiculous to anyone who didn't know about their following or understand about their online world. But the beast had to be fed.

She looked over at Zac. He had found a boulder in the grass and was standing on it, looking wistfully out across the fjord, making sure to give a good jaw angle. Lenny continued clicking, trying to make the most of the dramatic sky before the light gave out completely.

'Follow me.'

Without either asking for an explanation or waiting for them, Anders began walking again, past the nearest building downhill on the slope and towards the one situated behind it, slightly higher up. Both cabins were long and rectangular with irregular blackened timbers. The small, pretty glazed windows were seemingly placed at random and didn't sit quite square (clearly, how the facade looked hadn't been a consideration when they were being built; symmetry mattered for naught against a Scandinavian winter). As they approached, Bo could see that both buildings were a patchwork of materials: from a distance, all she had processed were the tufty roofs and aged timbers, but up close, sections of newer, blonde wood stood out against the older, blackened wood with huge pale boulders used as foundations, the line of them curving upwards slightly, and she wondered how these ramshackle, flimsy-looking buildings had held up to one storm, much less a hundred years of winters of them.

From this downhill side, the buildings appeared to have

three storeys, if the windowless stone basements were included. But following Anders around the corner of the hut to where it was nestled against the grassy bank of the mountainside, it seemed barely high enough for two floors, the tufted roof sweeping down in a catslide to her hip height, creating a sort of storm-shelter for the tiny door positioned there, out of the wind and away from the elements.

'It's like something from *The Lord of the Rings*. A little hobbit house!' she smiled, charmed.

'You know Tolkien took his inspiration from Norse folklore, yes?' Anders asked her, more than a little sternly.

'Oh yes, of course.' The others joined them, making exactly the same comments and Bo wondered how often he had heard them from other . . . well, tourists.

He opened the door – it wasn't locked; why would it be? – and ducking down slightly, stepped into a low-ceilinged room. It was as though the walls had been coated with honey, as the unpainted timber walls, floor and spindle furniture coalesced with two hanging paraffin lamps to create a golden glow of such warmth the tall black puffing stove in the far corner scarcely seemed required.

'I will come back,' he said, marching towards a door at the opposite end of the room.

They waited for the door to close again – and heard the sound of voices rise to their ear – before they started up themselves.

'I don't believe it,' Zac grinned, looking both bemused and disbelieving. 'It's like stepping back in time a hundred years.'

He was right, Bo thought, taking in the sight in a single sweep. The room was modest and sparsely furnished – a red and white woven rug on the floor was as close to decoration as it got in here. But minimalism was the least of it – the hanging paraffin lamps were all the confirmation she needed that there was no electricity here, much less Wi-Fi; could they get mobile data here? She vaguely recalled it had been raised in one of their discussions, the tone suggesting it was a sweet oddity but now, faced with the reality . . . Zac and Lenny were going to have breakdowns; their notions of a Robinson Crusoe existence still somehow assimilated decent broadband width. And although they could charge their phones with the portable chargers, where would they then charge *those*? It was incredibly warm in there though – radiators weren't required when the combination of the thick timber walls and that metal stove kept the space cosy.

She stepped further into the room, beginning to take in the details: cotton lace banners hung from metal poles in the lower halves of the windows, the cornflower-blue curtains to their side, limp but beautifully embroidered with yellow-eyed daisies. A square pine table was set alongside the window wall and draped with a spotless scalloped white cotton cloth; Bo could see that a bench was pushed under it below the window, and four chairs with gingham cushion-pads set around the remaining three sides.

There was a large dresser to the right of the door where she was standing, along the gable end, with plates and bowls set in an unbroken line along its racks. To her left was a black-painted cupboarded work bench, a butler sink and gas oven, all of which looked like they had been installed in the 1960s. A red whistling kettle sat on the hob, a pale blue enamel water pitcher on the worktop, some orange and brown patterned mugs hanging on hooks, an analogue radio; there was a hard duck-egg velvet settle to one side of the stove, a game of patience set out on a card table. A rocking chair was set in front of another window, positioned for the staggering view

– for the roof of the cabin in front fell just below the eyeline here – the dandelion-embroidered cushion on it still indented from where someone had been sitting.

'What's this then, do you think?' Zac asked, holding up a kitchen implement that looked like something a ninja would use.

Behind the closed door, the voices rose; the woman's voice was impatient and although not loud, still somehow strong – a match for her terse grandson?

Suddenly the door opened and the three of them swung round to find an elderly woman slowly walking towards them. Wearing black sheepskin bootees, a calf-length black wool skirt, floral blouse and a lavender cardigan, she was stooped and absolutely tiny, leaning heavily on a walking cane as she slowly made her away across to them with a beady, enquiring gaze. Her brilliant white hair, cut close at the neck, was left longer and set in waves around the temples, giving the effect that her long hair was pinned up. Her hands were marled with liver-spots and the skin so translucent and paper-thin, her veins were like purple tattoos. She was the oldest person Bo had ever seen, and yet also, strangely, one of the most beautiful, with strong, still-dark eyebrows, a high forehead, a beak nose and almond-shaped eyes.

If someone had put a tiara on her and called her a duchess, Bo wouldn't have been in the least bit surprised. What on earth was she doing in a primitive hut like this, miles from civilization with no electricity or help? What if she fell? Or there was a bad storm?

She walked up to their group in silence, openly assessing them like soldiers on parade, standing a whole foot shorter than Zac. Bo guessed she could barely be five foot tall.

'You have been on holiday already?' she asked Bo in

accented English, stopping in front of her and scrutinizing her particularly, taking in her too blonde hair and too tanned skin.

'We've just flown in from the South Pacific,' Bo replied, feeling it would be better not to get into the specifics of their lifestyle choices. She didn't think this woman would know much about blogging.

'The *where*?' the woman asked, sounding unimpressed.

'Other side of the world, basically,' Zac cut in, coming over with his famously smooth smile. 'Hi, I'm Zac Austen.'

'Zac Austen,' the woman replied, the words sounding hollow in her accent. Her eyes slid back to Bo again questioningly.

'And I'm Bo.'

'Bo?' the woman reiterated in the same tone. '*Bo*. And *Zac*. What are these names?'

'Well, my name's short for Zachariah and I'm a Kiwi. From New Zealand,' Zac said, still smiling. 'And Bo's from England but her name's actually Amy.' He cast a glance at her, knowing she would be rolling her eyes. Which she was.

'It's on account of my hair,' Bo explained. 'My mother used to love curling it when I was little, whenever I went to a party, and my father used to joke it made me look like Little Bo Peep. So Bo sort of stuck.'

'And I'm Lenny, short for Lenny,' Lenny drawled, refusing to kowtow to the old woman but nonetheless flashing her his signature lazy smile. 'I'm from Idaho in America. It was me who made the reservation with you.'

'Yes. I remember that name,' the lady nodded, looking not in the least bit charmed. 'Well, Lenny, my grandson is very cross with me for doing business with you out of season. He has threatened to take away my iPhone.' She arched an

73

eyebrow ever so slightly and after a shocked pause, all three of them burst out laughing at the scenario.

'– So you get coverage here then?' Zac asked hopefully.

'– You have an iPhone?' Lenny asked in disbelief.

'– Out of season?' Bo queried.

They had all questioned her at the same time, and the old lady looked overwhelmed momentarily.

Anders stepped forward. 'My grandmother rents out the farm through the summer months but only because we can get someone to stay out here with her to do the necessary chores. Clearly she is too old to do such things on her own now—'

His grandmother spoke across him suddenly, her voice a flurry of cross Norwegian.

He listened in silence and looked back at them all. 'She is very independent, still, for her age,' he said, looking between them and her; she nodded imperiously, satisfied. 'But the fact remains that she should not have let out the farm at this time of year when we cannot get someone to stay here with you.' He said the last bit looking directly at his grandmother again.

Bo looked across at Lenny. She clearly recalled his air punch when their request for the booking had finally been accepted. It *was* out of season but he had known – they all had – that it was perfect for the blog and so he had pushed hard, offering more money – no doubt because he knew Ridge Riders were picking up the tab. But their followers would love the rusticity, the isolation, the views and all the folksy, craftsy, self-sustainability hipster vibe. He wanted snow and marshmallow campfires and the Northern Lights – preferably all in the same shot – and this was the perfect place to supply it. It hadn't crossed any of their minds that there might have been a very good reason for the owner pulling up the drawbridge once the weather turned, that she was an elderly lady 'hosting' on her own.

'I would have told you all this and turned you away at my door,' Anders said flatly. 'Only it explains the brand-new skidoo my grandmother bought last month –'

Bo had to resist the urge to burst out laughing. She wasn't just toting an iPhone, that little old lady had bought a skidoo? What next? A Porsche?

But Anders wasn't laughing. In fact, he was looking more stern than ever.

'– So, as she has already spent some of the money you have paid, and she cannot pay you back, you are entitled to stay here. But I hope you are well acquainted with using out-houses, water butts and making your own fires, because she will not be able to help you.'

'Oh yeah, no worries mate,' Zac shrugged.

'And are you also prepared to check on my grandmother every day?' Anders fastened them all with a hard stare. 'I'm sure you understand—'

'Of course,' Bo said quickly. 'I'll check on her every morning before we go out, and in the evenings before we go to bed.'

'Good. She retires early but I come up every other day anyway and she has a walkie-talkie if she needs me. Plus her iPhone.'

Bo nodded, sure he had fractionally rolled his eyes.

'So then, the firewood is already chopped, although you will have to bring it in from the store yourselves. I suggest you do that every night before bed – it is not pleasant waking up to a cold house and having to go out to get the logs. Especially when more snow is forecast.'

'Is it?' Lenny asked brightly.

'Yes. Towards the end of the week.'

'And the Northern Lights?'

A wry look flashed through Anders' eyes. 'They're hard to see when the snow clouds are overhead.'

'Yeah, of course. Dammit,' Lenny nodded. 'Oh well, no worries. There's plenty of time and this place will look killer in the snow.'

'It *is* killer in the snow if you are not prepared,' Anders said, no hint of a smile. 'But you at least have the correct clothes.'

Lenny gave a sudden gasp. 'Oh, shit – clothes.'

'What?' Bo asked.

'Our clothes,' he said, looking back at them, wide-eyed. 'I left the bags in the car.' He looked back at Anders. 'And I left the car by the tourist centre. It said something about one-hour parking?'

'Oh Jesus, Lenny!' Zac cried, slapping his hand over his forehead and turning away.

Bo stared at Lenny in disbelief. '*No way* am I going back down there in the dark,' she said hotly, her eyes falling to the windows that now framed the black outdoors. 'It was all I could do to get up here in the first place.'

'Well, it's not just my fault!' Lenny pushed back. 'Did either of *you* remember? Well, did you?'

'Lenny, I hate to point it out but it isn't our jobs to remember that stuff,' Zac scoffed. 'You are paid to—'

Bo saw Anders and his grandmother watching them; they were both looking at them as though they were freaks with their too-tanned skin and hipster names and inability to remember something as basic as their actual clothes.

Anders caught her watching him and, for a second, they

said nothing, as though they were both on the outside of the moment, looking in.

'It is fine,' he said. 'I will bring them up in the morning. Give me your keys. I will move the car for you too. You will not be needing it here.'

He held his hand out and Lenny hesitated for a moment, deliberating as to whether or not this stranger could be trusted with them.

'Or perhaps you do not trust me?' Anders asked, looking almost bemused by the suggestion; it was all of the second emotion Bo had now seen him display.

'Yeah, no, no, of course I do, man,' Lenny said, dropping the keys in his palm. 'It's just . . . well, I thought there was a path from here back to the village?'

'There is. Two to four hours depending on your fitness. But it is a hiking path. Not for cars. And tricky at this time of year.' He shrugged. 'The skidoo can get you so far but not all the way. The last bit is too steep and, anyway, at the moment there is not enough snow.'

Bo looked at his grandmother. How on earth, then, did she ever leave this place? Or didn't she? Did her grandson bring her what she needed up here? There was categorically no way she would be able to hike from here to the water, that much was certain. She had to be in her early nineties, at least.

'So is the skidoo available for us to use?' Lenny asked hopefully.

Anders was quiet for a moment. '. . . It could be. For a price. Have you used one before?'

'All the time, man. I told you – I'm from Idaho.'

Anders nodded. 'Let me think about it.'

'Come, I will show you your lodging,' the old woman said,

unhooking one of the lamps from the ceiling and walking slowly past them towards the door.

Anders said something in Norwegian again – presumably offering to take them himself, but she swatted the suggestion away without even turning round. Bo shot him a grateful look as they left him standing in the room and followed after her in a polite single file, like ducklings to their mother. But his look in return was reproachful and wary. It was clear that as far as he was concerned, they were guests who had already outstayed their welcome.

Chapter Six

Bo stood at the window, watching as Anders loped back down the sloping grass area – it was most definitely not, in any sense, a lawn – his arms swinging and his orange rubber suit catching the moonlight. He was wearing a headtorch now and she saw how the beam stayed dead ahead, no anxious glances left or right, even though the darkness enfolded him like a witch's cape. He knew exactly where he was going, which step to place where, and in under a minute he had dropped out of sight again, en route back to the rib still bobbing on the water by the iron rungs. She didn't want to think about how black the water must look right now.

It was all of four o'clock.

'Well,' she said, turning back into the room. 'This is great, right?'

'This is *awesome*,' Zac said from his spot on the small sofa by the stove as he tried to get some mobile signal; surprisingly, there was at least some, although it flickered in and out of reach like a candle's flame dancing in the wind. Lenny had got the stove fire going and was trooping back and forth with fresh buckets of logs from the log store that adjoined the end of the cabin. The space was warming up quickly now. In contrast to the other cabin, this one had been shockingly cold upon entering – no one had stayed here for over two months,

Anders' grandmother, Signy, had told them, and clearly she didn't have the strength to keep fires going in here on her own.

Their cabin was almost identical to the old lady's: a principal kitchen/living room with a bedroom off to the far end, but theirs also had another small sleeping space in the eaves, which was accessed by a rudimentary timber ladder and loft hatch opposite the front door. Apparently the stone-built areas below had been the old stables, where they used to keep the sheep, goats and cows, but she had said there was just an old barbecue set and some rusted bikes down there now.

The outhouse was further down the grass path that ran between the two cabins, set back from the storehouse that they had seen standing to the right of these buildings when they'd arrived. Bo hadn't dared use it yet but Lenny had, declaring it 'cold but all right; take a torch with you'.

She came away from the window and joined Zac on the sofa; it was, blessedly, not as austere as the formal blue velvet one in the other cabin, but rather a squashy red style she recognized as being from Ikea. 'Do you think she actually does live up here, on her own, all the time?'

'Well, she's not on her own all the time – that guy said she has someone up here with her to help out with the lets in the summer period. And clearly he looks in on her regularly.'

'Still, she must be pretty tough to live like this at her age. You'd think she'd be crying out for creature comforts. This is a pretty hardcore lifestyle choice.'

'Precisely why I like her. Feisty,' he murmured, kissing the top of her head.

'But you'd think she'd go mad. It's not like there's anywhere she can walk around here, there's no telly, barely any reception. What does she do all day?'

Zac shrugged, throwing one arm around her shoulder and pulling her in to him as he started scrolling his photo gallery with one hand. 'Maybe that view is enough.'

'It is a hell of a view,' she murmured. 'And I suppose there's a lot of activity on the fjord in the summer for her to watch.'

'Too much activity,' he grumbled.

'She probably likes talking to her summer guests too; I imagine she's glad of their company.'

'Well if she is, I hope she has better social skills with them than she did with us. What was all that about, going on about our names being odd and looking at our tans as though we're diseased?'

'I am definitely too dark for my colouring at the moment. It does look a bit strange,' Bo murmured, holding out her arm and examining it.

'It looks healthy,' Zac argued. 'She's the one looking pinched and stricken.'

Bo smacked him lightly on the stomach. 'She's an old lady. Be kind.'

'She started it,' he grinned, chuckling as she whacked him again. 'Oh yeah?' he asked, forgetting about his phone and turning to tickle her instead, making her wriggle and screech. She tried to get away but his fingers had found her waist – or 'tickle spot' as Zac called it – and were showing no mercy.

'No, stop, stop,' she cried, gasping frantically with laughter, but she only succeeded in wriggling herself closer to him.

It was the sound of the clicking that made them both look up.

Lenny was shooting them again, his camera – which was always hanging round his neck – pressed to his face, the bucket of logs by his feet. 'No, carry on, guys,' he said, peering round the lens. 'This is great.'

But Bo cleared her throat and pulled herself back up to sitting again; the moment had passed. 'Don't use any of that, Len, okay?' she said, untwisting her jumper, which had spiralled around her torso in the tussle.

'Why not? It's great material.'

'Because it's private, that's why,' she said frustratedly, getting up.

'Where are you going?' Zac asked.

'To have a bath,' she snapped and she saw Lenny's eyebrows hitch up at her tone. They had been arguing more and more lately. 'And, no!' she said, pointing a warning finger at him. 'You can not photograph me there either.'

'Bo—' Lenny lapsed into a puzzled silence as she crossly filled the kettle and some saucepans with water from the rudimentary tap in the wall and put them on the stove for the first fill-up – the stove was operated by gas cylinder.

'Kids, stop fighting,' Zac murmured, lost to his phone again.

The small copper bathtub was situated in their bedroom at the end of the bed – not as any sort of design statement but purely because there was nowhere else for it to go. Still, it had an undeniably rustic charm that was all their followers' aspirations. Who wouldn't want to lie out in a hand-poured copper bath in the tiny wooden cabin of a Norwegian shelf farm?

While she waited for the water to boil, she wandered through to the bedroom to check on the fire in the small hearth. The flames were making the kindling crackle but it was still freezing in there – the red curtains were thinner than her knickers. Grabbing a pale green chequered wool blanket from the chair in the near corner, she pulled it around her shoulders and sank onto the bed, seeing if she could blow a little smoke ring with her own breath. Not quite.

The narrow bed had a striking red and white diamond-patterned patchwork quilt on it and she pulled that over too so that it covered her legs and tried to stop shivering. She was able to just hear the boys' voices in the next room.

'. . . to talk to her . . . getting really tricky lately.'

'. . . I will . . .'

'. . . just trying to do my job, man . . .'

'I know, I know. I'll talk to her.'

She dropped her head, knowing she had overreacted. Again. Lenny was right. He was just trying to do what they paid him for, and most of the time he made himself scarce at the appropriate moments. It wasn't like he was demanding to be around either – as long as he had his smokes and Cokes (or a beer, any time after five) he was easy company.

No, it was her. She was jet-lagged and cranky.

Turning to her side and tucking her legs up, she lay down on the bed, pulling the red and white quilt with her. This was going to be her home for the next few weeks and it was good to be here; if she felt overwhelmed by it right now, that was only because she was tired. She would feel better come the morning.

Things always felt better in the light.

'Ugh, what time is it?' she asked, feeling the hand on her shoulder gently rocking her awake. Blearily, she opened her eyes.

'Nine,' Zac said, leaning down to kiss her temple. 'Thought I should wake you now or you'll be awake at two in the morning instead.'

'Nine at night?' she repeated, sitting up. It was the same day? It had to be the longest day ever, surely?

The curtains were still open, but outside the darkness had settled into something solid and impermeable so that only her reflection gazed back at her. She realized the room was warm at last and that she had kicked the green blanket to the floor in her sleep.

The bath had been freshly filled and was steaming gently, and she could smell and hear something delicious bubbling on the stove. She looked at Zac in amazement. Exactly how much had happened whilst she'd been sleeping?

He cupped her face in his hands and kissed her tenderly. 'I love you, Bo Loxley. The future Mrs Austen.'

'Hold your horses,' she smiled up at him. 'Ain't nothing is set in stone till I get a ring.' She waggled her still bare engagement finger.

'And you will. It'll be the most beautiful one you ever saw, worth the wait for sure.' He kissed her again. 'When I propose next time, it'll be perfect, I promise.'

Next time? Bo's face fell as she remembered the agreement for the dummy proposal. During the course of their travels in the intervening period, she had somehow managed to forget all about it. 'No. I'm joking. It *was* perfect, I loved it.'

Zac shook his head, looking disappointed. 'But I messed up. I didn't have the ring, I rushed it—'

'And that's what I loved about it – the spontaneity; the madness of it. The fact that it was just the two of us,' she insisted, reaching up for another kiss.

But she could tell he was still annoyed with himself. The lifestyle they presented to their followers was so perfectly curated, he found it hard to accept when their private life fell anything short of that too.

She sighed as he got up from the bed and trailed his fingers in the bathwater. 'Still hot but you should get in before it cools; it took five trips with the kettle and all those pans to fill it. I can't believe you slept through it.'

Really? Five trips? 'Neither can I.'

'At that rate, I reckon we'll get through a gas cylinder every third day, boiling up the water like that.'

She hugged her knees up to her chest, clasping her arms around them. 'But there's no other way to wash, is there?'

He shrugged. 'I'll ask the old woman tomorrow how the hell they got the cylinders up here in the first place. They weigh a ton. I don't know how you're supposed to carry them up the path we took. How would you even get them off the boat?'

'Hmm,' she puzzled. It had been tricky enough getting herself off.

'Come, I want to show you something before you get in,' he said, picking up the green blanket from the floor and holding out his hand.

'What is it?' she asked, trailing after him as they walked through the next room. The smell of soup bubbling made her tummy rumble immediately. 'God, I hadn't realized how hungry I am. Where did you even get this?'

'Don't get too excited. Lenny remembered we didn't have any food, as well as no clothes, so he went to see our neighbour.'

'Oh no. Don't say we've taken food off her?'

'Only a couple of cans of soup that we'll replace tomorrow. She told him where some kayaks for this place are stored down by the water.'

Bo stopped walking. 'We're going to have to kayak into town and back for food?'

'And gas. Unless you can think of an alternative,' Zac shrugged. 'Come on—'

'Wait a sec.' She looked up at the hatch in the ceiling; a light was flickering and she could see a shadow moving across the rafters. 'Hey, Lenny,' she called up.

There was a short pause, then she heard the sound of heavy footsteps across the floorboards and his upside-down face appeared. 'Yeah?' His voice was benign enough but she could still detect the hurt in it.

'Come down here, will you?'

He frowned but did it anyway, descending the chunky ladder quickly. Like Zac, he was an expert climber. 'Yeah?' he asked defensively again.

Without a word, Bo wrapped her arms around his neck. He smelled stale – of beer, sweat and the dying base notes of nicotine – but then she doubted she smelled too good herself, right now. They all needed a bath after a day travelling. 'I'm sorry for being a moody cow earlier,' she whispered and kissed his cheek. 'You're just doing your job; I don't know what we'd do without you. You're amazing.'

He smiled, his dark eyes softening. 'It's all right.'

'I promise to behave from now on. You know I'm never good on the road, but we're here now and this place is just so . . . *us*. It's going to be amazing.'

'Yeah.' Lenny smiled back at her, always so ready to forgive.

'Talking of amazing,' Zac interrupted, reaching for her hand again. 'You need to come out here and see this.'

'What *is* it?' she asked, shivering immediately as they stepped out into freezing temperatures. She didn't have her coat on and it was like being plunged into an ice bath, making her gasp.

'This.' He didn't indicate anything in particular in the pervasive dark but she still, naturally, looked up.

A gasp escaped her. 'Oh!' she cried, turning on the spot in disbelief and momentarily forgetting the cold. She had never seen anything like it, the night sky not so much freckled with stars as machine-gunned with them. Whichever direction she turned in, the indigo sky was knotted, threaded and laced with white twinkling lights; it looked heavy with the weight of them, as though they might pull the entire canopy of the sky down to earth. 'It's so beautiful.'

'I know,' Zac murmured, draping the blanket over his shoulders and hers, and pulling her in to him. 'Lenny's gonna keep watch tonight. He's hoping the Green Lady will come out dancing for us, seeing as the skies are clear. He'll wake us if one does come out to play.'

'That would be incredible,' she murmured, captivated. 'It almost seems too much to ask for – all this and that as well.'

'I know. But this is what it's all about, baby. Just us and the universe.' He rested his cheek against the top of her head. 'This is all we'll ever need.'

Chapter Seven

Was it a dream?

The *thud-thud-thud* was constant, making her frown in her sleep and pull the blankets higher over her shoulders as she squirrelled down into the pillows. Beside her, Zac groaned. But the sound didn't retreat or pass over. It was getting louder and closer.

'What the hell?' she frowned, pushing the sheets back and propping herself up on her elbows, a tussock of blonde hair falling over her face; she blew it away again, trying to see out of the window, but the thin red curtains were drawn now. She could feel vibrations through the walls, the bed, her chest, and the windows were rattling in their frames.

Zac swore, getting up and instantly shivering as his feet touched the floor. He was wearing just his pants and a T-shirt – which was two more items of clothing than he usually wore to bed; he loved a cool room, but this was another level entirely. 'Damn,' he hissed, wrapping his arms around himself as, shivering, he pulled back the curtains and looked out.

The day outside was still limp, light more of a suggestion than an actual fact, and from her position in the bed Bo could see lights whirling outside. '*What* is going on?' she frowned, getting out of bed herself and also swearing immediately as her feet touched the floor. Pulling on her socks and yesterday's jumper over the thermals she'd slept in, she joined him at the window. 'Huh?' she muttered, as she saw a small helicopter hovering down slowly, aiming for the open expanse of grass just beyond the storehouse. 'Who's that?'

They watched as the rails came to a level touch on the ground and the blades began to slow. A few minutes later they had their answer as the door opened and Anders Jemtegard jumped down, a pair of ear defenders still clasped around his neck. He reached back into the cabin and pulled out a panoply of cases and rucksacks – their clothes! – and began walking up the grass towards the cabins as though they contained nothing heavier than children's packed lunches.

Behind him, in the background, Bo saw the door to the outhouse open and Lenny step out in his boxers and a sweater, looking ashen-faced and dazed; she laughed out loud as she realized how it must have sounded in there to have an unexpected helicopter landing a few metres away. He had probably thought the tiny structure was going to blow away completely in the downdraught. 'Poor Lenny!' she cried, laughing even harder as he tried to walk, looking thoroughly shaken.

Hastily, Zac pulled on his jeans and ran through the main room, opening the front door before Anders could get to it. 'Hey!' he said brightly, greeting him with one of his homie handgrips. 'So that's how you get around out here. Pretty cool.'

Bo heard what seemed to be the customary half-pause before Anders responded 'yes'.

'Good morning,' she smiled, coming through from the bedroom.

'Good morning,' he nodded, looking a little startled at the

sight of her; no doubt her hair was looking particularly wild right now. 'I have brought your bags.'

'That's so kind of you,' she said, walking over to take hers. Even after the luxury of last night's hot bath, it felt grubby to still be wearing the clothes she had worn all day and slept in all night.

'Coffee?' Zac offered hospitably, walking over to the kettle and half filling it.

'No. My grandmother will be expecting me. I am taking her into the village.'

'Really? Not even a quick one?' Zac pressed. 'We've got some really good Java,' he said by way of enticement, opening his own rucksack and rifling through it for a bit before finally pulling out the bag of coffee. 'Our small way of saying thanks for getting us up here last night. We hadn't realized what collecting the keys from you entailed. Sorry for putting you out.' He threw him an easy smile.

'. . . Just a quick one then,' Anders nodded.

'So, your grandmother seriously still lives up here on her own?' Bo asked, leaning against the back of one of the chairs as Zac got the coffee going.

Anders nodded.

'How old is she? If you don't mind me asking.'

'She is ninety-six. But this is all she has ever known,' he said, as though anticipating her next question. 'This is her life. There is no novelty to it for her; it is not hard or lonely. She knows no other way.'

'I guess the logistics of it makes a bit more sense now we've seen the chopper. That's a pretty cool way for a ninety-six-year-old to get around. Sure beats a mobility scooter,' Zac quipped as he unhooked the cups. 'How long have you been flying one of those things?'

'Sixteen years now.' Anders was dressed for the elements again in jeans, heavy walking boots and a red padded North Face jacket. His skin was tanned too she saw, now that he wasn't hooded and wind-blown, but unlike their tropical glows, his had a weather-bitten hue to it – reddening over the nose and cheeks indicative that he'd been chapped or burnt. There was a wildness to him, a feral undercurrent, as though he belonged more to the natural world than the human one.

'It's a cool thing to do, being able to fly. What made you start?'

'My job.'

Bo nodded, feeling exasperated. Was this a conversation or an interrogation? 'And what do you do?'

'I learnt to fly in the air force but now I run an outdoor experiences company – mountain bike expeditions, kayaks, fast fjord tours on the rib – and aerial trips,' he shrugged, indicating the chopper.

'Yeah?' Zac asked, looking intrigued just as Lenny walked back in. 'Hey, Len, where've you been?'

'In the outhouse, trying not to have a *freaking* heart attack,' Lenny muttered, nonetheless nodding at Anders in greeting as he passed. 'Morning.'

Bo burst out laughing again; he was still pale, and Anders grinned too, getting up to speed with what Bo herself had witnessed.

'And I see no one thought to light the stove,' Lenny said grouchily, going straight over there and resetting it himself. 'It's freezing in here.'

Bo caught Anders' gaze and she widened her eyes in an 'oops' gesture.

'Sorry, bro – we only just woke up. Here, have a coffee,' Zac said, bringing a mug over to Lenny and handing one to

Anders too. He came back a moment later with cups for himself and her. 'So . . .' he said, in an intrigued tone. 'Outdoor experiences, huh?'

Anders shrugged and took a sip – looking pleasantly surprised by the taste.

'How funny that should come up. *You* could be just the person we're looking for,' Zac continued. 'We could really do with hooking up with someone who has local knowledge of the area and can take us to all the best, most remote, most extreme spots.'

'I do not do the guiding in the winter,' Anders demurred. 'Only the summer. This is my off-season.'

Zac smiled, not easily deterred. 'Yeah but . . . a strapping guy like you, flying choppers, driving ribs, marching up mountain tracks; you don't do what you do because you *have* to. You do it because you love it. Isn't that right? All that stuff, it's in your blood.'

'Of course.'

'So then, even though you're technically off-duty, you might be convinced to join us on our adventures. We're not tourists, if that's what you're thinking.'

'No?' The sceptical tip to his eyebrows would irritate Zac, Bo knew; he prided himself on being regarded as a true nomad. 'Then what is it you do?'

'You ever heard of Wanderlusters?'

Anders shook his head. 'No. What are they?'

'Oh.' Zac looked surprised. He gave a bemused laugh. 'Well, they're us. Me and Bo. It's our blog – or, I suppose you might say, brand name. We're digital influencers. And we have over nine million followers each on Instagram.'

'9.45 to be exact and projected to become ten mill in twenty-three days although I'm on a personal mission to see if we can get it there for Christmas,' Lenny said, from his squatting position in front of the stove.

'You can be that specific about timings?' Anders asked.

'Critical mass,' Lenny shrugged, 'it gains its own momentum. Pretty easy to map and track!'

'And you?' Anders asked him. 'Are you a wonder . . . wonder what?'

'Wanderluster,' Bo said.

'Oh.'

'Nah, my official title is photographer and brand manager, but for that you can read general lackey: log carrier, flight booker, *fire starter* . . .' Lenny said with a sarcastic smile as he straightened up again.

'Right.'

'And we couldn't do without him,' Zac said, patting his friend warmly on the shoulder. 'Lenny's the one keeping this roadshow on the road.'

'So, you . . . travel around and take photos of it for your followers, is that right?' Anders asked.

'Exactly,' Zac grinned.

Anders frowned. 'But how is that different from being tourists – apart from having *lots* of people looking at your photographs?'

'Because we don't just come in and take photos and leave. We *live* each place we go to. Become natives. We don't do the whole five-star hotel with rainshowers and infinity pools shit. We want our experiences to be raw. Authentic. They've got to have integrity to them. Hence this –' he said, holding his arms up and indicating the rustic little farm. 'Perfect case in point.'

'So you are going to become Norwegian shelf farmers then while you are here?'

93

Bo heard the wry note in Anders' voice, even though his expression remained unchanged.

'Yeah – well, except without the animals. But we're certainly gonna live like them. No electricity or hot running water.' He gave an exaggerated shudder. 'It'll take some getting used to, especially in a Scandinavian winter.' He grinned suddenly. 'But Bo and I know how to keep warm.'

Bo looked away, embarrassed, hardly able to believe he had just said that. Anders looked taken aback too and Lenny just did his usual eye-roll, knowing better than anyone just how warm Zac liked to be.

'Well, I should go,' Anders said, putting down his coffee and making to leave.

'Whoa! Wait, wait, wait,' Zac said, pushing out his hands in a 'stay' gesture. 'We haven't finished discussing you helping us out.'

'There is nothing to discuss. As I told you, this is the off-season. I am not working.'

'But it wouldn't be working. This would be *fun*. Even better, this would be being paid to have fun.'

'Yeah, that's my gig,' Lenny said, stretching back into a standing position. 'Before he and Bo got it on, Zac here had his own cult following for his extreme selfies. He's climbed Huascaran in Peru, Lhotse in the Himalayas, the Gevora hotel in Dubai—'

'Got arrested for that one,' Zac shrugged.

'This is serious shit, not hiking on some trail with holidaying IT managers. Zac's known for going to places other people, even other climbers, wouldn't dare go. He's all about the challenge.' Lenny's dark eyes shone intently. 'You can guess what's brought him *here*, can't you?'

Anders didn't even try, refusing to engage. 'No.'

'. . . Mount Ankenes?'

'Mount Ankenes is not that high.'

'Nuh, but Zac here is gonna climb up and walk through the crevasse.'

Bo sighed heavily and shook her head. Mount Ankenes was notorious (in certain specialist circles) for being the most monitored mountain in the world. A giant crack, thirty metres deep and seven hundred metres long ran across the escarpment and would one day shear off completely; as Zac and Lenny delighted in telling her, it would trigger an eighty-five-metre tsunami that would barrel down the fjord, wiping out the villages of Hellesylt and Gerainger. Both villages would be destroyed, that was an advance fact – nothing could stop it from occurring and the debate was simply a matter of when, not if: any day now or sometime in the next thousand years. Zac was hedging his bets on the thousand-year event model, even though it was classified by the renowned International Centre for Geohazards as a Class Six risk, the highest.

'You are mad.' Anders stated it as a plain fact, rather than with any sense of awe.

'Very probably, my friend,' Lenny shrugged. 'But it will send his engagement percentage off the freakin' charts and, I'm hoping, get us up to the Golden Ten.'

'And that's worth potentially dying for?'

'That mountain's not going to fall down yet,' Zac said confidently, even though he couldn't actually know that for sure. Nobody could.

'For one thing, it's not something you can just *visit*. It is off limits to the public and only accessible by helicopter.'

'Which is precisely why we need you,' Zac said.

'There's nothing up there but a monitoring station.'

'I'm not going for the coffee.'

'It is security patrolled. There are cameras up there.'

'They'll have to catch me first,' Zac laughed, sticking out his tongue and widening his eyes like he had learnt at school, doing the haka.

But Anders wasn't amused. 'I won't do it. What you are suggesting is wrong. When the rockslide happens, it will trigger the biggest peacetime evacuation in Norway's history. It is not a joke. People could die.'

Zac leant his elbows on his knees, not at all perturbed by the prospect. 'Okay, well, look, just parking that particular idea for one minute – let's not get hung up on that one climb just yet. Len and I can go it alone if we really have to. But what's it gonna take to bring you on side for the rest of our stay, huh? For the next two weeks particularly, we need to find the inside track on this place and we need an expert to take us to all the best off-the-beaten-path places – rivers, caves, lakes, gorges, you name it. Lenny's been researching as best he can but there's no substitute for local knowledge. We could really use your help, man: you got the info, you climb, you got a chopper . . . You can name your price.'

'Why just two weeks? I thought you booked for a month?'

'Yeah, but that brings us up to Christmas and the end of our sponsorship arrangement here; after that we'll rest up a bit. Even Lenny's going home for a while.'

'I am?' Lenny asked, looking surprised.

'Well, aren't you?' Zac asked back, looking just as surprised. 'You don't wanna be here with me and Bo over Christmas. You got your own family, dude.'

Lenny paused. 'I guess.'

Zac looked back at Anders. 'Listen, as a bonus, we'll also tag you daily on our posts – and, trust me, that is advertising money *can't* buy. Nine million people daily seeing your company name on their screens? You'll have more business than you can handle.'

Anders looked underwhelmed and Bo wasn't sure he understood the dramatic impact appearing in their posts would have on his business. 'I don't want that much business, there's only one of me. And as I said before, this is my off-season.'

'You play a hard game, man, I'll give you that, but I'm a stubborn pain-in-the-ass and we need you. Come on, what will it take? Name your price. Hit me with a number.'

Anders merely blinked, his face made for poker.

'Okay, I'll start,' Zac said finally. 'Ten thousand?'

Anders' right eyebrow twitched ever so slightly. 'Fifteen. Assuming you mean dollars.'

'Sure – dollars, kroner . . . whatever you want.'

Wait, what? Bo looked up but Zac had that look on his face that he always got when he was 'doing a deal'. He was used to 'haggling' with the locals and always liked to buy their goodwill with a gesture of generosity.

Anders stared at him levelly. 'Dollars is better for me.'

'Zac—' she protested. But he simply held up a hand to silence her.

'Okay, dollars is good, if we agree to at least keep the Ankenes project on the table and up for discussion. Our sponsors *really* liked the sound of it when we talked with them. They think it'll make a great finale.'

'Zac!' Bo protested again.

'Babe, please,' Zac said shortly, without even looking at her. The words 'I'm busy' hung unspoken in the air.

'It can stay on the table but I make no promises,' Anders said bluntly. 'Right now, it's still a no.'

'I'm okay with that, I reckon I've got your number, man. So – have we got a deal?' Zac grinned, holding out his hand.

Anders shook it with more animation than he had shown at any other point in the past eighteen hours. 'Okay, deal,' he replied, nodding to the others, who were looking on open-mouthed. 'But I cannot start right now. I am taking my grandmother into the village and we will not be back until the afternoon, when it will be getting dark. We will have to start tomorrow.'

'Excellent,' Zac grinned. 'Good man. Tomorrow's great. That gives you time to get some ideas together for an itinerary and we need to get set up here today anyway – get some food in.'

'Tomorrow then.' And with a final, satisfied nod, Anders exited the building.

'. . . What?' Zac asked, seeing both Bo and Lenny's aghast expressions.

'Do you have any idea what the exchange rate is for the Norwegian krone to dollars?' Lenny demanded.

'About point eight?'

'*Point eight*?' Lenny scoffed. 'Try, to the power of eight.'

Zac's expression changed. 'Huh?'

'Fifteen thousand in kroner would've been just under two thousand in dollars!'

Zac's expression changed further still. '*What?*'

'I was trying to tell you,' Bo said, exasperated. 'But you wouldn't listen.'

'She was, man,' Lenny agreed. 'And you just blocked her out. Your pride just cost you – her, us – thirteen grand. You got robbed, bro, and you didn't even know it,' he said, slapping Zac sarcastically on the shoulder as he passed by, climbing up the ladder to his digs again.

Zac looked across at Bo, his face a curious mix of embarrassment and defiance. 'Well . . . it's money well spent, right? He's got a chopper and maps and . . .'

'One up on you,' Bo snapped. 'You know, you're always so sure you know what's right, but you don't! Sometimes, you're a bloody fool, Zac. You were right what you said to him just now – you are a stubborn pain-in-the-arse.'

'Bo! Babe—' But she was already picking up her rucksack and hoicking it into the bedroom with her. If nothing else, she had to get into some clean clothes.

Bo sat in the cabin looking out at the still fjord, the MacBook open on the table in front of her, her hand cupped in her chin. Zac and Lenny had gone down into the village on the kayaks to get a proper stock of food, leaving her to keep the stove going and to post something, anything, to the blog. With a dearth of any new significant shots yesterday or today, they would have to use something off the reel from the past few days on the road and she had been flicking through Lenny's library – but it was an uninspiring roster to say the least. There were some out-takes of her piggybacking Zac on the Eagle Pass but they'd already used that and it had garnered 306,782 likes so far, a good tally; anything over three hundred thousand was a decent engagement rate. Lenny had taken some shots of her, asleep in the taxi at Alesund on the way to the hotel, and there were some decent pictures of them both on the rib, Zac punching the air as they approached the waterfalls. With the orange jacket on, it was quite a striking image, albeit a little blurred and the lighting wasn't great. But perhaps a filter could sharpen it up and lift it? And the Ridge Riders badge on the arm of his jacket was clear to see.

Definitely one to consider. She wrote down the frame numbers and continued scrolling.

Up next was a sequence of shots showing her climbing the steep path to the farm last night, but having been taken from below, the angle was unflattering and the light (fading fast) was even worse down there in the woods than it had been a few minutes earlier on the water. After those came the pictures of her and Zac on the grass last night when they'd first arrived, but Lenny had already posted her spin and Zac's conqueror pose, so they were out too.

She came to the tickle fight on the sofa, her and Zac laughing, her eyes squeezed shut and head thrown back in exquisite agony as Zac grinned down at her. The sequence had a sexy dynamic energy to it, their teeth looking crazy-white against their tans in the honeyed room, as though they were being photographed in black light. She didn't like that her jumper had twisted up, exposing her taut stomach, even though she spent half the year being photographed in a bikini. All their followers pretty much saw her abs on a daily basis, and yet switch to the northern hemisphere and being bundled under layers of clothes and it made a sudden flash of skin feel somehow exploitative.

Still, they were hardly spoilt for choice with material at the moment. It was always like this during their transition days, and until they got into a rhythm here they would have to eke out what mileage they could from these holding shots. Reluctantly, she noted down the frame numbers again.

Tab, tab, tab.

She stopped as she came to another photograph of herself sleeping, this time bundled up on the bed in the blankets. Yesterday evening? After her tantrum. Her hair had streaked across her face, but her cheeks looked rosy from the flush of deep sleep. She bit her lip. She never liked being photo-graphed when she was asleep – the idea of someone standing over her like that, even if it was a friend . . .

The next batch was of her and Zac huddled under the blan-ket together, looking up at the crazily starred night sky. They were beautiful images, it was undeniable, one in particular showing the moonlight falling on their faces, partly in profile, Zac resting his cheek against the top of her head as they both looked out into space, searching in vain for the Northern Lights.

She hadn't realized Lenny had been photographing them then – from the angle, slightly above and behind them, she supposed he must have taken them through his window in the eaves. She had thought it was a private moment between her and her fiancé but, of course, there was no such thing. Bo immediately knew that was today's holding image for the grid – it perfectly encapsulated the heady freedom and inti-mate coupledom for which their followers so avidly loved them, and there was the rub, for clearly there was no way just the two of them could have captured that stunning image *without* Lenny being there. They needed him, he was excellent at his job. In order for her and Zac to be an Insta-famous couple, they had to live as a trio.

She captioned it, adding on all the hashtags that would bring them up on multiple search lists: wanderlusters, stars, starry, night, midnight, Norway, Norwegian, fjords, Gerainger . . . and pressed send. The little icon wheeled round and round and she wondered how long it would be before it picked up enough roaming reception and was able to upload.

She went to close down the images file but saw there was yet one more. Another one from outside? Was it better?

But as she clicked on it, she drew a breath and sat back in the chair.

It was of her, taken from behind again through the gap of a pushed-to door. She was lying in the bath, her long hair balled up in a messy topknot with tendrils dropping down at the sides. Her head was tipped back, one slim arm lolling lazily over the side of the copper tub, her tanned toes peeking from the water. Again, it was another beautiful image, encapsulating everything their followers tracked them for: something rustic yet chic, sensuous yet simple. Lenny's cherished 'engagement rate' would go through the roof but she didn't care – before she could check herself, she reached over and pressed delete.

She wandered outside with her phone, the yellow jacket back on. They had been here less than twenty-four hours and already it had proved its worth. In a climate and landscape such as this, warmth became a matter of survival and she sensed how ever-present and close that prospect was here. The sky was cloudy, the light completely flat, and the water lay heavily like a dark inert body nothing could move. According to Lenny, today was supposedly 'mild' but the chill had a biting edge to it, even though it was now just after midday and about as warm and bright as the day was going to get. The sun didn't appear to be rising beyond the top of the mountains but rather bobbing below the ridge line like a half-deflated balloon.

She wandered around the little farm, poking her head through the stable door downstairs – as Signy had told them, there was just an old barbecue and a few rusty bikes down there. She tried to peer in through the storehouse windows as the door was locked, but the storehouse was set off the ground on stone pillars, supposedly to keep animals and rodents from getting in, and she couldn't quite peer over the ledges. She took some arty close-ups of the weathered stones and blackened timbers instead. She found an old wooden barrow half buried in the long grass, a thickly rusted rake and some sort of stone wheel covered in moss, and shot those too. Everything here felt aged and long-forgotten, as though this spot had somehow slipped from the bonds of time to remain rooted in a fixed spot from the past, decades earlier than now.

Overhead, the sudden shriek of a bird made her look up. She didn't know what it was – an eagle? A buzzard? A hawk? – but the wingspan was immense, the pale-bellied bird wheeling in looping circles through the silent sky as though patrolling the fjord.

The sudden company made her realize how alone she was up here. It was a disconcerting feeling – seclusion and isolation were two entirely different experiences. On the plus side, it meant she had peace and quiet for recording some video footage for the Instagram 'stories' function – the other job Zac had tasked her with as he and Lenny headed off into town. She preferred doing these short videos to the photos precisely because they only remained up for twenty-four hours. Each short was only fifteen seconds long and she felt she could be more natural, relaxed, breezy, *herself* in them. There was something so judgemental and defining about the photos they posted to the squares: logged there for eternity, they seemed to stand proud as a visual record and testimony of what her life was. It felt like anything that went on there had to matter so much more, had to stand for something. Sometimes, usually when stuck in an airport, she would scroll through the feed herself, trying to see what other people saw: a young couple in love, laughing their way around the world, their hair too long, their tans too dark, their eyes too bright. Did they ever guess at how mundane their lives really were behind the squares? The travelling, the trekking to the photo locations, the hours of internet research . . . Those images didn't just happen. They were planned, edited and curated.

Yes, that was it. She was a curator of her own life.

Tossing her hair back from her face, she held her arm up in the air, the phone angled down towards her, the fjord at her back. 'Hey, guys,' she smiled to her own image on the screen. 'So we made it!' Bright smile. 'It's been a *crazy* few days – getting on planes, getting off them, getting on some more. But it was *so* worth it, because look where we are now: on a gorgeous little shelf farm in central western Norway.' She angled the phone so that it could sweep a panorama of the view. 'But we're settled now and see these buildings?' She angled the phone towards the cabins. 'That's our Home Sweet Home for the next few weeks. They're hundreds of years old. No hot water. No electricity.' She widened her eyes to camera. 'I know, right?' She laughed. 'But seriously, I—'

The phone stopped recording.

'Dammit,' she muttered, pressing upload and reset, tossing her hair back again and holding her arm back up. Bright smile again. 'Seriously though, it's amazing to be here and it feels *so* good to actually be cold again! Things you never thought I'd say, I know. I'm always the first to get my bikini on when the sun's out, but I'd forgotten how sort of *pure* the cold makes you feel, instead of that . . .' she pulled a face. 'Ugh . . . sticky, sweaty feeling. And of course Zac is like a freakin' *puppy*, bounding around and wanting to get back up a mount—'

'Dammit,' she said again as the screen flashed black once more. Oh well, that would have to do for the moment, she thought, pressing upload and wandering over the grass towards the boundary where the woods started up again. The gradient on the grassy expanse here was shallow but immediately below it, with the trees, the pitch straightened sharply again into an almost vertical drop and her stomach lurched at the sight of it.

She wondered when the boys would be back, her eyes falling to the mountains on the other side of the fjord, the waterfalls still tumbling endlessly, albeit silently from here.

'Hello?!' she cried out suddenly, liking how it felt to raise her voice. Release, of sorts. 'Is anybody there?' she asked into the void. But there was no echo. This place was too vast for that.

She turned to go back into the cabin. It was too chilly to stay out here for long and she needed a coffee to warm her hands against, but as she began to walk she heard the distinctive judder that had woken her that morning, and within moments the helicopter glided back into view through the thick clouds. It was like a giant fly with a bug-eye-shaped cabin, the landing rails like spindly legs.

She ran to the path between the two cabins, keeping well out of the way – she wouldn't be surprised if it blew her off the shelf – her hair blowing around wildly as she watched Anders land again. He really was a very good pilot – competent, confident, steady. Bit like him, as far as she could see.

She waited for the blades to come to a stop before she dared approach.

'Hi,' she said as Anders ran around the helicopter to help his grandmother out.

He glanced across. 'Oh, hey.'

'How was your trip into the village?'

He nodded. 'Fine.' He opened the door and Bo watched as

he slid his grandmother's arm around his shoulders and lifted her easily from the seat. He managed to carry her all the way up to where Bo was standing before the old woman, in stern Norwegian, demanded to be put down.

She really was tiny, only coming up to Bo's shoulders. Of course, she was hardly standing straight; the stick in her hand wobbled like a joystick and the old woman reached out, grabbing for Bo as she peered up at her through inquisitive eyes.

'Give me your arm,' she commanded and Bo obliged. She didn't dare not. Anders – having been effectively dismissed – walked back down to the helicopter and began to unload it.

'How was your trip?' Bo asked her as they began to walk in tiny pigeon steps up the uneven grass path between the two cabins. She wondered how Signy wasn't shivering in the cool air, as she had only a woollen shawl knotted over her shoulders.

'A waste of time. That doctor isn't old enough to tell me the time, much less read a blood result.'

Bo wasn't quite sure what to say in response. 'I'm sorry to hear that.'

'You enjoyed seeing Kristine though,' Anders prompted as he walked past them both, bulging bags in both his hands.

'Kristine?' Bo asked politely.

'My hairdresser,' Signy said, her eyes on the grass, and concentration on her face with every small step. 'She sets it for me twice a week.'

'How wonderful. I'd love to have someone do that for me.'

'You?' she scoffed. 'What do you need it for? . . . You're a young woman. Your hair looks beautiful down,' she said, panting slightly from the effort of walking and talking at the same time. 'My hair . . . used to be beautiful once. My pappa said it was my . . . how do you say it . . . my crown?'

'Crowning glory?' Bo suggested.

She grunted. 'I still remember . . . the day I first . . . put it up . . . I felt so sad . . . It meant I was no longer young.'

Anders, having deposited the bags inside, marched past them again, a trace of bemusement in his eyes as he passed.

'But you must still have been beautiful though? You're a striking woman, even now.'

'Even now. Huh,' she grunted again, a wry note sounding in her voice.

They reached the cabin and together they shuffled in slowly, Anders at their backs again. He was a fast walker – especially for one carrying several gas cylinders. He put them down with an exhale, kicking the door shut with his foot before going straight over to the stove to stoke the fire. Bo helped Signy into the rocking chair by the far window, quickly plumping up the dandelion cross-stitch cushion before she sat back against it.

'Here,' Anders said, coming over a moment later with a glass of water and holding out some pills in his hands as Signy unknotted her shawl. 'Take these now while I am here and can be sure you have taken them.'

His grandmother replied in Norwegian so Bo didn't understand what she said but her tone was clearly one of indignation; though she took them from him and obeyed, nonetheless.

Anders' eyes met Bo's as he turned away, a slight flashing arch of his right eyebrow betraying the level of patience that was required when dealing with his stubborn grandmother. 'Coffee?'

'*Takk*,' his grandmother nodded, closing her eyes and beginning to rock the chair gently.

Anders gave a wry grin as he looked back at Bo and she

became aware that there was an air of expectation in the room. 'Oh, who *me*? Uh yes, that would be lovely . . . if you're sure it's not a problem.'

'It's not a problem,' he said, turning away to fill a Bialetti coffee pot with water.

Bo shrugged off the yellow jacket. 'So do you have any other family in the area?' she asked, putting the question out to either one of her hosts as she sat down at the table, her hands absently smoothing wrinkles from the embroidered linen cloth.

Anders' gaze slid over to his grandmother quickly before he replied: 'No, it is just us. My parents died in an accident when I was very young. My grandmother raised me. Here, in fact.'

'Oh, I'm so sorry,' she said quickly, before adding, 'I mean about your parents, obviously; not . . . not growing up here, that must have been lovely.'

He shrugged, reaching for a large enamel tin and shaking out some coffee beans into a mortar dish. 'Mainly. It was lonely too though, sometimes. When you are a seven-year-old boy, all you want is to kick a ball with your friends. But here . . . ?'

'Oh, right!' Bo agreed, fully able to imagine the futility of kicking a ball about on this shelf. 'You would have lost a lot of balls.'

'It could have been worse. We are lucky to have this plateau. Some of the old shelf farms are on land so steep, the farmers had to tie both their children and animals to railings when they were outside.'

'To keep them from falling off, you mean?' Bo gasped. 'Seriously?'

He nodded.

'Oh my God!'

He cracked a half-grin, seeming amused by her wide-eyed astonishment. 'And you? Where did you grow up?' he asked as he began to grind the beans with the pestle.

'Oh, a place called Dorset, in the south of England,' Bo said, watching, fascinated. She'd never had her coffee ground for her by hand before. 'Nowhere as exciting as this.'

'I know Dorset.'

She looked up in surprise. 'You do?'

'I once had an English girlfriend from there. Sherborne.'

'That's not far from where I grew up,' she said excitedly. 'Do you know Wimborne?'

He stilled, seeming to think for a moment. 'I think we went there once. A horse race.'

'Yes, at Badbury Rings. A point-to-point, we call it. We always used to go to that.' She sighed happily at the memories as they rose, unbidden by this unexpected turn in the conversation. 'Do you know I've been all over the world and never once met anyone who knew my home town?'

He continued to grind the coffee. 'Do you go back often?'

It should have been an innocuous question. Instead she felt as though the ground had been whipped from under her. 'N-no,' she stuttered. 'No, I . . .' Her voice trailed off. She bit her lip, trying to gather herself. 'I really ought to. I keep meaning to. But the time just seems to . . . disappear, doesn't it? One minute, you're setting off on a six-month backpacking trip, the next thing you know, it's been four years.' Her voice rose shrilly at the end of the sentence and he glanced at her.

'Are your parents still living there?'

She forced a smile and nodded. 'Mm-hmm.'

He looked like he was about to say something but as he glanced over at her, taking in her frozen expression, the moment passed, his words sinking back down again, and a small silence bloomed instead.

She continued watching him grind the beans until she felt her heart slow to a steady pace again and the block in her throat cleared. He made it look easy. After a few minutes he stopped and poured the beans into the funnel of the coffee pot and put it onto the stove, keeping the ring of flames low.

A sudden snore made Bo turn, startled. Anders chuckled without turning round. 'She always sleeps when she comes in from the village. She refuses to lie on the bed and insists she will have a coffee, but she never does.'

'She's lucky to have you,' Bo smiled, turning back.

'I am the lucky one. She is all I have. My family. My home.'

Bo stared, feeling somehow saddened by the statement. On the one hand, their closeness was touching. On the other, he was a young man, still, and she was so old. At the very best, they had only a few years left together. What was he going to do then?

'Do you come to live here with her in the summer months too?'

'I would like to but my business is too busy. I have to be in town, dealing with the clients. But I come up every other day at the very least. Most days I can pass by with a group to bring supplies and check she is well. The tourists like to stop and have coffee here anyway and look at the view. Sometimes, if she is up to it, my grandmother puts on a demonstration for them, making the old traditional dishes.'

As if knowing she was being discussed, his grandmother gave another snuffly snore and Bo looked across at her. 'Do you ever get away from here?' she asked. 'Even just for a holiday?'

'But what is that? When people talk about holidays, they

mean escape from their own lives, from the pressures of their jobs, or being around other people, or needing to leave the city to be back in nature. I don't need that. All of those things, I have here.'

'So you're saying your life feels like one long holiday?' She smiled. 'How lucky.'

'Yes. I am.' He looked up at her. 'And you? Where was your last holiday?'

'Well we travel so much, the concept has sort of ceased to exist for us. We live on the road. Normal life for us is what most people would consider to be permanent holidays. We've just spent several months in Samoa.'

He took the pot off the heat, pouring the coffee into the mugs. 'So surely going home would be a holiday for you now then?' he said, handing her a mug.

She gave a noncommittal shrug. 'Yes, maybe.' Her eyes opened wide as the taste hit. 'Oh, wow! That is seriously good. Better than our Java.'

He looked pleased by the compliment, a small smile enlivening his eyes. It made him look dramatically different, as though the frost he wore had thawed, revealing colours and warmth beneath.

She sipped the coffee again, pleased herself that they had got off the topic of homes. 'This really is awesome.'

'Thank you.' He watched her. 'So where will you all go after this?'

Bo sighed. 'Well I'm trying not to think about it yet. We've only just got here. I want to get my feet under the table and enjoy being here. But Lenny's suggesting Sri Lanka.'

'So, back to the sun again.'

'That's what we try to do – switch hemispheres: hot, cold, hot, cold. It's a nightmare to be honest – I *always* end up with a cold every time we move place; in fact, I can already feel a tickle in my throat – but Zac says it shakes up the posts and makes the grid look varied.'

'The grid?'

'You know, the little Instagram squares on your feed makes a grid.'

'Oh.'

She smiled. 'I take it you're on Instagram?'

He hesitated. 'No.'

'Oh my *God*,' she laughed, astounded. 'You must be the only human under thirty who isn't, then!'

'I'll be thirty-one in June.'

'Well then, in June, it will be acceptable!' she chuckled. 'But not till then.'

He smiled, tapping a finger once in a while against the mug. For all his taciturn exterior, he was surprisingly easy company. Conversation didn't feel forced with him and silence didn't feel stilted. He somehow inhabited the space he was in with infinite ease and acceptance.

'Actually, I'm not being completely honest – I did open an Instagram account for the business last year, but I haven't done anything with it.'

'Oh, but you must, *especially* if you're in the tourist trade; it gives you a global reach. How many followers have you got?'

He thought for a moment. 'Forty something? Mainly my neighbours.'

She slapped her hands on the table. 'I know pot plants with more following than that!' she guffawed.

This time it was his turn to laugh out loud. 'Thank you!'

'Ahem!'

The cough made them both turn and they saw Lenny standing by the door, peering through at them.

'Lenny, you're back!' she smiled.

'What are you doing?' he asked, sounding sullen.

Bo held up her mug. 'Having coffee? Want one?'

He shook his head tersely, looking irritated.

'So how was it?' she asked, just as a peal of laughter suddenly curled through the crystalline air and she looked through the window to see Anna's distinctive tumbling hair as she and Zac crested the ridge.

'Oh, just look at this!' Anna cried, stopping as she took in the sight of the shelf farm, smoke puffing from the two chimneys. Zac was laden with shopping bags and Anna was rolling a small wheeled suitcase on the bumpy ground behind her.

'Who is that?' Anders asked as they watched them advance up the grassy path, Anna having to stop repeatedly to kick her bag the right way up as it continually toppled over.

'That's Anna, she's the marketing rep for the company we're endorsing while we out here,' Bo murmured. Why did she have a suitcase with her? More product for them?

Anders and Lenny watched as Anna passed by the windows. Bo had a feeling most men liked the look of Anna: curvaceous but athletic, her lively eyes made her appear to be laughing even when she wasn't. She looked like good company, feisty, bubbly. Sexy.

'Guys, in here,' Lenny called, still sullen. Had he and Zac had an argument in town? Or had Anna given him the brush-off?

'Ssh!' Bo hushed, pressing a finger to her lips, but Anders shook his head.

'It is fine. When my grandmother sleeps, she *really* sleeps. She's pretty deaf.'

A moment later, Anna and Zac were in the room too.

'Hey!' Zac puffed, dropping the bags by his feet and looking across at the cosy scene – her and Anders sipping coffee, Signy asleep in the rocking chair, the fire crackling quietly. 'What are you two up to?'

Bo held her mug up again.

Zac nodded. 'Oh. Is it good? As good as ours?' he asked, winking over at Anders matily.

'Better. Hand-ground in a pestle and mortar no less. Anders is without doubt the best barista I've ever met. You should have seen him in action.'

Zac's smile stayed stretched. 'Yeah? Well I can,' he panted. 'I assume you took loads of photos of him in action?'

'Photos?' The word escaped her like a wisp of smoke.

'Yeah, you know – those pretty shiny things we post everyd—' The smile faded from his face at the expression on hers. 'You didn't take any photos? Whilst you were having your coffee hand-ground by a real-life Viking in an historic shelf farm? You didn't think the fans would want to see that?'

Irony aside, she knew he had a point. She bit her lip – her nervous tic. 'I forgot.'

'*Forgot?*' Zac asked, annoyance in his eyes. 'You just forgot about the nine million people who care about this stuff?'

'I'm sorry. It was just coffee. We were talking.' She shrugged. 'It was a . . . a moment, not a stage set.'

'Oh, a moment, uh-huh,' Zac nodded, sarcasm radiating from him.

Anna cleared her throat. 'Hi, Bo.'

'Anna, sorry,' Bo apologized, mortified that she should witness their tiff. 'How are you?' she asked as Anna came over and they kissed on the cheek.

'Great, thanks. I'm so happy to be here,' she said excitedly. 'It feels like the days have dragged since I saw you all at

Storfjord. I've been counting down the hours.' Her gaze floated up to Anders, standing just behind Bo.

'Oh, this is Anders Jemtegard, and his grandmother there is Signy. They own the farm.'

Anna suddenly saw the sleeping woman in the corner. 'Oh –' she mouthed, as though any sound might wake her.

'No, don't worry, she isn't easily woken, apparently.'

'Oh good,' Anna grinned. 'Well it is a pleasure to meet you, Anders,' she said, holding out a hand.

'Anders has also agreed to act as our guide for the next two weeks,' Bo said. 'To ensure we can deliver the best posts. He knows all the hidden-away beauty spots around here.'

Anna was looking up at him intently, her eyes shining with intensity as their hands clasped. 'Have we . . . have we met before?'

'No.' Anders' reply was immediate. Typically brusque. They dropped hands.

'Are you sure? You look really familiar to me – and I'm great with faces.'

He shrugged but offered nothing further.

'I'm from Alesund. You don't have any connections there?' she persisted.

'No.'

Anna smiled her twinkly eyed smile, clicking her fingers and pointing at him playfully. 'Oh, it'll come to me. I'm sure we have met.'

Another shrug. He seemingly felt no compunction to make moments – or people – feel less awkward.

Bo spread her arms wide, indicating the rustic cabin. 'So what do you think of our little hideaway?'

Anna's hands flew to her cheeks. 'It's incredible! So tucked away! You can hardly see it until you are almost upon it. I have always wanted to visit one of these.'

'I know, I feel like I'm in a Tolkien novel up here. On the one hand, the farm is so tiny and snug, and on the other there's this vast, epic view outside the windows. It's insane.'

'Your followers are going to go crazy for it,' Anna agreed, turning back to Bo. 'And did Zac give you the good news?'

'No, what's that?' Bo asked, looking between them both.

'Zac!' Anna scolded him.

'Give me a chance!' Zac protested, his hands held up in the air. 'I got here the same time as you!'

Anna looked at Bo with her palms pressed together excitedly. 'The Sami – which is your style jacket – has already completely sold out online; within three hours of your first post going up, actually.'

Bo's mouth dropped open a little. 'Oh my goodness.'

'It's official – our customers can't get enough of you,' Anna squealed. 'You're already a hit!'

'Well, that's great!'

'And just wait till you try the rest of the collection. We guarantee you'll want to hike in it, ski in it, climb in it, sleep in it, even!'

So there was more product in that bag then, Bo thought to herself.

'I frickin' hope not,' Zac guffawed. 'Bo and I like to sleep au naturel. I don't want that changing!'

'Really?' Bo asked him, knowing she was blushing furiously. 'You said that out loud? You let those words actually come out of your mouth?'

Zac laughed, his tetchiness from a moment ago seemingly forgotten already. If there was one thing about Zac, he never held a grudge. 'Aw, you're going red. When did you get to be such a prude?' he teased, coming over and draping an arm over her shoulder and kissing her on the cheek.

'I'm not. I just don't think that it's anything anyone else particularly wants to know about, that's all,' she said wryly. 'Sometimes, you really need to apply a filter.'

'You don't usually care.'

'We don't usually have an audience,' she retorted, before adding, 'well, apart from Lenny.'

'Okay, okay, I'll keep shtum,' he murmured, sweeping her hair off her shoulder and kissing her neck instead.

'Zac!'

Lenny gave a loud groan, rolling his eyes in Anna's direction. 'Don't worry, you'll get used to it. They can be pretty nauseating to be around.'

'Hey, *I'm* not doing anything!' Bo protested as Zac looped his arms around her and hung off her like a sloth.

'So it's all true then?' Anna beamed as she gazed back at them both. 'True love?'

'The truest,' Lenny said flatly. He wasn't a big believer in affairs of the heart; most of his romances barely lasted the night. 'Come on, Anna, I'll show you your digs.'

'And I'd better put that food away,' Zac said, reluctantly letting go of Bo and, picking up the bags, heading back out of the door.

'Sorry, wait – what did you say, Lenny?' Bo queried.

He looked back at her, his eyebrow hooked just fractionally in the middle. He still looked irritable. 'I'm gonna show Anna where she's sleeping.'

'Anna's staying here? At the farm?'

'Yeah. We discussed that the other day.'

'But I thought she would be in the village. I mean, where . . . ?' She indicated to the cramped cabins with her hands. There was barely enough space for the three of them as it was.

'In the storehouse,' Lenny said, as though it was obvious, jerking his head back to indicate the blocky stilted building down the path.

'The storehouse?' Anna laughed, looking as shocked as Bo.

'Don't worry, it's not a storehouse any more – is it, Anders?' Lenny asked him. 'It's done up as a one-bed unit with a little living area. Why do you think *I'm* not staying in there?' He suddenly grinned at Anna again, giving a cheeky wink too. 'Lucky for you I'm a gentleman.'

Anna gave a surprised laugh, as did Bo – he was anything but that.

'Does my grandmother know about this?' Anders asked, looking displeased by the development.

Lenny's grin faded as he looked back at Anders, and Bo could tell he had taken against him. His easy-going, laissez-faire mentality was completely at odds with Anders' taciturn, almost formal, demeanour. 'Of course. It's all in the original booking. Ask her.'

'Well . . . she's sleeping,' Anders said, pointing to the sleeping woman, sarcasm hovering around the words.

Lenny shrugged. 'Well it is, anyway. Do you have the keys? We'd better get the stove going. If it was anything like our place, it'll be freezing in there.'

There was a pause, before Anders walked over to the dresser and pulled a set of keys from the drawer.

'Well, I guess I'd better help Zac unpack,' Bo said, returning her mug to the sink.

She walked over to the chair and took her jacket. 'Thank you,' she said, as she walked outside, Anders just behind her.

'For what?'

'Just all of it. The coffee. The chat. It was so nice and . . . normal,' she shrugged.

He looked down at her and she was surprised again by the dazzling colour of his eyes. 'No problem.'

Someone cleared their throat and they both looked up to find Lenny still standing on the path. 'You got the keys?' he asked impatiently. 'Anna's standing out in the cold.'

'There.' Anders pressed them into his hand. 'You know how the stoves work now?'

'Sure do,' Lenny said shortly. He turned away but Anders put a hand on his shoulder – at six foot three, he was a good six inches taller than him. 'Hey, there's something you should know.'

Lenny frowned. 'Yeah?'

'Next time you go to town, you don't need to carry the bags up yourselves.'

His face fell. 'We *don't*?'

'There are aerial cables down there, a pulley system to bring things up and down from the farm. Just clip the handles on and you're good to go.'

Irritation settled on Lenny's face like a cloud of flies. 'I really wish we'd known that an hour ago, man.'

Anders shrugged, turning away with a smile. 'Well, you do now.'

Chapter Eight

Reiten *seter*, Lodal, June 1936

It was a gentle day, the sun beaming with a kindly heat that warmed her bones without scorching her skin. Signy sang as she walked in long strides – well, the longest her legs could manage anyway. She hadn't grown in almost two years and she was still a good five inches shorter than her big sister, which felt like a keen injustice. If Margit was going to forever be the oldest, then didn't she get to be the tallest? Wasn't that fair? Her mamma kept saying she would grow again in the summer when the sun found her in the fields, but it hadn't happened last year, thanks to her broken leg and all those weeks spent stuck lying on her bed. But this year she was in the sunlight every day, and at night, saying her prayers, she always remembered to add on a plea for her legs to grow too.

Her shepherding stick was a downy birch branch she had found around the back of the *stabbur*; perhaps it had been used to prop the door open, for it was almost perfectly straight and the perfect height for her to use over the hillocks as she roamed with the herd. She knew the valley in its broad strokes from the occasional days spent here as a child whilst the adults worked, but the detail was new to her and she was enjoying exploring its nooks and crannies. Today, she had taken the goats to the pastures on the outer western edges of the valley, on the far side of the stream, where the ground began to rise up again, pine trees feathering the landscape in loose knots. Slowing her pace, she turned and checked the goats had all kept up with her; with almost two hundred nannies and kids, there were too many to stop and count individually, but her eyes scanned the ground for any drifters going astray.

Stormy had led something of a revolt several days earlier, deciding she wasn't yet ready to give up the day's lush grass for a return to the pens and had stubbornly kept grazing as Signy ran around dementedly, making her various different pitched calls and even, at one point, trying to *push* Stormy into action. It was surprisingly difficult to move a sulking goat, and, of course, if Stormy wouldn't budge, neither would the others; only bribing her with Signy's own treasured afternoon pear had eventually made her move, although seemingly feeling her principles had been compromised, the goat had petulantly cried in loud protest the whole way home.

Peace had been restored, however, and today Stormy was only a half-step behind her, her wet nose butting against Signy's hand every now and again. Signy smiled at the sight and sound of them all clustering behind her in a bottleneck, their little cowbells jangling on their collars. She had spent much of the afternoon stretched out on her tummy on a pale grey speckled rock that had at first glance looked like a basking seal, choosing names for the kids and laughing as she watched them frolicking in the lush pastures, picking their knees high over the grass tufts as they bleated little sounds that were at once joyous and melancholic; they were only nine weeks old but already they bounded and bounced with a dexterity she could never match. They still kept close to their mothers at this age, some of them wanting to feed even as they walked and the nannies protesting loudly in response, but in a couple of weeks it would be a different matter entirely and the urge to roam would kick in in earnest. She wouldn't get away with spotting her beloved gyrfalcons or counting butterflies then.

The valley lay cradled beneath her as she walked back in loping strides, the late evening sun still bright upon her face. The distant sheep looked like cottongrass tufts in the close pasture, the horse nosing the grass at a slow pace. The cluster of *selets* was on the other side of the stream from here and although she was too far away to make out any details keenly she could see general movement between the buildings – two figures carrying a filled butter churn between them to the in-ground cellar (Signy could tell from the way they held out their outer arms as counter-balancing weights), another sitting on a stool milking one of the cows, and two more threshing the long grass.

From here, the girls were as small as pepper pots but she knew she would hear their voices long before they became life-size again. For the past fortnight, this valley had rung with their shouts and calls, their laughter and squeals, as they settled into the freedoms of life away from their parents' watchful gazes, and Signy sometimes wondered what the eagles and foxes, the lynxes and squirrels must think from their hideaway homes, to have their quiet plateau suddenly filled up with farm animals and humans.

She sighed happily as she drew closer, knowing exactly what would happen when she crossed the stream; the pastures there were largely contained by rough stone walls – mainly to keep the sheep and cows in, rather than the goats, which would hop over them like daisies should they choose

– but within the topmost field, closest to the *selets* were more secure, higher-walled pens. She would leave the animals to range freely with the others there and run to help Ashild and Brit with making the last of the *sur-ost* (cottage cheese). It was a Tuesday today, which meant Ashi's *rommegrot* for dinner; whipped up from sour cream, milk, flour and served with cinnamon and melted butter, it had fast become Signy's favourite meal of the week, especially if they could have a slice of ham to go with it and some flatbread.

They had all fallen into a routine quickly, mainly because the others had done it before – they knew the shape and rhythm of the days here and fell into exhausted sleep when the sun was just nosing the horizon. Signy was sure she was asleep before her head hit the pillow most nights.

Margit and Sofie were in joint charge (although as far as Signy was concerned, that was only because Margit was happy for it to be that way), the two of them organizing the rosters and handing out chores. Signy, on account of her boundless energy, was sent out with the goats most days; the others had no doubt hoped the miles of walking might subdue her lively spirits but, if anything, the hours spent alone with just the animals meant she was even more sparky and talkative when she got back, always wanting another story around the fire. She had quickly acquired a reputation as the practical joker too, pouring jam in Ashi's boots and putting a toad in Sofie's bed one night. Kari, though not as prepared to be caught red-handed, was her accomplice in most of her japes and they had agreed whilst milking the goats one evening that playing tricks was far more fun than worrying about how to wear their hair, or which ribbon to thread in their blouses. They would stay forever free and wild and most certainly untamed by men.

Not that there was any risk of taming happening to either of them. Nils was the only man they had seen in two weeks, having returned to check on Sofie's ankle as promised a few days after the *buføring*. He had brought with him some of his mamma's *ystingsoll* pudding and word that a dead reindeer carcass had been found in the river up by the blacksmith's, before taking back with him their first batch of *setermat* products: butter, milk and brown cheese. But apart from ruffling her hair as he jumped off his father's horse, he had barely even noticed her, instead wasting all his time asking Sofie about her stupid ankle when it wasn't even hurt and never had been. The moment the men had gone, that first day, Sofie had jumped up from her perch on the rock – but only after the rest of the girls had all worked themselves silly, unpacking the materials off the animals and airing and cleaning out the huts so that even Signy, who worked harder and had more energy than any of them, had woken up stiff and aching the next day.

She had been itching to tell him the truth about Sofie's so-called injury; their father wasn't here now, things were different, they could trust Nils to keep the secret – at least then he'd see the truth about her. Why did he always look at her like she'd said something really interesting, when all she ever did was whine? And her jokes weren't funny *at all*, even though he laughed like they were. He should know what she was really like. But Kari, fully able to read her mutinous thoughts as Signy had watched him watching Sofie, had kicked her ankle hard under the table, warning her to keep quiet – and when she'd limped as Nils went to leave, he hadn't even noticed.

It had been a surprise to her how much she'd missed him, being here; it was the one thing that hadn't been as she'd expected. But then, she'd grown up seeing his face every single day. How could she have known how it felt to miss something she had never left? That hollow ache in the pit of her stomach wasn't something that could have been predicted. And besides, it didn't feel like she was missing him so much as losing him. He had always had time for her, growing up – happy to throw a ball over the hayricks with her, or to go on rambling walks together after church on Sundays, looking for vipers in the grass or beavers damming the river – but then he'd grown tall and his voice had deepened and everything had changed. She had been left behind, and when he did notice her, it wasn't as an equal but as an adult to a child.

She was almost down by the stream now, the white tufts of the cottongrass nodding gently in the evening breeze; it was so tall, the heads brushed beneath her hands as she walked, tickling her palms. She stopped to check on the herd behind her again, Stormy continuing onwards as she picked up on the sound of grain being rattled nearby in a bucket for the horse.

'That's it, nearly there,' Signy said, holding out her arm with her stick to contain them from spreading out too soon. 'Follow Stormy, follow Stormy,' she said as the animals passed by her quickly, a migration in miniature: bells jingling, heads nodding, hooves knocking on the stones in the stream. The kids bleated loudly as they were splashed by the others, running faster before doubling back to their mothers again.

Signy's eyes narrowed as they passed. She didn't need to count them – not that she could here anyway – but she had an innate sense of knowing when the herd was wrong, as though the very shape of it had been changed by the loss of one or two members. They were all with her now, she felt sure of it. But something . . . there was something. The hairs on the back of her neck rose and she looked back from where they had come. The sun – still above the mountains – threw dazzling, blinding white haloes like discuses straight at her; she shaded her eyes, scanning the grass-embedded rocks, the long shadows of the trees, the thick clumps of moss.

All was still, apart from a woodpecker bouncing in the sky towards the trees. She waited, feeling the sky become a thin membrane, taut and quivering above her. But then a goshawk cawed, piercing the tension, and she shrugged, turning back and splashing through the stream after her animals. Her mind was playing tricks on her. Of course they weren't being watched.

* * *

Bo sat up in bed, her neck at a slightly awkward angle; there was no headboard to speak of and the pillows were flat. Zac was in the bath – it was his 'turn' for the hot water. In order to keep gas cylinder consumption to a reasonable level, they had agreed to divvy up the days so that each of them had the bath every other day – Bo and Zac had it one day, Lenny the next. On their 'off' days, they would have to make do with washing themselves at the kitchen sink, which was a deeply unappetizing prospect. Lenny had told them that when he'd booked, Signy had said there was a nearby stream which people used for bathing, but washing in a river was one thing in July, quite another two weeks before Christmas.

Zac had tipped his head back against the bath edge and was humming 'Hotel California'. 'You need to shave,' Bo said, watching his Adam's apple bob up and down in his throat. 'You're turning into a bear.'

'Yeah?' he asked, raising a hand from the water and stroking his neck lightly. 'I'm quite liking it actually. It's warm.'

'It makes my skin itch,' she said, wrinkling her nose.

'But it's very "rugged man of the woods", don't you think?'

'Do you see Anders with one?' she asked, arching an eyebrow.

Zac sat a little higher and straighter in the bath. 'Oh – *he's* who comes to mind when you think of a rugged man of the woods?'

Bo shrugged. 'Well, isn't he? This is his shtick. A shelf farm in a forest on the side of a fjord.'

'Yeah, well – he's not far off this himself anyway,' Zac said, rubbing his hand over his chin as though it was a pelt and feeling the thick covering of bristles. 'Or maybe he just can't grow one as thickly as me.'

Bo opened her mouth in a silent 'o' before she chuckled. 'Oh, I see, right,' she nodded.

'What?'

'This is a competition. He flies helicopters but you can grow a beard? Is that it?'

Zac grinned, busted. 'I'm just saying.' He paused. 'And besides, I could learn to fly one of those things if I wanted – and then I'd be bearded *and* a pilot. And he'd just be a pilot. With bum fluff.'

Bo looked over at him from under her lashes, a bemused smile playing on her lips. She knew he was still smarting from Anders' outmanoeuvring of him this morning that was leaving him paying way over the odds for two weeks' work – although it said something about their income levels now that they could absorb the sum reasonably comfortably. Their brand had never been more influential and they weren't even yet at their peak. 'Mmhmm. If you say so.'

'Well, don't you?'

'*I* don't get why you care so much.'

'I don't, I just . . .' he trailed off, watching her as she continued to scroll through her feed.

She arched an eyebrow. 'Like winning?'

He grinned again, wolfishly this time. 'Can you blame a guy?'

She sighed. 'No, baby,' she said, knowing it was what he wanted to hear.

She came to a photo that Zac had posted an hour ago – he was sitting in the blue kayak, the shopping bags positioned precariously around him, with not an inch spare; it was a wonder they hadn't capsized. His stubble looked particularly dark in the image, his teeth especially white as he laughed at something, looking not directly to camera, but just off to the side of it. It looked natural and breezy but she knew it had been carefully contrived to have the essence of an amateur pic. Lenny loved the energy of reportage shots, always creeping about for an unexpected angle.

She glanced through the most recent comments for the post – they were almost entirely left by women crushing on Zac, all of them posting hearts or the heart-eye emoji, some of them asking him to marry them, others asking for more than that. It didn't upset or bother her; they were harmless fantasies, momentary knee-jerk impulses as these nameless women fancied a handsome stranger for all of a moment, before scrolling down to the next post.

Funnily enough, most of her fans were women too – it wasn't the case that if he had an almost all-female following, hers was all-male – and she was glad that other women liked her and found her approachable; she didn't want to have a legion of men fantasizing about her, even though she knew that, statistically speaking, a fair percentage of her almost nine million followers would be male.

But she also knew that the core of Zac's fans were men who had adopted him in the early days when, long before he'd met and linked up with her, he'd been a rookie climber with an ambition – and mission – to take the 'ultimate selfie' in every country in the world before he was twenty-five. It was those fans, the silent majority, who didn't comment on the pretty-boy pictures but immediately hit 'buy now' whenever he endorsed a new rope or climbing shoe or powder bag. They were the ones he was really communicating with; those women were just the cheerleaders making noise at the front.

Still . . . She looked up at him. 'Tell you what, let's put it to the vote.'

'What to the vote?' he asked, his eyes meeting her phone camera lens just as she clicked.

She smiled as she looked back at it on the screen. It was a cute photo: ever so slightly fuzzy but his eyes were animated and there was something amusing about seeing a bearded, muscular tanned man soaking in a bubbly copper bath.

'The beard,' she replied, bringing up the poll template and tapping out quickly: *Keep the beard? Yes/No.*

'There,' she smiled, pressing send and watching it try to upload. She held her arm up higher and it went on the third attempt. 'We can let the people decide.'

'How democratic of you, babe,' he murmured, dropping his head back again and watching her.

'I thought so.'

Her feed was a curious mix of sarcastic memes, adorable pictures of puppies, interiors shots – which was ironic for someone of no fixed abode – some fashion accounts, and assorted people they had met and connected with on the road.

The responses were immediate and she saw the numbers of messages in the top right of her screen begin to rack up, faster than she could count. 'Ooh, half and half so far,' she teased.

'Anna likes it,' he said, rubbing his jaw and chin again.

Bo arched an eyebrow. 'Does she?'

'She said she thought it made me look like Ryan Reynolds.'

'Then let's hope she votes Yes – along with the seven million other people you need on your side,' Bo said wryly.

'Are you gonna make me shave it off even if they do?'

'Of course.' She heard his low chuckle from the bath as she went back to scrolling again. She had missed so much on her feed over the past few days. '– Hey!' Her smile faded suddenly. 'What the actual fuck?' she frowned, clicking on an image that was familiar. 'Did you approve this?'

'What?'

Angrily, spine ramrod straight, she held her phone up for him to see the image of her relaxing in the bath. 'I deleted this picture! Why the hell has it been used?'

Zac peered at it for ten seconds before sinking back into his bubbles. 'Don't blame me. Lenny must have posted it. Looks good though. I like it.'

'That's not the point! It's too intimate, Zac! I didn't want it to be used. I deleted it for that reason – how did he even get hold of it?'

'I dunno, he must have had a copy in the cloud,' he shrugged. 'Listen, chill. It's not showing any of your bits. It's pretty. It's artsy. It's . . . what's that word?' he asked, looking up at the ceiling. 'Ambient. Yeah, that's what it is.'

'But he shouldn't be posting to the page without our

permission. You know he has to run anything that goes up past one of us first.'

'Oh, Bo – cut the guy some slack,' Zac said wearily. 'He's doing his job. That picture correlates perfectly with the brand.'

The brand. The bloody brand. Since when had she stopped becoming a private individual who couldn't even take a bath in private because the vibe worked for *the brand*? She glowered at him, remembering the hushed voices behind the closed door last night when she'd flown off the handle then too. Zac was getting as tired of this conversation as Lenny. But so was she. No one was listening to her or taking her seriously. There had to be a boundary, a cut-off point, didn't there? She wasn't public property.

She swung her legs off the bed and got up.

'Hey, where're you going?'

'To give Lenny a piece of my mind,' she muttered.

'Oh, Bo, no, wait,' he groaned. 'It's not worth it. It'll just cause tensio—'

But too late, she was already out of the door. 'Lenny!' she snapped, standing at the bottom of the stairs and calling up into his loft. 'I want a word with you.'

She waited but there was no sound. And the lights were off. He couldn't be asleep already, surely? She climbed the first few rungs of the ladder and peered in. It smelled of his cologne, worn boxers and T-shirts strewn across the floor like he was still a fifteen-year-old living in suburban Boise, Idaho.

He wasn't there. Where was he? Having a smoke?

Stuffing her feet into Zac's boots – the nearest to hand – she went outside, shivering immediately in the evening darkness. She looked for the tell-tale glow of a cigarette tip but not even the grass swayed in the still night. In the *stabbur* though, further down the path, lights pooled on the ground from the windows, two silhouettes moving past drawn curtains.

Oh.

She should have known.

She felt even angrier now. She had always made a point of never commenting on Lenny's love life; if sleeping around made him happy, she wasn't going to stand in judgement of it, but she could already see how this was going to play out: he would seduce Anna tonight and dump her by breakfast. It wouldn't be any different from the scores of other women he'd done this to except that he – and they – were going to have to continue to work with the poor woman for the next fortnight. He was a dog peeing in his own backyard.

Her hands balled into angry fists. She wanted to storm down there and give Anna the heads-up, but she knew she couldn't. It was none of her business. Anna was responsible for her own love life and Lenny was their photographer, done for the day, and what he did in his down time was nothing to do with her.

She turned – and started. Signy was sitting in her rocking chair by the window, watching her. For a moment their eyes met, and Bo gave a feeble, embarrassed wave.

Hesitating for a moment, feeling somehow exposed that she had been seen seething on her own, she walked back up the path and knocked lightly at the old woman's door.

'Come in.'

The voice was faint but Bo, with her ear to the door, entered. 'Hi,' she smiled, feeling awkward. 'I was just about to go to bed and thought I'd check on you,' she fibbed. 'Is there anything you need before I go?'

Signy looked at her for so long that for a moment Bo wasn't sure she'd heard her. Or was she simply seeing straight through the lie? 'You can heat some water and put it in the wash-bowl for me. I prefer to bathe at night. The mornings are too cold.'

'Sure. Of course.' Bo walked over to the sink and filled the kettle, setting it to boil.

'The wash-bowl is beside my bed,' Signy directed her, not turning round.

Bo stepped into the dark room; familiar silhouettes of a bedstead, chair and wardrobe looked back at her, a large apple-green jug, sitting in a deep bowl, on the top of a small dresser. She brought it back through, pouring some cold water into the jug. 'It's a beautiful night,' she said, walking over and perching on a chair by the table. Outside, the fjord lay cloaked in black velvet, silent and still.

'It will be the last time we see the stars for a while. Snow is coming.'

'Yes, Anders said that too. Not yet though, surely? It's crystal clear out there.'

Signy tipped her chin up fractionally, like a dog on the scent. 'It's not far away.'

'Do you think there's any chance of catching the Aurora tonight? We're so desperate to see it. Lenny was awake till three last night looking out for it. No joy, sadly.'

'Yes. It is quite the tourist attraction,' Signy muttered, her eyes on the sky.

Bo glanced at her. Was she just being defensive or did Signy seem to know to use the T-word pejoratively? 'Well, I really hope we get to see it while we're here,' she said benignly, hearing the kettle begin to boil. 'It's something I've always wanted to see, ever since I was little. Have you read the Philip Pullman book *Northern Lights*?'

'Why would I need to read about it when I can watch the real thing from my window?'

'Fair enough,' Bo smiled. 'I read it when I was little. Or rather – my brother read it to me. I'm afraid I got too scared reading on my own about children being killed.'

Signy scowled. 'Then why should it have been better when he read it?'

'Oh, everything was always better with him,' Bo said simply, a sigh spooling from her, her eyes on the black beyond – before she suddenly caught herself. What was she saying? She drew up the ramparts but it was too late. Signy was watching her; she had seen her flinch.

Her inquisitive gaze crept over Bo's features like fingers. 'Tell me why you have been away from your home for so long?'

'Excuse me?'

'You said it was four years since you had been home. That is a long time, unless you are deliberately staying away.'

'Not at all,' Bo said quickly. 'I just . . . lose track of time. One trip always seems to lead to another. But I'll go back soon.'

'Not for Christmas though?'

'We're booked now,' Bo shrugged. 'All paid up here for one thing, working until Christmas Eve for another. And I doubt we could get a flight back now even if we wanted to.'

'There's always a way back home,' Signy said firmly, making no secret of the way she scrutinized Bo's face, as though she were a palm to be read. 'What about your parents? Are they dead?'

'No.' The blunt question made Bo shudder.

'So then it must be hard on them, not having you home for Christmas for all this time.'

Bo felt her throat begin to close again, the pressure in her temple begin to build. How – exactly *how* – had they managed to get onto this? A minute ago she'd been having a silent tantrum on her own in the dark and now she was here, discussing with a near-stranger the one topic that was off-limits, even to Zac? 'They understand my career and my life decisions,' she said in a tight voice. 'They know that the nature of my job means my followers don't want to see Christmas in a sleepy village in southern England.' She looked at her nails. 'And besides, it's not like I don't ever see them – we chat on FaceTime every week and Zac and I meet up with them when they go on holidays. We regularly fly in to join them wherever they are.'

'So then you just don't join them at home,' Signy said, narrowing in on the pertinent point.

The kettle whistled, plumes of steam buffeting up against the low ceilings and Bo jumped up with relief. What did any of this have to do with Signy? And—

She frowned as she took the kettle off the flame, turning around to face the back of the old woman's chair. 'Wait – how do *you* know it's been four years since I've been home? I never told you that.'

'No. But you told my grandson.'

'Did he tell you?'

Signy scoffed. 'Of course not.'

So then . . . 'He said you were asleep,' Bo said, taking the kettle to the counter and pouring the boiling water into the jug, swirling the hot water with the cold with a wooden spoon.

'No. I was resting my eyes.'

'But you were snoring.'

'No. I was clearing my throat.'

Incredulous, Bo stared at the top of the back of the old woman's head. But even if she hadn't been able to see her reflection in the window, she would still have known she was smiling.

Zac was out of the bath and lying in bed when she wandered back over, pulling off her clothes and diving under the covers in one fluid motion before the cold could get her.

'Find him?' he asked distractedly, his attention on his phone.

'Who?'

'Lenny. Who'd you think?'

'Oh. No. He's down in the storehouse with Anna.'

'. . . Surprise, surprise,' he muttered.

'Yeah.' She picked up her phone where she'd left it on the bed, checking the time. It was barely eight and yet it had been dark for hours already. She hadn't remotely adapted to having only five hours of light a day, especially when their jet-lagged lie-in this morning and the guys' visit to the shops had all but used that allowance up today. Anders had stayed in his grandmother's cabin for the rest of the afternoon, only looking in briefly before he left to give them the heads-up for the next day's plan of a hiking trip to the Suitor waterfall; when he had left, the spectacle of the helicopter rising off the tiny plateau had drawn both men to the windows like little boys. Bo had made a pot roast, Anna a cherry pie and the four of them had played Monopoly afterwards, Catfish playing on Lenny's wireless speaker. Naturally, the entire evening had been uploaded in almost real time to the stories board via their four different accounts.

One thing was for sure, Norway was a hit. They were getting a great engagement rate for the few things they had posted so far to the grid, no doubt because of the novelty of her and Zac swapping a tropical island for a glacial tundra; people love looking at something new – even paradise gets boring when it's on loop.

'You were gone a long time,' Zac – clean-shaven – murmured, as though remembering their conversation, his foot beginning to root for hers under the covers. 'Did you join them?'

'No. I looked in on Signy and heated up some water for her to have a wash before bed,' she murmured back, skimming through the most recent comments in her Direct Message pile. There wasn't a chance of being able to answer them all, but she always tried to get back to at least a few people. There was the usual thread of heart emojis, some moons and stars, and hashtag *couplegoals* was trending . . .

You guys are so cute
I wish one day I meet someone to gaze at the stars with me
Love you two!
LOVE LOVE LOVE

. . . She froze. The taste in her mouth becoming metallic, the palms of her hands instantly clammy. She looked at the name; it was the same as before, the avatar picture too: distinctive, yet odd, somehow twisted – a close-up of a halved pomegranate, the jewel-like seeds spilling out lubriciously. She clicked on it, going into the profile but it was still a private account. Of course it was.

No followers. Following only one person. Her.

She went back to the feed and read the comment again. But she knew it was Him. She knew the tone if not the face.

I'm back, Bo. Miss me?

Chapter Nine

Bo shivered in the blue morning chill, waiting for a reply. She pressed her ear to the door, lest Signy's voice be faint, but nothing came. She put her hand on the doorknob and peered in. The little cabin looked untouched from when they had been sitting the night before – one of the chairs pushed back at an angle from where Bo had risen at the table, the dandelion cushion squashed, a lilac crocheted shawl draped across the back of the rocking chair.

She closed the door and walked through as quietly as she could in boots, wondering what to do now. The bedroom door was closed but the Bialetti coffee pot was on the gas ring; Anders had told her – before he'd left – that he'd pre-ground the coffee and left it ready to simply add hot water and steep; beside it was a mug and a small brown bottle with two pills on the wooden counter.

Bo looked across at the door again. There were no shafts of light seeping through the crack, no creaky mattress springs or the squeak of floorboards coming from behind it. Even though Bo had said she would be checking in this morning, if Signy was still asleep it might be best to make a little noise in here first, so as not to alarm her by suddenly standing by the bed like an apparition. She did look a fright – still in her pyjamas herself, Zac's chunky ironic snowflake jumper thrown on and her feet swamped by his boots. But after an almost sleepless night, getting up and coming over here, *doing something*, had been a welcome diversion. Was she just far too early?

Trying to make a reassuring amount of noise, she clattered around as she made the coffee, hoping the enticing aroma at least would tell Anders' grandmother that her visitor through here had come with kindly intent. She threw a couple of logs onto the stove, seeing how the still-warm ashes kindled immediately, then knocked at the bedroom door. Nothing.

She knocked a little harder. Still nothing.

'Signy?' she asked, her mouth close to the door. 'Signy, it's Bo. From next door.'

After another minute, she turned the handle and looked in. The old lady was lying in the bed looking almost flattened by thick blankets. And with good reason – it was freezing; a small fire had gone out in the fireplace at the opposite end and the room felt so cold, Bo half expected to see frost inside the windows. No wonder she didn't want to bathe in the mornings.

She shivered as she took in the sight of the bedroom in the weak morning light; she hadn't been able to pick out any of the detail in last night's gloom but in contrast to the frugal nature of the main room, the bedroom was decorative, feminine, even fussy: swagged embroidered cotton curtains were draped at the window, the floorboards all but obscured beneath a vast green, blue and yellow flatweave rug. The iron bedframe was black, with brass bedknobs, a decorative pale blue armoire was stencilled with scrolls and floral motifs, and a mirrored dressing table had a small lace coverlet pressed beneath the glass; on it was an enamelled hairbrush with pale nylon bristles upturned on the top, a tortoiseshell comb and an empty perfume bottle with a cracked rubber atomizer. A scalloped mirror hung on the wall above the fireplace, and on either side were two framed charcoal portraits – one of a woman, clearly Signy in her youth; the other of a man who must have been her husband. Both were strikingly good-looking. Signy, who looked to have been captured when she was in her thirties, perhaps early forties, looked haughty, elegant and strong, her head tipping back fractionally as though she was looking down on the viewer. Her husband had a more sanguine demeanour, with an unhatched smile flickering in his eyes, his hair swept back from the face to reveal a timeless bone structure.

Her gaze coming back to the bed, Bo took in a walking stick propped by the bedside table, a glass of water left on top, a set of dentures in another glass, and an antique wooden commode. The wash-bowl was on the dresser where Bo had left it last night, the empty jug to one side.

'Signy?' she said in a quiet voice. 'It's Bo. I've just brought you a coffee and got the fire going next door for you.'

Again nothing. The woman didn't stir. Her mouth was parted, as though she was mid-conversation, cheeks caving in slightly on the gums; her skin looked as thin as petals and she was as pale as a rose.

'I've also brought your pills in for you,' she said a little more loudly. 'Anders left them out before he went back to town last night.'

Nada.

She sighed. Putting the coffee and tablets down on the table, taking care to make some noise, she wandered over to the fire and put her hand out. Finding there was still some heat to it, she added some kindling from a bucket to the side and struck a match. The flames took instantly; the wood was all so well seasoned and the air so dry, no fire was ever out for long it seemed. She pushed a small mesh guard in front of the hearth and looked back at the bed. Still no response.

Wondering what to do next – short of playing the drums or jumping on the bed – Bo drew the curtains back, but even the light outside seemed to hesitate about coming in, barely making any impression on the dimness in the room. She went back to the bedside again.

'Signy? Can you hear me?' She placed a hand on the old lady's arm that was lying across the top of the blankets. It was icy to touch. 'Signy?'

She looked in fright back at her chest, searching for a rise and fall, but it was impossible to tell anything under those blankets. She scanned her face again, looking for a sign of life. Something. Anything.

No, no, no . . . Please don't say—

'I'm not dead.' Signy's eyes were still closed but a faint smile hovered over her puckered mouth. 'Not yet anyway.' Her words sounded muffled without her teeth in but a distinctive look glittered in her eyes as she opened them – it was the same look she wore in the painting. 'Maybe tomorrow.'

'Oh my *goodness*,' Bo breathed, a small incredulous laugh escaping her that this was some kind of joke. 'Thank God. I was really beginning to think—'

Signy winked. 'Party trick.'

Like her fake sleeping and pretend snores? 'That's a *party trick*?'

Signy shifted slightly. 'One of the benefits of being so old. Everyone's always expecting me to die any minute. I may as well have some fun with it.'

Bo chuckled. This woman was ninety-six years old and still pulling practical jokes on people?

'Help me sit,' Signy said, moving her arm up slightly. 'The

blankets are tucked so tight, it's like wearing one of my old girdles.'

With another smile, Bo hesitantly managed to pull her up to a seated position – it was easy enough, she weighed practically nothing – and stuffed some cushions behind her back. With an insouciant air Signy slipped her teeth in and swallowed down the two pills Bo had put on her table.

Carefully, worried she might spill the coffee, Bo handed over her mug and watched as she brought it to her lips, closing her eyes in pleasure as she drank.

'That is good,' she said in a low voice, sinking back a little into the pillows.

'Is that your husband?' Bo asked, looking over at the charcoal portrait again.

Signy looked over at it, her expression becoming almost liquid as her gaze settled on the man's face. 'Yes. He was the best man I ever met.'

Bo watched her. 'I can tell you loved him very much.'

'Loved?' Signy said sharply. 'He is dead, the love isn't.'

Bo's mouth parted. She had never heard anyone say such a thing before. 'Were you together long?'

The old woman closed her eyes, as though sinking into the memories. 'Lifelong. And we were blessed with five healthy children.' She opened her eyes again after a moment, a tiny frown creasing her brow as she saw her visitor still standing there. 'You can go now.'

'. . . Oh.' Bo felt taken aback. 'Well, if you're sure.'

Feeling strangely disappointed by the brisk dismissal – the old woman was unpredictable and capricious, yet interesting too – she crossed the room, turning back at the door. She was about to say that she'd look in that evening, but Signy had closed her eyes again and was smiling as though the weak light coming through the window was sunlight warming her face; as though in her world, everything was brighter.

The rap at the door had a spring to it, and a moment later a head of sleek, blow-dried brunette hair peered round the corner.

'Good morning!' Anna beamed, seeing Bo and Zac sitting at the table quietly together and letting herself in. Zac was taking an arty close-up photo of his steaming coffee cup against the gnarled wood of the table. He had already snapped a spider making a web in one of the corners of the window and a picture of his socked feet, crossed and up on the table, a view of the still-dark fjord beyond his toes. Anything, in fact, to avoid talking to her. He had been a hive of industry since he had woken to find her gone, his initial alarm immediately switching back to hurt pride again, and she knew he was still smarting from her rejection in bed last night. It was the first time she had ever rolled away from him but she couldn't bring herself to care about that right now; she still felt a million miles away. She had bigger monsters to deal with than his wounded ego, and since coming back from checking on Signy she had sat staring out of the window, waiting for the light and lost in thought. Why – why had He come back?

'Hi, Anna,' Zac said, pushing away his iPad. 'Coffee?' He held up the coffee pot on the table.

'That would be amazing, thanks,' she said, laying her jacket – a Ridge Riders one too, the same as Bo's but in red – on the back of the chair and joining them at the table. 'Hey, you shaved your beard off!'

Zac rubbed his hands over his smooth jaw. 'Yeah. The people had spoken. Bo put it to a poll.'

Anna laughed as she looked between them both. 'How brilliant!'

'Well, *she* certainly thinks so,' Zac replied, throwing Bo a benign look.

'And I do too. You look great!'

'I thought you said I looked like Ryan Reynolds with the stubble.'

'Well, now you look like . . . Michael Fassbender without it!'

Bo forced a smile, trying to kickstart herself into action. Vaguely, she knew he would like that comparison. She also noticed Anna was perfectly made-up, her lashes brushed lightly with mascara and a slick of gloss on her lips. She was wearing skinny white jeans, a black and red folk-style knitted jumper and Sorel snow boots, a pair of white furry earmuffs clasped around her neck. Bo, in her boyfriend jeans, plaid shirt, bare face and tousled hair felt distinctly underdressed in comparison. It had been a long time since she'd dolled herself up. Why would she? The places they went to never called for it – fine restaurants, dinner parties and black-tie balls weren't part of their landscape. 'Did you sleep well?' she asked flatly, tucking her unbrushed hair behind her ear.

'Actually no, not really,' Anna said with a sheepish smile.

Bo felt her stomach drop and she hoped to God Anna wasn't going to share confidences about her night with Lenny. 'Oh, I'm sorry to hear that. Was it too cold?' she asked, giving her an out.

'No, it's not that – the cabin's lovely, but I don't think I'm used to the sound of silence. It's so *loud*.' She bit her lip and gave them both a quizzical stare. 'Does that even make sense?'

'Oh, it does,' Zac grinned, knowing exactly what Bo had been thinking as he poured her a mug and handing it over to her. 'We get the same thing but in reverse. Cities we take ages to adjust to now; weeks, really. And if we're under a flight path, forget it.' He shook his head. 'Silence is the reward for seclusion but it does take some getting used to.'

'Well, I look forward to acquiring the habit,' she smiled, copying Bo and wrapping her hands around her mug too. 'So, where are the others?'

'Well, Lenny's upstairs –'

Bo automatically arched an eyebrow, but she wasn't surprised he hadn't stayed with Anna last night. In his world, that counted as being 'tied down', which made him feel 'claustrophobic'.

'Hey, Len – are you ready yet or what?' Zac called up the ladder.

'Coming. I'm just sorting the cameras.' His voice was muffled but they could hear the sound of his footsteps on the boards as he moved around above them. '*Ow!* Fuck!'

Zac laughed. 'Keeps banging his head on the rafters,' he said confidingly. 'That's the third time so far today. He's not a morning person.'

'Who is?' Anna sighed, resting her chin in her hand, her eyes roaming the basic, yet cosy cabin. 'And our guide – Anders? Is he up from the village yet?'

'He should be here any minute.' Zac checked his Apple watch. 'We agreed a ten o'clock start. We need a little light to see by, at least.'

'Will he come by helicopter again? That was so cool last night.'

'Not sure. It must be heavy on fuel.' Zac shrugged. 'He might come by rib, the way we came.' He shrugged up his eyebrows. 'Or maybe he'll arrive by camel! Who knows? He's a real action man. Norway's answer to Bond.'

They heard the sound of Lenny coming down the ladder, his camera bag slung across his body as he descended, wrinkling his Led Zepp tour T-shirt. 'Hey, guys.'

'Hey, Len,' Bo mumbled, seeing how he didn't throw any intimate looks Anna's way and construing it as a bad thing: if he'd already slept with her, then this was just the first of many rejections Anna would have to get used to.

Anna, though, seemed unperturbed. She certainly wasn't watching him longingly or overtly trying to catch his eye; well, not unless the mascara and lip gloss were for his benefit.

Bo looked down into her coffee, realizing she didn't care either way about the team's love lives; she didn't feel up to 'work' today – photographing waterfalls was not high on her list of priorities right now. She wanted to hide away, for it to be just her and Zac for once, the way it used to be – not the illusion of it with a small entourage in tow and a vapour trail of nine million ghosts, Him watching her from behind a screen.

Standing beside her, Lenny reached across the table to pour himself the last of the coffee and a whiff of stale BO wafted over her like a nuclear cloud. Instinctively she turned away. It was his turn to get the bath tonight and frankly it couldn't come soon enough.

'So, we all set?' Lenny asked, noticing her flinch and a scowl settling over him.

'As soon as— Oh good, here he comes now,' Zac said, watching as Anders suddenly appeared on the plateau, arms swinging, head down as he walked at speed up the grass, as though unaware he had just hiked a near-vertical path. He was wearing his orange waterproof gear again, a large backpack strapped to his back, flashes of his scruffy blonde hair escaping from the hood like fur trim.

A minute later there was a brisk knock and he was standing in front of them all, expectantly. 'You are ready?' he asked, his eyes scanning the motley group and lingering particularly on Anna, looking so bright and perky in her beautifully co-ordinated outfit.

'Sure,' Bo sighed, draining the coffee and scraping her chair back. She supposed the sooner they went, the sooner it would be done. 'Let's do it.'

Anna's expression wavered as she took in Bo's muted outfit. 'Uh, Bo – are you going to change?'

'Hmm?' Bo looked down at herself dispassionately.

'Well, I was just thinking – if we're going to a waterfall, this would be the perfect time to wear the matching waterproof trousers with the jacket, wouldn't it? I mean, not that I'm trying to tell you how to dress,' she smiled. 'But it does seem like a perfect opportunity, doesn't it?' She bit her lip anxiously, waiting for Bo to respond.

'That's not a problem, is it, Bo?' Zac said, answering for her as he pushed his chair back too and stretched. 'I'm already in mine.' Bo noticed for the first time he was wearing the branded trousers in black, with a matching long-sleeved charcoal thermal top.

'Two hundred thou,' Lenny whispered under his breath as he passed by with his breakfast can of Coke, clearly trying to incentivize her.

'Bo?' Zac pressed with an impatient tone, seeing how she didn't react. 'We're good to go when you are.'

'Uh, yes, of course,' she mumbled, bringing herself back into the moment. 'God, yes, of course, what was I thinking?' She slapped her hand on her forehead as though she was a dunce. 'I'll go and change.' She walked into the bedroom and closed the door behind her, feeling an overwhelming urge to cry, but she pressed the heels of her hands to her eyes and took a few deep breaths instead, trying to calm herself down – all she had to do was wear a pair of trousers; it was hardly unreasonable.

She knew she had to get it together. She was overreacting, still spooked by last night's email, but he wasn't real. He was just a faceless coward behind a screen, probably on the other side of the world; the threat was implied, not real. She would never meet him. He would never get near her. Not again . . .

The collection of Ridge Rider outfits were draped over the wooden spindle chair in a rainbow medley, the tags still on and with the slightly chemical odour of factory-fresh clothes. She stepped into the yellow waterproof trousers – no cool black or grey for her; they fitted well but as she looked down at herself, she thought that with the jacket on too she looked like a Teletubby.

Still, everyone was waiting.

'Okay, great!' Zac said as she came out of the room again, eyes down. 'See? That wasn't so hard, was it, babe?' he asked, small barbs still prickling his words.

'Oh, you look so cute! How do you pull that off?' Anna exclaimed, clasping her hands together happily.

'It's okay then?' Bo asked doubtfully, looking down at herself.

'Just wait till Head Office gets a sight of you.'

'Let's go then,' Anders said briskly, not passing comment as he turned and led them all out of the cabin, Zac on his heels like an over-eager student.

'Yay! Let's do this,' Anna said, doing a little air-punch behind him, using her and Zac's catchphrase.

Bo followed her with a sigh as she zipped up her coat and pulled up the hood, all sound instantly becoming muffled, like voices below a duvet. Lenny brought up the rear as he shrugged on his jacket and locked up behind them. Bo glanced in the windows of the other cabin as they passed – was Signy up from bed yet? Sitting at her rocking chair by the window? – but at this time of day, the glass only reflected her own yellow-bundled image back to her.

Anders set a brisk pace. He was taking them to the Suitor waterfall, a four-hour round trip by foot from here, which, with the limited daylight, was going to be tight if they wanted rest-stops and time to take footage too. The waterfall was close to the farm as the crow flew, but with no designated path for much of the hike and having to go up first before they could get down, he had warned them the going would be slow and potentially treacherous in places, for although the early snow had largely thawed, some ice patches remained.

Bo wasn't sure they had the weather for it today, as they marched in file like soldiers on a training exercise. Just as Signy had predicted, she could feel snow in the air; the sky had clouded up overnight – robbing Lenny of yet another Aurora – and was now as woolly as a bobble hat but nowhere near as warm. Not that that mattered – she was panting and pink-cheeked within minutes as they went straight into a steep hike.

The Suitor was one of the most famous sites in the area and sat directly opposite the Seven Sisters fall, which she had gazed upon in an almost constant meditation on the opposite side of the fjord since arriving at the farm. Anders had explained that if they wanted dramatic shots, there was another waterfall, Storseterfossen, just behind Gerainger itself, which had a sherpa path running directly behind the water; but when Zac had looked it up on TripAdvisor, it had come up as the fourth most popular activity in the region – far too mainstream for their tastes (or their followers'). They had to do it 'authentically', Zac had insisted, which translated as 'doing it the hard way': finding a waterfall without a path to, from or behind it, and taking their pictures there. 'The journey's the destination, man,' Zac had shrugged, when Anders had looked at him like he was mad.

Turning their backs on the fjord, they followed a steep path tracking up and away from the farm, heading into the trees again; for the first fifteen minutes, Anna kept up a stream of hearty, excitable chatter but as the gradient refused to give and the trees kept on coming, acres of forest still above them, she lapsed into the breathless quiet of the rest of them. This was the reality behind the filtered images – hard slog.

Behind her, Bo could just detect Lenny snapping away intermittently – even with her hood up, her ear was acutely attuned to those distinctive clicks – but apart from that and the snapping of twigs beneath their boots, the silence rolled like a storm cloud, sometimes gathering up birdsong within its embrace, but more often feeding on itself and becoming louder, stronger, bigger.

Fifty minutes in, without a break or even a slowing down, they were at 1,800 metres above sea level, lingering patches of snow freckling the grass at these higher altitudes, the air as clear and pure as diamond chippings.

'We'll take a short rest here; there's no more path beyond this point,' Anders said, walking over to a boulder and sitting on it with the same casual action of a commuter taking his seat on the train and beginning to read the paper.

Lenny groaned. 'I hope that's not his way of saying we've just done the easy bit,' he muttered, immediately sinking into a cross-legged position on the grass as Anna dramatically sprawled spreadeagled like a shipwreck survivor beside him.

'I think I'm dying,' she groaned. 'You guys are all so *fit*. I've got to get to the gym.'

'Nah. You look in excellent shape to me,' Lenny replied, giving her an obvious visual sweep. 'Smoke?'

'Ooh.'

Bo watched on from beneath lowered lashes, feeling like she was watching them from behind a wall of glass. It distantly occurred to her that if they were still flirting then perhaps that meant they hadn't got it on yet? And if that was so, then she could still get to Lenny first and warn him off – the last thing they all needed was an ugly split and an atmosphere for the next two weeks. But not yet. Not now. She looked away, losing interest in them. *He* was filling up her head and she could concentrate on little else.

The ground had plateaued here at the top of the mountain, the sheer cliffs rolling up to a sudden but gentle stop. It wasn't a view that could be ignored and as she stared out, letting the view wash over, her eyes began to focus and notice details as her gaze followed the terrain rolling away into the distance: snow-speckled, forest-furred mountains becoming grey bumps, becoming just a haze as the mountaintops rippled out towards the Norwegian Sea on the horizon.

At the sight of it, she felt her spirits begin to rise like a spring sap. The big view made her feel small, and that made her feel better. Her own troubles, such as they were, seemed so inconsequential when she stood on a mountaintop and saw the world at her feet. It was a curious mix of euphoria and invincibility, coupled with a feeling of being utterly insignificant. And it was this feeling that was the reason she did this. It was the high that kept her going.

Bo looked across at Zac. He was standing off to the side, looking into the distance like Columbus searching for America, but she could tell from the set of his jaw that he was still hurt. Wounded. She had practically leapt from his touch last night, his enquiring hand reaching over in the same moment she had seen the message, and it had been a sucker-punch to his ego.

Glancing over at the others – Anders was poring over a map, Anna and Lenny each rolling a cigarette – she walked over to him and slipped her hand in his, glancing up at him anxiously as he stared ahead. 'Hey.' She squeezed his hand, her voice barely more than a whisper. 'Still love me?'

It was a moment before he squeezed back. 'Just about,' he said in a low voice.

She felt her heart ache as she watched him; he was such a boy in so many ways. 'I'm really sorry about last night. I was just . . .' What did she say? She had never told him about the troll, not really, not all of it. With followings the size of theirs, it was statistically impossible to please everyone or have everyone like them. They were both resigned to – if not fully inured to – the jealous, mean-spirited and sometimes outright cruel remarks and jibes some strangers felt entitled to make. And this guy had always been clever – nothing was ever too explicit, there were no outright threats, he was savvy enough to make sure he didn't do anything that would give either Instagram or the police something to work with; but an undercurrent of menace still dripped from every word. He might have talked about wanting to *humiliate* her, *punish* her, *degrade* her – but he always signed off with smiley face emojis. He had only harassed her for a few months but during that time, he had posted a comment every single time she put up a new image; and although she received comments in the thousands, she always found herself scrolling through to find his; it could take hours, it had become a compulsion but she had needed to know if he was still out there.

And he had been, as constant as a shadow, until one day, quite suddenly, it had all stopped. She remembered it well – the shocking vacuum. It was the first time she had shared a photo of herself with Zac, a month or so after they'd got together, when she'd felt sufficiently reassured they had some kind of future together. She had never shared anything of her private life before that night, she had scrolled for almost two hours through the comments trying to find his response but there had been nothing, nor the next day or the day after that. Zac's presence had scared him off. Coward that he inevitably was, he had seen that she wasn't alone any more, that she was less vulnerable. But even though he had been silenced, still the question had always niggled in the back of her mind – was he still there, watching her through a screen? Or had something happened to remove her from his life – maybe he'd been in prison? Or his own life had improved, he'd got married himself? Or perhaps he'd been doing this to other women like her and simply shifted his attention? Worse, he'd begun harassing real women in his actual life? Or perhaps he was dead – hit by a bus. Cancer. Karma . . .

The questions had lingered, even though for three and a half years there had been nothing; and slowly, slowly, she had allowed herself to relax, to believe she was free again. So why now? Why had he come back? What had she done to tempt him from his hibernation? She was clearly still with Zac. Why couldn't he just leave her alone?

'Hormonal?'

It was a moment before she clicked back into the present

again. '. . . Yeah . . . right. That.' It was as good an excuse as any. She could hardly explain it all now, out here, anyway.

He glanced down at her and caught sight of her expression. 'Hey, it's okay,' he whispered, turning to look at her fully and clasping her face in his hands. 'Of course I still love you. I'm nuts about you. I just hate it when we fight.'

'Me too.'

'I love you so much, baby,' he whispered.

'I know. And I love you too.' She blinked up at him, waiting to be forgiven, waiting to move on. She closed her eyes as he kissed her but in the background she heard the click-click-click of Lenny's camera and an '*Awww*' from Anna.

'God, they really are so cute,' Anna stage-whispered to him. 'We used to wonder, sometimes, if maybe it was just a publicity thing.'

'Nope. Suck-face the entire time,' Lenny drawled in a bored voice.

Bo pulled away; she wanted to grab the camera from Lenny and stamp on it, tell him to keep his cynical opinions to himself, but she didn't stir. Zac had asked her only last night to try harder with him and she would. She would even let it go about the bath picture. This time.

Anders, having folded away the map again, was sitting on the rock, his elbows splayed on his knees, watching them all impassively. He seemed to feel no inclination to become their friend, or become a closer part of the group: there was no chit-chat or small talk or joke-telling or anecdote-swapping. It was as though he had told himself he was their guide, pure and simple, and that any contact beyond getting from A to B and back to A again was outside his job description. Which was odd, because he had been such easy company the day before when she had sat with him in his grandmother's cabin.

Although he never said or did more than was absolutely required to make his point – no arm waving or hyperbole – there had been animation within his stillness. No fuss hadn't meant no fun.

Anna and Lenny dragged their last draws on the cigarettes and stamped them out on the ground, a small puckered circle of raspberry gloss around the neck of Anna's. A cold gust ran at them all and Bo shivered again – though she was warm from the hike, the wind chill was inescapable and she pulled up her hood again. Snow was definitely coming.

'Given that there's no more *up* to climb, please tell me we're going down?' Anna smiled as she walked over to Anders. She had a slight grass stain on her white jeans and mud had spattered up her calves but she still looked like a model on a campaign shoot.

'Yes, but this is where the hard work begins.'

'What?' Anna half wailed, half laughed, turning back to Lenny as she pulled a series of funny faces.

'Oh man, didn't I just know he was gonna say that!' Lenny groaned.

'We need to be careful across this stretch.' Anders stood up and was addressing them all. 'The land here is steep and the grass may be slippery as we go down. Walk in a single line behind me and keep your eyes on the ground. If you slip or trip here, you won't stop till you hit water.'

'Excellent!' Lenny quipped, hoisting the camera strap over his opposite shoulder and stretching out his neck.

'You will hear the waterfall before you see it but do not stop to take photographs until I have found somewhere safe for us all to stand, okay?' He looked at them all in equal turn. 'No picture is worth dying for.' And when there was a silence, he added with a frown: 'I hope we are all agreed on that?'

'Of course,' Bo murmured, but Zac and Lenny were a full beat behind her. Many times Zac had risked his life getting the ultimate selfie shot – one time in Yosemite, he had pulled a line between Higher Cathedral Spire and the nearby cliff face and halfway across the tight-rope, dangled upside down by just the karabiner at his waist. The resulting image was one of his most notorious – his hair falling vertically downwards, the whites of his eyes dominating as the sky switched places with the very, very far-away ground – and Bo still didn't like looking at it. She suspected he didn't like being read the health and safety act by Anders either but he had little choice: the balance of power was with their guide right now; he was the only one who could get them where they wanted to go so they had to play by his rules.

They followed him down the face of the cliff, the grass brushing their left shoulders. It was precipitously steep and they all fell into a solemn silence of concentration that was only punctuated every so often by Anna giving tiny squeals or gasps, before a breathy laugh escaped her, along with a nervous but still jaunty 'sorry!' So much for being seen but not heard, Bo thought, her nerves beginning to fray as she picked her way down the trail carefully. It had begun to sleet, making the grass wet and even more treacherous.

The climb down was hard going on their thigh muscles and made all the worse for the slow control the descent required. But sure enough, as Anders had predicted, they grew aware of a growing roar like distant planes as they steadily dropped height, traversing across the mountain. Occasionally, Bo couldn't resist snatching a look up as it grew to a deafening din, but there was nothing to see – not until they suddenly stepped out from the trees and walked into a mist as thick as soup.

The spray spritzed them all and Bo reached for her phone and started recording, pushing her hood back so that she could feel it on her face. Anna's instinct was the opposite – pulling her hood up to protect her hair and trying to get out of the way – but Bo, Zac and Lenny were straight into photographing and recording every magical first moment of it. They were the Wanderlusters, after all.

'I said no stopping!' Anders barked, making them all jump and comply. 'Come down here.' He walked them over to a small grassy area downhill. It stretched back towards the trees, away from the spray, and though not quite level there was enough room for them to spread out.

Bo shot him an apologetic look as they gathered together.

'This will be the base,' Anders said tersely, shrugging off his rucksack.

Taking that as their cue, Zac began unpacking his ropes and axes. Bo went for the lunches.

'This is amazing!' Lenny hollered, his voice barely audible over the sound of rushing water as he took in the panorama with his photographer's eye, using his fingers to make a frame as he scanned left to right and back again. Zac meanwhile was looking up and down the waterfall, trying to establish where exactly they were. He and Lenny had pored over photographs and maps at the table together last night but it was hard to make out the shape of it when they were so close.

Anders pulled out a laminated image from his pocket and showed it to them. 'So we are here,' he said, pointing to a photograph of The Suitor. It was roughly bottle-shaped, with a narrow neck at the top splitting into multiple tributaries lower down where the rocks beneath jutted out, dispersing the waterflow. From where they were standing, Bo could see the gradient below become slightly more shallow as the cliffs sloped like a slide down into the sea. They themselves were situated just above the halfway mark, at the bottom of the neck section and immediately below the most concentrated vertical drop. At the top of it, the water came over the rocks with such force, it blew out as well as down.

She shivered again and looked across at Anna. 'I'm glad I changed into the waterproof trousers after all!' she called over the roar.

'I wish I had!' Anna shouted back, indicating her skinny jeans. 'My vanity will be the death of me!'

Bo laughed, feeling her mood improve once more. This scenery, the hike, making up with Zac . . . she felt the shadow of the troll recede again. He only assumed the power *she* let him have – that was what the policeman had said to her the day she'd tried to report him, to do something. This man didn't know where she was or with whom. He wasn't a real threat, he was just the idea of one. Look at what he'd *actually* said last night: had she missed him? There was no doubt he wanted to intimidate her but, ultimately, it was just a question, that was all.

'Can we please eat first before you go into Boy Scout mode?' she asked Zac as he began roping up. He had got that look in his eyes, the one he always got when he was near a slab of vertical granite. 'I'm starving.'

'You're always starving,' Zac winked at her. 'But you go ahead, I just wanna do one drop first,' he said as he spooled out the coils of a climbing rope and clipped on his karabiner belt. He kept restlessly casting his gaze up and along the waterfall, looking for potential belay sites and she knew these were the moments *he* lived – and travelled – for: adventure and discovery. Pushing himself to the limits. 'You with me, Len?'

'Sure, man,' Lenny said, already swapping his hiking boots for soft-soled climbing shoes.

'Then let's do this.'

'Well, *we* all need to eat,' she sighed, knowing better than trying to stop them, and settling herself on the rock, handing out the home-made rolls she had made earlier. Anna took one, Anders too, and the three of them began to eat, watching as Zac and Lenny began scrambling up the rocks together.

'Does your photographer rock-climb?' Anders asked her, his eyes on the guys.

'Only to get into position for the shots. He's pretty good but he leaves the really technical stuff to Zac.'

'So Zac's a professional climber?' he asked, his gaze trained on the way Zac was almost swinging himself up the cliff. It seemed to Bo he was showing off a little, knowing he had an audience. He didn't usually climb that fast.

'Yes. Well, in as much as people follow him to watch him doing stuff like this. It's what he's known for – mad mountain-climbing selfies. It sort of evolved from his original goal of becoming the youngest person to visit every country in the world before he was twenty-five.'

'Did he do it?'

'Yeah, he did, but last year, a twenty-four-year-old did it too.'

Anna slapped her hand over her mouth. 'I'm sorry, I shouldn't laugh.'

'But it is quite funny,' Bo agreed, grinning too. 'And next year, it'll probably be a nineteen-year-old on his gap year!'

'How did Zac take it?' Anders asked her as she offered around the Cokes Lenny had packed.

'Not well. He's pretty competitive.'

Anders looked back up at Zac scaling the cliff face like it was hot to the touch. 'Yes.'

'So, Bo – how did you guys meet, can I ask?' Anna asked, looking up at her with a fan-girl expression.

'Me and Zac?' Bo's gaze fell to the ring-pull as she went to open her can. '. . . It was such a random thing, really. He's from New Zealand, I'm from England and yet we met when we were both asked to do a promotion with the Java tourist board. There's this lovely little place called Kampung Pelangi, which means rainbow village; the whole thing had just been painted – and I do mean every single house – painted with rainbows. They thought it would bring more tourists to the area and that our respective pages had the diverse spread that would cover most demographics: I had the spiritual, arty, yoga-loving crowd and he had the rad, adrenaline-junkie types, backpackers, gappers . . .'

'So you met in Java,' Anna said with a sigh. 'Even that is cool.'

Bo smiled. 'It's a beautiful place. Really beautiful – but the town was tiny. We stayed there a few nights doing our own thing by day, but come the evenings there wasn't much else for us to do but hang out together, chatting in the bar.'

'What were you doing in the days?'

'Well, I was off visiting temples and markets. But Zac was climbing all the volcanoes,' she said, rolling her eyes. 'Surprise, surprise.'

'They're still active in Java, aren't they?' Anders frowned.

'Naturally. That's how he likes it,' she shrugged.

'Was it love at first sight?' Anna asked, widening her eyes excitedly, wanting the scoop.

'To be really honest?' Bo hitched up her eyebrows. 'No.'

'No!' Anna almost fell off her perch on the rock.

Bo wrinkled her nose. 'Well, all his action man thing – I thought he was a bit ADHD at first. He couldn't ever sit still, shut up . . .'

'No, no, no,' Anna laughed, shaking her head. 'It can't be true.'

'It was like being lumbered with a puppy.' Bo glanced up at him on the rocks. 'Still is, to be honest,' she laughed. 'Zac's such a people person. He loves everyone, wants to be everyone's friend.'

'But he won you over in the end,' Anna sighed, quite determined to get to the happy ending.

'Won me over. Wore me down,' Bo quipped with a non-committal shrug.

Anna guffawed, loving the inside track. 'Well, it's as well he did,' she said wistfully, before looking over at Anders. 'Do you know about these guys?'

Anders shook his head.

'They went supersonic when they hooked up. It was a match made in Insta-heaven: Bo with her beautiful, wistful, spiritual images and Zac with his adrenaline-fuelled, crazy stunts, both of them so gorgeous. It's no wonder they took over the virtual world.' She sighed.

Bo smiled, but Anders continued eating his roll in silence – clearly not the least bit interested in her and Zac's success – his gaze flashing back up the waterfall every few moments. Bo wondered whether he wanted to be up there too. Zac was screwing an eye into the rock and looping through the rope, Lenny below him on a ledge, his camera pressed to his face as he captured it all. Boys off having their adventures.

Bo felt the flutter of a few frozen, wet flakes on her cheeks; the sleet was getting heavier, the flakes bigger. She held out her hands and watched as a couple fluttered into her palms.

Anders looked around them, a frown creasing his brow as he finished eating and rubbed the crumbs off his hands. 'The weather was set to worsen tonight but this is coming in sooner than expected.'

'We should probably get some shots done sooner rather than later, don't you think?' Anna asked her.

Bo suppressed a groan. She would have liked to sit and admire the view for a few minutes, to rest up a bit and actually appreciate this place, rather than merely document it. And besides, there was still a bread roll going spare. A snowflake landed on the tip of her nose and she crossed her eyes trying to look at it. 'I agree, but I need Lenny. We'll have to wait for him to come back here,' she said, looking over to where the guys were climbing: Lenny was a third of the way up the drop now and kneeling on a narrow ledge, his attention solely traced on Zac as he searched for handholds, getting as close to the water as he could. Bo already knew what her fiancé was doing – looking for a dip, a hole, a cubby, somewhere just shallow enough to press himself against the back of the waterfall for some 'behind the falls' footage. Being roped up to the rock-wall, he would be safe enough against the pressure of the tumbling water. Should be, anyway.

She went to reach for the extra roll.

'. . . Well, I can take the pictures for you,' Anna suggested. 'It's better than nothing.'

Bo looked up at the white sky again. She supposed Anna had a point. The clouds were thick, the sleet falling like wet feathers from the clouds, no brightness anywhere. The weather had well and truly set in for the day; Signy's and her own instincts had been right. Reluctantly her hand dropped, away from the food. 'Okay, sure.' She had another gulp of her drink and stood up. 'Anders, there's a spare roll there if you want it.'

She had offered it to be polite, expecting him to refuse in

an equal display of manners. 'Thanks,' he said instead, reaching for it and taking a huge bite.

'Why don't you stand on that rock there?' Anna called. Bo turned to see she had clambered down the slope a few feet and was standing right beside the waterfall. Leaving Anders to the last of the lunch, Bo walked to the side of the fall and looked down to where Anna was pointing: a narrow seam of rock – more of a lip than a ledge – protruded six to eight inches from the cliff face, for a run of six feet; it was easily enough to get a foothold on, and as it snaked towards the fall itself, it bellied out into a small basin maybe two feet wide, the rushing water pooling there momentarily before spreading and spilling over the edges on the final approach to the fjord.

The deafening roar of the water made her heart beat faster, her feet tingle; it was like standing in front of a steaming engine or a puffing dragon. 'Um, I'm not sure,' she hesitated. 'That's pretty close to the falls.' Right beside them, in fact.

'Yes, but there's enough room to plant your feet in that shallow pool. It's only the spray that'll be an issue really, but if you keep the hood up . . . it would really show off the range's technical waterproof properties.'

Two hundred thousand pounds. That was the deal they had struck to promote the collection. And if the clients wanted to show off their waterproofability . . . Could she really say no?

'Okay,' she said, handing her phone over to Anna and taking a deep breath, carefully stepping off the grass.

'No!' The shout made her turn. Anders had jumped to his feet, the roll dropped in the grass. 'You can't go in there. The water pressure is too great.' He ran over.

'But she's not going into the *middle*!' Anna exclaimed, as

though that point was obvious. 'Bo's not going to stand under the waterfall, just at the edges here. Where it's calm. Look, the rockwall here is nearly dry.'

Anders looked across at Bo, ignoring Anna completely. 'One misstep and you would be swept over.'

'I appreciate your concern, but it's fine. Like Anna says I'm only going to stand at the sides. Don't worry, I've stood in hundreds of waterfalls.'

'In the tropics, maybe, but not a Norwegian fall in winter you haven't,' he said. 'The recent mild spell has melted much of the early snowpack; the rivers are fuller than usual. And the temperatures are unsurvivable.'

'Oh, thanks to Ridge Riders, I'm perfectly warm – and fully waterproof too,' she said with a cheesy smile and giving Anna a thumbs-up. Anna did the same back.

A wet flake landed on the tip of Bo's nose. She had to resist the urge to stick her tongue out and catch it. 'Trust me, I have no intention of falling in.'

'Bo—'

'Anders, really. I'm fine. You're our guide, not bodyguard. This is what we do.' She took a tentative step forward, aware of the weight of his disapproving stare as she angled herself into the sheer rock wall and went to pigeon-step across the river's exposed bedrock.

'Then wait!' he said with an exasperated tone. 'I will show you where to stand, at least.'

'Okay.' She shrugged, as he side-stepped past her with ease.

'Right, take my hand. These rocks are very slippery.'

'No! *Really?*' she teased – he was pretty easy to rib with that taciturn demeanour of his – letting his hand squeeze around hers, his grip was so tight her knuckles blanched as she awkwardly made her way along the rocks too. 'You getting this, Anna?' she hollered. She didn't want this effort to be in vain.

'Yes!' Anna shouted back, her voice faint beside the water.

Moving so close to the waterfall, it wasn't just the full impact of the roar or the mist that hit them, but the whirling air too that was displaced by the rushing torrents, whipping Bo's hair around her face. The spray and wind combined was freezing but Anders seemed oblivious, his head bent as he looked for the right footholds, his body leaning in to the mountain. With her one free hand, she pulled the hood back up.

The depth of the basin was greater than it had looked from the bank and it was up to their ankles here. They were both wearing fully waterproofed hiking boots but she could already feel the pressure of the water trying to push her feet from beneath her. In spite of her breezy, possibly even cocky, words a moment ago, she keenly felt that the line between beauty and danger was a thin one here. He was right – a Norwegian waterfall in winter wasn't like anything she had ever experienced before.

'There. Now that's as far as you go,' he said, not releasing her hand until he was sure she had a secure footing. She leant back against the rock face. The pool, though wider here, stretched barely two feet in front of her. It was round enough to sit in, but that didn't feel like much consolation when that was all that was stopping her from sliding down this rock face into the inky waters of the fjord.

'A bit further over would be better!' Anna yelled from her spot on the bank, waving her arms to indicate where she wanted Bo to go. 'If you can!'

'No!' Anders shouted back hotly. 'The water pressure is too strong.'

'It's only for a second!'

Anders stared at her, disbelief and then a bolt of anger colouring his face. '. . . *No*,' he said shortly, but there was finality in the word. No further argument would be brooked.

Anna gave a shrug.

Anders looked back at Bo. 'Do *not* move,' he said in a stern voice. 'Tell me when you want to come back and I will get you.'

She nodded, but ironically his caution was only serving to make her feel more nervous. She pressed herself in harder to the wet rock wall as he tried to get round her again, their waterproofs rustling against each other as he momentarily pinned her to the rock before his foot could find the grip to inch away on the other side. She gave an awkward smile as he passed over her.

'Excuse me,' he murmured, his eyes flashing to hers and away again. But she felt that funny drop in her stomach that she had got the first time she had seen him. Something about his eyes made her . . .

'Bo! Look at me!' Anna shouted, her phone already up to her face. 'Can you move your arm? We need to see the badge!' she added, pointing frantically at the badge on her own red jacket.

Anders moved further to the side, still on the rocks but out of frame now. He crouched down, watching on. Bo gave a shiver. Without him there, she suddenly felt uncertain. Immediately in front of her, the tiny plateau she was standing on dropped sharply from sight, whisking the lower falls down to the sea so that it felt like she was balanced precariously on the very lip of the waterfall. She felt like a dust mote, a single raindrop, a solitary snowflake – alone, exposed, vulnerable . . .

She couldn't hear the click of the camera for once, but she knew it was on her and she moved in the way she knew how to – slowly, to prevent blurring. Arms out. Arms up. Head back. Head down. Hood down. Hood up. Bent leg. Looking to the side – giving them lots of different options to choose from. And all the while flashing her bright smile, never faltering.

'Bo!' Tentatively she looked across to see Anna waving at her excitedly from the bank again. 'Put the hood down! Hood down!' she cried, pulling her own hood up and down to make the point clear.

Bo shivered. The sleet was feeling icier by the minute and it had to be several degrees colder here than it was on the bank, but she did as she was asked, feeling the mist immediately spritz her hair. She smoothed it back with her hands, blinking and gasping as the spray drenched her. It was shockingly, shockingly cold.

'Okay, are we good?' she called after a few minutes, turning to leave the rock pool. She put one foot forward onto a submerged rock, but as she transferred her weight, it moved beneath her, sitting loose in the water.

'No!'

She heard Anders shout from her left but she didn't see anything – her ankle was twisting as the stone rolled, throwing her off balance, her arms wheeling, a scream escaping her like whistling steam. She was falling . . .

Everything seemed to happen in slow motion then – she knew she couldn't keep herself upright but she desperately fought to land herself in towards the slope, her cheek scraping against stone, one knee slamming heavily against a submerged rock. The pain shot through her like a white light but she barely registered it as, prone on all fours, the water rushed in where it could – up her trouser legs, under the hem of her jacket, in at the cuffs and neck. It was a level of cold she couldn't articulate, robbing even the breath from her. All she was aware of, over everyone's shouts, was the roar of the water . . . the cold . . .

And then a hand. A hand closed around her wrist like a steel vice, pulling her up and out of the river like a caught salmon. Her feet didn't even touch the ground as she was unceremoniously half dragged, half carried back to the bank, water emptying from inside her clothes like an upturned bucket.

'What the *hell* did I tell you?' Anders shouted at her, his face contorted with an anger that whipped the relief from her and filled her with a fresh fear. 'You could have been killed! You *would* have been killed if you had gone over! You understand that, yes? Right now – you would be dead. Dead!'

His hands were tight upon her arms, his eyes colder than the water she had just fallen into. Shocked hot tears splashed from her eyes as her lungs filled with desperate breaths. She wanted to tell him she was sorry but the words wouldn't come. She was shaking violently, stunned and in pain, soaking wet, still frightened, too bewildered. It had all happened so slowly – and yet too fast to react.

'Stop shouting at her!' Anna yelled hotly, clambering over to them. 'Can't you see she's in shock?'

Anders released her but Bo thought she might drop to the ground without his support. Her muscles wouldn't seem to work. Her body seemed to have a life of its own, the muscles absolutely rigid and spasming. 'I *said* this would happen!'

'Well "I told you so" is not going to help anyone now!' Anna cried, seeing how the water was still sloshing from inside her clothes. 'God, she's really wet and shivering.'

They both looked at her with worried expressions.

'. . . We have to get her back to the farm,' Anders said, his voice suddenly different. Concerned. For some reason, it sounded more scary than when he'd been shouting.

'But that's a two-hour hike!' Anna protested.

'Then we had better start,' he snapped, making to head back up the slope.

Bo tried to obediently follow after, to mitigate for the inconvenience she had caused, but as she put her weight on her right leg, she cried out, stumbling forward.

Anders turned, startled. 'What now?'

'M-my knee,' she panted, still shivering wildly, unable to meet his gaze. 'I h-hurt my knee when I f-fell.'

There was a pause, Anders' expression changing again – this time from concern to fear. 'Stand on it,' he said, watching her closely.

She tried, but as soon as she put her weight on it, she cried out again and stumbled forward. He caught her easily, setting her back to upright as though she was a toppled chair. Slowly, she brought her gaze to his, frightened of the quiet rage she knew she would see there. 'I d-don't th-think I c-can walk,' she said quietly, her teeth chattering.

A face appeared above the bank. Lenny, his eyes wild with fright and framed by his long, dangling hair. 'Fuck!' he cried, slapping one hand to his forehead as he took in the sight of Bo shivering wildly, her gaze distant. 'What happened?'

It was a rhetorical question. Surely it was perfectly obvious what happened. The real question was what they were going to do about it now. Here.

Everyone except Bo was watching Anders. He looked back at them all with an expression of unchecked disgust before turning and looking around at the area. The woods butted up almost to the edges of the waterfall, but for the small exposed area of grass where they had lunched. It was turning gradually white – the sleet coming down harder now and beginning to settle, the weather beginning to close in fast.

He tutted, shaking his head and looking furious. He turned to them all again. 'If she can't walk then I'll have to bring the helicopter round, there's no other way to get her back,' he said with a hard expression. 'Which means going back to the farm and picking up the rib first.'

'You're not going to leave us here, are you?' Anna asked, looking panicky.

'No. But only because there won't be enough room for all of you to come back in the chopper. You'll have to follow me – but we'll be going at my pace, which is fast. I won't wait for you. She needs to get back in the warmth as quickly as possible.'

A skitter of stones down the embankment made them all look up as Zac's frantic expression suddenly peered down at them from the bank too. 'Holy fuck! Is she okay?' he panted, his hands still powdered white, karabiners jangling at his waist. 'Bo? Baby?'

Bo looked at him but he sounded very far away; it was as though she was seeing him underwater. She felt her good leg buckle beneath the weight of supporting her.

'Bo!' Zac cried, readying to jump down to them.

'No, stay up there. We're coming back up,' Anders said, scooping her up and climbing off the rocks, carrying her quickly to the trees where he settled her down on the grass, right beside the trees. It was dry there – well, drier – away from the mist and the roar, the sleet that was becoming snow . . . She wasn't sure if she was still shivering now; her body felt curiously detached from her and she couldn't feel much except for the pain in her knee like a radiant heat.

'Christ, look at the colour of her, man,' Zac fretted, going pale himself as he got close to her.

Bo saw their faces all turn to her again. What were they saying? She kept catching the tail end of words.

She saw Anders look across at Zac; they seemed to say something to each other without using words. 'We need to act quickly. Anna, come with me,' he commanded. 'You can get the fire going back at the cabin and run a hot bath for her. Zac, you come too.'

'What? No! I'm not leaving Bo here!'

'Lenny can stay with her. But if you and Anna fall behind and I get separated from you both, I need you to be responsible for getting Anna back safely.'

'But—'

'*You're* the one with mountain experience. I can't have two people stranded out here. The weather is getting worse.'

'For fuck's sake,' Zac said through gritted teeth, looking down desperately at Bo. 'How is this even happening?'

'Zac, it's fine, man. I'll take good care of Bo,' Lenny said. 'I won't let anything happen to her, swear on my life.'

Anders shrugged his coat off. 'Keep her warm. Get this on her.'

'Sure thing,' Lenny said, taking it and bundling it around her.

'But won't you need your coat?' Anna asked Anders. 'It's so exposed on the top of the mountain.'

'I won't feel it when I'm walking. I'll be fine,' he replied briskly. 'Now let's go.'

From behind her glass wall, Bo watched them climb up the grassy slope, their backs retreating from her, little blocks of colour that became smaller and smaller until within a few minutes they disappeared out of sight altogether, leaving her and Lenny behind. Zac kept turning every few metres, his pale frantic face looking to her like a bleached-out dot. She wished she could keep her eyes on the spot where he had slipped into the trees with the others but it was hard to keep her eyes open. She felt so sleepy now. So tired . . .

'It's okay, Bo, you're gonna be okay,' she heard Lenny say determinedly, a shiver trembling through his body as he wrapped his own bulk around her, trying to create a windbreak. 'We'll be fine. Totally fine. They'll be back for us in no time, you'll see.'

He didn't sound convinced.

Chapter Ten

It was like floating. As her eyelids fluttered against the light, her ears strained for sound but nothing came. She felt like she was being cradled in a cloud – weightless, drifting . . . She could sense light, bright light, and a heaviness upon her, pressing her down onto something soft.

With effort, she opened her eyes, closing them almost immediately as the light rushed at her like ghouls, making her flinch and startle. After a couple of moments she tried again. This time, her body was braced and, slowly, she was able to focus: her brain making sense of the flaming copper bath, the spindle chair with a yellow jacket hanging on it, the square that was a window, an almost celestial light blazing through.

Her fingers twitched as she saw that she was in bed, half buried beneath a pile of covers that made it difficult to move. She realized she couldn't feel her arms or legs – she had no idea if they were lying straight or splayed, such was the leaden heaviness in her limbs, and she wondered how long she had been here and if she had once moved?

Turning her head on the pillow, she saw Zac curled up beside her. He was lying on top of the covers, fast asleep, but something – her movement – must have disturbed him because he stirred, a small spasm flickering across his face before his eyes met hers in shock, startling them both. He sat up, his body as rigid and tense as an arrow. 'You're awake.'

'I guess so,' she said quietly. 'What . . . what happened?' But even as she asked, images flickered through her mind: the white froth of water; the black rocks; an orange warmth; his face against the trees . . .

'You slipped and fell in the water. You were hypothermic. But everything's fine now. You're safe.'

Safe. She looked around at the sparse bedroom, the place they were calling home for the next few weeks. 'How did I get back here?'

'Anders brought the helicopter round.'

'The helicopter?' she repeated weakly. Surely she should remember that?

'Yeah, Lenny said it was pretty hairy watching – there wasn't much room and the only bit where he could land wasn't flat. Credit to him, from everything Len said, he's a damned good pilot. Anders was back with you in an hour and forty; it could have been a *lot* worse. The weather came in so quickly.' He frowned. 'Jeez, on the way back we were walking into the wind and visibility was so bad, Anna almost stepped right off a ridge.'

It was all she could do to pucker her brow. 'But she's okay?' she asked weakly. She felt nauseous, unsettled, something niggling at the corners of her mind.

'Yeah everyone's fine. We've all just been worried about you. You've been out cold for nearly twenty-four hours.' She had? 'Do you remember getting in the bath?'

She blinked again. 'No.' No Lenny, no helicopter, no bath.

'Nuh, you were really out of it. Anders was properly worried for a bit, started saying we should get you up to the hospital in Alesund for some warmed IV, but I knew you'd be fine. Anna and I got this place like a furnace while Anders was bringing you back – stove roaring, steaming bath, hot pans in the bed the old-fashioned way, hot-water bottles and every blanket we could find – which was nine in all by the way. You were like a reverse princess and the pea,' he grinned.

'Thank you,' she said in a stripling voice. 'I'm sorry—'

'Hey, what are you sorry for?' he hushed. 'It's not your fault.' He reached over and kissed her temple and she closed her eyes. But she remembered Anders trying to stop her, his words of caution, his stern expression as she'd larked about in the water – all for the sake of a nice photo.

'Where is everyone? It's so quiet.'

'Anna and Lenny have gone into town to get stuff for dinner. They'll be back in a while.'

'Lenny—'

'Don't worry, he's fine. He got a bit of a chill too but Anna let him have a bath at hers when you guys got back yesterday.'

'Is he okay?' she whispered.

'More worried about you than anything. The snow came in really hard after we left but he somehow managed to stop you from getting colder and your condition deteriorating. He was a bit of a hero, to be honest.'

'Hero? Not Anders?'

Zac sighed and gave a reluctant nod. 'Yeah, him too. Goddam heroes everywhere you look.' He reached behind him for a water glass and handed it to her. 'Here, drink up.'

Bo did as she was told, too weak not to, taking several small sips and suddenly realizing her lips were dry and chapped. She pushed the glass away again. She felt drained and still shivery. 'Is he here, Anders? I should thank him.'

'No.'

Strangely, the word felt like a rock, cold and hard upon her chest. He had gone. She leant her head against Zac's chest. 'Well *you're* my hero,' she whispered, closing her eyes and feeling the heaviness of sleep press down on her again. Unable to resist.

It was dark when she stirred again – not the midnight velvet of twilight, but the diaphanous silk of dawn, a feeble poke against the tumbled clouds that clung to the mountaintops as though magnetically fastened there.

Bo stared out of the window at the slowly rippling blue symphony; the nights were so long and dark here, curtains weren't required to keep the light out. But she had been in this room for thirty-six hours now and her body – and in particular, her bladder – felt suddenly, desperately awake. With a sinking heart, she remembered the outhouse. Oh God, what she wouldn't give for an en-suite right now. But nature was calling . . .

Heaving herself up into a sitting position, shivering at the slightest breath of air against her body, she winced and gave a small gasp of pain as she tried to move her right leg; she pulled the mass of blankets away to get a look at her knee. She had been put into a heavy pale blue flannel neck-to-ankles nightgown that could only have belonged to Anders' grandmother and she had to rustle up the skirt to see her own skin. She flinched at the sight of the dramatic bruise that spread out from the kneecap like a black rose, the leg swollen and stiff-looking. Pressing her hand to it lightly, it felt hot to the touch, a small ridge of swelling pressing into the cup of her palm.

Beside her, Zac slept again – open-mouthed and snoring slightly, but still beautiful. He was wearing Ridge Riders thermals, the first signs of another beard beginning to speckle his jaw and cheeks once more. She wondered if he had left her side at all. On the side table sat a tray: tomato soup and hot chocolate, both now covered with a thick skin.

Feeling weak and light-headed, and unable to stop a small groan of effort, she tentatively got her feet to the floor and tried to stand. Her knee instinctively didn't want to lock but there was no bolt of anguish, no white shock of pain if she kept it bent, her heel off the floor. She stood for a moment, letting her body readjust to gravity.

Feeling the dizziness pass, she took the topmost blanket from the pile and, wrapping it over her shoulder, limped towards the door and looked out into the living room. Everything was still. The stove to her right was still warm but there was no beam of light coming from Lenny's loft. Every one was asleep.

Shutting the bedroom door lightly and keeping her weight on her good leg, she managed to get another few logs on the fire, pushing gingerly at the warm cinders with the poker before her bladder impressed itself upon her consciousness again. She hurried, limping, to the front door. Zac's climbing boots had been left there and, although far too big, she slid her feet in, opening the door wide and—

Her mouth dropped open. She stepped out with a look of utter astonishment. Snow had fallen heavily at some point – or possibly constantly – since she had been brought back here, and now everything was white. Utterly pristine and perfect, it was a sparkling wonderland, the world blanketed into a pillowy softness: the trees looked padded, bushes sprang like marshmallows, and Signy's cabin immediately behind only just seemed to peer above the ground like a half-risen soufflé.

Turning around the side of the house, she looked down

towards the fjord at water so dark, it was as though ink had been dropped into it. She gave a shudder at the sight, the cold touch of it a still-visceral memory. She saw the menace below its serene surface now. This remote wilderness had a breath-taking beauty that stirred the soul. But it was still a wilderness.

The snow creaked underfoot with each painful step as she hobbled as fast as she could towards the outhouse, Zac's boots threatening to fall off with every tread, gripping the blanket ever tighter to her shoulders. It was too cold to be out here in just a nightie and blanket and boots. She needed layers, thermals. That yellow jacket. But she hadn't known about the snow when she'd stepped out, and her bladder wouldn't be denied a minute longer.

With fumbling hands, feeling her teeth begin to chatter again, she let herself into the tiny hut, her body trembling with relief as she passed water. But even in the space of a few minutes, the chill that had set seed in her bones two days earlier, bloomed again in full power as though it hadn't ever gone but merely slept, her muscles going into microspasms as the cold marched through her like an ice army.

She tried to run back, but her knee and the too big boots would not allow it and a day and a half without food had left her weak. She staggered up the sloping path and back to the cabin door, fumbling with the latch as her skin made contact with the freezing metal, and she all but fell into the cabin again, panting from the effort.

'Bo?' She heard the voice behind her, concern singing out. But the heat inside the cabin was clamouring to greet her too, wrapping around her like a woollen scarf, the contrast of cold-to-warm too sudden, too great and before she could reach the wall or grab anything to hold on to – she felt herself crumple to the floor.

'Bo?'

She blinked. Anders face was upside down and peering over her with an expression of alarm. Oh God, not again. 'I'm . . . I'm fine,' she stammered, trying to push herself up to a sitting position.

'The hell you are,' he muttered, taking her by the elbow and steadying her as she took a few deep breaths. 'What were you thinking going out in the snow in your condition?'

'It's nothing. I fainted coming in from the cold, that's all,' she said, shivering again as a gust of wind blew in through the still-open door, dousing her like a bucket of iced water. He reached back and slammed it shut without a moment's consideration for the rest of the cabin's occupants. What time was it anyway?

A second later the bedroom door opened, Zac's sleepy face appearing. 'What the—?' he mumbled, before taking in the sight of her on the floor. He rushed over. 'What happened?'

'Bo went outside in a nightdress,' Anders said, looking back at her like a cross parent. 'Wearing just a nightdress. In the snow.'

'I didn't know it had snowed. I needed the loo. What was I supposed to do? Go in the sink?' She dropped her head, feeling exhausted again. Even that exchange had drained her.

Everyone was quiet for a moment and she realized her teeth were chattering and her fingers pulled agitatedly at the blanket again, but it felt as thin as a pillowcase and woefully underequipped for the job.

'We need to get you off the floor,' Anders said, stepping forward to hoist her up. But Zac rose too, blocking him, and, holding her by the elbow, helped her to stand. Anders moved back again, out of the way.

'Okay?' Zac enquired, holding her up.

'Yes, I'm fine,' she muttered, even though her vision had pixelated again. 'I wish everyone would stop making a fuss. I just need to eat something.'

'Make some toast, would you, mate?' Zac asked Anders, gripping her arm tightly.

Anders walked over to the stove and threw in another log. The night's cinders had already reddened since she had passed by a few minutes earlier and she saw a first, rekindled flame begin to flicker and kick. He sliced some bread and placed it under the grill.

'You need to get back into bed,' Zac said.

'I don't want to be in bed,' she protested feebly. Why was her head pounding so much? It was her knee she had hurt.

'Then sit down beside the fire. You need to get warm again,' Zac said, taking her over to the small sofa, seeing how she limped. He set her down carefully and it reminded her of Anders handling his grandmother on the way back from the village. 'You can't keep getting cold like this.'

'Well, it's a bit bloody hard not to when you can hardly walk and you're living in an unheated cabin in the snow with an outhouse for the facilities,' she grumbled. But even as she said it, she marvelled at how Signy managed it. Bo stared at the floor, feeling wretched and pathetic. She was even wearing the old woman's nightdress!

She sneezed suddenly – and then again. 'Oh.'

Zac pressed his hand against her forehead and sighed. 'And now you're hot.'

'Now I'm hot? Make your mind up.'

'You've got a temperature is what I mean. No doubt the one you always get when we come somewhere new.'

It felt like a failing of sorts. 'Excellent,' she whispered sarcastically, leaning back in the chair and resting her cheek on the cushion, staring into the fire. She felt pummelled, achy, and simultaneously hot and cold.

Zac shot Anders a weary look. 'This isn't working.' He raked his hands through his hair. 'We're going to have to rethink. We clearly can't stay here while Bo's sick; the facilities here are going to make her recovery too tough. There's a metre and a half of snow out there. She can't keep going out in that.'

'I agree. Pneumonia is a real risk for her right now,' Anders said matter-of-factly.

Zac looked over at him, clearly irked by Anders' dispassionate responses. 'If we leave, will we get a refund?'

Anders shrugged. 'No.'

'Oh, well, great. Just great. This is all working out rather nicely for you, isn't it?' Zac snapped. 'You take our money but talk us into leaving anyway? You never wanted us here in the first place.'

'What I want doesn't come into it,' Anders said simply. 'My grandmother has already spent what you gave her. You can stay for as long or as little of the month as you wish but I cannot give you back the money you have paid.'

Bo watched from the sofa as Zac began to pace. 'Well, then we'll just have to move her into a hotel until she's well enough to manage being back here again,' he said. 'It's not like it'll be long – a few days, tops.' Zac looked across at Anders. 'It's the Union Hotel, right? The big one in the village?'

Anders nodded. 'But it's closed for eight weeks for annual refurbishment and repairs. Reopens the first week in February.'

'Of course it does,' Zac said, with a shake of his head. 'Right, fine. Where else could we try?'

'There are no hotels open in the village at this time of year. Everything closes when the A63 is shut and the Hellesylt ferry stops.'

Zac was silent for a moment. 'Unbelievable. So then, what are we supposed to do? We can't all leave here. We're being paid to promote the extreme Norwegian lifestyle. *This* is what they want from us,' he said, indicating the remote cabin. 'This is what they're paying for and that money is what we're living on.'

Bo sneezed three times in succession. 'Ugh.'

There was a long pause as both men looked across at her. She supposed she looked ridiculous in the flannel nightie.

'There is another solution,' Anders said calmly, his quiet voice cutting through the tension.

'Yeah? And what's that?'

'She can come and stay with me. In the village.'

Bo's head jerked up.

Zac frowned. 'Say what now?'

'I've got two bedrooms and two bathrooms. She can have her own space there whilst she recovers. I'll be out in the day with you anyway so she will have plenty of time to rest and if you meet me there each morning, instead of me coming up here, then you can see her every day too.' He looked at Zac passively.

'I dunno, man,' Zac murmured in a low voice, eyeing Anders suspiciously.

Anders shrugged and gave a bored sigh. 'It's up to you. You need a solution, I'm giving you one. But if you can think of anything better, take it. I don't care. You've already paid me for the accommodation and my time. It makes no difference to me what you do.'

From behind hot eyes, Bo watched Zac regarding him with outright suspicion and she dropped her head on the cushions again. Honestly, what on earth was he so frightened of? All she wanted was a central heating system and a bathroom and a vat of tea.

And anyway, what other choice did they have?

'Well, I guess we could talk to Anna – see if her bosses will fly with that,' Zac said finally. 'Bo would only be gone for a short time, after all. A few days in the warm and you'll be right as rain, won't you, baby?'

Bo nodded. 'I'd be better in half that time if someone would just feed me,' she muttered grumpily. 'Is there *any* sign of that toast I was promised?'

'Oh yes,' Anders remembered, walking back and opening the oven, pulling out a blackened slice from the grill. He turned back to them with an unapologetic look. 'I shall start again.'

Bo blinked, hoping this wasn't an omen as to the standard of his cooking. She didn't want to survive falling in a waterfall only to be finished off by his dinners.

The sound of movement overhead made them look up, as feet appeared on the ladder and Lenny climbed down, wearing a pair of socks, cactus-printed cotton boxers and a navy sherpa fleece. 'I thought I heard a noise,' he mumbled, looking weary.

'Great use you'd be in a burglary,' Zac quipped as Bo took in the sight of his sleep-addled face. His five-o'clock shadow looked closer to eleven and he had bags beneath his eyes; even his tan seemed to have faded.

'Lenny,' she murmured, reaching an arm towards him.

'Hey, you're up. I didn't even see you sitting there. You're disappearing into the furniture. How you feeling?' He crossed the room and kissed her on the forehead, pulling back with a frown and pressing the back of his hand there too.

'Better.'

'You don't feel better.' He turned back to the others. 'She's got a fever.'

'Yeah, and Anders thinks pneumonia is a risk too. She needs to get warm and stay warm. She can't be going out in the snow every time she needs the loo . . .' Zac said.

'That's true.'

'So we're making alternative arrangements for her. She can't stay here when she's so sick. Anders has said she can stay at his for a few days. In town.'

Lenny's jaw dropped open. 'You're kidding?'

'No. Why?'

Zac looked puzzled, Anders offended. Bo was embarrassed.

'Because, I mean, we don't . . . we hardly know him.' He turned to Anders. 'No offence, dude, but you can't think we'd let her go stay with just anyone? You could be an axe murderer for all we know.'

'Len – first off, Anders is the guy who saved her ass on the mountain. I hardly think he's going to do her harm at his house in the village.' But the expression on Len's face suggested he still thought it was a moot point. 'And secondly – what's with the "we"? She's *my* fiancée.'

'I know that, but you know what I mean. We're a family, the three of us. I care about her too, you know I do.'

Zac softened, patting him on the shoulder. 'Yeah, I know you do, man, you're a brother to us both. But this is the only viable option. Bo can recover properly in town and we'll stay here and fulfil our obligations with Ridge Riders. It's only a short-term thing and then everything can go back to normal again in a few days; it's the best option in the long run. You'll see.'

Chapter Eleven

Lodal, mid-June 1936

Signy walked like an old woman, bent forward at the hips by the haybale on her back, her muscles screaming for relief. The bale weighed almost more than she did and if she were to fall forwards she would struggle like an overturned beetle to get back up again, but her legs kept moving over the uneven ground. She may be small but she was mighty – that was what her pappa always said.

'This is the last of the fourth line,' she panted, twisting and letting the bale roll to the haybarn floor. 'Just one more to go.'

'Thank goodness,' Brit puffed, dropping her head and resting her cheek against the pitchfork for a moment, both of them aching and weary and out of breath.

It had been a race against time all afternoon, the girls trying to beat the grey clouds that had peeped over the horizon soon after lunch and made slow but ominously steady progress across the sky towards them. The hay had been drying for nine days now, Sofie and Margit – as the biggest and strongest – in charge of scything the grass, working their way across the fields in a diagonal pattern, as Kari and Ashild followed after them, tossing the strewn cut grass onto the hayracks to dry. They had cleared so much grass that all the hayracks were now full; and although they continued to scythe, the younger girls raking the cut grass into windrows on the ground instead, the dried hay needed bringing into the barn for storing before the men came up to transport it back to the farm. Luck had been against them, though, and every time they went to bring it in there had been a heavy dew or a cloudburst, just enough to soak everything through and push them back again. The hay couldn't be stored in the barn unless it was completely dry and they had planned on clearing the hayracks the next day, but the unexpected dark clouds had changed those plans. Signy had come down from her long hours spent walking the outfields only to be put straight back to work again as the others – red-cheeked, their hairlines streaked with sweat – hurriedly loaded the hay onto the small horse-drawn cart, or alternatively hand-twined small bales pushed through the baling box her father had made, carrying them up to the barn on their own backs.

The slow clop of Bluebell's hooves outside announced the arrival of the next load and, straightening up with a wince, Signy moved out of the way.

'Nearly there,' Kari said breathlessly, reaching her pitchfork over the side of the cart and immediately beginning to toss the hay into the barn. 'Another cart-load, I reckon.'

Signy stepped out and looked up at the sky, breaking into an immediate run back down the path. It was purple and pregnant with rain. There was just one more rack to clear but that would take a few minutes even with all of them working on it. Each rack was made by five wires strung tightly between tall spruce poles, and from a distance, when they weren't in use, the racks were almost invisible to the eye, the spruce poles standing out of the ground like coppiced woods. But when they were laden, with five layers of overlapping long grass drying on the wires, they looked like dense hairy walls, striping the fields; Signy had always loved playing cat and mouse around them with Nils and the other boys when they came up for Midsummer's Eve. But there was no time for playing games now. She could clearly see the silvered rain sliding towards them like an advancing blade, coming up from the valley, breaching their plateau.

'Hurry!' she called, seeing Sofie sitting on a rock, her elbows splayed on her knees tiredly as she took a break, waiting for the cart to return. 'It's coming!'

Sofie looked up, then jumped too. The storm had stolen a march on them, and together with Margit they all began grabbing the hay from the wires in armfuls. With no time to wait for the cart, Ashi threaded the twine as they pushed the hay down into the cubed wooden baling box. It was an odd-looking but ingenious contraption her father had invented: a tall, narrow box accessed by a hinged door on one end and with a wooden levered 'stamper' to push down and compress the grass from above. If it was rudimentary, it was also effective.

'Hurry!' Sofie said, glancing back across at the advancing storm.

'I'm going as fast as I can,' Ashi replied as the first bale was formed and released and she had to thread up for the next one. It was a fiddly job, best done by little fingers.

Signy pulled the first bale free and, knotting it tightly, heaved it with a groan onto her back, beginning the incline up to the haybarn again. It was so heavy and she felt so tired after hours of walking with the herd today, that with each step, she wasn't quite sure if her knees would give out, but within a couple of minutes she had tossed it onto the barn floor for Brit to pitch, and was running back down again.

Fat drops began to pelt the ground, not many, not yet, but they were large like bullets.

Kari and Bluebell were already back in the field by now, the horse nodding quietly as the cart was frantically reloaded with loose hay. Signy blinked hard as she felt the raindrops strike her forehead and cheeks; no one could afford to get wet. Wet would almost certainly lead to ill and the *seter* was no place for that, with neither doctors nor other adults around.

She and Ashi baled another pile. In the distance, a rumble of thunder made them all stop and turn for a moment, waiting – breaths held – for a lightning strike. They counted.

One. Two—

There! It was close. Two miles away.

Sofie shrieked but Signy laughed with delight. Her first storm at the *seter*! The rain was suddenly falling quickly, densely, and the girls fell into a sort of dance, hopping from one foot to the other as though they could dodge the raindrops.

'Quick! Hurry! That will have to do!' Margit cried, tossing a last armful of hay onto the cart and taking Bluebell by the reins, turning her as tightly as she dared without spilling the cart and walking briskly up the path. Sofie followed, pulling her cardigan over her hair. There was still a line of hay remaining on the wire nearest the ground. It was the driest, having been placed there first and protected by the upper layers above it, but Signy knew it couldn't be helped – the storm was upon them and it would simply have to get wet and dry out again later. At least now they would be able to clear the windrows and get the new batches drying on the racks before they rotted on the ground. So much hay was required to get them through the winter months – both as bedding and feed for the animals, and if it was a long hard winter, as this year's had been, they couldn't afford to waste a single straw.

With a last burst of effort, she hoisted the final bale onto her back and with her hands securing it at the base, ran staggeringly towards the barn.

'Hurry, Signy!' Kari called, beckoning her on with frantic hand movements. Signy grinned, feeling her muscles burn. She desperately wanted to stop, but part of her also loved the drama of it all, the six of them out here battling the elements together.

'Is it wet? Is it too wet?' Brit asked, pulling her in through the door with a desperate tug and immediately inspecting the bale as she let it fall to the ground. Signy fell to her knees, panting, her cheeks a mottled red stain as raindrops fell from strings of her hair.

'Only superficially, I think,' Margit said, patting at it with her apron. 'If we store it by the door, where there's most airflow, it should dry out okay.'

Signy's hair was plastered to her head, fat drops dripping down the collar of her dress and mingling with the sweat of her exertions. 'That . . .' she panted, still on her knees, 'was brilliant.'

Another rumble of thunder made them all look up again, seeing the rectangle of bruised sky through the open barn doors as another lightning fork split the heavens.

Ashi squealed, covering her ears with her hands and squeezing her eyes shut. 'I *hate* storms!'

'I love them!' Signy breathed, eyes wide as she got up to her feet and staggered over to the window to look; the old small whetstone her father had replaced lay discarded on the ground by the wall there, lifting her up just high enough to see out. The rain had come in so hard, she already couldn't see the crumbling stone wall at the bottom of the nearest field and it was as though the encircling mountaintops had been flattened down by the sheer force. The goats were safely locked in their pens but the sheep were huddled in the near pasture under the aspen tree and the cows were lying down beside the walls.

'It looks like this is going to settle in for the night,' Margit sighed, standing by the open double doors and scanning the sky for signs of respite or light. But it was darker now than at midnight.

'Well we can't stay in here then,' Sofie said. 'We need to get into dry clothes and eat something. We'll have to make a run for it. Last one out locks the doors!'

She sprinted out before the others could respond, but they were only a half-second behind her, flying through the door in a scurry of shrieks, their arms wrapped over their heads.

The haybarn was situated above and behind the cabins on the opposite side to the stream; getting back to their huts should only take ten, fifteen seconds at most but the rain was driving down, puddles already pooling on the hard ground. They would all be soaked.

'What? No! . . . Wait!' Signy cried, reacting too late, distracted as she was by the splitting sky. But she had already lost. The others were sprinting down the path, their heels kicking up, splashing through the puddles as they hurled themselves towards the shelter of their cabins.

Signy ran out and freed one of the pinned-back doors, swinging it shut and refastening it internally. The rain pounded at her back like fists, the cold a sting against her skin. She ran around to get the other door and was pushing it shut, eyes squeezed to slits against the rain, when she suddenly screamed.

It was a scream that carried over the storm, making the animals startle and the girls stick their heads back out of their cabins.

'Signy?' Margit cried, running back out into the rain. 'What is it? What's wrong?' she asked worriedly.

But Signy couldn't reply. She could only point at an area in the corner where the haybales were stacked in a tower. And beside it, a pair of feet.

The man stood in the haybarn, his cap held in his hands as the six girls fanned around him, eyes casting up and down as though scanning him for knives. Signy couldn't take her eyes off him. If this man did mean them harm, could they – six teenage girls – defeat him? He didn't look to be much older than them. He was neither tall nor strong-looking like Nils, but he had a polite mouth and clear hazel-brown eyes that burned from beneath a thick dark fringe.

'Who are you?' Margit asked, her voice hard, but a tiny tremor betrayed her nerves as her hand gripped tighter around the primitive hay knife – it was the first thing she had grabbed upon hearing Signy scream.

Sofie was standing behind her right shoulder, appraising the man with open curiosity, her chin jerked high in her usual air of superiority; in spite of this, she seemed to have decided Margit could be the lead on this matter.

The man's gaze didn't deviate from Margit's. 'My name is Mons Bjorstad. I am a clockmaker from Trondheim.'

'Trondheim is a long way from here,' Margit said evenly.

'Yes, it is,' he agreed. 'I have travelled for a long time to get here.'

'You are alone?'

He nodded.

Signy narrowed her eyes, watching him, remembering the particular sensation of having been watched a week earlier. She had felt it on several occasions since then – had it been him? Or were there others? Was he lying? The man's face was lightly streaked with dirt and his eyes drooped slightly at the outer edges. He looked fatigued but he didn't have the colour of a man who worked outdoors, nor the same coarse accent; his hands had long, tapered fingers and were neither calloused nor rough. If a clockmaker was to have a 'look', perhaps his was it.

'Where are you travelling to?' Margit continued.

'Loen. Down in the valley yonder.' He jerked his chin towards the village out of sight from here.

No one said anything. Loen was their home. They knew every person who lived there, and they also knew that almost no one ever came to visit. The village was remote with no through path and clustered around the inland lake Lovatnet.

Margit's grip tightened slightly around the neck of the knife. 'And what is waiting for you in Loen?'

'A commission from the *lensmann*, Martin Omenas.'

'Omenas?' Sofie echoed sharply, side-stepping forwards to stand in front of Margit now. 'What does *he* want *you* for?' she asked, walking past him a little too closely. It was something she often did to put men, quite literally, on the back foot.

But Mons didn't step back; he merely leant a little instead, watching her as she walked, and Signy could see him tracing her beautiful face, as though it was a book that could be read and understood. 'He heard about my work with astronomical clocks.'

'Astronomical clocks?' Sofie scoffed. 'What on earth are they?'

'They represent the solar system using the geocentric

model,' he said calmly. He had a steady gaze and his voice when he spoke, although quiet, was certain and self-assured. To Signy's eye, he seemed intelligent and educated; noble in action, if not high born.

Kari and Ashild tittered, as Sofie scowled at him. It was quite apparent that none of them had ever heard of a geocentric model, much less understood how that might be shown on a clock.

The stranger – Mons – looked back at Margit again, their leader. 'I am sorry if I caused alarm. That was not my intention. I had hoped to reach the village tonight but was caught by the storm. I only wanted to take shelter through the worst of it before carrying on. I did not mean for you to ever know I'd been here.'

Margit stared at him for a moment longer, her grip on the knife lessening; Signy could see her sister was of the same mind that he posed no apparent threat. 'No,' she said finally. 'It is fine.'

'I will leave immediately and trouble you no further,' he said, bowing his head, before replacing his cap and making to move past them.

Signy looked up at her sister; she could hear the storm at their backs, the rain pelting against the roof and window and walls, the thunder rumbling in rhythmic rolls across the sky.

'Absolutely not.' Margit's voice was clear as a bell. He stopped. 'You can't possibly go out in this. You must stay for the duration of the storm – we insist.'

Relief brightened his face as he smiled. 'Well, thank you. That is very kind.' He nodded his thanks to each and every one of them. 'Thank you.'

'I'm Margit Reiten,' she said. 'And this is my sister Signy. Our father owns the summer pastures up here. Brit, Ashild and Kari Jemtegard,' she said, pointing out each of them. 'Their family's farm abuts ours in Loen, and Sofie . . .' Margit caught herself, remembering her friend's sensitivity on the issue. 'Sofie Doving is our dear friend and neighbour.'

'It is a pleasure to meet you all,' he said, his attention coming quickly back to Margit, as their unofficial representative; it was both politic and polite, but as Margit smiled back, her gaze seemed to catch with his, tangling in it.

Signy looked between them both.

'Well, you must be tired and hungry,' Margit said finally. 'Come with us. The cabins are over here. You can rest whilst we prepare dinner. We were about to eat anyway.'

It was raining harder now – if that was even possible – but though they all threw their arms protectively over their heads as they ran down to the huts again, this time there were no girlish squeals or shouts; Signy looked back to see Mons fastening the haybarn door for them before he followed.

'Please, do take a seat by the window,' Margit said, setting the hay knife in the corner and pointing to the small table with bench chairs. Signy knew they had been planning *kokeost* cheese and rolls for dinner, but she said nothing as her sister reached for the smoked ham hock hanging from a hook in the far corner of the cabin. Sent as a treat by their mother, they had been saving it for Midsummer's Eve but with a guest to feed – albeit an unexpected one – there were standards to uphold.

Sofie and the Jemtegard girls had retreated to their respective cabins to change into dry clothes and retrieve their small luxuries too, and when they returned fifteen minutes later, Brit had put on a slick of lipstick, Ashi had tied a blue ribbon in her hair and Kari was wearing her favourite embroidered neckscarf. They came bearing the side of salmon they had had curing for the past three days; Ashi was a superb fisher-woman and every Sunday he'd taken to hiking to the lake in the next valley where – in exchange for a day's respite from duties – she would return with a new catch. It had become their weekly fresh treat.

'Please, do not go to any trouble on my account,' Mons said, seeing how they draped a lace cloth over the table and Margit fetched a red candle from the drawer.

'No trouble,' Margit smiled, her eyes flashing to him like darting fish before she turned and began slicing the ham.

With the five girls working in the small cabin kitchen, it was cramped and felt to Signy like they were the goats in the pen, all bustling against each other. But it wasn't just space that was tight; the air suddenly felt compressed too, like it was stoppered inside a champagne bottle, fizzing with some alchemic change. Amongst all the jostling elbows, Signy glimpsed the furtive glances back at the handsome stranger sitting by the window, and she felt the urge to give in to hysterical laughter. Apart from Nils' visit the first week, they had been deprived of the company of any male under the age of fifty for almost a month now (and given that Nils was their brother, the Jemtegard girls hadn't been thrilled by his presence anyway). This Mons man could have had two heads and trotters for feet and they would still have flirted with him.

'Do you play?' Mons asked Margit as she brought a stack of blue plates to the table. He was pointing to the small guitar on the wall; it was their father's, reserved for the special occasions when he and the rest of the village came up here.

'No,' Margit demurred. 'That's my father's.'

'That is a shame. I suspect music played up here sounds sweeter than in the valleys.' Margit had straightened up but he kept her on the spot with a direct gaze that seemed to exclude the rest of them. Signy saw two pink spots colour her sister's cheeks and she was amazed – she had never seen her blush before.

Margit went to turn away—

'Margit sings,' Signy said hurriedly. 'Mamma says she has a better voice than the nightjars.'

'Is that true?' Mons asked her, looking grateful for the opportunity to keep her there, keep her talking.

'Oh no,' Margit said bashfully, with a shake of her head.

'Yes, it—'

But before Signy could protest it, Margit added, 'How about you? Do you play any instruments?'

'Only this.' He reached into the pocket of his woollen coat and pulled out a slide harmonica.

'Well, perhaps you could play a little for us whilst we prepare dinner?' she asked.

'I would be glad to, if you would sing in return?' He smiled, his gaze capturing hers again, and Signy saw how it scooped her sister off the ground, cradling her in the air.

The others looked at each other and Signy knew they could see it too, this thing, whatever it was between Margit and the stranger.

The sound of the latch made them all turn round as Sofie walked in, looking sensational in the pale lemon cotton dress she had made her father take in at the waist three times. Her dark hair was slicked back as though she had been caught in the rain – even though it was less than ten steps from her cabin to here – and she had lightly stained her lips.

Signy saw how Margit's face fell at the sight of her friend; Sofie looked ravishing, as she well knew. 'Have I missed much?' she asked the staring crowd.

Signy felt a flash of anger arrow through her at Sofie's

game. She was toying with the man, determined to make him fall in love with her in revenge for how he had refused to bend the knee earlier, making her look foolish as her scornful words were thrown back in her face.

But Mons simply smiled. 'Not at all. Margit and I were just making a pact. I will play after dinner, if she will sing,' he said in his quiet voice, looking back at Margit and wrapping her up once more in a soft gaze. 'What do you say, Margit Reiten? Will you sing for me?'

Chapter Twelve

Her cheek against the cushion, Bo listened to the sound of the boat pulling away, the deep gurgle of the propellers under-water as the rib slowly reversed in a half circle and glided into the frame of the windows. From her position on the sofa, she could just see Anders checking behind them, one hand on the throttle; he was kitted out in his orange waterproofs again, his hood up as snowflakes dotted the air between them. He looked like a teacher on a school trip: stern, cautious and steady as Zac and Lenny and Anna – having taken up pos-itions on the seats and holding on to the handrails – joked and larked about, their hooded heads moving animatedly as they laughed and talked, excited about the day's forthcoming adventure. Anders was taking them round to a precipitous gorge. It was a long way further up the fjord and involved another long hike when they got there – and Bo felt nothing but relief that she didn't have to go out there with them too.

She hugged the hot-water bottle closer and watched as Anders eased the boat into gear and led them away, the wake behind them a startlingly bright scar against the dark water. She tracked them for as long as she could but in under a minute they were out of sight, the signature frozen silence of the fjord settling again like a smothering blanket.

For several minutes she didn't move, except to breathe and

blink. She felt tucked into a fog and far, far away from any-where. She had little sense of being here, in Anders' house, alone – not that it mattered where she actually was. She was a stranger wherever she might be – none of these places were home. Not the cosy shelf farm a mile up the water, not the beach hut in Samoa.

From her bundle of blankets on the chair, she looked around at the place where she had been left; things had moved quickly once the arrangement had been decided – her unforeseen convalescence was throwing out an already tight timetable and Lenny (uneasy though he was with the plan) was also adamant they couldn't lose the light of another day to getting her sorted out. In the week since they had arrived in Norway, they had lost a day to travelling, another to set-tling in and welcoming Anna, there had been the disastrous trip to the waterfall, and then of course yesterday, when she had slept constantly and Zac had kept watch. Lenny had had to pad out yesterday's posts with yet more throwback fillers, but their fans wanted an adventure to feed on, they needed fresh material and her 'chill' was holding them all up.

So while Zac, Lenny and Anna had hiked and kayaked their way back down to town with lunch supplies and climb-ing equipment in the rucksacks, Anders had packed a bag for her and brought her back to town in the helicopter. It had taken less than five minutes to get to the village by air – they were no sooner up than they were going down again – and the same again in his orange Defender from the heliport to the house. He had guided her, sneezing and shivering, into the sitting room where she was lying now and piled her up with cushions and blankets, then got a fire going; he'd made her coffee and toast and pulled a tub of frozen soup from the freezer to defrost in time for lunch, so that by the time the others had arrived, pulling up at his jetty beyond the window, she was as comfortably ensconced as if she'd been there for days. The house had all the creature comforts of a village home – a TV, hot running water, a fully working kitchen, integral toilets . . . and after such an embattled week at the shelf farm, these pedestrian details felt luxurious beyond measure.

Dropping her head back in the pillows, succumbing to a coughing fit, she switched on the TV, letting her gaze roam over the room. She was vaguely surprised to find she liked it; it was masculine but not brutally so: bookshelves stuffed with paperbacks covered the opposite wall; a pair of old leather chairs – the seats cracked with age – were positioned in front of it and a vast mottled mocha-and-ivory shaggy sheepskin rug was spread on the wooden floor, in front of the wooden fireplace to her left. Her perch, a contemporary three-seater cream wool Ikea sofa, was positioned in front of the large square-paned windows that gave onto the water, with an industrial-style floor lamp arching over her like a solicitous butler.

It was a more stylish room than she might have predicted; to date, she had only ever seen him in rugged outdoor survival clothes and so had assumed he was someone who invariably rated substance over style – certainly the bafflement-bordering-on-scorn on his face as he watched her and Zac doing their Instagram 'thing' had suggested he didn't buy into aspirational lifestyle culture.

Yet the room still revealed something of who he was – and what he cared about – in the details: in spite of his ultra-controlled personal demeanour, he wasn't meticulous at home according to the grey-marl sock rolled up and peeking out from under the corner of one of the chairs; a well-thumbed copy of a rib-boats brochure on the side-table was no surprise. The still-white wicks on the candles on the fireplace told her he'd never lit them and didn't entertain. There was a Swiss army knife opened to the bottle opener on another table. Stacks of curling-paged climbing and skiing magazines. A mountain bike wheel was propped against the side wall.

She channel-hopped for a while; there was a lot of biathlon coverage and slalom racing, which although in Norwegian didn't need translating, but she eventually found an English-speaking channel playing old episodes of *Columbo*. She watched without taking any of it in. The room was almost oppressively warm but she couldn't stop shivering and she hugged the hot-water bottle harder, just as the sound of a door clicking echoed in the hall.

She stiffened, suddenly alert. 'Hello?' she called, lifting her head an inch off the cushion.

'*Hei?*' A voice called out, footsteps coming closer.

A woman peered around the door – silver short hair, pale green eyes and wearing jeans, a turquoise ski jacket, damson-coloured hand-knitted jumper and hiking boots. She nodded and came further into the room; she was carrying a small leather Gladstone bag and moved with brisk authority. 'You must be Bo?'

Bo nodded, feeling too alarmed-slash-exhausted to speak.

'I am Annika, Anders' neighbour. He asked me to look in on you.'

He had? 'Oh. But—'

'I am a doctor.' She gave a small shrug, lifting the bag in her hand as though that alone proved it. 'Retired now of course, but I help out when required.' She walked over to the sofa and sat down on the edge of it, pulling out a stethoscope. 'He said you fell into the water,' she said briskly, putting the earbuds to her ears and warming the suction cup against her hand by breathing on it several times and then rubbing it.

Bo watched, mesmerized. 'Yes.'

'That wasn't very clever. How are you feeling?'

'Well . . .' Bo went to demur.

'Because you look like hell,' Annika said, leaning in to put the stethoscope against Bo's chest. 'Breathe in for me. And out.' She listened, moving the instrument a few inches here and there. She frowned. 'Sit up for me.'

With a struggle, Bo leant forward and Annika repeated the procedure on her back too. Without another word, she took off the stethoscope and put a thermometer in her ear. 'Open,' she said, taking a tongue depressor next and examining Bo's throat; she palpated her glands and finally looked at her with clear-eyed scrutiny. 'You're very tanned. Where have you been?' she asked with the same suspicion as Anders' grandmother. Bo wondered whether the answer would have any effect on the diagnosis.

'Samoa, in the South Pacific. We've only been here a few days.'

'Hmm. You got all your innoculations?'

'Yes.'

'Well the long flight and the change in climate won't have helped,' Annika muttered, packing everything into her bag and looking back at her again. 'You've got a nasty cold and a chest infection that I don't like the sound of. You're going to need antibiotics; there's a crackle in the bottom of your lungs we'll need to keep an eye on. Trust me, you do not want to get double pneumonia out here.'

'No,' Bo agreed feebly.

Annika stared at her – not unkindly but with a directness Bo was unused to. 'Have you eaten?'

'A little toast.'

This seemed to please her. 'Good. Eat little and often and keep your strength up. And drink plenty of fluids.'

'Anders has left me some soup for lunch.'

'Will you be able to manage it on your own?'

Bo nodded, just as she felt another coughing fit come on. '. . . Oh yes,' she spluttered finally. 'I'll be fine.'

'Hmm.' Annika looked unconvinced. 'Well, I'll come back and check on you later. I'll leave my number on the kitchen table if you need anything. In the meantime, I'll go to the pharmacist for you and we can get the antibiotics course started for that chest infection. Are you allergic to anything?'

Bo shook her head.

'Fine. Stay here, keep warm, don't move unless you have to. I'll be back in a while.'

Bo nodded as Annika got up and headed for the door again. 'Thank you,' she said weakly, just as she began coughing again.

'Don't thank me. It's Anders putting himself out,' Annika said over her shoulder, the front door clicking closed again a moment later.

When she awoke, *Columbo* had been replaced by *The Golden Girls*, but there was a small brown bottle of pills on the coffee table in front of her and the fire had been restacked. Bo blinked, trying to bring herself up to speed with events. She felt so disoriented still. Had that lady – Annika, was it? – come back? And Bo had slept through it?

Checking the time, she was astonished to see it was after two o'clock. How long had she been asleep for? The light would begin to fade soon and the others would be heading back here.

She reached out an arm and picked up the pill bottle, rattling it lightly. It sounded dispiritingly full. *One tablet. Three times daily. Five days. Course to be completed.*

Gathering her energy, Bo got up. The pain in her knee was still there but the swelling had gone down a lot and it was becoming easier to walk, the stiffness letting up with use. She hobbled into the kitchen for a glass of water: bitter-chocolate-painted units were topped with pale blonde worktops and there was a small round table with orange chairs; all the crockery was plain white from Ikea and the cutlery serviceable steel. The Tupperware tub of soup sat on the draining board, defrosted now and ready to be heated.

Feeling a faint thrill of delight that the cooker was electric, she watched the ring glow red within seconds as she put the pan on and waited for it to bubble. She leant against the counter, stirring the soup sporadically, her eyes flitting over the collection of waterproof jackets hanging from a hook behind the door, the solitary washed-up plate and cup on the draining board, the crumbs still on the breadboard . . . A wall calendar with images of the fjord was open to December, the white date squares sporadically filled in with commitments in blue ink. She couldn't decipher his handwriting nor understand Norwegian to read what any of them said but she saw that the squares for 10 December onwards had been grouped together by a red bubble and scored through with *Instagram.*

She frowned, feeling curiously stung by the slight. It felt dismissive and disparaging, as though he couldn't even be bothered to know their names.

She took her humble feast over to the table and began sipping slowly, her eyes closed from the effort it took. She couldn't taste anything and her appetite had deserted her for once but she managed to force half of it down before conceding defeat. The activity had depleted her and she dropped her head, feeling spent. She needed to lie down again. Leaving the dishes in the sink, she slowly walked through the rest of the house, looking for the bedroom; she might feel more rested if she slept in a bed and not on the sofa.

There was a small study fronting onto the lane, pinboards thick with layered papers that fluttered like feathers in the downdraught and photographic brochures for Geraingerfjord Guided Tours folded in piles on the desk. There was a downstairs cloakroom too with a toilet, yet more coats and pairs of walking boots and wellies turned upside down on sticks. The staircase upstairs, opposite the 'front' door, was narrow, winding around on itself; there was a small bathroom at the top and two bedrooms set on either side. But which was hers?

She peered into the one on the right. Was this the guest room? The bed had been dressed with a thick white duvet, a fringed charcoal-grey blanket draped across the lower half. It had an old painted wardrobe and chest of drawers with a large jug and bowl set on the top and a worn rug on the floor. In the corner, she could see a door leading to another small white-tiled bathroom.

The room opposite was almost a carbon copy, but here the duvet was navy, the blanket across it red and the furniture was more modern – walnut she thought. It had a more masculine energy to it, and her instinct was that this was his room, but the bag that had been packed for her was propped against the end of the bed. Without needing further invitation, she peeled back the covers and fell in. She tucked the duvet close around her neck and curled up into a tightly wound foetal position. Within seconds, she was asleep again.

*

'Hey. Goldilocks.'

She groaned. But her arm was squeezed again and she felt herself gently rocked side to side.

'Wake up.' She opened one eye. Anders was staring down at her. 'You're sleeping in the wrong bed. This is my room.'

'Huh?' She tried to wake up, to compute what he was saying.

'Wrong room. You're in the other one.'

She frowned. 'But my bag—'

He glanced down and saw the rucksack at the foot of the bed. His expression changed. 'Oh. I must have put it in here by mistake.'

'What time is it?' she murmured, not wanting to move.

'Four.'

'Four?' She looked out of the window in front of her – the sky was a rich indigo again, the last of the daylight just a ribbon trim along the horizon. Forcing herself to sit up, she looked around with fresh eyes, noticing a photo beside the bed. It was of him with a woman: brown-haired, blue-eyed, light freckles. A rich mouth, good teeth. Beautiful.

He saw her looking. 'You'd better come down immediately,' he said abruptly, taking the photograph away and sliding it into the bedside drawer. 'Zac wants to see you before they have to head back.'

'Oh . . . sure,' she murmured, feeling affronted by the hostility in his actions. Snatching the photograph like that was plain rude. And was it her fault he had put her bag in the wrong room?

'Hey!' Zac said, greeting her with outstretched arms as she staggered downstairs a few minutes later and into the living room, still clutching her hot-water bottle, still shivering. He, Anna and Lenny were all gathered around the fire that she saw had almost gone out again and which Anders was once again prodding into life. 'How are you feeling?'

'I was sleeping,' she mumbled. 'I think I've slept most of the day.'

'Good. Best thing for you,' Zac said, kissing her on the forehead and wrapping her in his arms. Bo closed her eyes, letting herself relax against him. 'The more you rest now, the quicker you'll recover.'

'Hope so,' she murmured into his chest. 'How was the trip?'

'Amazing!' Anna beamed. 'Anders took us all the way to some falls way, way down the valley where we got some incredible footage. We never would have found it on our own. Go on, Lenny – show her.'

Lenny shuffled forwards, already tabbing back through the screen on his camera. He took the strap off his neck and handed it to her. 'Tab right.'

Bo did as she was told, eyes aching as she took in the harsh polar palette of white and black, gunmetal and navy; it made her shiver again just to look at it. Much of the footage was of Zac scrambling up an almost sheer overhang, his face burning with concentration, fingers clawed.

'That's a great one,' Anna said, peering over her shoulder. 'You can really see the give across the shoulders there,' she murmured, pointing to the jacket he was wearing. 'Our patented four-way stretch.'

Bo felt the energy leave her again. 'Yes.' She stopped at another photograph of Zac standing astride a chasm, one leg on each steep bank. Lenny had taken it from below so that he looked like a Titan bestriding the earth.

'Love that one,' Lenny chuckled. 'Once we get a filter on it.'

Bo flicked faster, disinterested – it was all shots on the kayak, shots at lunch, most of just Zac but some with Anna and Anders in too. Anders wasn't smiling in a single one. Anna wasn't *not* smiling in a single one . . .

'They're great,' Bo smiled weakly, handing Lenny back his camera and shuffling over to the sofa again. Pulling the blankets back around her, she sank down into the cushions, looking back at them all through hot, dry eyes.

'Oh, Bo, you look terrible,' Zac murmured, coming to crouch in front of her.

'I'm fine. I'll be better in no time now that I've started a course of antiBs.'

'When did you do that?' he frowned.

'Anders' neighbour popped in. She's a doctor.'

'Oh, Anders, that's so nice of you,' Anna said, smiling sweetly at him.

'Not really. The sooner she is better, the sooner she can go again.' Anders rose to standing. He was still wearing his waterproof clothing, the orange rubber squeaking lightly with every move.

Bo sighed; she wasn't sure whether he intended to come over as abrupt as he did, or whether it was a lost-in-translation thing.

'You should go now,' Anders told them, his eyes falling to the windows.

Already? Bo looked at Zac in despair.

'It's so dark already,' Anna said nervously, looking back out.

'It's not as bad out there as it seems from here, but you'll need to leave now if you don't want to be hiking that path in the blackness.'

'Come on, guys,' Lenny said, zipping up his jacket again with a sigh. 'Better get those headtorches on.'

Zac stroked Bo's hair with a hand, his gaze as soft upon her as feathers. 'I hate leaving you like this.'

'I'm fine,' she murmured but she didn't want him to go either. They had had less than five minutes together.

He reached down and kissed her temple. 'I'll see you in the morning, baby,' he whispered, kissing her again.

'See you in the morning,' she whispered back, feeling his hand grip hers tighter for a moment before he reluctantly stood up.

'Look after her for me, man,' Zac said, zipping up his jacket again and looking over at Anders standing impatiently by the door. 'She's my everything.'

'Yes.'

There was another pause and then, through half-closed eyes, Bo heard the rustle of them all leaving.

'See ya, Bo,' Lenny murmured.

'Sleep well. Get a good night's rest,' Anna said sweetly, pressing a hand lightly to Bo's shoulder as she passed.

The front door clicked shut and she heard the sound of their steps on the terrace, the clomp of their boots on the jetty and then their voices as they climbed back into the kayaks again, Anna squealing lightly as she tried to climb into hers in the dim light. There were a few splashes as the oars began to cut through the water and then that thick, loud silence again, rolling back in like a sea that had been momentarily parted.

Bo was watching the downhill racing in Austria, the Norwegian commentary a sort of white noise against the clatter coming from the kitchen as pans were lidded and drawers opened and closed. The smells that came through in wafts kept making her nose twitch.

Anders hadn't come back through since having his shower and changing out of his outdoor clothes, so it was something of a surprise when he popped his head through the doorway and she saw he was wearing a grey waffle top and navy checked flannel lounge pants. His shaggy blonde hair was shampooed and he looked shiny-clean. Bo vowed never to take hot running water for granted again.

'Dinner is ready.'

'Thank you,' she smiled, forcing herself up and – because he was watching – managing not to wince too much as she put her weight on her knee; it was definitely improving.

She limped after him into the kitchen. Steam was still drifting along the ceiling like low-lying clouds, a riot of saucepans all stacked into each other in precarious towers by the sink. But the smells . . . oh, the smells.

She sat down at the table, clocking that there was water for her, a beer for him.

'Ordinarily I would offer you one, but . . .' He shrugged.

'No, it's fine,' she said, looking over as he came across with two plates.

'Lapskaus – a Norwegian stew,' he said, setting it down in front of her. 'Good for feeding a cold.'

'It smells good.' She closed her eyes and let the steam cover her face for a moment as he began to eat, focusing on his food with the intensity men always seemed to have for filling their stomachs; she supposed he had had a very active day.

She picked up her fork. 'So your grandmother played a trick on me when I went in to check on her the other day,' she said lightly, feeling the need to be a good guest and make conversation.

His eyes flicked up to hers momentarily. 'Oh yes?' he asked, but a smile was already hovering. 'What did she do?'

'She pretended to be dead.'

The smile cracked into a full-wattage beam. 'Yes. She does that. It is her party trick.'

Bo grinned. '*I* nearly died.'

'My grandmother has a wicked humour. But you should take it as a compliment. It's a sign she likes you.'

Bo looked bemused. 'What does she do to the people she doesn't like?'

'Puts frogs in their beds.'

Bo's mouth dropped open; it had been intended as a rhetorical question. 'She does not.'

Anders shrugged. 'She is known for her tricks. All her life she has played them. She says why should she behave just because she is old.'

'Fair point, I guess.'

They ate some more, the silence between them was companionable and slack. In the background, the radio was on, but barely. From the tone of the presenter's voice, it sounded to Bo like they were reading the shipping forecast.

'This is so delicious,' she said, even though she was eating feebly, managing only the smallest of bites.

'It is good you have some appetite. That and the antibiotics will act quickly now.'

'Thanks again for putting me up like this. It's really kind.'

'Not kind. It is the only practical solution.'

Bo nodded, wondering yet again whether his abruptness was intended or not. There seemed to be a chasm between what he said and what he did – acting kindly, but speaking gruffly. 'So – you live here alone?'

There was a slight pause before he answered. 'I do.'

'And you don't get lonely?'

His eyes flashed her way, almost like a warning. 'No.'

She remembered the photograph of the girl beside his bed but something in his demeanour told her not to ask. He was a private man, and she fell silent again.

'How about you? Don't you get tired of being *with* people all the time?' he asked, his eyes on his food.

'Um, well, yes – I guess sometimes it can get a bit much.'

'Lenny is always with you?'

She sighed. 'Oh yes, Lenny is always with us.'

He sat straighter, reaching for his beer. 'It must get tiresome.'

'Well, it can do. I mean, he's our friend, he's a great guy. But . . .' Her voice trailed off. 'It would be nice to have *some* time just on our own, you know?'

'So then, get rid of him.'

'It's really not that easy.'

'Why not?'

'Zac and I had been together a couple of months when we realized that our being together and the shared posts we put up had really begun to inflate our following numbers – lots of his fans had begun to follow me and vice versa,' she shrugged. 'But once you get to a certain size, over a million, say, it's like interest on a capital sum, it just keeps ticking over all the time, the numbers getting bigger and bigger. We'd noticed our posts got more likes when they showed the two of us together, which was fine – but that meant we both needed to be in shot and there's only so many couple selfies you can take before they all begin to look the same. Plus, we had an increasing number of brands approaching us for endorsement work because they loved that we were a couple so our revenue really took a leap. We realized we could actually make a career from just "being together" but it meant we needed a photographer, someone who could travel with us and help develop us as a brand.'

Anders shrugged as though he saw the logic in it. 'How did you meet him?'

'Luck really, it was just a chance thing. We were in Sumatra and Zac got playing in some volleyball game on the beach; Lenny was on the team and they started chatting afterwards, hit it off, went for a beer . . .'

'What was he doing in Sumatra?'

'You mean, apart from bumming around, living on 75p a day?' She rolled her eyes. 'He was out there looking for some iconic bass guitarist in a band from the Seventies; he'd heard the guy was living out there and Len wanted to do a photo shoot with him. He was convinced *Rolling Stone* would make it a cover story and give him his big break.'

'And did it?'

She sighed. 'Poor Len couldn't even find this guy; he'd been out there for weeks by the time we met him and he was running out of money, so when Zac mentioned we were looking at getting a photographer, he put his hand up for it.'

'So he wasn't a blogger too?'

'Nope. He'd never heard of us. But Zac realized he was exactly what we needed – someone with no ties, who would travel anywhere and everywhere with us, plus who could keep up with him on the mountain. That's a pretty big ask.'

'Does he mind following you both around? What about his own life?'

'We're pretty much his family now. Life's not been particularly easy for him.'

'Is it easy for anyone?'

'Well, no, but—'

'Is it easy for you?' The question seemed to have an edge to it.

She hesitated. 'There have been dark moments, of course. But Lenny was badly bullied at school. His father OD'd. He's had a tough time.'

'So this is his escape?' Anders asked.

'Yes, maybe,' she agreed.

'And you?'

'What do you mean?' she asked.

'Why do *you* do this?'

'Do what?'

'All the non-stop travelling. You are escaping something too?' It was a typically forthright comment.

It was a moment before she could speak. 'Actually, I think of it as embracing new adventures. It's a positive decision, not a negative, and I consider myself very lucky to lead the life I live. I'm basically paid to do what I would otherwise be paying to do.'

He nodded fractionally as though in agreement, as though his previous question *hadn't* been combative. 'Good for you.'

But still she felt pricked by his comments. 'And besides, friends are the family you choose, right? I love my parents and I speak to them regularly. We FaceTime every week, but I want to lead a different life to theirs. I don't want to live in the same street, with the same neighbours, doing the same job day-in, day-out. Zac and Lenny understand that, they're my family now.'

'But if you and Zac are engaged, doesn't that make him a raspberry?'

'You mean a gooseberry,' Bo corrected, pleased he'd got something wrong with his otherwise faultless English. 'And how do you know we're engaged anyway?'

'He called you his fiancée earlier.'

'Oh. Yes . . .' she mumbled. 'Well, yes, we are although it's not official yet.'

'You're not wearing a ring. Is it a secret?'

'No,' she fibbed, not wanting to have to explain to him Zac and Lenny's double-bluff.

'Did your fans go mad when they heard?' he asked and she heard the wry note in his voice.

She bridled. 'Actually, that's what I mean by it's not official yet. It's not a secret, per se, but we're keeping it to ourselves for a little while. We'll go public with it when he's got me a ring.'

'When will that be?'

'Sometime soon I guess.'

'Out here?'

'Maybe.' She shrugged.

'Don't you want to tell people about it? In my experience, women always want to talk about their engagements and weddings.'

'Well, we're happy keeping it private. I don't want nine million people congratulating me just yet.'

'Why not? That would be a nice thing, surely?'

She gave a snort. 'Trust me, not everyone out there is nice.'

Anders took another sip of his beer, watching her. 'No?'

'Of course not.' And when he kept staring at her, she added, 'You've heard of trolls, I take it?'

'There are plenty of trolls in Norway,' he smiled, his eyes softening.

His joke diffused her indignation too. 'I don't mean in folk tales,' she grinned, before sighing heavily as she remembered what she did mean. 'No, I mean the sad bastards who hide

215

behind a screen and can't feel complete in themselves without tearing me down in some way.'

Anders' eyes narrowed slightly. 'And you have many of those?'

'The law of averages means I must have several hundred, if not thousands, lurking in a crowd of nine million.'

'What kind of things do they say?'

'Oh . . .' she sighed. 'It's usually just bitchy comments like they hate my top or my hair or my bum looks fat, or I've got an annoying voice, or Zac's too good for me.' She shrugged. 'Nothing serious. Just stuff that . . . brings you down a bit really. Mostly it doesn't bother me.'

'Mostly?'

'Well, of course, some of them are worse than that.'

'How?'

She stared down at the half-empty soup bowl. 'I've had a few death threats . . . Dick pics. They're pretty bad.'

He frowned. 'What does Zac say about it?'

She inhaled sharply. 'Oh . . . well, I don't . . . I don't really tell him about them. I just delete them immediately.' She gave a shudder. 'There's no point.'

'But why not?' Anders looked stern now.

'Because it's just . . . par for the course really. We all know a certain amount of abuse is unavoidable.'

He looked incredulous. The colour had flared on his cheeks. 'You accept harassment as a *norm* for your job?'

She swallowed. When he put it like that . . . 'But it's remote. Faceless. The threat is . . . theoretical. I don't know these people. I'll never meet them.'

'So they have never tried to make actual contact with you?'

'No – well, I mean, one did. Once. But it was a while ago now. I can handle it. I won't let him frighten me.'

'Him? So then you're being harassed by a man?'

'Yes.'

'But you haven't told Zac about him?'

'No.'

'You must,' he insisted.

'No.' *Her* voice was firm now.

'Why not?'

She stared down at her plate. 'Just because.'

But Anders dipped his head lower, tangling her gaze insistently with his. 'Because?'

Bo looked at him. 'Because nothing can be done. I tried once before. I went to the police but they can't get his details from Instagram without a warrant and for that there needs to be an actual crime committed.'

'But if you told Zac, he could scare him off.'

'How? By thumping his chest?'

Anders looked away, frustrated. They both knew she had a point. 'This guy who tried to make contact with you. What did he do?'

She bit her lip, resenting the cold sweat even just the memories brought out in her. '. . . He broke into my hotel room when I was taking a bath. He took some of my stuff and left a photo – a Polaroid – on my bed for me to find.'

'Of himself? You've seen him?'

'No. It was a pomegranate cut in half, with all the seeds coming out. He took it from the fruit bowl.'

Anders frowned. '*Why?*'

'I've no idea what it's supposed to mean, but it's the image in his avatar,' she shrugged. 'It was his way of showing me it was him.'

He stared at her for a long moment. 'That is intimidation.'

'Not technically a crime, though.'

'Breaking and entering then?'

'There were no signs of forced entry and I couldn't prove what had gone missing.'

'And what did go?'

'A piece of jewellery. Some . . . underwear.'

Anders sat back in his chair, watching her, and she looked away again. 'Did he do anything after that?'

'Nothing so . . . direct. There were a few comments of course – did I like the gift? Was it lavender bath lotion I'd used? When was I going to wear the new dress I'd left out on the bed?' She bit her lip. 'Anyway, I met Zac pretty soon afterwards and that seemed to scare him off.'

'So then he was intimidated.'

'Maybe. Maybe not. All I know is he dropped out of my life again – no more comments, no more gifts. I even thought he was dead for a while. Until he made contact again a few days ago.'

Anders frowned. 'When?'

'Just after we got here.'

'But when exactly?'

Why did it matter? 'Uh . . . it was the night before we went to the waterfall.'

Anders stared at her. 'And that was why you were so quiet that morning?'

She nodded, amazed he'd noticed.

'But you still haven't told Zac?'

'I told you, there's no point. It would only frustrate him. And besides, there's no need. I take precautions now – I make sure that every post we upload *doesn't* reveal our location. I won't let him find me again.'

'And Zac and Lenny know to do that too?'

'Of course. It was Lenny's idea. He said it's a good safety

measure anyway. We'd be mobbed if our followers knew where we were. We once did a store opening in Kyoto for a Japanese brand we'd endorsed and the authorities had to shut the street. We couldn't even get a coffee. It was terrifying.'

'But this . . . this guy . . . he must know you're in Norway right now.'

'Sure, but Norway is a big place, right? He could follow me here and spend ten years looking and never find me.'

Anders inhaled deeply, sitting back in his chair and looking back at her with an expression not so much of sympathy, as pity. 'This is fucked-up.'

'I know.'

'There are maniacs everywhere. Much less, ones that have fixated upon you.'

She pressed her lips together. 'I'm fine.'

'Are you? It seems to me you were wrong about what you said to me at the waterfall.'

She frowned. 'What did I say?'

'That you needed a guide, not a bodyguard. If you ask me, a bodyguard is exactly what you need.'

It was a moment before she realized the scream was her own. That it had come from her. That her body was still trembling from the terror.

The door burst open, bright light from the landing falling in gracelessly as Anders' wild silhouette filled the door frame.

'What is it?' he asked, dashing in, looking around the room as though he expected to find an intruder in there. 'Are you okay?'

'I . . . I . . .' she panted, looking at him vacantly. *Was* she okay? Why was she crying?

'You were screaming.'

She stared at him, open-mouthed. She didn't know what had happened, only that her heart was pounding so hard she thought it might leap from her chest. She closed her eyes, trying to remember; and she felt it again: the trace of the nightmare, the old one she thought had gone – the sensation of rolling, landing upside down, the growing darkness, his fixed, unseeing eyes . . .

'Here, drink this.' He was holding out the glass of water.

She sipped it, realizing how dry her throat felt.

'Better?'

She nodded.

'Do you know what happened?'

She kept her eyes on the duvet, feeling ashamed that she had woken him, that she had let her carefully lidded fear escape. 'A bad dream, that's all.'

He pressed the back of his hand to her forehead. 'You're burning up.' He walked into the bathroom and she heard the sound of a cabinet being opened, the rustle of tin foil. 'Here, take this, it'll reduce the fever.'

She swallowed it down with water and he took the glass, setting it back on the bedside table.

'Try to get back to sleep.'

She nodded, her hair rustling against the pillow. But as he went to shut the door again, pushing back the light, she felt the terror surge again like a wave, the darkness trapping her. The dream was still waiting for her, the menace a shadow that lived behind her eyelids. 'No!'

The door flew wide open. 'What's wrong?'

'Not . . . not the dark,' she mumbled but her heart was pounding again. 'Leave the light on. Please.'

He stared at her for a moment, his shoulders dropping an inch.

'I'm sorry,' she whispered, feeling the tears come, the panic too big to push back tonight.

'It's fine,' he said after a moment. 'Don't worry.'

'No, I'm sorry,' she said again, feeling humiliated. Pathetic.

He came and sat on the end of the bed. 'Don't be. Just lie down. I'll stay here until you go back to sleep.'

She stared at him, gratitude suffusing her. 'You will?'

He nodded. 'It's fine, you're safe now. Go back to sleep.'

Safe now.

She slid down the pillow, its cool crispness soothing against her hot skin. She closed her eyes again, the light from the hall spilling over her like sunlight and Anders sitting beside her in silence, keeping watch.

Chapter Thirteen

Morning oozed like a cracked egg, the weak light spreading and touching every corner of the room. Bo stirred, her eyes moving rapidly behind closed lids before she sensed the difference somehow – this was not her bed, not her room, not her boyfr—

Her eyes flew open. Anders was asleep on the bed, lying on his stomach, his head turned towards her. He was more off the bed than on it, his long legs dangling over the ends as he occupied the bottom third of the mattress, as though trying to keep his distance. He was lying on top of the duvet, wearing just a pair of blue checked flannel pyjama bottoms. How had he slept through the cold? And why was he sleeping here?

More to the point – she looked around, suddenly realizing they were in his room again – why was *she* sleeping here? She tried thinking back but last night felt foggy, indecipherable. She remembered . . . she remembered the bad dream. He had been helping her. Promised to wait till she fell asleep . . .

She looked at him as *he* slept now; it was the first time she had studied him properly and it was like seeing him for the first time. All her impressions of him till now had just been composites of scruffy, wind-tangled blonde hair and orange rubber hoods, angry eyes and hostile reserve. But in sleep, there was a softness to him that he cast off in the day; she saw his lashes were black and thick, with a pronounced curve; that his brows were perfectly straight, his lips a full brownish pink. In fact, get past the thick stubble and the wild hair, he was almost beautiful. Animalistic.

His eyes opened – as though sensing her scrutiny – and for a moment, it was like looking into the stare of an eagle: a superior, unknowable creature, wild and free. He blinked into full alertness and pushed himself up. 'Did you sleep?'

She nodded. 'Yes, thank you.'

He dropped his head again and sighed, a bone-aching weariness in the sound. 'Good.' He rolled his shoulders back, pressed his ear to the shoulder and repeated it on the other side. He looked back at her. 'How are you feeling now?'

'Actually . . . better.' She felt amazed by the realization.

'Yeah?' He reached up and pressed a hand to her forehead again. 'Your fever's broken at least.'

She nodded. 'Yes, I feel better.'

'Annika said the antibiotics would start to kick in today. Although you are not out of the woods yet.'

'No.'

'It is important you continue to rest.'

She looked around the room. 'Why am I in here again? Didn't you say this was your room?'

'I figured seeing as you had slept in the sheets already, you were better to stay in here. I didn't want your germs.'

Bo couldn't help but smile. It wasn't the most chivalrous reason she'd ever heard. 'Well, no.' She gave an apologetic wince. 'Sorry you ended up sleeping in here anyway.'

'. . . It's fine.' He stared at her for a moment and she felt that odd sensation that always came when their eyes met – as though the mountains were pushing back, tectonic plates suddenly shifting. She couldn't shake the feeling that, although near-strangers, they somehow understood each other, like old souls that had met before in another life. '. . . Well, I'll go and get your medicine. You are due another tablet.'

'Okay, thanks.'

'Can you manage a coffee?'

She smiled. 'A coffee would be amazing.'

She watched him get up, his bare back lean and surprisingly tanned for a man who didn't take holidays. He shrugged on a sweatshirt from the chest of drawers and walked out of the room, his footsteps heavy on the stairs as he went down.

Bo looked around the room again, finally taking in all the little details she had been too delirious to notice yesterday – the pile of dirty clothes spilling out of the laundry basket, the vintage Bullitt poster on the wall, the push-up bars on the floor. And on the bedside table, a small square of dust where the photo had been of him and the beautiful smiling brunette. She wanted to slide open the drawer and look at it again, but she knew it would be a violation of trust, and after everything he had done for her last night . . .

She heard him come back upstairs after a few minutes, carrying a tray of his freshly ground, freshly roasted coffee, honey toast, fresh water and her pills. 'Eat,' he said, setting it carefully on her lap. 'I'm going to shower.'

He disappeared into the bathroom next door and she heard the water come on, the low hum of him singing quietly – singing! – reverberating through the walls. She smiled to herself as she ate her toast and she was still smiling several minutes later when he wandered through, wrapped in a navy bathrobe and towelling dry his hair. 'What?' he demanded, casting a quizzical look her way as he walked over to the chest of drawers again.

'Nothing.'

'You're smirking,' he said over his shoulder.

'Yes, well, I just didn't have you down as a shower singer, that's all.'

He paused, straightening up momentarily, but an abashed amusement had enlivened his eyes. 'Oh, I see. You heard that?'

'Oh yes,' she grinned, picking up her coffee and sipping from it. 'I heard that.'

'Do *you* sing?' He had pulled out a pair of jeans and was rifling through his T-shirts.

Her throat went dry. He wasn't going to change in here too, was he? 'Almost never.'

'Well, perhaps you should try it.'

'You haven't heard my singing voice. It's generally considered a mercy if I don't.'

He gave a small snort of amusement, shutting the drawers and walking over to the wardrobe. She watched, aware of the strange intimacy into which they had been thrown – her lying in his bed, watching as he gathered his clothes from his own bedroom.

'Hey, I want to ask you something,' she said, as much to keep him distracted from the situation as anything.

'Okay,' he said, reaching up and bringing down a sweater from the shelf.

'What's my name?'

He turned to her, one eyebrow hitched quizzically. 'You don't know your name?'

'No, *I* know it,' she said archly. 'But do you?'

'Of course.'

'So what is it, then?'

'Bo.'

'Huh,' she mumbled, regarding him critically.

'Why are you asking me that?'

'Because in your calendar in the kitchen you've written that we're *Instagram*, which is pretty rude,' she said pointedly. 'And yesterday, you called me Goldilocks.'

'Yes – because you had been sitting in my chair, then you ate my soup and then I found you sleeping in my bed.' He shrugged. 'Like the nursery story. And you are already named after one, right? Little Bo Peep. Goldilocks.'

'Oh! . . . Well, I guess that's pretty clever.'

He shrugged, turning back to close the wardrobe door. 'Perhaps.'

'So if I'm Goldilocks, what does that make you, then? The big scary bear?'

A trace of a smile twitched the corners of his mouth as he left the room. 'I suppose it does.'

Bo laughed, holding the cup close to her face, just as footsteps suddenly sounded on the stairs. They both looked up in surprise as first Zac, and then Lenny, appeared in the doorway.

'—Hey!' Zac looked pulled up short by the sight of them both: her eating breakfast in bed, Anders robed.

Anders looked equally taken aback, frowning at the intrusion. 'What the hell?'

'W-we been down there calling you,' Lenny said in panic as his eyes swivelled between the two of them.

Anders frowned harder. 'I didn't hear you.'

'You're late,' Zac said to him coolly, in a voice that set Bo on edge – even though he wasn't looking at her. 'We agreed a ten o'clock start. It's now half past.'

'Sorry, I overslept.'

'Yeah?' Zac queried, his tone light but Bo sensed a vein of

steel running through it. 'And why was that then?' They both knew it wasn't the over-running of time that was bothering him.

Anders glanced back at Bo – as though asking her how much he should divulge – and she immediately wished he hadn't. It looked loaded, complicit, as though they were guilty of something.

'I had a bad night. Nightmares. From the fever,' she said quickly, willing Zac to look at her instead. 'Anders very kindly got me some water and medicine, so he had a pretty broken night too. It's my fault he overslept.'

There was another pause as her explanation was taken and weighed up, as though it was barely plausible. 'And how *are* you feeling today?' Zac asked, finally looking across at her.

'Better. A lot better.' She smiled as brightly as she could manage, trying to appease him.

'Well, it's about time. You've spent most of the past two days asleep,' Lenny muttered.

'Yes, sorry about that, Len. I realize it's an inconvenience to you,' she said, her voice heavy with sarcasm.

'Are you well enough to come back?' Zac asked.

'Oh . . .' she faltered. She wasn't ready to give up electricity and hot running water just yet. 'No. Not quite. I'm sorry.'

'The doctor's started her on a course of antibiotics,' Anders said. 'She needs to rest and stay warm until at least day four.' He walked across the room, his clothes in his arms.

'Well, if I didn't know better, dude, I'd say you were quite enjoying having my fiancée as a house guest,' Zac said with a smile, but Bo saw the jealousy flaming in his eyes.

Anders stopped in front of him and looked down at Zac, knowing exactly what he was insinuating. 'No. But it's the right thing to do.' And he walked out, slamming the door of the other bedroom behind him a moment later.

Bo felt slapped by the words.

Zac watched him go before turning back to her with a shrug. 'Manners of a pig,' he muttered, coming over to her.

'Zac!' she hissed.

'What? You can't say that wasn't rude.'

'*You* were rude first! Casting . . . aspersions about like that!'

'Aspersions? What else am I supposed to think when I walk in and find my fiancée laughing in bed and some random dude walking around the bedroom getting dressed!'

'First off, I'm *sick*. Never been less sexy, if that's what you're getting at. Secondly, he's not random, he's your guide. Thirdly, he was only getting his clothes because this is *his* bedroom but I fell asleep in the wrong bed yesterday and got my germs everywhere so he's let me sleep in here instead. And finally, he's got a girlfriend! He's not remotely interested in stealing yours if that's what you're thinking.'

Zac frowned. '. . . Has he?'

'Look!' she hissed, yanking open the drawer and showing him the photograph.

'Huh. Good-looking girl,' Zac murmured, handing it back a moment later.

'You owe him an apology,' she said in a low voice, closing the drawer again.

'Oh, Bo, c'mon—'

'I mean it, Zac. He's been nothing but kind – that is *all*.'

Zac sighed, but his jaw was jutting forward, as it always did when he was riled.

'Zac? Promise me?'

He sighed again. '. . . Fine, I promise.' He shot her a guilty look. 'Look, I'm sorry, okay? But it's just . . .' He raked his fingers through his fast-growing hair. 'Well, what am I supposed to think?'

'Uh – trust me perhaps?'

'I know that in principle, but it's not easy being away from you like this, that's all. It's not how I thought it'd be out here.'

She softened. 'I know. Me either. But it won't be for long.'

'Really?'

'I feel *so* much better today. I'm definitely on the mend. A couple more days and we'll be back to normal again, you'll see.'

'When you say a couple, do you actually mean . . . tomorrow?'

She chuckled. 'I don't know. *Maybe*. No promises.'

Zac smiled, his eyes soft and puppy-dog again. He took her hand and kissed the back of it. 'And then just you wait till I get you back again . . .' He leant in and nuzzled her neck, his breath hot on her skin.

But Bo tapped him on the shoulder. 'Uh, Zac . . .' she said, pointing towards Lenny, who was still standing in the doorway, watching on with a scowl on his face.

'Oh, come on, man!' Zac cried, getting up from the bed. 'Seriously? Is nothing sacred?'

'What? I'm waiting for you.' Lenny shrugged, turning and disappearing down the hall. 'You knew I was there.'

Zac followed after him, pushing him on the shoulders like a boisterous big brother. 'What? You're asking me what?'

Bo listened to them go, tramping down the stairs in their hiking boots, Anna's melodious voice making a trio as they joined her in the kitchen.

A minute later the door of the spare room opened and Anders came out too, the rustle of his clothes seeming extra loud as he passed by her door and down the narrow corridor in purposeful strides. But he didn't pop his head in to say goodbye or remind her to take her pills or offer to take the tray down.

She was an unwanted guest here, after all, and he was only doing what was right.

The day passed slowly. The unremitting exhaustion of fighting an infection had passed now that drugs were on the case, and she couldn't while away the hours in a heavy slumber in the same way. She spent much of the morning on the sofa lying under the blankets, watching 1970s American TV and only getting up to prod the fire, but after a few hours and only one short nap, she was restless to move about. Annika had popped in again and checked her over, seeming pleased by her overnight improvement from cusp-pneumonia to 'just' a heavy cold, but she was busy and hadn't stayed for more than ten minutes, leaving Bo alone again in the quiet house, in the hibernating village.

She sat at the kitchen table, stirring her soup and wondering what the others were doing. She had forgotten even to ask where they were going today, their time together so contracted as they endlessly raced against the encroaching darkness. Annika had told her the sun didn't rise above the mountaintops at all here between December and February and Bo felt the same low light reflected in herself, like she couldn't get up to full power.

With a sigh, she picked up her phone that had been left out on the coffee table, as she realized it had been three days since she had used it last. A new record! What had she missed, she wondered, as she scrolled through her feed again, whizzing past images of fruit smoothies and sheepskin boots, ski slopes and dogs being funny. But it wasn't them she wanted to see. She was looking for Zac's face – where were they all today?

What were they doing without her? She hoped Lenny might have posted something, that there would be just enough signal to carry their day in the mountains down to her here in the valley.

Growing impatient, her feed was too long, she clicked on the search button and found Zac's account. It was odd to be on the outside of her own life looking in, she thought, as his grid came up, full of action shots and sticking closely to its agenda – black granite, neon ropes, virgin snow and inky water: Zac kayaking, Zac climbing, Zac leaping across a stream, Zac eating lunch on a rocky outcrop, Zac hiking. But there was one of him and Anna that caught her eye. They were standing back to back on a boulder, the fjord just a back-drop behind them. Zac was bent forwards, Anna on his back, her legs kicking up like a beetle. She was laughing, looking to camera, the red of her jacket and the white of his teeth visu-ally gripping. 'Living free. #livefree #livebrave #ridgeriders #wanderlusters #norway #outdoors #ad.'

Bo felt a stab of jealousy at the sight of it. She knew that it was just a photo opportunity taken in her own absence, part of their contractual obligations to post at least one image per day; but something about the energy of the two of them chimed. The image worked. And it was getting good engage-ment.

She scrolled through the comments, seeing the usual litany of heart-eyes and lightning bolts, pink hearts and muscle arms. But interspersing them, she saw, were queries too: '*Where's Bo?*'; '*Who's she in the red?*'; '*Did you guys break up?*'; '*OMG are they a couple now?*'; '*Marry me, Zac!*'; '*Who dat?*'; '*Everything ok with Bo?*'; '*U guys still together right?*'; '*Bo + Zac 4ever*'. Ridiculously, she felt flattered that some of the follow-ers had noticed she wasn't in the picture at the moment, that

Anna – photogenic though she might be – was no substitute for her.

Wanting more details, or another angle, she tabbed onto his Stories – it began with footage of his feet as they clomped through muddy snow, his laugh slightly too loud against the mic as he fooled around with Lenny, instigating a snowball fight which Anna then joined in too, scoring a perfect bullseye at his phone. Occasionally Anders was in shot too but he was usually hanging back and waiting to get on, turning away any time he thought he was in shot, that familiar expression of bafflement and disdain on his face seeming even more pronounced today.

Bo felt her tension with Anna transfer to him instead. It had been hovering at the edges of her consciousness all day, like a flicker in the light. Had Zac apologized to him this morning, she wondered? And did Anders even deserve it, after what he'd said about her?

She had insisted Zac do the apologizing, but only because she had needed to deflect from the stinging hurt that she had felt after his comment; it had been harsh, even by his standards. Yes, he was peremptory and almost contemptuous of their group, she knew that; he didn't buy in to their lifestyle or pretend to understand or rate their careers. Yet one-on-one he was different . . . easy company. And after his genuine concern last night, she had thought they were even becoming friends; she had never opened up to anyone about *Him* before and she'd begun to think that perhaps the upside of a terse temperament was being a good listener. But his comments that he didn't want her around, that he was only doing the right thing, had cut her. More than that, it bothered her that it upset her.

Well, he wouldn't have to put up with her for much longer, she resolved, pressing the back of her hand to her forehead again. Her temperature was down, almost normal again and she was no longer shivering constantly; the cough was already less than it had been and, apart from a light aching of her limbs and some sinus congestion, she was almost okay. She was just about walking without a limp now that the bruise was going and if she kept up with the round-the-clock meds, there was no reason why she couldn't leave here with the others when they came by tonight. She was in a much better state to finish off her recuperation at the cabin and she wouldn't stay somewhere she so clearly wasn't wanted.

She clicked onto Lenny's profile and blankly watched his Stories too, beginning to get bored now – it was the same material but from different angles: footage on the rib; the snowball fight; Anna laughing shyly at lunch as he trained the camera on her, playfully boasting he'd make her the 'next Bo'.

That annoyed her. As though he was the king-maker.

It was the same on Anna's account too. Bo had noted the number of followers Anna had when she began to 'follow' her after their first meeting which was just good manners; it had been in the six hundreds but now she saw she was above five thousand, three days in, and Bo knew that was the Wander-lusters effect; that was just how it worked. People were beginning to notice Anna and to talk about her. Bo wasn't there but Anna was? Instagram relationships very often fin-ished with a golden bullet, stopped dead in their tracks with neither any warning nor explanation to their followers, and those poor people who thought they knew them so well just because they saw what shoes they were wearing that day or what they were eating for lunch, in reality didn't have the first clue about what really went on in their idols' lives. And they never would.

Bo bit her lip. If people were beginning to talk and wonder

about Anna, shouldn't she reach out and post something? The last thing she – or Zac – wanted was conjecture and gossip. With 9.5 million people watching on – according to Lenny's latest update – a whisper very rapidly became a shout.

She looked down at her untouched chicken soup, twirls of steam still rising from the bowl and instinctively began decluttering the table, pushing the local newspaper out of the frame and the small pile of envelopes that had fallen through the letterbox that morning. She decided to shoot it as a short video, capturing the steam trail as it floated up. Just four seconds' worth, then she overwrote '*On the mend*' in flesh-coloured type. It wasn't much, but it was something.

She uploaded it to both her grid and Stories and before she had even swallowed a spoonful of soup, the likes started coming. The notifications were set to silent for this very reason, as they began pinging onto her home screen in a fast-rolling scroll.

She clicked on a few as she ate, feeling better with every sip: '*Oh no, what's wrong?*'; '*You ok?*'; '*What happened?*'; '*Where's Zac?*'; '*Bone broth! The best!*'; '*Love you, Bo!*'; '*Be better!*'; '*You got this!*'; '*Get well soon sista*'; '*Where is this?*' . . . She wasn't sure her own mother could have shown more concern; in fact, she was pretty sure her mother would have been more concerned by all this emoting from complete strangers; she found the social media world bewildering and distasteful. 'But these people don't *know* you, Bo! Why on earth do they care about your holiday photographs? I can barely bring myself to look at your aunt's snaps and she's my own sister!' her mother had said that day in her kitchen, when Bo had announced she wanted to 'make a go' of the Interweb-thing (as her parents called it) and travel the world.

She hadn't been back since. It had been almost four years

since she'd gone home but sitting there, in someone else's kitchen, unwell and medicating with home-made chicken broth, she felt a sudden, violent yearning for the real thing. She wanted to see her parents' faces again. The last time they'd been in the same room together had been in May when she and Zac had met up with them for a week in Thailand, en route to Samoa. (Bo didn't think she'd ever forget Zac's face when her dad had suggested the two of them went to play mini-golf together.)

But even that wasn't the same. It wasn't home. It wasn't grey skies and sheets on washing lines, the cat sitting on the garden wall, and towels drying on the Aga. It wasn't wellies by the door and post on the mat, apple turnovers as a week-end treat and roast lamb on Sundays. It wasn't somewhere like this. She had knowingly, willingly and urgently swapped routine for novelty, the familiar for the new and that had been her choice, her only way to cope. But right now—

No.

No. Pushing the thoughts away, knowing she was feeling weak and self-pitying, she took the bowl to the sink and washed up; she even dried up too, such was her desire to do something other than go back to that sofa. But even wiping down the surfaces, sweeping the floor and descaling the taps couldn't delay the inevitable and she found herself back there within ten minutes, staring at the wall again. She was bored. Bored. Bored. Sitting around wasn't good for her. Dark thoughts began to crowd her and she became morose, so the discovery not only that the fire was almost out, but that the log basket was empty too, pleased her more than perhaps it should have done. She slid on the far too large pair of muck boots that had been left by the door – this was fast becoming a habit – and, pulling on one of Anders' rubber jackets, wandered out in clompy footsteps in search of the log store, her fingers clutching it closer to her as the biting temperatures immediately snapped . . .

She shivered as she turned the corner to the back of the house, the dark still waters of the fjord stitched to the end of the terrace and stretching away like a bolt of silk. The mountains on the opposite side of the bay were as perfectly reflected as a mirror, so that she could even see the birds flying high above the town. A white-breasted dipper was standing in the shallows, a blue kayak tethered with an orange nylon rope to one leg of the ramshackle jetty, a gull sitting at one end of it. A pristine silence framed the view as though the world was being held in a glass vial.

The log store was attached to the small storehouse on the left-hand side of the path. It was like a miniature version of the house and exceptionally pretty, with a red door and a window beside it. Was there . . . ? She looked around. Was there any way to carry the logs?

She peered in the shed, hardly able to move for all the equipment in there: rubber suits in various sizes dangled from hangers on a wire, kayak oars stood bunched in a corner, mountain bikes balanced on racks . . . She saw a rough suede log sack lying limply across one of the saddles and grabbed it.

Loading it up, she staggered back into the house and with audible groans of effort disgorged the load into the large wicker basket. It was a job that would have been made significantly easier if she'd changed into shoes that actually fitted, but she nonetheless repeated the unwieldy process three times, until the basket was full and logs were spilling onto the sitting room floor.

With a sigh, finally feeling she had earned her rest, she took the log sack back to the shed, tossing it carelessly onto the bike again and making to leave. But something made her stop. She felt . . . watched. Not alone.

Heartrate spiking, she looked more carefully around the small space. 'Hello?' Her voice sounded timid. Ridiculous. It was probably just a mouse. Or weasel. Lenny had told her they had lots of weasels out here. 'Is someone there?'

But then she saw it, in the shadows, just peering between the limp arms of the rubber suits – a face. Pale and hauntingly beautiful, the woman appeared to be almost swimming out of the dark, as though surfacing from the fjord's own icy depths. In the absence of colour, of light, the finer details of her appearance were unclear, but there was a directness in her gaze that was both intimate and challenging.

Bo pushed the wetsuits along the wire and stared at the portrait. It was propped up on a workbench, the woman's gaze hypnotic. Disconcerting. Bo felt like the woman was looking right back at her, which was ridiculous – she knew that; but after a few moments, as she pulled the suits back again, restoring everything to its original state, and as she walked back up the path, hunched over and shivering in the cold, she felt the woman's gaze still upon her, calling her back. What was it about the portrait that had unnerved her?

In the house she stood motionless for a moment, feeling rattled. She didn't want to abuse Anders' trust or violate his privacy . . . and yet her feet moved anyway, taking her upstairs to the bedroom and the bedside cabinet; feeling bad, she opened the drawer. The photograph he had snatched from sight lay there, radiating a pull she couldn't quite understand. Sinking onto the bed and taking her time, she studied it with a scrutiny that hadn't been possible in his presence, with a temperature, with Zac.

It was definitely her. The same woman in the portrait. Clearly his girlfriend.

For the second time in half an hour she felt, if not quite envious of another woman, certainly challenged. And, again, she didn't know why. Was it just curiosity? Sheer nosiness? After all, why should such a striking portrait be hidden from sight in a storage shed and yet the same woman's photograph be kept beside his bed? Why have this image out, but not that one? And who was she? Bo found it hard to conceive that there could be a woman out there who knew Anders in the way she knew Zac. He seemed so absolute in his reserve, one-dimensional almost. She couldn't imagine him having a tickle fight with someone or brushing their hair as they sat in the bath. She hadn't even heard him laugh. A smile was shocking enough.

Replacing the photo, she went downstairs and brought up Instagram, doing a search under his name. He had told her he had an account for the business, but what about personally? Oh.

It had a hit. One Anders Jemtegard.

She clicked on it, feeling a giddy kick of victory as she saw those true-blue eyes and knew it was him. He looked different, though – his hair was short and he was clean-shaven, his face not as angular as it was now. He looked younger, more innocent somehow. His expression wasn't guarded, his body language more expansive.

He only had eighty-two followers; he was following twelve, and he had posted a sum total of nineteen photos – most of which seemed to have been taken in a city, not a mountain in sight. But they had real warmth to them, they felt honest – not edited or filtered or stylized. They hadn't been taken by a professional photographer or curated. They were amateur snapshots depicting a happy life, or rather a happy couple – for the woman, definitely his girlfriend, was in most of them too. There was one image in particular that Bo couldn't stop looking at: the two of them were sitting in a park, a colourful striped rug stretched out between them. Anders had one knee up and his girlfriend was leaning back on it, her hands over her stomach and laughing wildly at something; he was laughing too but gazing down at her with a tenderness that was almost painful to witness. Bo clocked the date, in faint type, in the bottom corner. It had been taken on 15 August 2013. It was the penultimate photograph. The last, she saw, had been taken eleven days later at a concert – bright lights drenching a distant stage, hands in the air, their heads angled together but only their eyes visible as they attempted a selfie.

Why had he not posted anything after then? Had they broken up? He seemed a completely different person in those photographs to the man she knew now, and she had an instinct that something had happened to him. Changed him.

But what?

Chapter Fourteen

Lodal, June 1936

Signy held her breath as the crown was laid on her head. The girls gave a collective gasp as Margit adjusted her hair and pulled her costume straight.

'There,' she whispered, looking back at her little sister proudly, her eyes shining with unusually vivid intensity.

'Do I . . . ? How do I look?' Signy asked her, apprehension lurching like nausea as she heard the crowd gathered outside, waiting.

'Like a princess.'

It wasn't true of course. Real princesses didn't wear lace-up boots or have sunburn on their cheeks but Signy beamed anyway, wishing she could see herself fully; the only mirrors up here were the back of spoons and the lake on a still day. It felt strange not to be in the loose, gauzy cottons of her summer dresses and her hands ran over the tight velvet bodice, her fingers rippling over the dense red and gold embroideries; the thick, full black skirt all but obscured by the pristine white apron that cloaked it. But it was the crown – made of birch twigs and blossoms – that really marked her out as special tonight: the Midsummer bride.

'Are you ready?' Margit beamed, leading the way to the door. 'Your groom awaits.'

With a proud nod, Signy let her sister open the door and she walked out of the cabin to the waiting villagers all gathered around, seeing how the happiness shone in her mother's eyes to see her toeing the line for once and looking appropriate in traditional dress. It was an honour bestowed upon the youngest girl and she felt her heart swell as the village cheered her out. Her groom, Johan Muldal, the blacksmith's youngest son, looked on in trepidation. A year younger and three inches shorter, even than her (which was really saying something), he had run scared from her ever since she had thrashed him for kicking the heads off some Black Vanilla orchids that everyone in the village knew were rare.

But she took the nervous hand he held out now and as the fiddler began to play, they both followed him over the grassy path, beyond the cabins, past the hayricks and down to the dell by the stream. Behind her, Signy could hear Kari and Ashi giggling, Brit, Sofie and Margit all talking in excited voices as they were shadowed in turn by the boys and young men who also made up the procession. Some of the villagers were carrying flaming torches, not for the light – for even at almost midnight the sky was still lit, a pale blonde with violet threads – but to ignite the bonfire the men had worked all day to assemble. It was taller than a house, drier than a desert, a steeple pointing to the gods to bring abundance and good harvest to the valley. The animals had all been gathered into the closed pens for the night, away from the roar and light and searing heat, and Signy had been so excited she had even let Stormy get away with raiding some wild carrot left over from an old vegetable plot on the way down from the pastures today.

They stood before the unlit fire, the village swelling in a crowd around them as the parson mock-married them to symbolize new life and the new season, offering up prayers and thanks. As he finished his proclamations, a great cheer went up and the men threw their torches like spears into the steeple. In a rush, it went up, great flames tapping the sky, vying for brilliance, sheer blinding brightness.

Signy gasped, feeling the thrill of fear as she felt the heat almost immediately, the villagers' faces glowing in the light. The fiddler began to play again. Johan dutifully took her hand and spun her – or did she spin him? – and she felt her heart swell as everyone else began to dance around the fire in whirling couples – her parents, Margit and Brit, Kari and Ashi, Sofie and . . .

Nils.

He was turning her with practised deftness, a bewitched smile on his face as she twirled prettily beneath his fingers, her dark hair flying out like a witch's cape. She too was in traditional dress – the heavy black dress with corseted bodice, her apron beautifully, intricately embroidered with red and blue flowers. But she had cast off her shawl now and for the first time, Signy saw how the scoop of her neckline dipped dramatically lower than anyone else's, revealing a daring sweep of smooth, velvety skin. Signy's eyes narrowed at the sight of her rising and falling bosom as she and Nils danced on and on – Sofie's father would never have modified it as such, but as the tailor's daughter, she had learnt at his knee and was an accomplished needlewoman herself.

Had he seen? Signy could not find Sofie's father in the crowd of onlookers, but as she and Johan circuited the fire, she saw other eyes were on Sofie too – some scandalized, others appreciative.

The music finished in a flurry of bow strikes and with a cursory, but careful, head bob to her very relieved groom – her crown was less comfortable than it was beautiful and threatened to topple with every turn – Signy took it off and ran to find the other girls before the next dance began.

The beer was already flowing, some aquavit too, and she could see the older women filing to and from the *stabbur* bringing out the food for the feast: cured mutton leg, boiled ham, smoked salmon and pickled herrings, potatoes, flat-breads, cheese, jams . . .

'Hey,' she panted, finding Kari picking up thick bunches of bird cherry branches.

'Hey, want to help?' Kari thrust an armful towards her. 'The trolls won't be casting any spells over *our* cows this summer.'

'You don't actually believe that,' Signy grinned as Kari loaded her up.

'I have no idea what I think, but just in case,' Kari shrugged, walking up to the stables. 'I believe in covering all bases.'

Signy followed after, looking back down the slope to see whether Sofie and Nils were still dancing, but from this vantage all the dancers were silhouetted by the flames; it was impossible to tell who was who. 'So did you see her?'

'Who?'

'What do you mean who? Sofie!'

'No. Why?'

'Her dress. It's indecent! Her father will be so ashamed. I can't believe you didn't notice.'

'I'm sure no one did. All eyes were on you Signy, dearest. You are the Midsummer bride after all.'

Signy glowered. All eyes had most definitely *not* been on

her, Sofie had seen to that. Nils, for one, hadn't been able to tear his gaze off his dancing partner.

They were at the stables now, Kari ducking low as she walked in and began fastening the cherry branches above the animals. Signy stood by the doorway, arms laden, looking back at the action. She could see her mother helping to carve the mutton, her father standing in a group with some other men, including the sheriff, Martin Omenas.

Mons Bjorstad, the charming stranger she had found in the haybarn, was standing with them too; Omenas was his employer of course, the reason he had travelled here in the first place. None of the girls had seen him since he had stayed over in the spare cabin that night, as he had left for the village early the next morning, but though he had gone almost as quickly as he had arrived, the memory of him had somehow remained, like a shadow on the wall. Several times, Signy had caught her usually diligent sister staring into space as she sat on the milking stool and once, she had come into the cabin to find her touching their father's guitar, as though it was a cat to stroke.

Still, whatever flirtation they had enjoyed, he wasn't the reason her sister's eyes had looked so bright today, her cheeks pinked with feverish anticipation; nor was he why she had brushed her hair so many times Signy joked she would soon be bald. Word had reached the girls that Rag was coming to Midsummer's after all, and it had been like setting a match to tinder.

In fact, she could see him now, tethering his horse and weaving his way through the crowd, fashionably late. There was a repressed energy to his movements, confidence brimming from him as he was eagerly greeted by his fellow neighbours. 'Rag is here,' she muttered.

'Where?' Kari asked eagerly, forgetting all about the trolls and evil spirits and popping her head back out to look. She followed Signy's gesture. 'Oh! He is even more handsome than before.'

Was he? Signy could see him in profile, his dark silhouette like a cameo against the flames. But it was true – even in outline, he was beautiful: white-blonde hair swept back off a high forehead, straight nose, cleft chin. His presence caused a stir, and not just amongst the girls, Signy saw men responded to him too, as though bowing to his invisible power.

'Handsome is not enough,' Signy said with scorn. 'He is a brute.'

Kari shot her a sideways grin. 'Oh, you're not still peeved because he knocked over your snowman, are you?'

'Of course not! That was years ago,' Signy huffed, although in truth, it did still rankle and was certainly on her list of reasons not to like him. But still, she watched along with Kari, seeing how the men eagerly grasped his hand and slapped his back, like he was a hero returned and not merely a trainee soldier.

Just a few feet away, Margit was standing with Sofie and Brit, the three of them with their backs to the men as they watched the dancing. The fiddler was working himself into a frenzy as the revellers danced through the night, the flames the real spectacle as the bonfire blazed, unstoppable now.

As the dance ended, another cheer erupted; the beer and high spirits were in full flow. Signy watched on Rag – noticing the girls – made his excuses and wandered over to them. They turned in unison, Brit's delight at his unexpected return apparent even from this distance.

A few minutes passed, the conversation polite and formal until the fiddler lifted the violin again. Signy saw his hand go out – and Margit take it. They walked into the dancers' fray, people inclining their heads to watch and comment as the dance began. They all knew it was the match that must happen. Both were of age, both from the two most prominent families.

Signy looked across at Mons. He was watching them too, like the rest of the village.

'Signy, look,' Kari breathed, as Margit and Rag set up opposite one another and bowed gracefully, decorously. 'Aren't they a beautiful couple? You're going to have such gorgeous nieces and nephews.'

'Oh, hush now,' Signy hissed crossly, looking back at Mons again.

But he had gone.

'Where is he?' she frowned.

'Who?'

'Mons Bjorstad. The clockmaker.'

'Him? Who cares?' Kari said dismissively, unable to take her eyes off the dancing couple.

With Mons gone, Signy looked at the dancers again too – Rag had changed over the spring; he had grown more powerful in his physique: his shoulders broader somehow, his rangy legs now more muscular. For sure, he was the most striking man she had ever seen, but he held no interest for her; her eyes sought out only one and she found him with another start. It felt like a jolt to see him now; even though she always made sure she was back from the pastures when the men were due their weekly visit to take back the week's produce, Nils hadn't returned to the *seter* at all since his initial visit checking-up on Sofie's 'injury'; Kari had told her their father had needed him on the farm during the ploughing and sowing periods but although the haying had begun, they had been in *habølla* – the quiet time – for at least a week now; he was free surely?

She watched as he stepped back into the frame, going to stand by Sofie. He said something, something which made her jerk her chin in the air – and then nod. He was asking her to dance again. It was a public statement of interest, people were bound to notice – and comment.

Signy saw how Nils' shoulders dropped in relief as they joined the dance too, Sofie defiant and gleaming in the firelight, her dark hair shining, skin aglow. And as the fiddle started up and the dancers began to move, the flames danced but Sofie danced harder – twisting and leaping, touching the blonde sky with her own fiery fingers as she enchanted her partner with her passion and grace.

On and on they whirled, almost the entire village stopping to watch, and Signy saw then how it would be; she felt a rock in her throat, tears pressing against her eyes as the two premier couples, the town's new generation, danced in the twilight: Margit would marry Rag, and Sofie would have Nils. They were good matches all round – land with power; beauty with land. And when at last the music stopped, the cheer that erupted could have flattened the mountains. The young men bowed as the girls curtsied and they returned to the spectators, all of them panting and flushed. Signy saw their father taking Margit proudly by the chin and kissing her cheek. He was ruddy from the beer and in high spirits. Martin Omenas was too, and though the two men did not shake hands together, confirming a pact, it was evident they were both of the same mind as to the desirability of the union.

'I guess we should go back,' Kari sighed, taking the last armful of branches from Signy and fastening them to the eaves of the stable. 'You are the Midsummer bride, after all.'

'It's not about me,' Signy said flatly. It never was and never would be. But together, they lolloped back into the village, arms swinging, skirts rustling.

'Hungry?' Kari asked, steering her over to the table where the food was laid out. They ate with their fingers, a ravenous hunger coming upon them as the excitement and anticipation for the party was swapped over for the reality of a late night.

Signy was licking her lips after a chicken drumstick when she felt a hard pinch against her arm.

'Ow!' She turned but no one was there; a man was walking away, though. Dark-haired, light-footed. Elegant hands . . . 'I'll be right back,' she mumbled to Kari, dropping the bone on the ground and hurrying after him.

She followed him over to the aspen tree, the one where Bluebell liked to nod in the shade in the heat of the day. It was set back from the fire here, in the shadows.

'Mons?' she whispered, seeing how he hid behind the trunk.

'Come here,' he hissed, motioning desperately for her to move out of sight.

Tentatively, she approached. 'What is it?'

'Is it true?' he asked her, a bleakness in his eyes.

For a moment she didn't know what he was referring to – but then she saw the look on his face and she knew it was how she had looked watching Nils dance with Sofie.

'Are they betrothed?'

'Not . . . not formally. Not yet. But it is expected,' she said quietly.

He looked away, nodding, his gaze on the distant pass through to the next valley.

'It has been assumed since they were children that a match would happen.'

Mons looked back at her. 'Does she love him?'

'I . . .' Signy realized that she didn't know. 'I'm not sure. I think so. All the girls are wild about him.'

'Does he love her?'

'How could he not? Everybody loves Margit.'

'Yes.' Mons dropped his head down, looking like he might fold in on himself.

Signy watched him, seeing his anguish. It leapt through him like a jumping fox. 'Do *you* love her?' she asked, almost in a whisper. But the question didn't need to be asked. The answer lay in his hung head and slack shoulders.

'I can think of nothing else. These past few weeks have been a torment. I could find no reason to get back up here without arousing suspicion. I thought tonight would never come. And yet now I'm here, I find I daren't approach her . . .'

'But you scarcely know her. You were here just a night.'

'I know and I didn't sleep then either. I can neither understand nor explain it, but that night her sweet voice filled my head and hasn't left it since. I didn't even close my eyes in bed. I tried to believe that if I kept sleep at bay, I could hold off the morning from ever coming and . . . stay here forever.'

Signy looked back towards the crowd. Margit was still standing with their pappa, with Rag and the others. But her gaze was cast down, and every so often she would look around, as though searching for someone. Was she looking for him? For her?

'I thought it was fate, bringing me all the way up here – to meet her.' He looked at her with a fierce sorrow. 'I have been counting the days for this night to come. But now I learn it is already too late. That she is lost to me before she was ever mine.'

'I'm so sorry,' Signy said sympathetically. 'I know how bad it feels.'

He stared at her for a moment. '. . . You? But what would you know of love? You are only a child.'

Signy's mouth parted in dismay. 'I'm fourteen! I'm just . . . little, that's all! But I'm growing this summer. I've already grown an inch.'

He regarded her for a moment, before looking away again. 'I'm sorry. Of course you have.'

Signy felt the blood rushing through her head, anger and indignation a combustible mix. Why did no one ever take her seriously? Why did they always treat her like a baby? Why did they never think her feelings mattered too? 'I'm going back,' she muttered, clenching her fists and beginning to stomp away.

'Signy, wait,' he called after her. '*Please.*'

Reluctantly, she turned back.

'Would you do one thing for me?' And he reached into his jacket pocket and pulled out a small, slightly wilted posy of flowers. 'Put these under her pillow. Don't tell her. Don't say anything. Just hide them there.'

'What?' she frowned. But she already knew the fable; everyone did. If a girl slept with the flowers under her pillow on Midsummer's, that night she would dream of her future husband.

He stepped forward and pressed them into her palm, curling her fingers around them tightly. 'It might be the only thing left to me. The only cause for hope.' And without another word, he turned and walked back up the hill, skirting the crowd, staying in the shadows.

Signy watched him go, feeling torn – the match with Rag was her father's greatest ambition. To usurp it in any way would be to tear down his long-cherished wish. And yet . . . she had seen the way her sister and Mons had looked at each other that first day. Had the hundred strokes of her hair been done for Rag – or him?

She looked at the flowers in her hand again. Would it be so bad to do as he asked? They were just flowers, there was no actual harm in the request, was there? It was only an old wives' tale anyway, no different to Kari's trolls and the bird cherry branches hanging over the cows. Carefully she slid the posy into the pocket of her skirt, the white apron concealing it in deep folds, as she rejoined the party. It was a whimsy and a hope. Nothing more.

What harm could come from it?

Chapter Fifteen

It was so dark by the time Anders got back, all the lights were on in the village houses, reflecting into the water like pin-pricks through a sheet of tin. Bo heard the putter of the engine as he brought the rib in to the mooring outside, but as she stood by the window and watched as he cut the power, threw over the ropes and walked up the jetty, she saw that he was alone.

'Where are the others?' she asked, pulling the blanket harder around her shoulders as he came through the door a minute later, pulling off his boots with the opposite foot, droplets of melted snow on his orange rubber jacket.

His eyes flashed up to her, as though irritated to find her there. The friendliness of last night had dissipated completely and only this morning's hostility remained – but was it because of her friends, or her? 'I dropped them at the bay on the way past. We were late in leaving again and there wasn't time to bring them back here first.'

'Oh. Right,' she said, feeling a crashing disappointment to have missed her fiancé again; they had spent less than five minutes together in the past few days and most of that had been spent bickering. Meanwhile, his and Lenny's stories had continued to come off the mountain throughout the afternoon – more laughs, more japes without her – and it had felt like a peculiar form of torture to be watching from the wrong side of the glass. In particular, she felt that if she heard Anna squeal – on camera or off – one more time, she might slap her.

Her eyes fell to the bag she had left packed, ready by the door. Anders saw it too in the same instant, his gaze coming back to hers for a protracted moment before he turned away abruptly. 'I'm going for a shower.'

She heard him take the stairs, two at a time, as she looked into the vacuum of where he had just been. She didn't understand this man. He didn't want her here and yet she had never asked for this. And *she* wasn't the one who had insulted him this morning.

As she heard the water come on, she slipped back into the sitting room, hoping she hadn't used up all the hot water; anticipating that she'd be going back to the shelf farm tonight, she had treated herself to a bubble bath. It would be her last such luxury for a while.

She didn't know what to do with herself – what to do or where to go – and was still perched on the edge of the sofa when she heard him come back down the stairs ten minutes later. She heard him go straight into the kitchen, where his footsteps stopped abruptly; then they started again and she looked up to find him standing in the doorway.

'You made dinner.'

'Just a chicken pie. I thought it was the least I could do, something to thank you for letting me stay here.' She noticed that he was wearing a shirt with his jeans, and that he had combed his hair. Was he going out? '. . . But you can freeze it if you want.'

He frowned. 'Did you go to the shop?'

'Yes.' A large blocky building on the waterfront, she had

discovered it was also the post office, pharmacy and dry cleaners too.

'But you're sick.'

'Almost better now. I had intended going back with the others tonight. I don't want to impose on you any longer than I already have.'

At her pointed words, he shifted his weight uncomfortably. 'Look, about this morning—'

'No, really, I get it,' she said quickly, cutting him off, not wanting to get into it and have him stumble across her inexplicable hurt. 'I do. And I completely understand. You didn't ask for any of this. A week ago, you had no idea we were about to descend on your grandmother's farm, much less that you would have to end up nursing me.'

'It's fine.'

'It's not, though. You don't know me. And then, on top of everything, you had to spend a night babysitting me just because I was having some . . . *stupid* nightmare.'

'It didn't sound stupid last night.'

She looked away. Had she screamed out more than once? Before she had woken herself? How bad had it been? 'Well it was. All nightmares are intrinsically stupid, aren't they? They don't mean anything. Not really,' she mumbled.

He gave her a wry look. 'Unless you subscribe to the widely held belief that they reveal deeper feelings we don't want to acknowledge – like anxiety. Or fear.'

She looked up to find him looking at her closely, as though waiting for an explanation. Sometimes, the way he looked at her – she almost felt he *knew*. She looked away again. 'Well, anyway, I'm not fearful and I'm better now; that's the main thing.'

'No you're not. You sound like you're talking underwater.'

She was so shocked by his frankness, a bark of laughter escaped her. 'Thanks!'

He shrugged, but there was a faint smile on his lips too. They looked at one another for a long moment and she felt them falling into a truce of sorts, the awkwardness from this morning beginning to thaw.

She hugged her arms around herself. 'So you're off out then?' she asked, trying to feather lightness into her voice.

'Briefly, yes.' He looked down at himself with slight bemusement. 'Annika is having her Christmas party tonight. I said I would look in.'

Oh great. More time on her own, Bo thought to herself. 'That's nice. She's lovely, so kind.'

'She is.' A small silence bloomed. '. . . You would be welcome to come along if you like.'

'Oh no, no, I couldn't,' she demurred quickly, shaking her head.

'Because you are sick?'

'No. I really am feeling a lot better. I just took another aspirin. Should keep me going for the next few hours.'

'So then . . . ?'

'It's sweet of you to ask but the last thing you or anyone else wants is me gatecrashing the joint. Go, be with your friends,' she said, waving him away. 'I'll be fine. I've got a fire. I've got pie. I've got *Columbo*. What more could a girl ask for?'

He watched her. 'You've been stuck inside for three days now. You're going out of your mind.'

'No. No, I'm not.'

But he wasn't listening. 'What have you got to wear?' he asked, looking at her grey-marl tracksuit that made her look like an eighties jogger. 'Jeans?'

'Uh, I don't know – maybe, yes, but nothing else that would be appropriate for a party I don't think. Listen, though, it's fine. You go.'

He hesitated, looking at her for a long moment as though she was trying to take something from him, before he said: 'There's some clothes that might fit you in the bottom drawer upstairs.'

'But—'

'You need to get out.'

She pulled a face, on the one hand desperate to get out of here, on the other – 'Are you *sure*?'

He rolled his eyes, looking strained. 'Go. You're making me late.'

With an excited squeak, she shuffled past him and, grabbing the packed bag from the door, hauled herself upstairs. Pulling the clothes out in a hurry, she found her skinny black jeans but no party top – no shirt or blouse, not even a clean T-shirt. She had here only the ghastly blue nightdress, a bra, two pairs of pants and no socks.

Going over to the chest of drawers, she opened the bottom one. A waft of scent was released: fresh but powdery too; she couldn't place it. Inside, was a lace shirt; *nope*. A sea-green cashmere jumper; *pretty but too warm*. A red and white striped Breton. *Oooh* . . .

She put it on quickly, finger-combed her hair, pinched her cheeks and came down the stairs three minutes later.

'That was qui—' he said in surprise, his voice faltering at the sight of her in his girlfriend's top.

'Yes, thanks for this,' she said, pulling at it slightly. 'And don't worry, I'll wash it before I leave. Your girlfriend will never know.'

'It doesn't matter.'

'Oh, but it does, trust me,' she argued. 'We know about these things. I'd go mad if Zac loaned out my clothes to another woman.'

Without another word, he handed her the yellow Ridge Riders jacket.

'Do I need this if we're only going next door?' she protested as he shrugged on his North Face one that looked suitable for tracking polar bears.

'It's snowing outside. Zip it up and put the hood up too. Is your hair wet?' he frowned.

She sighed but did as she was told, giving a shocked gasp as he opened the door and an arctic blast blew in. 'Oh my God, my mother would just *love* you,' she shivered, clutching the jacket tighter to her and stepping out into the night.

Annika's house – not so much next door as up the lane and over the road – was a perfectly symmetrical white feather-lapped cube, with a steep roof and sage-green windows and front door. Tiny white lights hanging down like icicles traced every frame, including the eaves, and illuminated pointed stars were affixed to the windows. Even the orchard of dwarf fruit trees had twinkling lights draped on the canopies, so that the house and garden looked sugar-sprinkled with fallen stars.

Anders walked slowly for her, checking her knee was okay, that she wasn't getting out of breath, that she was warm enough . . . He gave her his arm to help her balance on the icy paths. But she only suffered one coughing fit and she liked the feeling of the cold against her cheeks. After days under duvets and in front of a fire, the freshness of it felt purifying.

The front door was unlocked and they walked through a storm porch into a good-sized room where a large crowd was gathered, drinking and talking, children running around some 1970s furniture that was unwittingly chic. Faces turned towards them as they walked through, pushing down their hoods, friendly hands outstretched to Anders as he passed, curious gazes fastening upon her. Bo smiled and nodded but she was already questioning the decision to come – she couldn't hear any English being spoken and she felt strangely exposed, being out without Zac. He was always the more gregarious of the two of them, covering for her anxiousness when they were out, keeping the attention on him and safe-guarding her.

'Are you up to an aquavit?' Anders asked her. 'It is warming on the inside.'

'Sure,' she nodded. She could do with something to take the edge off her nerves. She followed him into the kitchen, instantly spotting Annika by the worktop. She was rolling out gingerbread dough with a group of children standing beside her, all talking at once with shaped dough-cutters in their hands; another group of children were sitting at the large pine table decorating batches of gingerbread that had already been cut and baked.

'*Hei!*' Annika smiled, calling across the excitable chatter as she spotted them and waving with a floury hand. 'You made it!'

Anders waved back. 'Yes!'

'How are you feeling?' Annika asked Bo, looking at her too.

'So much better! Thank you!'

'You look better! It's remarkable. That tan I think!'

A little hand appeared in front of Annika, trying to swipe some dough, and Bo laughed as she lightly rapped the boy's knuckles. 'Agh-agh-agh,' she admonished, saying something to him in Norwegian.

'Anders,' a deep voice boomed from behind and they both turned to find a tall bearded and bespectacled man standing there. He said something else too, something she couldn't understand.

'Hi, Harald,' Anders smiled, immediately speaking in English and shaking his hand. 'Sorry I am late.'

The man nodded, casting a glance at Bo and replying in faultless English himself. 'You were working again, huh? I saw your boat coming in tonight.'

'Yes.' Anders nodded. 'This is Bo, a client. She is staying with me for a few days.'

'. . . The sick girl?' Harald asked in surprise. 'But you are better so soon? Annika said you were very unwell. She was concerned about you.'

'Harald is Annika's husband,' Anders explained.

'Ah, well, thanks to your wife I'm feeling a *lot* better,' Bo said quickly. 'The antibiotics have really helped.'

'You are taking them regularly I hope?' He glanced at Anders with a weary smile. 'My wife gets very agitated if people go too long between doses. It's all to do with keeping the chemicals at a consistent level in the bloodstream, you know.'

'Right. I'll remember that.'

'Would you care to sit down? Perhaps you are tired.'

'No, really I'm fine. It's nice to be up and out for a bit. I've spent the past three days cooped up and I'm itching to spread my wings.'

'Well, we are glad you have joined us. What would you like to drink? Something soft?'

'Actually, is there any aquavit left?' Anders asked him.

Harald grinned. 'He is giving you the full Norwegian experience, huh? Follow me.'

They squeezed through the crowd, Harald guiding them to the next room. Bo marvelled at where all these people had come from. Their initial exploration through the streets a week earlier had felt like walking through a ghost town, and even earlier today, in the store, she had only seen three people in there and one of them was the guy behind the counter. (Bo could see him in the corner here, too.)

'What a turnout you've got! Is the entire village here?' she asked, as Harald stopped at a small drinks table in the dining room and poured them both a drink. Dean Martin was singing 'I'll Be Home for Christmas' in the background.

'No,' he chuckled. 'That really would be a squeeze. We're bigger than we might appear. About two hundred and forty residents now. Anders helped tip us over when he moved back here last year.'

'Last year?' Bo looked at him in surprise. 'But I thought you grew up here.' He had told her his grandmother had raised him on the shelf farm.

'I did. But then I left.'

'The lure of the big city lights,' Harald smiled, patting him on the shoulder warmly and squeezing it fondly. 'We lose all our young to Oslo but the best eventually come back.'

'You lived in Oslo?'

'For a while.'

He was his usual non-committal self but Bo was intrigued. Was his girlfriend still there? Was that why she kept a drawer at his? But why had he come back? For his grandmother?

'Anyway, Oslo's loss is our gain,' Harald said, turning his attention to her. 'And where is it you're from? You're Australian?'

'British.'

'Ah. And what has brought you here out of season? This place is very different in the summer months, you know.'

'Well, that's why we wanted to come now really.'

'We?'

'Me and my boyfriend Zac. We're travellers. Well, travel bloggers. We stay all over the world in the most remote, off-the-beaten-track places we can find.'

'Is Gerainger off the track?' Harald asked with a quizzical smile. 'We have almost two million visitors annually.'

'I know but . . . well, that's why we've come during the quiet spell. Plus we're staying at Anders' grandmother's farm which is fairly . . . hardcore.'

'Yes it will be,' Harald said, nodding with a knowing look. 'And how have you managed with that?'

'Well, getting hypothermia and then *almost* pneumonia was rather problematic with no central heating or hot running water,' she chuckled. 'Hence, why Anders stepped in to help out for a few days.'

Harald looked across at him with a proud expression. 'He is a truly good man.'

Beside her, Anders shifted his weight, embarrassed.

Harald laughed, slapping him hard on the shoulder. 'How long will you stay in the village?'

'Well the rest of our group are still up there. I'm going back tomorrow.'

'You have missed your friends?'

Bo waggled her head. 'Mmm, yes and no.'

'No?'

'It's actually been really nice to have some time to myself. We . . . because of the size of our online following, we have to travel as a group.'

'You mean an entourage?' Harald asked, looking amused.

'Oh, I wouldn't say that,' she said quickly.

'I would,' Anders said drily.

Harald laughed loudly.

'No,' Bo said defensively. 'We only have Lenny – he's our photographer-slash-manager; he comes everywhere with us, organizes our trips and itineraries.'

'And then there's Anna too,' Anders prompted.

'But she's just the marketing rep for the company we're currently in partnership with. She's only with us for a couple of weeks,' she protested. 'She's not normally with us.'

'And you're *all* staying up at the farm?' Harald asked.

'Yes.'

'That must get intense.' He looked across at Anders questioningly. 'Especially at this time of year. Once you're up there on that ledge, you're stuck there. It's not like there's anything else around besides the view; you can't even move freely.'

'That view could *never* get boring and I like the seclusion of it,' she shrugged. 'But I guess it's a Marmite thing.'

'Marmite?'

'You either love it or hate it.'

Harald looked across at Anders. 'I thought the farm was only available for summer lets.'

'So did I. But my grandmother took the money, bought a new skidoo and forgot to tell me anything about it until they all turned up on the doorstep.'

Harald laughed loudly again; it was a generous boom, like a tuba in a hall of violins. 'God bless your grandmother, no one gets in her way.'

'That's for sure.' Anders grinned too, looking as though he'd been loosened at the stays. In fact, he looked completely different, full stop, tonight – seeing him out of his work clothes, relaxing with friends, his energy was totally different.

The reserve that felt like a forcefield when he was around her and the others, was completely gone here. He was softer somehow. A flesh and blood man, rather than the bionic automaton guiding them up and down mountains. People kept touching him – patting his shoulder or shaking his hand as they passed by on their way to the kitchen – as though he was a favoured son, casting her curious glances as they went and she knew the tan drew more attention to her than even her accent. But not once did she think any of them recognized her; there was nothing grabbing in their looks, they didn't want selfies or a shout-out. For the first time in a long time, she didn't feel watched.

Bo drank her aquavit, not caring that it burned her throat, and she happily held out her glass for a refill when Harald offered it, the sharp edge of her nerves already blunted.

'So, I imagine you've been enjoying the heady luxuries of staying at Anders' house then, whilst you've been sick?' Harald asked, as he poured. 'Television? Internet?'

'Hot running water's been the best thing,' she agreed. 'Wifi, I've been less interested in. It's been surprisingly good being off social media for a bit.'

'Bo is one half of Wanderlusters,' Anders said, with no apparent trace of sarcasm. 'She and her fiancé have nine million followers.'

'Nine mil—?' Harald's eyes bulged. 'And you like that?'

Bo felt a surprised laugh escape her. It wasn't the question that usually came after people heard that. 'It's fine. It's a job.'

'I thought you said it was a lifestyle?' Anders challenged, his usual inscrutable stare making her shift her weight.

'Well, it's both. It started out as a lifestyle and then I started getting paid to lead it.' She shrugged, looking between them both. 'But in order to lead it, I need to be able to fund it, so . . .'

'But doesn't it feel . . .' Harald frowned. 'I don't know, what is the word . . . ? Intrusive, all these people watching you?'

'Sometimes, yes. I don't like being recognized when we're out. I like to feel there's a line between online me and real me.' She felt Anders' gaze settle harder on her.

'So you mean that these millions of people following you aren't really seeing the real you? But then isn't that deceitful? Misleading?'

'No, I think of it more as they see a slice of my life and who I am, just not all of it. They see twenty per cent. It's a curated version of my life – edited, sanitized, prettified, filtered. They can watch me, without really seeing me.'

'That's an interesting distinction: they can watch you but not see you,' Harald mused, nodding wisely. 'So, what does it take to give them this twenty per cent? I assume you are guilty of photographing avocados on toast?'

Bo laughed out loud; even Anders grinned.

'Maybe once or twice,' she admitted. 'But I try to post two to three photos to my grid each day—'

'The normal Instagram images,' Anders clarified for him. 'They call it the grid.' He shrugged, as though it was a free-mason's handshake.

'And then at least five or six fifteen-second videos to my storyboard.'

Harald looked intrigued. 'And can you do that quickly or does it all need to be decided beforehand? Do you have meetings about what you'll show?'

'Well, this is where our photographer comes in. We'll plan various trips and excursions and he'll then shoot reportage-style throughout that. He probably takes two, three hundred images a day.'

'*Three hundred?*' Harald looked scandalized.

'Minimum. That's split between Zac and me but for every image we post, it takes probably twenty, twenty-five frames to get a decent one.'

He looked bewildered. Lost. 'But I don't understand – you're a very pretty girl. Surely it is easy to take a photograph of you? Don't you agree, Anders?'

Anders looked like he might choke. 'What?'

'She is pretty, no?'

He frowned as though he didn't understand the question. 'Uh . . . yes. She's fine.'

Harald had a mischievous smile on his lips.

Fine? She's fine? 'Well, thank you,' Bo said lightly, refusing to let the slight settle on her. 'But I might be blinking in one snap, or the wind's blown my hair in my eyes, or there's a shadow on my face, or the silhouette's wrong.' She shrugged. 'It can be harder than it looks.'

'Well, I had no idea,' Harald murmured, looking startled by the prospect. He glanced at Anders. 'I guess that's the difference between digital and film. Back in my day, you simply couldn't afford to take so many frames. Every single one cost money to be developed.'

'Yes, I guess.'

'I suppose you might argue that photographs meant more back then?' Harald suggested.

'Oh, but I disagree,' Bo said. 'People document their lives in a way now that they never could before.'

'Yes, but in so doing, haven't they devalued the form?' Harald debated. 'When everybody's taking multiple shots just to get one decent "selfie", it doesn't mean as much as when there were only limited chances to capture an image. There's no sense of permanence now because everyone's always on to the new, the next thing.'

Was he right, she wondered? It was a valid point.

'And I hate how nobody prints their photographs any more,' he said, getting on to a riff. 'Posting them is the new photo frame! You can't have a picture in your house where just your family and friends will see it, it has to be on the internet to be validated by strangers.' He tutted. 'It makes you wonder what would happen if a pandemic wiped out the human race and this planet was visited hundreds or thousands of years from now by another race – they would think that humanity ended in the 1990s! There would be almost no physical evidence of us because all the images are sitting on hard drives that no one would know how to work any more—'

A hand appeared on Harald's shoulder suddenly and he turned. A short woman with light brown hair and kind eyes blinked back at them and then at him. She said something in Norwegian.

'Yes, of course,' Harald murmured, turning back to them. 'I'm sorry, you'll have to excuse me, Annika is wanting us to do the tree decorations now. Duty calls.'

'No problem,' Anders nodded.

'Help yourself to drinks and food,' Harald said. 'There is *risengrynsgrot* over there.' He looked at Bo. 'If you have not had it before, you are in for a treat. My wife's is the best in the province.' And with a smile and a wink, he disappeared back into the kitchen.

'Risenwhat?' she asked Anders.

'It is a porridge, with sugar and cinnamon and butter – a very traditional part of Norwegian Christmases.'

'Then I think I should try some,' she said; if nothing else, she hadn't had supper and that aquavit schnapps had gone to her head. 'I can record it too, post a little footage.'

'Really?' Anders sounded reluctant.

'Yeah,' she sighed, feeling the same herself. 'People are already asking if Zac and I have broken up, just because I've not posted for a few days.' He tutted but she held out her glass for him to hold as she reached for her phone from her jeans pocket. 'It really is something when you can't even be sick without the conspiracy theorists having a field day.' She blew out through her cheeks. 'But that's how it is, right? Roll with the punches. The social media show must go on. People want daily contact, even if it's just seeing the colour of the varnish on my toes.'

Anders frowned, shaking his head imperceptibly and staring at her as though *she* was a conundrum. 'Come on, then,' he said, leading her over to the buffet table. There was a vast spread laid out but the porridge was seemingly very much the centrepiece, being kept warm in a jug-eared silver tureen. He ladled some in a bowl for her and she began recording, showing his earnest concentration as he sprinkled on the cinnamon, sugar and butter. His face softened ever so slightly as he handed it over to her but the realization that he was being filmed saw him immediately arch out of shot and lapse back into his customary scowl. She laughed as she stopped recording. 'You don't have to look *quite* so horrified, Anders,' she grinned, uploading the post. 'It is only a camera, not a gun.'

'Now, can you just quickly be Lenny and film me having a bit of it?' she asked, handing the phone to him before he could say no. 'It'll prove to the followers that I am still alive and kicking in Norway and that rumours of my death have been greatly exaggerated.'

He gave a sigh but did as she asked, filming her as she took a first, tentative sip. 'Mmm-mmm!' she said, doing her best Nigella and widening her eyes as the flavours hit. 'My God, that's delicious,' she exclaimed, immediately going in for a second spoonful. She closed her eyes in bliss and then looked to camera. 'Guys, this is a traditional dish called *risen*—' She looked at Anders for help.

'*Risengrynsgrot*,' he said from behind the camera.

'Right, that,' she grinned. 'It's basically porridge, cinnamon, sugar and butter and it is *delicious*.' She took another spoonful – only this time . . . She grimaced. 'Ugh, what's . . . what's that?' she asked, spitting into her hand.

Anders chuckled. 'That's a scalded almond.'

'What? *Why?*' she complained, staring down at it.

'Tradition has it that whoever gets the almond will be first to marry.'

'Tradition . . . ?' She looked straight to camera. 'Oh, jeez . . . You heard it here first, guys,' she winked.

'And your prize for finding the almond will be a marzipan pig.' Amusement continued to speckle his voice.

'A marzi—?'

'It's stopped recording,' he said, abruptly holding the camera back out to her as though it was a hot coal.

'Oh. Thanks.' She grinned, taking it from him. 'Do I really get a marzipan pig?'

'Along with a husband, yes,' he shrugged but his eyes were dancing. He somehow always managed to say so much more with his silences than his words. 'You cannot say we Norwegians are not generous.'

She smirked at his quip, playing the video back and holding the phone out so that he could see it over her shoulder. It was highly amusing – her grimace and surprise, his dry comments. And with the Christmas tree, twinkling lights, music, shrieking children and all the party guests in the background, it oozed authenticity. A genuine Norwegian Christmas. The fans would go mad for it. She uploaded it with a smile.

Slut.

The word flashed behind her eyelids every time she blinked, it glowed on the other side of the road as she looked to cross, it sucked out the brightness of that happy, festive room. Together, they walked in silence back to the house.

It had been a great night up till that point. She had had three aquavits – enough to make her head swim and her smile easy – and at first, as her phone buzzed constantly in her back pocket, she had shared some of the responses with Anders. A fair few of them had been about him: '*Phwoar! Hello Blue Eyes*'; '*Viking style*'; '*Who heeee? #yesplease*'; '*Deets!*'; '*Zac who?*'

'Well, *you're* a hit!' she had laughed but he had looked away, refusing to engage. The prospect of global adoration hadn't seemed to flatter or excite him and he'd turned down flat her plea to take a stand-alone photograph of him, '*due to popular demand*'. But the schnapps and festive mood had loosened her up and she had snuck a few of him anyway whenever he spoke briefly to other friends and neighbours; she found and tagged his Geraingerfjord Guided Tours account, watching as his number of followers ballooned from forty-seven to over three thousand in forty-five minutes. She had planned to show him his dramatic new following at the end of the night by way of a thank you, for it had been a great night.

Things had been easy between them. They had talked, even laughed, he had introduced her to various people from the village and it constantly surprised her to see not only how popular he was, but how fiercely loved too. Everyone slapped his shoulder that little bit harder, holding on to him that little bit longer, as though he was precious, rare. People had begun dancing too, but she and he had stood and watched from the sidelines, talking intently and trying not to look as embarrassed as they felt. It was the only time things had felt awkward between them. Personally, she wouldn't have minded a dance, she felt in the mood to let go and buoyed up by the festive spirit here, but unlike Zac – who had been known to drop into a Caterpillar in the supermarket if the right song came on – it went without saying that Anders wasn't a dancer; even with his friends, there was a reserve to him that felt bulletproof, nothing could infiltrate. The old version she had seen of him in his Instagram profile might have danced, but not this one.

She had swayed a little though, she had let her head feel heavy on her neck as she enjoyed the vibe. But then the noise had started to come in via her back pocket, a static that steadily drowned out the music. She had wanted to convey the night for what it was: a cosy, local Christmas party – nothing staged or aspirational, just an old-fashioned community celebration with children baking gingerbreads and decorating the tree, Abba in the background and old ladies sitting in chairs by the fire. So how had that somehow been construed as her cheating on Zac?

One comment had been all it took to trigger the landslide. *'OMG see how he looks at her.'* It had been posted on the first video as she'd filmed Anders ladling the porridge; he'd only been in shot for a couple of seconds and for most of that he was scowling. What were these people seeing that she wasn't? Clearly something, because plenty of others had taken up the cry too, wanting the details, demanding to know where Zac was, who *'the hell this guy'* was, had they split?

It had killed the party dead, for them both. Anders' easy good mood had faltered as the accusations had continued to flood her feed, visibly upsetting her, causing her to withdraw. And it only tainted things further when he was drawn into the virtual fray too; she regretted tagging his details, for no doubt some of the haters would target his page directly too and what if his girlfriend saw it? What would she think to see him drawn into this mess?

Bo had kept the troll's comment from him. She felt shamed by it somehow. Not for Him the triplicate question marks and disembodied shock; no emojis or online emoting. *Slut.* It was a label. A judgement. A verdict – taking the smile from her face and the shine off her evening. She had asked to leave, both ruining his night and offending him in the process.

She stood back as he retrieved the key from under a rock by the wall and they walked into the quiet, dark house. The last embers of the fire in the sitting room cast a thin veil of flickering light across the floor and bled a little into the hall. She took off her coat and boots, watching his back as he moved into the kitchen.

'Want a drink?' he asked.

'No, I'm fine,' she mumbled, knowing she'd had enough. Possibly already too much. Aquavit and antibiotics didn't mix. She went and stood by the kitchen door.

'I meant like a coffee or cocoa,' he said tersely, glancing back at her. 'You should have something to warm you up again. It's cold out there and you're still not well.'

'Are you my nurse now, as well as guide and bodyguard?'

He shot her an inscrutable look as he went over to the fridge and took out the milk.

'What?' she asked testily, the buzz from the schnapps suddenly an agitation; she felt upset. Angry. Humiliated. The online abuse was a virtual scream in her face and now *he* was being tricky with her? 'Why do you always look at me like that?'

'Like what?'

'Like . . . I'm ridiculous.'

His brow creased further. 'I don't think that.'

'It sure looks like you think that. Anytime you see me doing my job you give me this look of sort of . . . weary despair.'

'Well, I'm sorry if it seems that way,' he said, pouring the milk into a pan. 'You are of course free to live and work however you want.'

'But you don't approve,' she pushed.

He gave her a direct stare then. 'Do you need me to?'

'No,' she said defiantly.

'Exactly.' He walked back to the fridge, returning the milk.

She watched him, feeling like he was trying to provoke her with his constant calmness; his lack of response to anything, ever, felt exaggerated. Unnatural. He took a jar of cocoa from the cupboard and heaped a couple of spoonfuls into two mugs, stirring the milk as it began to heat. There was such precision in his movements. Control. 'Why *are* you so disapproving of me?' she said again, pushing him for an answer, refusing to move on. 'I want to know.'

He looked at her squarely then, his too blue eyes boring into her. '. . . I simply do not understand why you would continue to put yourself in such a vulnerable position.'

'I'm *not* vulnerable!'

'You are being harassed by a man who once broke into your bedroom and you have just received countless insults and hate mail from strangers. I saw it happening, how it upset you. It is madness to put yourself through it.'

'But it's not, I'm used to it. It's nothing. And *he's* nothing. He's not real.'

'He's real all right,' Anders said with a worrying tone.

Bo stared at him as she felt her heart jack-knife. Why would he say that? Was he trying to frighten her? She felt hot tears press against her already hot eyes; her medication was wearing off. She needed to go to bed, she knew. And yet—

'It must be *so* nice being you, Anders. Living a life where everything's simple and stress-free, looking down on the rest of us. I mean, you've just got it all figured out, haven't you? You're a veritable saint – coming back here to look after your grandmother, living on muesli and hiking mountains by day, keeping a drawer for your hot girlfriend.' His darting glance was like a warning, making her heart pound harder, but she couldn't stop. 'Admit it – that's really why you're upset. You think she's going to see those comments and wonder if perhaps what all those people are saying about us is true. You're not concerned about me being upset or vulnerable. You're angry with me because I just made your life complicated, that worst of things.'

'I'm not angry with you,' he replied but she watched as he stared into the pan, stirring the milk with furious concentration. Her words were hitting their mark.

'What's your girlfriend's name, anyway?'

He didn't answer and Bo got the message instantly: she was off-limits.

'Okay, then – why did you leave Oslo?' There was provocation in the question, in her voice, and as his head whipped round, she saw she had a genuine response from him. Finally. She had seen the way he had frozen when the topic had come up earlier. Why was he so cagey about it? People left small villages for big cities all the time. They left the cities again too. What was the big deal? 'If your girlfriend is still there, why did you come back here?'

He turned away again but she could see a pulse in his jaw now as he poured the milk carefully into the mugs before bringing it over to her. 'Take this to bed with you. It'll help settle your sleep.'

Settle her sleep? She looked incredulously at the mug he was holding out to her. 'You're not my *mother*.'

He stared back at her impassively, less than a foot away. He smelled of soap and . . . trees. Woodland. A smudge of engine grease. Suddenly he felt big, standing there, his masculinity and unspoken physical power a growing awareness between them. 'No. But apparently she'd like me.'

Ordinarily, it was the kind of dry response that would at least elicit a glimmer of amusement in his eyes. But there was nothing. Contrary to appearances, she saw he was angry too; the very composition of him had changed, as though his muscles were made of stone.

'Why won't you answer my question?' she demanded, refusing to let him wriggle off the hook, deploring how her stomach floored every time he turned his gaze to hers. She saw the way his eyes travelled over her face, as though trying to see beyond the skin, to understand her.

'Because this isn't about me.'

'Yes it is,' she said belligerently. 'I asked you a question and I'd like an answer.'

'No, you're upset, a little bit drunk and you'd like an argument.' He pressed the cup into her hand and walked past her with his own. 'Turn the lights off when you come up.'

Chapter Sixteen

'Baby, you're back!' Zac's arms folded around her, his voice in her hair, even as the rotor blades still whirled. 'I wasn't expecting you till tonight at the earliest. Christ, I've missed you.'

Bo closed her eyes. She hadn't been able to get out of the helicopter fast enough. If she had thought Anders had been surly before, he had taken it to a whole other level now, greeting her in the kitchen this morning with nothing more than a flick of his eyes. She had stood there momentarily, her 'germy' bedsheets rolled up in her arms as he had hunched over the paper, drinking coffee and eating toast, and the reluctant apology she had planned on giving had stuck in her throat; instead they had driven to the heliport in silence, flown over here in silence . . .

'I feel like I've been gone for *months*,' she mumbled into his shoulder, feeling so relieved to be back with him that she wanted to cry. He rocked her from side to side, his arms so tight around her that it felt almost difficult to breathe and she blinked, only able to see the sky above his shoulder, the tops of the trees. When he released her, she dropped her bag from her shoulder, looking around at the small ledge that had briefly become home. She felt a stab almost of pain at inhaling its wild beauty again – so unmodernized, untouched; the purity of it was almost too much to bear. Its jagged and dramatic sharp edges had been temporarily softened and rounded by the now regular snowfall. The day was beautifully clear, a pink dawn rising to clear skies and she felt like she was up with the eagles on this rocky perch again, surrounded only by trees and water, the sky within fingertip distance.

In the cabin, she glimpsed movement behind the dark windows and then a face – Anna waving, a white towel wrapped around her, bright in the gloom. 'What the—?' she muttered, just as the door opened and Lenny walked out – or rather, swaggered. 'Oh. It's like that, is it?' she murmured to Zac as he came over to them both.

'It's so like that,' Zac murmured back.

Dammit. With the events of the past few days, her intended warning to him about the perils of mixing business and pleasure had completely left her head.

'Our wanderer returns!' Lenny said, stopping just in front of them. His grey jeans were just about falling off his hips and there was a coffee stain on his sweater; he looked unkempt and like he was deliberately growing a beard. 'How you feeling, Bo?'

'Better,' she smiled as he hugged her hard, his arms constricting around her like boas. She pulled back stiffly.

'We missed you. It wasn't the same here without you.'

He was being kind but Bo knew that wasn't true: she had seen their stories yesterday; she had heard him tell Anna he'd 'make her the new Bo'. 'Thanks. The drugs have well and truly kicked in now and it's good to be back. I'm looking forward to a little normality at last.'

'Well, I can help with that,' Zac said, grabbing her in his arms again and swooping her down into a dramatic lunge and kissing her passionately, before returning her to upright again so suddenly that her hair flew over her face. She gave a surprised laugh. 'Consider normal service resumed.'

She tried to push all the blonde back from her face. 'Did I miss much?'

'Oh you know – a gorge here, a waterfall there. Just the usual.'

Bo supposed it was usual – when other people were off sick, they missed meetings; she missed mountaineering. 'It's been looking good on Stories though.'

'Yeah?' Zac asked, kissing the top of her head and stroking her hair back, gazing down at her as though she was heaven-sent. 'You been keeping up?'

'Of course. It wasn't like there was much else to do.'

'So then I take it you're aware the trolls have been out in force?' Lenny asked with his usual bluntness. 'The internet is convinced you two have broken up.'

'I know,' she said, drooping slightly. 'And, for the record, I blame you.'

Lenny looked defensive. '*Me?* Why?'

She glanced across at the cabin before she hissed, 'For featuring Anna so heavily in the Stories.'

'But we couldn't exactly keep her out,' Zac frowned. 'She was there.'

'Yes, but she's been in almost all the footage – and she's supposed to be *behind the scenes*?' She hadn't meant the comment to come out quite so pointedly. 'If people don't know where I am and all they're seeing is her . . . what are they supposed to think? And she does giggle a lot.'

'You sound jealous, Bo,' Lenny smirked. 'What's wrong? Don't you like Anna taking all your attention?'

'It's not that,' she said defiantly. 'But I don't need my feed being spammed with three million cries of #SaveBo #teamBo.'

'Well, to be fair, you didn't exactly help things either by cheerleading for Bond's new fan club last night.' Zac jerked his head down towards the helicopter where Anders was jumping out.

'I wasn't *cheerleading*,' she gasped, irritated by the mere suggestion. 'I went to a traditional Norwegian Christmas party with a local and was sharing some of its customs with our followers – because that's what we do. That is the point, isn't it? Authentic experiences?'

Zac pulled a face. 'Ye-a-h, but like you said, it's also about how it reads.'

'Some folks might definitely have interpreted you and him as flirting,' Lenny said.

'We were not flirting!' Bo said hotly. 'Don't be so ridiculous!' She looked at Zac. 'You don't think that, do you?'

'No, of course I don't. Len, leave it, stop stirring the shit-stick,' Zac said, shaking his head. 'It doesn't matter anyway. She's back now. People will see the truth soon enough.'

Lenny gave a careless shrug. 'Hey, whatever – on the plus side, all this are-they, aren't-they is playing well with the fans. We're up to 9.6 now and engagement is up to 52 per cent, which is *un*heard of. They're loving the drama. Keep 'em hanging a bit longer and let them speculate, I say. Hell, you could even mock a big fight, a little break-up, if you want.'

'No!' Bo snapped, appalled by the very suggestion. 'I've been gone for *three days*. Since when did our lives become a soap opera?'

'I completely agree,' Zac said soothingly, looking down at her with a sombre expression on his face. 'I'm just glad you're back. I was worried about you.'

'Why?'

Zac jerked his head towards Anders still down at the helicopter, lifting out bags. 'Well, he's hardly Mr Sociable, let's face it,' he scoffed, speaking in a low voice. 'I thought he might bore you to death. Christ, he's barely said a word on our expeditions, has he, Len? Literally won't volunteer any sort of conversation. It's as though talking somehow *pains* him.'

Lenny guffawed. 'Yeah.'

Bo forced a smile, not liking this turn of conversation either, and yet unable to deny the truth in their words. 'Well it was fine,' she said placidly. 'He was . . .' She shrugged, remembering his kindness when she'd been ill, his easy conversation at dinner and at the party, his brusque comments yesterday morning and his stonewalling in the kitchen last night. 'Fine.'

'*Fine?*' Lenny echoed, looking between her and Zac before giving a shrug. 'Well then, that's great. It was fine,' he said sarcastically. 'I guess we were worried out of our minds about you staying with a silent stranger for no reason.'

The sound of creaking snow made them all turn to see Anders coming up in long-legged strides, a couple of bags from the grocer's in one hand and two gas canisters in the other. His eyes met hers for just a fraction of a second; it was only a glance but it felt like a shove, their 'argument' last night (could it even be called that?) like a wall between them.

She swallowed hard as he passed. Why exactly *had* she been so agitated with him last night? He had been right – she had been drunk (her head this morning had told her that) and she had been rattled by the haters' comments. But why had she taken it out on him? Why did his opinion on her choices even matter to her? And why was it so hard now to say sorry?

'Morning, mate,' Zac said brightly, tipping his head in greeting. 'Thanks for bringing her back safe and sound.'

Bo knew this was the moment to say it – to chime in with her thanks too and to acknowledge what he had done for her; but like the apology she also owed him, it blocked her throat like rocks in a landslide.

As he walked by, Anders simply nodded in reply.

'Rude bastard,' Zac muttered under his breath as Bo stood on in dejected silence. Anders strode ahead and as her eyes followed him, Bo suddenly saw Signy sitting at her window, observing. Bo turned away, feeling miserable, feeling guilty, but this time she found Lenny watching her too.

Always there were all these people, watching. Watching, watching. Wanting something from her.

'You okay, Bo?' Lenny asked, looking at her quizzically. 'You still look kinda peaky.'

'Do I?'

'You're sure you're well enough to be back here? You don't want to spend another night in town?'

She scowled again. 'Are you trying to get rid of me, Lenny?' He probably wanted to make a star of Anna again for another day.

'Of course not. I'm just worried about you is all.'

'Well I'm fine.'

'Come on, let's get you in from the cold,' Zac said, picking up her bag, and the three of them followed in Anders' footsteps up the path between the cabins. But where he turned right, they turned left into theirs and as they passed by, she could hear Signy's voice, stern again, and Anders' – low and agreeable – coming from around the corner outside their door. They were going out already?

'Zac, has anyone been going to check on Signy while I've been gone?'

'Well, Anna tried but she said she's always up and dressed when she goes in in the mornings,' he shrugged. 'And at night, she's already in bed when we get back.'

'Oh.' Not for them the 'playing dead' trick then?

They walked into the cabin, stamping their snowy feet on the mat and Bo gave a shiver of relief at the warmth there – only to shudder. Things had become dramatically more 'relaxed' in the intervening period since she'd been here last: clothes hung off the back of the chairs, newspapers and a map were scattered over the sofa, a cluster of empty beer bottles stood by the door; dirty dishes were piled up in the sink, five red wine bottles and the dribbling stubs of two red candles were left on the table and the whole place smelled of wet socks and damp towels.

'Oh, come on!' she said, surveying the chaos and feeling her mood sour further. This wasn't the 'homecoming' she'd been anticipating. 'You can't be serious? I get a cold and you start living like students?'

'What?' Lenny asked, looking around in bafflement and seeming genuinely blind to her complaint. 'What do you mean?'

'Oh, I'm sorry,' she said sarcastically. 'I say students, but what I really mean is *pigs*.' She put her hands on her hips and looked straight at Zac.

'It's not that bad, is it?' he asked, scanning the room.

'Zac – I am not staying here if you don't clean this place up. I mean it. I'll go straight back to Anders' place again and stay in town.'

But her heart pounded heavily at the threat – that was now the last place she could go; she could never go back there. Zac stared back open-mouthed, panic scurrying over his face like mice. 'Len, mate! You wash, I'll dry,' he said hurriedly, squeezing her around the waist and planting a kiss on her cheek. 'We'll have it tidied up in just a bit.' He smelled of beer, she realized and she noticed his eyes were red-rimmed and bloodshot. He was hungover to *hell*. They both were. How had she not noticed it outside?

'And you're going to need to wash afterwards. You stink.' She wrinkled up her nose. '*Both* of you.'

'Yeah?' Zac looked hurt as he sniffed his armpits. 'Oh yeah, maybe you're right.'

'Oh yeah, maybe I am,' she mimicked, just as they all heard the sound of the helicopter starting up again, that distinctive *dud-dud* beat making the plates rattle in the dresser. It was Anders' day off and he was taking his grandmother back into town for her second weekly trip; the boys ran to the window to watch, laughing at the incongruity of the image of the old lady with the white hair wearing earphones and rising into the sky, until she was looking down upon the fjord like a queen.

But laughing wasn't what Bo felt like and as she went into the bedroom, the door closed behind her with a slam.

She was straight back into it. With Anders having the day off, Zac and Lenny (not forgetting Anna) had planned to go skiing at Stranda. It was an hour's drive and two ferries up the fjord and it was a peculiarly subdued journey, as everyone's respective hangovers began to bang in their heads. But Bo threw herself into the action with a vim that belied her still-embattled body. She was determined not to give the haters any more ammunition; she would be in every shot, and in every shot she would be smiling. Happiness was always the best revenge, wasn't that what they said? Well, let them see her with Zac. Back together. Stronger than ever. Let the gossips and the naysayers go hang. Enough about Anna. Enough about Anders. That was all just noise. She knew the truth. She knew what made up the other 80 per cent of her life that her detractors never got to see.

Her Ridge Riders ski kit – a black Bond Girl-style all-in-one with yellow trim – fitted like it had been made for her and she threw herself down the quiet slopes with unusual abandon: she beat Anna on every run, even Lenny too on some; only Zac could still outgun her, and by the time they stopped for a late lunch, red-cheeked and with burning thighs – at three o'clock, the night clouds already sailing in – their collective mood had lifted. Clicking off their skis, they all bustled, laughing, into a mountain restaurant, ravenous and feeling reborn. Bo, feeling the endorphins ricocheting through her, led the charge. She was worn out but happy as they all collapsed into a booth by the window, and she had almost, very nearly all but forgotten about her falling out with Anders.

'Well, she's definitely back,' Lenny said, nodding at his screen as he scrolled through the images he had taken.

'My baby is back,' Zac murmured, his arm slung behind the back of the bench seat as he kissed her hair again, and Bo felt a private swell of victory as she stared at the menu, unable to risk darting a glance in Anna's direction.

Anna had been quiet all morning and had only become quieter as Bo bested her on every run. The rivalry was unspoken but she knew they both felt it. Anna had overstepped the mark in her absence but the dial was being set back to normal now and she didn't like it. Anna had been basking in Bo's spotlight and, whether it had been inadvertent or not, it was clear she had enjoyed the attention. She had liked being the #girlinred.

'This is almost reading like a catalogue shoot,' Lenny said, flicking his eyes over to Anna. 'Your bosses are gonna die when they see this shit.'

Anna gave a tight smile.

Bo looked around the restaurant. It was a small octagonal hut at the top of one of the pistes, fitted out in an industrial style with exposed steel rafters and planked counters. The waitress – speaking faultless English – was quick to come over and take their orders for a round of beers (hot chocolate for her) and soups. There were another five or six groups in there, helmets and bobble hats hanging on hooks and dripping melted snow onto the floor, a couple of kids walking in the typically awkward snow-boot gait, their salopette braces already down by their waists as they headed for the toilets.

'That's a great one,' Lenny said, holding up his camera to show them all – it was an action shot of Bo carving a turn, her body looking lean and strong as she angled in to it, a spray of snow reaching to the screen, her mouth open in delight, teeth looking super-white against her tanned skin and rainbow-reflective goggles. Looking at it, she could almost believe herself that it was the most fun she'd ever had and not a forced display of defiance. But she had faked it till she made it, for she felt happy now. Back on track. She dropped her head contentedly onto Zac's shoulder.

'God, my girl is hot,' Zac said proudly, squeezing her knee. He had been all over her since her freak-out about the state of the cabin, trying to make it up to her, and she felt bad now; it hadn't been the mess that had triggered her tantrum.

'That's going to be a sell-out for sure,' Anna said, looking at the image over Lenny's shoulder. He was already writing up a caption. '. . . Hmm, I might ring head office and see what stock they've got on it. Don't post it just yet, okay?' she said to him as she got up and, shrugging her jacket back on, went outside to make a call; reception was better out there.

'I need a slash anyway,' Lenny said with a sigh.

'Nice. Thanks,' Bo muttered sarcastically.

'Oh yeah, she's back all right,' Lenny quipped.

'I'll join you, mate. Before the food comes,' Zac agreed.

'What are you? Teenage girls?' she scoffed as he shuffled off the bench seat and the two of them rock-walked across the room together.

Bo gave a sigh. Reaching across the table, she picked up Lenny's camera and continued scrolling through the images. Lenny had really gone overboard on the number of frames today – it was a clear day, the light was good and the fjord, lying like a sleeping dragon, made for a stunning backdrop.

Lenny had been right though, the three of them in shot did look suspiciously professional, throwing all the right shapes and silhouettes for the camera as they passed. Yet again, Anna was squarely in a lot of the frames, although that was hardly surprising given that she and Lenny were now sleeping together; he was bound to be distracted by her for the short-term. Very short-term.

On and on she scrolled, eventually getting back to the images of this morning taken from inside the cabin as she'd arrived home: her hug with Zac, her jumping out of the helicopter, arms wide, hair flying behind her. And then before her return – inside the cabin with Anna: Anna, looking post-coital and running across the space in just her towel, one hand up to hide her face; a tray set with two steaming coffees and almond croissants; Anna looking surprised – wild-haired, hungover and not entirely happy – as she peered around the bedroom door, waiting for her bath.

Before all of that, came the night before. It looked like it had been rowdy, the three of them sitting with several bottles of red wine, their arms splayed on the table, and charred cork marks on their hopelessly laughing faces as they played Ibble Dibble, one of Zac's favourite drinking games.

Bo felt a pang of envy at the sight of them all carrying on without her. Not that she expected them to sit in chaste silence and do crosswords in her absence but, still, did they have to have quite such a good time? Nonetheless, it was quite comical to travel backwards from their dishevelled appearances at the end of the night, to their more put-together selves earlier in the evening. Anna had cooked, she saw. Zac had been playing solitaire with a deck of cards. Lenny had got his guitar out.

'Right—' She looked up as Anna sat back down on her chair opposite. 'They're contacting the factory to get another batch out as soon as possible.'

Bo replaced Lenny's camera on the table. 'They can do that? Respond to market demand that quickly?'

'It will mean limiting numbers on other styles, depending on how much fabric is left. But they've said it'll be worth it if the response is the same as with the Sami jacket. Trust me, that suit is going to fly as soon as you post.'

The waitress came over with their drinks order, setting down the beers. Anna gave a small groan of protest as she lifted hers.

'Feeling a little delicate this morning?' Bo smiled, sipping her hot chocolate and wondering whether she could broach the topic of Anna and Lenny being together. She was dying to know more but she felt on the back foot. She and Anna had spent hardly any time together and nothing at all one-on-one; they didn't know each other yet; they hadn't got drunk or cooked for one another, whereas the others had had three days to bond with her. They had all knitted together as a team in her absence and Bo was conscious of being left to play catch-up. On the chairlifts, as the hangovers had receded, she had listened as they repeatedly cracked jokes about something or other that had happened yesterday or the day before, as though they were all now bonded for life. Incredibly, Bo had felt sidelined, even though she could see how much Zac was trying to bring her back into the fold again.

'What? Oh, you mean . . .' Anna rolled her eyes, blushing a little. 'I can't keep up with them. I don't know what I was thinking drinking all that wine last night.'

'They are pretty hardcore,' Bo agreed. 'Take my advice – don't even try. The hangovers aren't worth it.'

'Yes, you're right.' Anna stared at the table, seeming embarrassed. Her personal situation with Lenny had blurred the boundaries of this professional relationship and Bo could already feel how it changed things – and that was before they'd even broken up. What would it be like then? 'But thank goodness for this today,' she said, jerking her chin to indicate the ski resort. 'It has been the best thing for clearing a sore head.'

'Yes. I feel better for it too,' Bo agreed. 'Resting is all well and good but after a certain point, I think you just feel more "meh" for moping around, you know?'

'We are all so glad you are back.'

Bo smiled, knowing that was a lie. 'Your bosses most of all, I bet,' she said simply.

'Well,' Anna shrugged. 'You are vital to the Wanderlusters image.'

Yes she was. 'It's definitely good to be back in the frame again,' Bo sighed, keeping her voice neutral. 'It was all such terrible timing with that stupid accident and then me falling sick just as we were getting going. I'm so sorry it's all been so *messy*.'

'Hey, no! We are just glad you are okay. It was not your fault.'

Bo's eyes flashed up to her. No, it wasn't – or at least, not entirely. As she recalled – and the memories were pretty hazy – Anna was the one who had been pushing her, directing her. Bo never would have stepped onto those rocks ordinarily. Shouldn't Anna take some responsibility for what had happened?

But Anna didn't appear to be one afflicted by introspection. Instead, she leaned in a little closer, a sly look coming into her eyes. Girl to girl. 'Tell me though – was it really okay being with Anders at his house? I mean, he is so *difficult*.'

A chill swirled around her, as though a door had been opened and a draught slipped in. 'Yeah.' Bo shrugged, looking down into her drink. 'I mean, it's not like he wasn't around much.'

Anna's voice had changed – becoming lower, intimate, secretive. 'It is so strange. I know I recognize him. I just do not know where.'

Bo tried to think for her. 'Well, I don't know – could it have been at a trade convention perhaps? You both deal with the outdoor market, after all.'

Anna wrinkled her nose, looking sceptical. 'No, I don't think so.'

'Or uni? Apparently, he used to live in Oslo.'

'Oslo. Hmm, maybe. But that is a big place and I've only been a handful of times. I thought Alesund would be the connection. That is the main town around here.' She sighed, just as the guys re-emerged. 'Oh well, it will come to me.'

Zac flopped down beside her heavily and nuzzled her cheek again, kissing her temple as though he'd been gone for two years and not two minutes.

'Oh, good – beer,' Lenny said, taking a deep appreciative glug. He smacked his lips together, a giant slug of foam on his upper lip as he looked across at her and Zac for a moment. Then he reached over and squeezed Anna's thigh, before draping his arm around her, his hand grazing her breast as he kissed her lingeringly, his tongue darting between her lips.

Bo shot Zac a look – their display was so overtly sexual – but he just shrugged.

The waitress came back with their lunch – huge bowls of soup and buttered buns – and Bo, feeling her tummy rumble at the smell of it, dived in. She was halfway through before she noticed the others (not Lenny, he was always starving) didn't seem to share her appetite. 'What's the matter?' she asked, seeing their still-full bowls. 'Don't you like it?'

'Mushrooms,' Zac muttered, by way of explanation.

'My hangover is worse than I thought,' Anna smiled wanly.

Lenny looked up from his spoon. 'I think it's great.'

Chapter Seventeen

Lodal, July 1936

Signy stood at the window and looked up into the mountains, her eyes a narrow squint. It was up there somewhere, watching. Waiting. She had heard the wolf's howl and it had made her sit up in bed, her heart jack-hammering. Margit hadn't stirred – lips parted, features soft, she looked kind even in her sleep. But Signy was the shepherd; it had become uniquely her job – whilst the others rotated the chores of milking and haying, churning and picking – it was agreed that she had the stamina, the wanderlust and the connection with the animals. She must protect them.

Tiptoeing into the main room, she looked out across the moonlit meadows. The pastures were empty of course – she herself had put the animals in the pens – the hay drying on the ricks swaying like horse manes in the light breeze. The snowball-headed cottongrass by the stream glowed bright like globes, thick shadows covering the ground as the almost-full moon tiptoed above the sleeping valley.

In the cabins opposite, everything was still. Kari slept like a bear – Signy knew nothing would wake her – but there was no movement in either hers, with Brit and Ashi, nor Sofie's. She alone had heard the wolf.

But then again, she felt she had almost been waiting for it. She had sensed its eyes on her for the past few weeks as she herded the flocks to and from the outfields and she had come to realize from the way the hairs rose on the back of her neck that it wasn't a human gaze but a predator. A hunter. Her instinct told her so.

The animals knew it too. They had been increasingly skittish, collectively shunning the higher ground and its rocky outcrops – they picked up scents she could not and had begun to stay close; even Stormy had stayed nearby. And so unbeknownst to the other girls, knowing they would only panic if she told them, Signy had begun to take a threshing knife on her trips; furious indignation wouldn't count for much against a wolf's jaws, and she now obsessively counted her flock even though it was unnecessary. If one was taken, she would just *know*.

The cardigan her mother had knitted for her for Christmas was on the back of a chair and carefully – avoiding the creaky floorboards – she shrugged it on over her pink embroidered nightdress and crept outside. Her rubber boots were kept at the door to the cabin and she stepped onto the mossy path, shivering in the night chill.

She buttoned up the cardigan as her ears strained for sounds of disturbance in the stables, but as she got closer all she heard was the occasional snorts and grunts of dozing animals, hooves scratching against the hay.

The howl came again, a sound that made her skin creep, and she pivoted on her heel. It wasn't close, but nor was it far. It had come from the east just over the ridge and was closer than it had been, of that she was certain. Unless, of course, there was more than one.

She needed to know. It was unlikely, but if there was a pack circling them, the threshing knife wouldn't be enough and they would need to send for a hunting rifle from the village in the morning. She couldn't shoot, but the very sound of its blasting barrels might be enough to frighten them off.

At a fast clip, she began to march, arms swinging – past the *stabbur* and the haybarn, the cabins behind her. The ground was on an incline here, the valley already beginning to bowl upwards to the peaks, moss-covered boulders bobbling the land. A great grey owl called from the low branch of a birch tree and she heard the scrabble of squirrel claws scampering up trunks as she passed by. The sky was far from dark – rather it was dim, as though a tint had fallen over the earth, and she could see almost perfectly, stumbling only a couple of times in her haste, her heart pounding.

She used her hands to help her climb near the top as she scrabbled up the last sections, pulling herself up to her full unimpressive height as she finally made it and looked down onto the neighbouring valley. The lake where Ashi fished shimmered like a silver plate, the pale moon like a pearl globe on its surface. Shaped like a kidney bean, a small tree-dotted island sat towards the back of it from here, the cluster of winter fruit trees her grandfather had planted sixty-five years before reaching back from the dimpled edge of the shore.

Signy squinted again, looking for a movement or sound to catch her attention. Had they come here to drink? The stream that led off from it ran directly down to the *seter*. Her body felt taut and primed, animalistic itself, as she scanned the dusk. She was hunting a hunter and she felt the pulse of the natural world beat through her; she belonged to this and it belonged to her.

A splash came to her ear and she braced, dropping down to her knees out of sight. But the noises that followed were not lupine and she pressed herself yet further down onto her stomach as a small blue rowing boat edged out of the dark shore into the moon rays, the strong certain stroke of oars breaking the glassy surface as it headed for the glistering centre.

The voices carried like torches in the night – bright and flickering, drawing the eye; chattering and excited, catching the ear. Their faces were too far to see from here but as he rowed to the centre of the lake, the moonlight caught on his white shock of blonde hair.

No!

Signy gasped, feeling the tears spring and blurring her wolf-sharp night vision; she brushed them away hotly, her breath ragged with anger as she watched the girl stand and pull her dress over her head. And for a second, she just stood there, legs astride for balance, gloriously naked and bathed in moonlight. The lambent beams stroked over her pale skin as her breasts and belly, hips and legs gleamed like Rodinesque marble. He stared up at her like she was a goddess, his fingers fumbling at his own shirt as he couldn't rip his eyes off her. And then she swung her arms up into a point and curved into the water, the ripples from her splash making the boat rock.

'Wait for me!' he shouted as he wriggled out of the shirt, leaning back to undo his trousers and pull them off as she began swimming away with graceful strokes.

Signy gasped as he stood and balanced too, the moon hitting him like a spotlight. She had never seen a naked man before and her eyes widened that he should look like *that*. In the next instant, he was also in the water, surfacing briefly to whip his hair back before chasing after her, slicing through the water with a dedication and concentration that could only result in one thing. Success.

She would be his.

Nothing else mattered. And certainly no one.

* * *

'Signy?' Bo stood over her, the cup of coffee and two pills in her hands. 'It's me, Bo. I've brought your coffee.'

She put them down on the table and walked over to the fire, prodding at the almost-out ashes before selecting the best log and setting it on top. Then she drew the curtains, sighing at the view. 'It's snowing again.'

Actually, it was snowing so hard it was almost dizzying to watch, huge fat flakes whirling and twirling like pirouetting ballerinas and obscuring the waterfall on the other side of the fjord. Everywhere she looked was white – the sky, the ground, the forest – as the trees' branches dropped low below the weight, shedding their loads in sporadic, startling bursts as squirrels scampered or birds landed upon them. The thick grass roofs had lost their tussocky textures now, swollen into smoothness, and even the smoke from their non-stop puffing chimneys was lost in the snowscape.

'I know you're not dead,' she said with a smile, coming back to the bed and looking down upon the old woman. Her eyelids were shut but Bo could see her eyes moving behind them. 'And I know you're not asleep either.'

Signy's eyes opened, immediately pinning Bo with her hard, accusing stare.

Bo frowned, the smile dying on her lips. 'What is it?'

'I don't like people who upset my grandson.' Without her teeth in, the words were muffled but Bo understood her perfectly.

'What?'

'You heard me,' she said, holding her arms up and out and waiting wordlessly for Bo to hoist her into a seated position.

'I don't understand . . . What has he said to you?' Bo asked a minute later, as she finished arranging the pillows behind her and straightening the blankets.

'Nothing. He did not need to.' She reached over to the glass and put her dentures back in, rolling and stretching her cheeks a few times to get them into position. Finally, she smacked her lips together. 'But I know him well and I know when he has been hurt.'

The word vibrated within her. 'Signy, I haven't hurt him. I wouldn't.' She *couldn't*. It was blindingly clear that she was inconsequential to him.

'I know that look on his face and he had it yesterday when he brought you back here.' She regarded Bo with a fierce look. 'I thought you were different.'

Bo tried to catch up; he had looked as impenetrable as ever to her. 'Well . . . well, how do you know it wasn't one of the others that upset him? He's been spending his whole days with them and I'm sorry to say he really hasn't gone out of his way to be friendly with anyone. He doesn't join in with their conversations or jokes.'

'Pah! He doesn't care about them; they are an irrelevance. He doesn't waste emotion on things or people that don't matter. My God, if life has taught him one thing, it has been that.'

'What do you mean?'

Signy shot her a sharp look. 'Never you mind. But I know what I'm talking about. You don't get to my age without learning a thing or two, and I know about people – who you can trust; who's good; who's worth it. And I can see he likes you. He trusts you. And he doesn't trust many.'

'With all due respect, he hardly knows me.'

'Doesn't he?' The question was like a probe and Bo swallowed, remembering the confidences she had shared with him, telling him things she hadn't told Zac – but only because it had felt safer being one step removed. It had almost been like telling a counsellor or therapist. 'Do you think that every person who comes into your life, you will need to spend *years* getting to know?' Signy asked. 'Pff! Some – the special ones – come already matched. You fit together like pieces in a puzzle. Don't ask me why, they just do. And it is so with you and Anders; I knew it when I heard you talking together from my chair.'

Bo looked down, feeling her heart knocking against her ribs for there was a slant of truth in the old woman's words: she *did* feel she knew him better than a week's acquaintance would ordinarily suggest. He was easy to be around and she could sit in silence with him, which was always an issue for her; silences had made her jumpy ever since . . . ever since that night. But they also clashed. He hurt her with his brusque manner and careless words, and though he and she might recognize *something* in each other, it wasn't necessarily good. She felt judged by him, as though she disappointed him in some way. 'I think you're reading too much into it,' she said quietly. 'He's been very kind to me but he has made it perfectly clear that ours is a professional relationship. We're not friends, nor does he want us to be.'

'You are mistaken.'

'No, we had a disagreement the other night and that's why he was upset. He's angry with me, not hurt by me.'

'People disagree all the time; it means nothing. If you ask me –'

But Bo hadn't, she thought.

'– You are allowing your opinions of him to be swayed by *your* friends. They do not understand him, he doesn't play their way, therefore they do not like him. But I wonder – would you care so much about their feelings if you knew they didn't care about yours?'

Bo felt a wave of indignation rise up in her at that. What was she insinuating? That they'd all been having a better time here without her? She remembered the photographs on Lenny's camera – they certainly hadn't been moping about, missing her. 'I don't know what you're talking about. Of course my friends care about me.'

Signy's eyebrow hitched up. 'I have watched you from my windows, all of you. There is not much more for me to do, after all. I see everything,' she said enigmatically.

Oh, great, Bo thought to herself. Now she was the all-seeing eye? 'Well, luckily for me, I'm used to being watched. We all are, it's in the job description,' she said tightly, all out of patience for this conversation now. Like her grandson, Signy had managed to offend, insult and hurt her. Was it a family gift? She walked over to the door again, wishing she hadn't bothered coming round. So much for being kind to the elderly. 'Drink your coffee while it's hot. Anders will be here in twenty minutes.'

Signy stared over at her, watching her disengagement with an expression that might – in certain lights – look like regret. 'He is not what you think,' she said, more softly now.

Bo was quiet for a moment. 'But who ever is?' she said with a shrug before closing the door.

Chapter Eighteen

He arrived at the farm as if by stealth – it was impossible to predict how he would travel: as Zac had mocked the first morning, it might be by land, sea or air. Not that she was watching for him. The falling snow was simply mesmerizing and she sat side-on on one of the chairs by the window, her knees tucked under her chin, watching the flurries, snow falling upon snow. It felt like the world was filling up, the hard angles of the mountains now rubbed out, even sound itself becoming rounder, plumper, softer. The view over the fjord would have been utterly perfect were it not for the numerous brown beer bottles sticking out of the snow on the window-sill. 'Nature's fridge,' Lenny had said when she'd asked him about them.

'Hey, man,' Zac murmured, glancing up from the table. He was writing up the latest blog post. 'Coffee's made if you want some.'

'No thanks,' Anders said, stamping his feet on the mat to dislodge the snow. Bo deduced he must have arrived by skidoo; she'd have heard the helicopter and seen him come over the ridge from the water. He pushed his hood off, sending another shower of snow onto the floor, and unzipped the jacket, his gaze catching Bo's as she sat by the window.

'Hi,' she said, giving a weak smile and wondering if Signy

had told him they'd had words this morning. She reached for some small talk, something to hide their uneasiness with each other. She didn't want Zac to know about the argument. How could she explain it to him when she still didn't understand it herself? Being upset by the troll had been one thing, but why had she turned on him? Why did it matter what he did or didn't think about her? '. . . No helicopter today?'

'Visibility is too poor. I took the skidoo.'

Zac looked up again. 'Ah! The new one we financed for you?'

Anders shrugged. 'It's good.'

'So then our being here isn't *all* bad. We've brought you *some* good cheer.' A note of sarcasm edged the words like a frill and Bo knew her fiancé was frustrated by Anders' impermeability. He was used to befriending everyone he met and he was almost affronted that Anders had rebuffed his attempts at friendship.

Anders looked at nothing in particular. 'It is fine that you are here. And I think you are coping surprisingly well with the basic facilities.'

'High praise! Well, I did tell you – we're wanderers, not tourists.'

Anders nodded like he didn't care either way, coming further into the room. 'So I have a different plan for today,' he said, standing like he was about to give a sermon. 'It does not involve waterfalls or caves but I think you will like it.'

'Yeah? I'm intrigued. Spill.'

Anders looked confused. '. . . What?'

'Spill. Spill the beans,' Zac said, attempting to clarify. 'Tell us.'

'Oh.' Anders looked wrong-footed by the colloquialism and, Bo thought, momentarily vulnerable. He was so used to being in control. 'Well, I need to get my grandmother her Christmas tree so I thought you could come with me and we will get you all one too. For here.' He indicated the cabin. 'I assume you will want one? Christmas is in five days.'

Bo bit her lip. Was it really only five days to Christmas? She had lost track of the dates since her accident and falling sick, and the remoteness of the farm meant that with no shops or TV, they were fully out of the festive loop. She realized she hadn't done any shopping at all. Was it too late to send a parcel home? When was the last shipping day from here? Her mind began to race . . .

'You want us to go *shopping* for *trees*?' Zac asked disappointedly, as though Anders had suggested going for a pedicure together instead.

Anders didn't move but Bo could see the suppressed sigh ripple through him. 'We would not buy it. I meant we get it from the forest. We cut it down ourselves.'

'Oh!' Zac's eyes widened. That changed things entirely. 'Are you allowed to do that?'

'Of course. This is my family's farm. We own the land and whatever is on it.'

Zac looked over at Bo, excitement all over his face. 'That sounds pretty fucking A, wouldn't you say, babe?'

Sometimes Bo thought he was twenty-six going on twelve. 'I would.'

'I mean, how – what's the word? Higgle?'

'*Hygge*,' she supplied.

'How *hygge* is that? Cutting down our own tree.' His eyes brightened further still. 'And perhaps we could do some logging as well?' he asked Anders.

'Sure. If that's your idea of a good time,' Anders said in typical wry fashion. 'The stocks are beginning to get low anyway.'

'The fans will lap it up. Me as a Norwegian lumberjack . . . Wait till we tell Len. Hey, Len!'

'Heard you,' Len's muffled voice came through the floorboards.

Bo arched an eyebrow and looked across at Zac. She had presumed Lenny had stayed over in the storehouse with Anna. Unless of course Anna was up there too?

'Like it?' Zac called.

'Sounds great,' he replied in a monotone.

'Well, move your ass then and get down here. What are you doing up there anyway?'

Bo closed her eyes, not wanting to hear the answer. If Anna was up there with him . . . But the sound of the latch turning was answer enough, for a moment later Anna herself was stamping her snowy boots on the mat too. 'Morning!'

Uh-oh.

'Coffee's on the stove if you want some,' Bo said, knowing this was where it was going to get awkward. It had been a one-night thing after all then, exactly as predicted.

'Thanks. Hey, Anders,' Anna said, passing him.

'Hey.'

'Want a coffee?'

'No, I'm fine.'

He looked so awkward, standing stiffly in the room while Anna made herself at home, clattering about confidently, knowing where all the cutlery was kept and which cupboard held the cups.

Why did he hold himself apart, Bo wondered, just as Lenny's heavy tread came down the ladder too.

'Morning all,' he mumbled, looking wild.

'Anna's getting the coffee if you want some?' Bo said,

watching as he crossed the room and trying to gauge their body language.

'Yeah, thanks,' he said, throwing her a sarcastic smile as he opened the fridge. 'Because coffee isn't actually the drink of the devil.' He pulled out a bottle of Coke, taking a swig and swallowing down a burp.

'Oh yeah, sorry,' she muttered. He never drank coffee, hence his sugar-drink addiction. She'd just been so distracted, scrutinizing him and Anna together . . . She noticed they hadn't greeted each other yet. And that Anna was keeping her head down as she poured the milk.

It was definitely off between them.

'So, Anders, we went skiing yesterday,' Zac said, finishing his post, slamming the laptop shut and tipping back in his chair. 'Place called Strandafjellet?'

'Yes, I saw. It looked good. Lots of powder.'

'You saw?' Bo asked, forgetting momentarily that they weren't 'officially' talking.

He looked across at her and again she felt like he was pushing her, unbalancing her. 'If you remember, you linked me up to your account so I am now one of your nine million followers.'

There it was again, that sly disassociation. He followed them but not really. Not because he wanted to.

'Uh, uh, uh. 9.7 million followers,' Lenny corrected him. 'And we're within a fairy's fart of 9.8.'

'Right,' Anders said flatly.

'Did you see my action shot of Bo?' Lenny went on, oblivious.

'Of course.'

Lenny arched an eyebrow, waiting. '. . . And . . . Did you

like it?' Bo knew from his tone what he was thinking: blood; stone.

'It was good.'

'Good?' Zac laughed. 'It's great! Lenny here's the man! A lot of pro sports photographers couldn't have got that shot. He had to lie down in the middle of the piste to get the angle right. One missed turn by Bo and she would've sliced right into him.'

'Nice,' Bo said sarcastically, wrinkling her nose. 'Powerful image right there.'

'That was a dangerous thing to do,' Anders said sombrely. 'Other people might not have seen him. It could have caused an accident.'

Zac, getting up from the chair, groaned. 'Oh my God, chill the fuck *out*,' he part-wailed, part-laughed, throwing his arms around like a gibbon. 'It was quiet. It was fine. And he got the shot.'

'And, thanks to that, the suit you wore, Bo?' Anna interjected. 'Already sold out. Like that.' She clicked her fingers. 'All online stock gone in an hour, they told me.'

'That's my girl,' Zac said, wrapping his arms around Bo and kissing her cheek. 'Star quality.'

Bo gave an embarrassed smile, opening her eyes to find Lenny, Anna and Anders all watching. Everyone always watching them. All the time.

Bo went to get her phone, which was charging in the bedroom. She shrugged on the yellow jacket as the others pushed their feet into their boots and traipsed outside. Pulling up the hood, she glanced down at her notifications on the way out. Six missed calls – all by an unidentified number, no doubt marketing spam – and myriad direct messages. But one caught her eye, the one she was forever watching out for.

I know ure fucking him.

With every footstep, the snow creaked like old barn doors. It was pristine, virginal; the silence inside the forest, beside the fjord, somehow amplified and lifted. The branches of the conifers were bent almost to the ground, the snow upon them as thick as her arms and the dotted tracks of animals – rabbit, deer, lynx – laced the snow. Their own footprints were, by comparison, heavy and sluggish behind them, enormous oval depressions that smashed and scattered the tightly drawn surface.

Anders was setting his usual brisk pace up the steep slope and making no allowance for her having been unwell, seemingly having forgotten altogether. It was back to normal – for all of them.

Bo, feeling shaken by the troll's latest contact, was hanging around the back of the pack, letting Anders and Zac go ahead. They were carrying the axes, which must have weighed six pounds each and Zac's face when Anders had presented them outside had made Bo realize he had assumed they'd be felling the trees with chainsaws. Lenny, naturally, was bringing up the rear and Anna was two paces ahead of her, sounding breathless and tired already, a lit cigarette perched between her fingers. They were all walking in a single file through the woods, the fjord to their left, the indigo water glimpsed in fringed snatches through the trees.

Bo kept looking up at the treetops, staggering as she went. It was easy to underestimate the sheer size of these coniferous giants until she went and stood beside them. Most were at least six metres high, with branches so strong and thick, the 'skirts' were two, three metres in diameter – far too big for the wooden cabins, they wouldn't even get through the door. Everything about the forest felt ancient and overscaled. How would they ever find anything to fit?

But unlike their usual treks, they didn't have to go far this time, Anders stopping and putting down his backpack within ten minutes of setting out. The crop of trees was significantly smaller here, a young copse set within the forest like a small patch within a quilt. Zac immediately buzzed around, patting the trunks like they were mates in the bar and declaring which trees he thought were best.

'I like this beauty,' he said, pointing to one decisively. Bo heard the click-click-click of Lenny's camera. 'Good shape. Not straggly at the top but not too wide at the base.'

Anders gave a cursory glance over. 'No,' he said, turning his attention straight back to unpacking his backpack.

'No? What do you mean no?'

'That one is three metres. You can't go over two and a half at the most. The ceilings.' He put his hand above his head to make the point.

'It doesn't look three metres from where I'm standing.'

'Well it is.'

'You sure?'

'Yes.'

A spasm of irritation flickered across Zac's face. He didn't like being told 'no'. 'Then we're going to have to agree to disagree, buddy. I've got good spatial perception and I think the size is fine. I like it and I think it'll look great in our cosy cabin. Don't you, Bo?'

'Huh?'

'Don't you think this is the one? Straight, bushy, good shape.'

'Uh . . . Sure.' She smiled at Zac but she could feel Anders' disapproval towards her radiate like a heat beam across the snow.

'Okay, fine,' Anders said lightly, bringing over hard hats for them all, goggles for him and Zac. 'You can have that one. Have you ever felled a tree before?'

'Nope. But it's on my bucket list.'

'Okay. So then the most important thing to know is that we're going to begin by cutting on the side which we want the tree to fall. Which is . . . there,' he said, pointing uphill. 'There is space for it to land without damaging the other trees. And it will be the right way round for dragging back.'

Bo inwardly groaned. She hadn't thought about that – they were going to need to get these trees back home again.

'When we cut, we come in at a forty-five-degree angle to create a notch. I will swing. Then you. We create a rhythm, okay?'

'Sure.'

Anders put on the goggles. 'Please, stand back,' he said to her, Anna and Lenny.

But Lenny, camera already to his face, was if anything inching closer. Hearing the silence, he looked up. 'What? You don't mean *me*, surely? I've got to get in there; capture the action.'

Anders merely arched an eyebrow in reply.

'Just get back, Lenny,' Bo muttered.

'Oh, come on.'

'We've already had one disaster on this mountain,' Anders said. 'Let's not make it two.'

Bo flashed a glance over at him. Was that blame in his voice?

'Jeez,' Lenny groaned, rolling his eyes like a teenager but stepping up the slope to join them.

Everyone waited – camera and camera-phones poised. Anders walked around the tree once, assessing it, before readying the axe at the base. Then, with a deep inhale, he swung it over his shoulder and brought it back round, slicing straight into the trunk.

The sound reverberated through the forest, a few unseen birds in neighbouring trees taking flight and sending great beams of snow pattering to the ground.

Zac copied him, looking more hesitant but only for the first few strokes. Within minutes they had a rhythm. They each recorded it all, Anna supplying a running commentary. 'Yeah, that's it . . . nice stroke! . . . it's getting there . . . not much more . . .'

Bo wished she would shut up.

'Okay, and let's stop,' Anders said, panting lightly and pushing back the goggles. He inspected the notch. It was deep, cutting into the halfway point of the tree. 'Good. Now for the other side.'

With not a minute to rest, they began cutting from the opposite direction until another notch was carved. They stopped sooner than they had on the first side, only the slenderest margin of wood fibres remaining intact; Anders was looking up at the tree, one hand held in the air. 'She's going . . .' he said, even though the tree appeared completely motionless.

Bo waited, breath held nervously. Was he absolutely sure the tree would definitely fall uphill?

But a moment later, a deep, plaintive creak issued from the tree as it slowly, elegantly, toppled over. Uphill.

'Nice work,' Anders smiled, reaching over to shake Zac's hand. Genuine animation! Everyone looked amazed.

'That was incredible!' Zac grinned, turning to their cameras and pulling various muscle-man poses, including the obligatory foot-on-the-stump shot.

'Well, I'm glad you liked it,' Anders said. 'Because now we have to do it again.'

Zac's smile faltered. 'Oh, shit, yeah.' Both of them were red-cheeked and panting, sweat at their hairlines as they took off the helmets, and Bo knew Zac had been overdoing it, playing to the camera and forgetting this wasn't the only tree to fell. Or drag home.

Both men sank into the snow for a rest, Zac falling back dramatically like a snow angel.

'Bo, go sit on the stump,' Lenny said, readying the camera again. 'Let's get some shots of you while they recover.'

She did as he asked, drawing her knees up and hugging her arms around them, pixie-style, tipping her head one way, then the other. The yellow jacket was paying dividends again, warm and waterproof and a good contrast to the black-green palette of the trees. Another great shot; she already knew how this would read: the Wanderlusters at play in the Norwegian forests, cutting down their own Christmas tree!

'Okay, great,' Lenny said, releasing her from modelling duties.

'So which tree are you having, Anders?' Anna asked, lighting up another cigarette. Bo hadn't realized she was such a heavy smoker.

'That one.'

'*That* one?' Zac laughed at the sight of it. There was no doubt it was one of the smallest in the copse. 'But it's just a stripling. I've seen toilet brushes bigger than that!'

It did look pathetically feeble. The branches were bushy enough and the shape pleasingly symmetrical but it was knee-high to the rest of the trees in the forest.

Anders shrugged. 'It is the right size.'

'Well,' Zac grinned. 'At least it shouldn't take us too long to get that one down. Hey, we can get Bo to sneeze on it, that should do the trick,' he guffawed.

Bo met Anders' gaze for a moment but he looked away instantly, refusing to connect, and she felt that faint nausea in the pit of her stomach again. They couldn't leave things like this; they needed to clear the air and she knew it had to come from her. She had been the antagonist after all – drunk and wanting an argument, like he'd said.

'Ready?' Anders asked him.

'Sure. Anytime,' Zac replied lackadaisically, as though he hadn't been tired at all.

'Actually, I'd like to have a go,' Bo said as they both stood.

'What? Why?' Zac asked, looking confounded.

'Why not?'

'Because you're—'

'A woman?' she interrupted, fixing him with a defiant stare, daring him to say it.

'No! I was going to say unwell. You've been unwell and you're not back to full strength yet.'

'Did that stop me skiing yesterday? Or hiking up here today?'

Zac, looking bashful, held out his axe to her. 'Fine, then.'

Bo was tempted to ask – in the name of female solidarity – whether Anna wanted to have a go too, but given that she was supposed to be strictly behind the scenes, decided against it. Besides, she didn't think Anna had the same need to hit the bejesus out of something in the way she did. Her earlier upset in the bedroom had morphed into anger now. She was fed up of being bullied, intimidated, harassed. Since when had she become a victim?

'So you saw what we did, yes?' Anders asked her as she weighed up the axe. It was surprisingly heavy. 'Stand in a wide stance and make an across-the-body motion. Do not go straight down or you will chop off your feet.'

She shot him one of her sarcastic smiles. 'You do love to go straight to the worse-case disaster scenarios, don't you?'

Anders didn't smile back. 'Because they are there. The risks are real.'

It was the longest he had looked at her and she wished he didn't look so pained by it. 'I've got it. I understand,' she said quietly.

'Let me go for the first five strokes, just to get the cut going.'

'Okay.'

He circled the tree again almost ritualistically, assessing it, before looking back at the trees surrounding them. 'It will go this way,' he said, pointing out the fall line.

Standing on the opposite side of the trunk to him, she watched and waited as he got himself into a balanced position, slowing down his breathing again. And then he began to swing.

Bo counted . . . Two, three, four, five . . .

Her own arm swung, the axe cutting into the groove with a satisfying *thunk*. She laughed, delighted, pulling back for him, before repeating it. Over and over they swung, getting caught up in the rhythm, and when Anders' hand came up for her to stop, it felt too soon.

They walked to the other side and five strokes each was all it took before he stopped her. She held her breath again, feeling the suspense as the tree – beautiful and lush – held firm and stood tall for one final moment before toppling graciously to the floor, like a crinolined Victorian lady in a swoon.

Bo clapped excitedly, feeling a rush of pride in herself.

Anders walked up and shook her hand, his enveloping hers like a bear's paw. 'Well done,' he said, a smile in his eyes that for once didn't knock her over but lifted her up, and for a second she wondered if he'd forgiven her for her behaviour.

But he let her hand drop, turning to the others. 'Now we need to get these back.'

'And then, rest,' Zac said.

'And then, logging,' Anders corrected with a smile. 'You still want to be a Norwegian lumberjack, right?'

Even travelling downhill, it was hard-going. Lenny was no use at all, of course, his camera to his eye as he photographed Anders and Anna, and her and Zac carrying the trees back. Zac had suggested dragging them but Anders had replied it was a matter of personal taste whether he liked having a Christmas tree with needles on or not, which had made everyone else laugh.

In spite of Bo's stand for equality when it came to chopping the trees, carrying them was another matter and she had only lasted a few minutes taking the greater weight at the base. Anders had managed to loosely wrap the trees by rolling them in a sheet of muslin folded in his backpack, pinning the branches up and in, so that the tree could be carried, tip down.

Zac was breathing heavily three metres behind her, urging her to go faster, but what had taken ten minutes to climb, took almost double that to get down with a tree to carry and they collectively breathed a sigh of relief as they emerged into the farm's clearing.

'Thank *God*,' Anna groaned, dropping the tree on the path and easing out her arms with a grimace of pain. 'I'm not going to be able to move tomorrow.'

Bo didn't think she would either. She had woken up with stiff legs from skiing yesterday; now she could add back and arms to that for tomorrow.

'I'll take it from here,' Anders said to Anna, lifting the tree easily onto his shoulder and taking it round to his grand-mother's cabin.

Anna looked on in disbelief. 'He totally didn't even need me to carry that with him,' she gasped as he disappeared around the corner. Tomorrow's aches could have been entirely avoidable.

'Maybe he thought you wanted the genuine lumberjacking experience too?' Bo suggested.

'But I am Norwegian! *I* don't need it!' she cried, still stretching out her arms.

Bo laughed.

'Come on then, let's get ours up. I'll take it for this last bit,' Zac sighed, hoisting their tree onto his shoulder too, just as he had seen Anders do, but he staggered forwards, his knees buckling under the greater weight of it.

Bo helped to steady him by catching the tip end and taking some of the weight.

'It's fine. I've got it,' he grunted, trying to find a better hold.

'Zac, let me help.'

'I said I've got it. Let go.'

Bo gave an impatient sigh. It was quite clear that he would fall the second she let him take the full weight. 'This is a much bigger tree than Anders' one. He couldn't carry this alone either. It's fine. We'll both take it.'

Zac's eyes narrowed slightly as he saw that she was mollifying his ego, but he gave a grudging nod of consent regardless.

'Anna,' Bo said. 'Anders said there's a large bucket in the stables downstairs that will be ideal for standing our tree in. Could you get it? And, Lenny, why don't you make yourself useful too and help fill it with earth?'

Lenny frowned. 'What earth? Everything's covered in snow!'

'Then dig, man. Dig!' she smiled, as Zac slowly, carefully walked round to their front door and opened it.

'Where shall we put it?' she asked, trying to stop the back end of the tree from swiping everything off the walls and surfaces as he walked ahead of her.

'By the window?' His voice was strained from the effort.

'No,' she mused. 'It'll block out the light, there's too little as it is.'

'Well it can't go by the stove. It'll be too hot, the needles will fall off,' he panted.

'Bedroom?'

'Hardly fair on Lenny,' he muttered.

'But he's not going to be here. He's going home for the holidays.'

'No he's not.'

'*What?*' Bo almost dropped her end of the tree, making Zac stagger. She caught hold of it again.

'Must we discuss this now?' he cried, turning hopelessly, looking for a space.

'There.' She pointed to the far corner, opposite the front door. 'Put it down in the corner there.'

'But then it's obscured behind Lenny's ladder.'

'Oh, just put it down, Zac,' she snapped.

Taking the tree off his shoulder, they laid it out on the floor. Outside, she could see Anna and Lenny with the bucket, but they weren't digging, they were arguing. It was the first time Bo had seen them talk to each other all day, she realized.

She saw the tight anger in Anna's face, the lazy shrug in Lenny's shoulders and she knew everything she had feared was coming to pass. But she couldn't deal with their doomed affair right now. She turned back into the room and straightened up to face him, her hands on her hips. 'What do you mean that Lenny's not going home for Christmas?'

'I was going to tell you. I only just found out myself.'

'Found out what exactly?'

'He's got no one to go back to. His mum and step-dad are on some cruise in the Caribbean – they figured he'd be with us. What's the point in him spending all that money to go home if no one's there?'

'Okay then, fine – he doesn't go home. He goes to see friends. Or takes a spa break. I don't care, but he's not staying with us!'

'Why not?'

'What do you mean why not?' she cried. 'Zac, it's Christmas. There have got to be times when it is just the two of us. He cannot *always* be here.'

Zac sighed, dropping his head. 'Bo, we've been over this—'

'Yes! And you're not hearing me!' she said, pressing her hands to her chest. 'Look at me, Zac – we *need* some private time together. We need it. Things have been tricky recently – you must have felt it too? Ever since we got here, it's like we've been permanently out of sync. First Anders joined the ranks, then Anna—'

'She's nothing to do with it.'

'I'm not saying she is directly, and neither is Anders. But it's everything collectively, don't you see that? We are never alone. Ever.'

'We are in bed.' He winked at her and she knew it was his way of trying to get her off-track.

'This is serious, Zac. We can't continue like this. Sometimes I think your main relationship is with Lenny, not me. *I* feel like the spare part.'

'That's just crazy.'

'Is it though? You never listen to what I have to say on things.'

'Yeah? Like when? When have I not listened to you?'

Bo didn't even hesitate. 'The other day when I tried to stop you from agreeing to pay Anders in dollars.'

'That was different.'

'No, it wasn't different; it was typical. And coming here, for example – it was *your* idea after you read about the mountain that's gonna fall down. Then *Lenny* negotiated where we'd live – in a cabin with no central heating or hot water. Excellent choice, Len. He even arranged for Anna to be out here with us, providing a very nice upside for him in the process but which is now going tits-up outside as we speak.'

Zac gave a weary sigh. 'I am so damn freaking tired of having the same argument over and over again, Bo. How many times do we have to go over it? We cannot do this – we cannot be *us* – without him.' He stared at her incomprehendingly. 'We are two hundred thousand followers short of hitting ten million. The fans are loving this place. They're loving what we're doing. And we can't do what we're doing without Lenny.'

Bo blinked at him. He really didn't get it. 'You see, that's the problem, Zac. When I talk about 'us', you talk about the brand. For you, they're one and the same.'

'Because they are!' he cried.

She crossed her arms. 'So if the blog folded tomorrow, if we just stopped posting: no more photos, no more Stories . . . would there still be an us?'

Zac looked at her like she was mad. 'Wha—? Why are you even asking me that? It's a pointless question. Why would we stop? This is the dream! Everyone wants what we have, to live like this. They want to *be* us.'

It wasn't an answer to her question and her heart plummeted further with his every word. She tried again, pushing him. '. . . I'm speaking hypothetically Zac, would you still want to be with me, without ten million people watching us?'

He stared at her. '. . . Of course I would.' But the hesitation had been there. They'd both heard it. He simply couldn't imagine what it would be like for them to go back to being just a couple in love. He had bought into the hype. He believed the life encapsulated on the grid was the real Zac and Bo; that was where his reality lay. But hers . . . hers was on the other side of the lens – or the grid. For her, their real life lay in what they didn't show – their whispered conversations on the pillow at night, sharing a spoon for pudding, going for a walk just for a walk's sake . . . She felt a glaze crackle across her heart as she realized it had been weeks since they'd shared a moment like that together. Oh God. When exactly had this happened to them?

Zac blinked, watching the emotions flicker across her face. 'Look, I know you find it hard to let people in. You went on the road for very different reasons to me. I just wanted adventure, but you . . . you needed escape.'

'Oh. No—' She turned away, not wanting to talk about this now. Not ever.

Zac walked over to her. 'Yes. A terrible thing happened to you, Bo. Your brother died in your arms. You were trapped with his body for three hours before help came.' She scrunched her eyes shut, her head turned away from him, but he clasped her with a tight grip, making her face him, face *it*. 'I can't even imagine what it must have been like for you, baby, in the cold and the dark like that. And I know how hard it is for you sometimes, to shake it off. I sleep next to you, remember? Your nightmares are my nightmares.' His voice softened further still. 'So I get it, I know why you ran. But being here with me because you can't face going home, is a different thing to being here with me because you want and choose it for itself. And when you go on and on about Lenny being the root of our problems, or the blog, or the fans, I'm scared that what you're really saying is – it's me. Us. This. That you don't actually want *this* life, it's all just a diversion from the one you're too scared to go back to.'

She stared at him, her mouth agape. Was he right? Was all of this just an elaborate deception from herself, a way to not have to think or feel about her past? For a moment, her words and thoughts wouldn't come, the room disappearing as her eyes blurred with hot tears. 'No, I . . . I do choose this. I choose y—'

But the sound of scurrying feet made them both turn as Anna and Lenny carried the bucket in between them, both of them hunched over and straining at the weight of it. Bo pulled away roughly from Zac, turning her back to the room as she quickly dried her tears. She didn't want them to see her crying.

'Where . . . ?' Lenny panted.

'Uh . . . here,' Zac said, glancing across at Bo before taking the weight of it from Anna and helping Lenny carry it to the corner.

With a sniff and a deep breath, Bo turned back with a smile stitched on. But as her gaze met with Anna's, she immediately saw she wasn't the only one upset; Anna's mascara had smudged ever so slightly beneath the lashes; she had been crying too. What had Lenny said to her out there?

A moment of unspoken solidarity flashed between them as the guys grunted, getting the heavy bucket into the perfect position.

Lenny dropped his hands to his thighs, trying to get his breath back. 'The ground is fucking frozen, man. Frozen! I had to use a pickaxe.'

Zac slapped him on the back. 'And you've done a great job. Come on, let's get this baby up and then we can chill.'

Bo kept quiet – even if it wasn't the time to remind him about the logging, his words were still ricocheting around her. Did he really think those things? Was the problem not with him or Lenny or the blog, but her? And if it was, what did that mean for them?

She watched in silence as, with loud grunts of effort, both men hoisted the tree off the floor and positioned it over the bucket, Lenny scrabbling furiously to dig a hole in which to place the trunk. Only, as they tried to straighten it . . .

They all looked up at the sound. The tree was wedged at a catastrophic angle, a good forty centimetres too high for the ceiling, and the bucket was tipped onto its bottom rim, unable to sit flat.

'Ah!' Anna said quietly into the thick silence.

'I guess we could cut the top off,' Lenny suggested after a minute.

'But then it'll be out of proportion if we just hack the top off and have these massive branches splayed against the ceiling,' Zac frowned. 'I don't get it. It looked the perfect size in the forest.'

'Yeah, because everything else was huge in comparison, man,' Lenny drawled. 'It's called per-spec-tive.'

'No shit, Sherlock,' Zac muttered.

They all stared up at it dejectedly.

'We could go cut another one,' Lenny suggested.

'Oh, could *we*? Well, if you're gonna do the cutting this time instead of standing around taking pictures—'

'Hey! *I* was working up there, making you look good.'

Zac muttered meanly under his breath, looking furious, and Bo knew the real reason he was angry was because Anders had been proved right. What was more, he'd known he'd been right even as he'd agreed to help fell it. He had known this would happen, that Zac would be left looking foolish.

She glanced through the still-open door. In the window she could see through to Signy's cabin – the lights were on, and the fronds of their tree were just visible, reaching beyond the frame. It was standing proudly upright and Anders was fastening on red ribbons. Bo turned back to the comedy of errors on their side of the path.

'I know what we'll do,' Zac said decisively. 'Lenny, you take the top, I'll push the base.'

'Where are we . . . taking it . . . ?' Lenny grunted, trying to dislodge the top of the tree from its new groove in the ceiling, the whole thing coming unstuck quite suddenly and almost sending him sprawling in a spray of pine needles.

'Just here,' Zac said, lifting the base and – with the entire tree held at an angle just off horizontal – positioning it at the

319

bottom of the ladder. They straightened it and the top of the tree immediately disappeared, unobstructed, straight through the hatch up to Lenny's loft.

'There. Perfect,' Zac said, wiping his hands together.

'Oh yeah,' Lenny scowled, seeing how the branches splayed onto the rungs of the ladder and made access to his room nigh on impossible. 'Just perfect.'

Chapter Nineteen

Lodal, early August 1936

Signy walked slowly through the wild orchard, reaching up to pull cherries from the bough, to weigh an apple in her hand. She took a bite, sliding down the smooth trunk of a damson tree, and sat in the grass, watching as light glittered off the surface of the water, the leap and splash of a fish sending wrinkles out to the shore. On the opposite side, the little blue rowing boat nudged the grassy bank, keeping secret the stories held within its timbers on the nights it glided silently under the moon. Signy stared at it, one hand carelessly caressing Stormy's kid, Clouds, who was seeking rest in the shade, her nose nuzzling against her palm.

The summer felt endless, the days without end, the never-setting sun playing in the sky and making them all restless. Sleep was short in spite of their exhausting days and everyone was edgy. Kari had said it was because they all had their curse but Signy wasn't so sure. Several times now she had crept from the cabin at night, the moon picking out her path as she stole up the slopes and lay on her belly to watch as the midnight swimmers rowed the little boat into the centre of this silvered lake, their laughter curling in the silence.

Did the others know about the lovers? Or sense it some-how? The very fabric of their companionship had become abrasive: Kari and Ashi kept fighting, Brit had fallen sullen and even Margit was distracted and short, disappearing on long walks for 'time alone'. Of course, they had been up here in the valley for nearly two months now. Apart from the Mid-summer festival and the weekly visit from one of the farm labourers, they had had no respite from each other in all that time, no other distraction. They had told all their stories, read their books, darned all their knitting. Tempers were bound to begin to fray.

Which was surely why it should have rung alarm bells that Sofie was so happy. In the weeks following her discovery, Signy had watched on in mute dismay as Sofie had set about her chores with an enthusiasm and grace never seen before. She smiled as she milked the cows. She told jokes as she churned the butter. She glowed from the inside as they all bathed in the stream and even Kari had begrudgingly remarked she looked even more beautiful than usual.

Signy longed to confide in Margit or Kari, to tell them what she had seen. But how could she? Her sister was set to be engaged to Rag, and Kari's own brother was hoping to pro-pose to Sofie. If the truth about their trysts was to come out, the matches that had been preordained by all their families would be in tatters.

Even worse than that was the friendships that would be lost. Margit loved Sofie. She saw only the good in her – the vulnerability and frailties, the unfairness of her position in being born to a cotter. If she was ever to discover that her dearest friend had been betraying her in this cruel way . . . If Kari and Ashi and Brit were to find out that their brother was being humiliated, a cuckold even before the proposal . . . It could tear the village apart. So she kept her silence – but she watched and she waited. Like the wolf circling the plateau, she stayed just out of sight.

She knew he was out there. She felt his lupine presence like the breeze on her skin, and sometimes she thought she could see him so clearly in her mind's eye – his head low, shoulders slinking, paws padding silently on the grass, yellow eyes fixed upon them – it was as though he was the one trotting beside her and not Stormy headbutting her knees. She took the knife everywhere with her now, hiding it every evening in a crevice in the aspen tree just over the stream as she returned from her day's herding. She knew the wolf could go almost a month without eating and it had been three weeks since she had first heard its howl. He had to be hungry, he had to be waiting for his moment to strike. And when it came, she would be ready for it.

She could feel it coming on the air, the season at its peak now. The temperatures had soared, making their physical work more laborious and their nights stickier, and yet change was already on the march. In another month, things would be entirely different again, the summer over. Their work at the *seter* was almost done – the lambs and kids had grown leggy and plump, the bulk of the winter hay was now gathered and stored, and their dairy yield was up on last year. And in the valley, after a wet spring and dry summer, she knew there would be an early harvest; within two weeks, the men in the village would be bringing in the crops.

Already the nights were gently stretching and darkening and the girls were beginning to anticipate their return to the village – their mothers' embraces, their sweethearts' smiles. Signy wondered whether Margit would look for Rag; he was due to go back for military training after the harvest. Would their engagement be announced before that? She hadn't asked her big sister about her dreams the morning after Midsummer's night but the posy had been found nonetheless and was now set in a small glass vial beside her bed, the flowers papery and faded in the heat.

To her surprise, Signy had taken comfort in the sight of it. She had always ridiculed her friends' superstitions but now she saw it was a portent. For twice in the past week, she had waited for the howl and then the soft click of Sofie's door, following her up to the lake – and twice Rag hadn't shown. Sofie's mood had blackened sharply, and Kari had warned her only this morning to keep well away after Sofie kicked a milk churn at her for staring at her 'the wrong way'.

Maybe, just maybe, Destiny – if that was what it was called – was getting back on track.

* * *

'Signy?' Bo said in her morning voice. 'It's me, Bo. I've brought your coffee.' She set the mug and pills down on the nightstand and walked over to the fire, poking and prodding it, before rolling on a log and replacing the guard. 'It's stopped snowing,' she sighed, pulling back the curtains and looking up at the clear lilac sky as only the wispiest skeins of cloud drifted overhead.

She turned back to find Signy already watching her, looking straight down her nose like Queen Victoria lying in state. 'Ah, you're awake.'

'Not dead yet,' Signy muttered.

Bo walked over and without needing to be asked, helped her up to sitting, plumping and rearranging her pillows behind her. She waited as Signy put her teeth in and swallowed her tablets.

'How are you feeling today?' Bo asked.

'Why do you care? You're not my nurse.'

Bo sighed. Oh dear. It was like that this morning, was it? 'No. No, I'm not. But I just want to be sure you're okay and there's nothing I can do for you? It's so isolated up here.'

'*Splendid* isolation, I think they call it,' she said fiercely.

Bo suppressed a sigh. Eight o'clock was early to start an argument by anyone's standards. Was it the only way she could wake up, perhaps? 'Your Christmas tree looks great.'

It was the right thing to have said and a smile softened her. Finally. 'Yes. Anders always gets it just right.' Her eyes glimmered shrewdly. 'He said yours is far too big.'

Bo refused to rise to the bait. 'I'm afraid so, yes.' Lenny had had to climb the ladder last night wearing his coat to protect him from the needles – although she couldn't imagine how he was going to get down again this morning. It was one thing pushing up against the branches, quite another coming down on them. 'But anyway, even if it had fitted, it's still pretty sorry-looking. We don't have any decorations for it of course, so it's just standing there, naked as a baby.'

'That is why you are going to Alesund today?'

'That's right. Anna says there's a Christmas market down by the wharves. We're going to meet the rest of her team while we're there too.'

'Anna? Now she's the hussy?'

Bo stiffened. Why couldn't Signy just . . . play nice? 'No, she's the *marketing rep* for the company we're endorsing out here,' she said patiently. She would not be riled by her today. She would not.

Signy pushed her head a little further back into her pillow. 'Hmph, I know what I saw.'

Bo took a deep breath. If what Anna and Lenny got up to was none of her business, she failed to see why Signy should make it hers. 'Well, anyway, we're making an early start today on account of the journey. So if you're sure you're okay . . .' She went to turn away but Signy held her hand out suddenly, her eyes beseeching. Warily, Bo walked back and took it in her own. It was warm, like a heat stone. 'What? What is it?'

'You need to start protecting yourself, girl. I was young once too. I know what beauty can do to a man. They need to possess it. It turns them inside out and makes them crazy.'

Bo looked at her. Was the woman confused? Suffering from dementia? 'Well, talking of crazy, I heard an interesting fact about that,' she said smoothly. 'Apparently more people go mad under the midnight sun than the midday moon. Have you heard that? I would have thought it was the other way around. All those hours of darkness.' She gave an exaggerated shiver.

But Signy was not fooled. 'Don't change the subject. You know what I'm telling you.'

'I really don't.'

'I understand you, girl. I *know* you!'

'How exactly? How can you know me?'

'Because you remind me of myself,' she said, regarding her closely. 'I believed I could control my life too. I thought there were rules and that the game was fair. If I heard a wolf howl, I believed there must be a wolf.'

'I'm sorry, I don't follow,' Bo faltered. 'What . . . wolf?'

'Nothing is as it might seem. People are not what you think. What happens to you is not always within your control and you must learn to accept that, to give yourself up to it.'

'You mean, I should just drift?' The old woman was talking in riddles, it was hard to keep up.

'No, not drift.' She closed her eyes and Bo could see her reaching for the word. 'Submit. It will all happen anyway, one way or the other.'

'What will?'

'What is meant to be. You can fight against it, but you will only tire yourself. And I can see that you are tired, girl.'

Bo felt a catch in her throat. *Jamie. Home.*

She blinked hard, pushing tears away, standing up abruptly. 'I've got to go. The others are waiting.'

But Signy's words followed her to the door like arrows on her back. 'Feelings cannot be ignored, girl. No matter how hard you try to resist, they demand to be felt. Remember that. The heart wants what it wants.'

Chapter Twenty

There was no snow in Alesund, only rain, the damp art-deco streets glimmering, lights shining invitingly from shop windows. Anders had parked his orange Defender in a car park overlooking a small wharf with colourful houseboats moored alongside, and their odd group had fractured into shards – Anna heading back to the office to 'catch up' on paperwork (Bo privately thought she had looked desperate to get away from Lenny), Anders making for a chandler's that had parts he needed for the rib, leaving her with Zac and Lenny, their usual threesome.

Anna's directions had been vague to say the least – 'straight ahead, make a left at the water, keep the water to your right, follow the lanes in' – but somehow they had found their way to the Christmas market anyway.

Certainly Christmas had found its way to the market. It wasn't big. Not like the flashy Pinocchio-and-candy-cane-styled ones of Strasbourg and Vienna and Prague, which filled grand cathedral squares, where sellers sold their goods from pretty, peaked cabins that looked like elf grottoes, where dramatic light installations criss-crossed overhead and hot chocolates costs ten euros. Rather, a series of utilitarian white awnings and tents lined a single, narrow cobbled street and strings of fairy lights were hung artlessly, wherever possible.

But there was a charm to it – some of the sellers had outdoor heaters to stand by, shoppers stopping momentarily to blow on their hands and stamp their feet, striking up conversations and sharing a smile with strangers; a brass band was playing at the far end; children were running past in wellies with sweet-filled cones; and the small cottagey shops on the opposite side of the lane had opened their doors, offering special exhibitions, hot food and somewhere to sit, talk, sing carols even.

Zac held her hand loosely, leading her through the crowd as they drifted from stall to stall, sampling locally caught smoked salmon bites, handling folk-tale-inspired woodcuts, 'testing' home-brewed aquavit . . . They found a stall selling Christmas decorations made from birch wood – a delicate star, an intricately notched snowflake, a miniature Christmas tree, an ornate sleigh, giant bells, silhouetted reindeer – and Bo, compensating for their late start to the festive season and wanting to get into the Christmas spirit even if she had to buy it in, took five of everything. Further along, they came across a colourful passementerie stall laid out with ornate braids, tassels, trims and cords, and again with a zeal bordering on fervour, she bought ten metres of red velvet ribbon, intending to copy what she'd seen on Signy's tree: simple bows tied to the tips of the branches.

'Do we need bows if we've got the wooden bits?' Zac asked as she handed over the money.

'They're not *bits*, they're decorations. And yes we do, because I may just put the bows on the tree and use these around the cabin – you know, hanging at the windows and from the rafters.' She gave a happy shrug. 'Make the whole place more festive. Homey.'

'Homey, right,' Zac murmured, looking at her anxiously just as her phone rang.

She answered it, seeing the worry on his face at her use of the 'H' word. 'Hello?' she said. But there was no reply. 'Hello?' She frowned as she pulled away again and disconnected. That was the third time it had happened, this morning alone.

'Who was that?' Zac asked as she clicked on the call log.

'Unidentified caller,' she said with a bored groan, even as her heart tripped into a gallop. 'I've obviously ended up on some marketing list. I keep getting spammed.'

'Don't answer them. Once you pick up once, that's it – they'll never leave you alone.'

'I usually don't,' she muttered. 'You distracted me.' All she could think was – was it Him? This couldn't be coincidence, surely? The resumption of messages and silent phone calls?

They moved along, stopping again as Zac wanted to sample yet more schnapps, pretending to analyse and weigh up the flavour of this batch, as opposed to the other two stalls further back. 'Try some,' Zac said, offering her a tot glass.

'It's eleven o'clock and that's your third shot,' she said pointedly. 'I'd prefer we had a coffee.'

'This'll keep you warmer,' he shrugged, dispatching it himself instead.

She watched, sensing a note of defiance in the gesture. Although nothing had been explicitly said, a slightly sour tang seemed to have lingered between them after their conversation yesterday; he hadn't reached for her in bed last night and in the car on the way up here, she had found herself wondering where their talk might have led had they not been interrupted by the others.

Zac's general mood hadn't been improved either, by Lenny having to hack his way down from the loft like an Amazon explorer this morning; even worse than raging about it, he had stayed pointedly silent on the matter as he patiently picked pine needles from his hair whilst having his Coke and toast, the tree's ridiculous oversizedness in the small cabin standing as a totem of Zac's lost battle with Anders – he had pinned his colours to the mast and got it wrong. Again.

Knowing his pride had been dented once more, Bo reached for his hand as they continued walking through the rain, Lenny behind them clicking away and switching between snaps and video. As much as she could, she tried to ignore him – it made for better footage anyway – but she noticed other people were beginning to look: his crouching, leaping presence was attracting attention, making people stare and wonder why he was filming the two of them, and that led them to wonder who she and Zac might be. Her jacket hood was pushed up, largely obscuring her face, but she detected the growing murmur rippling through the crowd, surreptitious looks darting across the passage as they took in her and Zac's tans, her bright hair, their accents . . .

'Zac, I think we should make a move,' she murmured, touching his sleeve.

'Why? We've only just got here.'

'I know but . . .' She glanced around. 'I think we're being recognized.'

He looked around them both ways, finding eyes already upon them. 'So?'

'So it's narrow here, a one-way street. I don't like it.'

Zac groaned. 'You're not still freaked about Kyoto, are you? That was completely different.'

'No, I know . . .'

His patience sounded tested. 'This is an entirely different scenario, Bo. It's a family thing, everyone's out doing their last bits of Christmas shopping. They're not interested in us, even if some of them do recognize us.'

'Wassup, guys?' Lenny asked, wandering over, seeing how they'd stopped.

'Nothing,' Zac shrugged.

'Bo, you cool?' Lenny enquired, frowning as he saw her face.

'Sure,' she shrugged, but Zac was wrong; this wasn't about Kyoto. Those phone calls she kept getting – it was Him. She knew it. Somehow he had got her private number. And if he had got that . . . what else had he found out? Did he know where she was? Could he be here? Was that why he had started up again? He had found her once before. Why not again?

She held Zac's hand tighter, trailing him and casting worried glances about the crowds as he headed for a food van, carols wafting from a radio on the counter. 'Hey, you hungry? They've got some pastries over there.'

She forced a weak smile. 'Great.'

'Len?' he called back.

Wordlessly Lenny put up two fingers in a peace sign. He was photographing them standing in front of the truck, no doubt to show the followers how they were 'keeping it real'.

'You want *two* pastries?' Bo asked.

'Hey, it's cold out here.'

Zac shrugged and placed their order. 'Four pastries, two coffees and a hot chocolate,' he said, reaching into his pocket for change.

'Hei – excuse me.'

Bo swung round at the voice, even though it was soft and hesitant. A teenage girl with plaits and a beanie was standing there, her eyes wide as though she was looking at Taylor Swift. 'Are you Bo?'

Bo fixed her smile in place as she tried to steady her frantic heartrate. She mustn't let the panic win. She didn't want another fight with Zac, not when yesterday's showdown had been left so unresolved . . . 'I am, yes.'

'And that's—?'

'It is,' she said quickly. 'Would you like a photo?' A shared selfie was the quickest way to end encounters like this. Once people had got *proof*, they didn't want to linger or talk – all they wanted was to show it, share it. Taking the selfie wasn't about this actual moment but the ones that came after, when everyone else got to see it. The validation afterwards counted for more than the actual experience.

'That would be amazing!' the girl gushed as Zac turned and – seeing the situation – immediately engaged a full-watt beam. Together they stood closer to the girl, moving their heads in, knowing exactly which angle to get, all of them looking at themselves on the screen. Lenny, naturally, was photographing them being photographed. 'Thank you so much. I am a big fan of yours. I hope one day to live as you.'

'Thank you. It's lovely meeting you,' Bo smiled as she moved off. See? she reassured herself. Not so hard.

'God Jul!' Zac called out, looking very pleased with himself for knowing Happy Christmas in Norwegian and giving her a thumbs-up.

'God Jul,' the girl laughed, calling it back in a completely different way and shaping her hands into a heart shape.

'God, that language really doesn't sound like it looks,' he tutted as they turned back to get the drinks and snacks from the truck counter.

'No.' Bo watched the girl move off, telling herself she had

to stop overreacting. The girl had been friendly and sweet, wanting nothing more than a photo with them. What if those calls were innocent too? Wrong numbers, slipped connections, a telesales worker in India . . . Rationally speaking, there was simply no way He could have traced her number, not unless he worked for the phone company and what were the chances of that? It just wasn't possible. There was nothing to worry about.

'Uh, guys?' Lenny said.

'What?' Bo asked, glancing over her shoulder. A large group had swarmed around them, phones in hand and expectant smiles on their faces – the floodgates seemingly broken by one teenage girl.

'I think you're wanted.'

Bo sat in the coffee shop, exhausted, her shopping bags by her feet, hands around the mug. It was the first coffee she had had since breakfast, the one at the market having been cold by the time they had obliged with all the selfie requests. Even Zac had seen the sense in splitting up after that – they were far less likely to be identified if they went round separately and they needed to do their own shopping anyway.

It had also been more fun. As something of an ascetic when it came to personal belongings – never wanting to own more than he could carry – Zac wasn't a natural shopper. He didn't need more socks (they had sponsors for those), he didn't wear cologne and they had no home to decorate; joke presents were their thing and she had found a zorbing ball set for him. But that didn't mean she couldn't splurge on other people and she had enjoyed hitting the shops in earnest for once. Finding anonymity on her own in the crowds, she had drifted into the city centre, admiring the opulent window displays and finding herself singing along to cheesy Christmas songs as she browsed and queued at the tills. She had smiled a lot and said 'God Jul' to at least ten people, and as her shopping bags began to bulge, as she began to mingle and blend with the crowds – rather than standing apart from them – she had finally felt the Christmas spirit descend upon her. So what if it was commercial and touristy? It was also *fun*.

She had bought presents for her parents, Zac, Lenny, Anna – it seemed only polite when the girl was working with them up till Christmas Eve – and, somewhat surprisingly, for Anders and Signy too. She hadn't planned on it. There was clearly no expectation of gifts on either side – frankly, a civil word would do Bo; this morning's 'lecture' from the old woman had left her almost as rattled as the silent phone calls. But she had gone into the cashmere boutique lured by the ruffled cardigan in the window for her mother and the ice-blue travel blanket had just jumped out at her – it would highlight Signy's beautiful, merciless eyes, be light enough to drape over her shoulders and yet warm enough on the bed for those really cold nights. She didn't need to do it, but if they were going to be neighbours over the Christmas period and they were staying in her property, it was only good manners. And because she had bought for Signy, she had felt she needed to get something for Anders too, settling on a burnt-orange cashmere scarf from the same shop; he'd no doubt hate it but she thought it would be a good colour on him and perhaps useful when he was on the water. At the very, very least, it was another wrapped and ribboned gift to place beneath the giant tree and add to the Christmassy vibe in their cabin. After all, it was better to give than to receive, right?

It was continuing to rain outside, the inside of the windows steadily fogging up and obscuring the world as if a rubber was erasing a pencil sketch. The cafe was small with navy walls, scuffed wooden floors, leather butterscotch sofas and high-stooled industrial workbenches for seating; ebonized open bookcases were filled with tall packets of coffee beans. An enormous roasting machine was set behind the counter where home-made cakes, brownies and pastries were set out, and music played quietly in the background. There was a great hum of conviviality about the place, several people working there on their laptops, and best of all, Bo was certain no one had recognized her. For several minutes, she just sat there, watching these strangers going about their lives in peace. It was nice to just be part of the moment for once, rather than trying to define it or capture it. But then she remembered Lenny's parting words at the market: she needed to post, post, post today. They were at 9.85 million followers now, and he was on a mission to hit ten million by Christmas. And she hadn't posted a single thing. What was wrong with her at the moment? She kept doing too much living and not enough working. She took out her phone and snapped a selfie – chin in hand, winsome smile, damp hair, hot coffee. Writing 'Shopper's reward' as the caption and tagging #wanderlusters, she uploaded it. Then she took some arty shots of the coffee house, of her presents, her drink . . .

She used the tag 'wanderlusters' every time she posted, so did Zac, so did Lenny, but as she watched the icon circle round and round, she realized that she had long since stopped checking in on it herself; the traffic volume was simply too high. With nothing better to do, she clicked onto the thread now though, curious to see what was there.

It was a disconcerting experience, like seeing her own life being played back to her in a film, for not only did the post contain the images she, Zac and Lenny themselves had uploaded, but those of nameless, faceless strangers who had seen them, spotted them out and about.

There! As if as proof, the images at the very top of the grid were the ones taken just a few hours earlier in the Christmas market. She saw the one with the girl with plaits who had started it all off, her bright-eyed smile and genuine excitement, Zac glowing with the flattery of the situation, her looking strained.

But there was more than that. Much more. There was a photo and some videos of her and Anders at Annika and Harald's party. She felt a lurch of disappointment and wondered who had taken it; it felt like a betrayal somehow, catching her at a private occasion: their heads were angled in as they talked closely, trying to hear each other over the music, her laughing, her hand touching his arm briefly as he said something that appeared to be amusing. It was preceded by a grainy shot of her and Zac at Oslo airport, eating lunch, clearly en-route to here. Before that, was one of them on a plane, only the tops of their heads visible as they watched a film – it looked as though the person taking the shot must have reached into business class from the galley (queueing for the loos perhaps?). Another of them leaning on the counter at the car-rental desk . . .

And further back, as she started scrolling faster, not liking how this felt, she saw them jogging on the beach in Samoa; them walking hand-in-hand over the Pont Neuf in Paris; them on their phones in a cafe in Ubud; her trying on a dress in Marrakech – taken through a shop window; them in a bar in Sydney; them arguing in the street in St Petersburg . . . Back and back it went, the past three and a half years preserved here like a global photo album that anyone could add to. It acted as an almost perfect timeline of their travels. If anyone wanted to know where they had been in October 2015, they could find the answer here (Costa Rica, having a kitesurfing lesson).

She didn't want to keep checking and yet she couldn't stop looking. It was so shocking to see herself through strangers' eyes, not knowing she was being watched or photographed. It was both intrusive and intimidating, yet also flattering too, for how many other people had this privilege of seeing their lives from the outside? And much of what she saw in the images she had forgotten about – the fishing trip in Kenya; that jacket she wore in Rio; her severe bob in Tokyo; those Raybans that never slid off her nose when she looked down in Mexico; Zac's beloved Red Sox baseball cap that he lost in Banff. That hotel bedroom in Sri Lanka—

She stilled, feeling even her blood pause in her veins. No, she would never forget that. It was scorched in her brain, the moment she had come out of the bathroom and known – just known – that He had been there. It was almost as though his scent had tainted the air. She had immediately seen that the top drawer had been left fractionally open and known her underwear had been rifled through, perhaps taken. The bedcover had been too neat as well – she had been lying on it beforehand reading a magazine, her own physical impression left on the duvet like a fossil, but now someone had smoothed it, pulled it down tightly, proprietorially. And of course, the photograph had been left for her to find on the pillow.

And now this photograph was posted with all the others.

A thought came to her and she gave a physical judder – because how many of these other images had come from Him too? The ones taken through the shop windows or across from the street? Him sitting at the next table in the airport or walking a step behind her in the souks? Had he been watching her all this time – not through the screen, but in life?

She felt hot. She felt cold. She felt sick. She felt—

'Bo?'

She almost jumped a metre in the air, giving a small scream that made everyone start, including Anders. 'Hey. I'm sorry,' he said quickly, holding up a placating hand and dipping his head low in embarrassment. 'I didn't mean to disturb.'

'Oh. Oh God, Anders, it's you.' She dropped her head in her hands, her fingers raking her hair tight at the temples as she stared at the woodgrain of the table, trying to calm herself. She was jumpy. On edge.

'Who did you think it—? Bo, are you okay?'

She forced a smile, forced herself to look up. 'Yes. Absolutely. I'm fine. I'm sorry I was just . . . miles away.'

His gaze fell to her phone, now face up on the table, her image replicated thousands of times in a grid. His eyes narrowed.

'What are . . . what are you doing here?' she asked, covering it with her hand and trying to play it cool. 'You went to the chandlery?'

'Yes. I got what I needed.' He was watching her closely, his eyes tracking over her and seemingly seeing the paleness of her cheeks, the fearful brightness in her eyes.

'What a coincidence seeing you here. Of all the coffee shops in all of Alesund . . .' she joked weakly.

'I buy my coffee beans here,' he said, jerking his chin towards the ebonized cabinets.

'Oh. That really is a coincidence,' she mumbled, looking over at the shelves before fading into the middle distance again.

'I'm getting a coffee. Do you want another?' he asked,

drawing her back. 'There's another forty minutes before we're meeting everyone back at the car.'

'. . . Sure. That'd be great. Thanks.'

She watched as he walked over to the counter and ordered, his movements minimal and sure. Nothing was ever extraneous with him. He had none of Zac's hyperactivity or over-enthusiasm. None of his hyperbole and superlatives. He was utterly contained, kept within himself. Nothing leaked out or bubbled over.

He brought the coffees over a few minutes later, a small Danish pastry on a plate. 'For you. You look like you could do with the sugar. You're pale.'

'Oh. Sorry.'

He shot her a quizzical look. 'It wasn't a criticism.'

'No,' she said, lacing her fingers around the base of the mug and staring in at her drink; she thought she could get high on the smell alone.

'Bo – what has happened?'

She looked up, feigning disingenuousness. 'Hmm?—'

'And don't say nothing. You look terrible.'

She stared into her coffee again. What could she say? She couldn't draw him into this.

But he already knew. 'It's Him isn't it? That guy. You had the same look the night of the party.'

The night of the party. Her mouth parted in a little 'o' for a moment as she remembered her behaviour that night and how badly she'd behaved, taking out her frustrations on him. 'Listen, about that—'

'Forget it. It's not important,' he said, swatting away her apology before she could even get it out. His eyes met hers – clear and strong. Straightforward.

'No, it is,' she insisted. 'I have to apologize. I was out of order and I *am* sorry, I don't know what came over me. I can't explain it. I have no excuses.'

He watched her and she found she couldn't hold his gaze. It felt too searching, somehow, as though he knew all her hiding places. 'There was a lot going on,' was all he said, but for once, the silence between them felt loaded and thick. 'Now tell me what's happened. What has He said?'

She sighed, knowing he wasn't going to let it go. For some reason he had made her problem his own. 'Only more of the same. It's become daily again,' she said, staring at her finger-nails.

'Then that's harassment. Report him.'

'Honestly? If it was just that, I think I could cope with it.'

'Then what?'

She bit her lip, looking back at him again. 'I just found this.' She pushed her phone towards him and he looked at it blankly. 'It's a thread for a hashtag that we use all the time. It means anyone wanting to connect with us, be part of our com-munity, can come here, post here. Only – I've not looked at it. For *years*. It's for the fans more than us. I just write it automat-ically every day without ever thinking about it. Me, Zac, Lenny – we all use it.'

'Where are they?' he asked, straightening up and looking around for them.

'We split up. We were recognized at the Christmas market and the crowd got really big . . . I don't cope well with it: everyone knowing who we are when we don't know who they are back.'

He was watching her closely. 'Are Zac and Lenny coming here?'

'No, I'm meeting them back at the car.'

'So then . . .' Anders sat back in his chair, his knee accidentally butting hers under the table. He seemed more relaxed to hear the guys weren't coming, but he still gave a heavy sigh. 'You said you clicked onto this page . . .' he said, jerking his chin to indicate her phone on the table between them, prompting her.

'Yes . . . And then I found that.' She tapped the image on the screen with her fingernail.

Anders picked it up, his frown deepening as he scrutinized the shot of the hotel room. It was innocuous enough – until the backstory was explained. He looked back at her. 'This was your hotel room – where he broke in?'

She nodded. 'Yes. No one else could have taken that photo except him. Look, you can just about see the photo he left on the pillow.'

His mouth tightened at the sight of it.

'What I want to know is – why is it up here? This forum? This has nothing to do with Wanderlusters, it was taken before I ever met Zac. If he took that photo as some kind of . . . souvenir of what he'd done –' she repressed a shudder. 'Why post it at all, much less here? It means nothing to anyone else apart from Him.'

His gaze slid over to her. 'And you. It's his way of telling you he was there, and that now he's here too – he's every-where. Maybe it's his proof that he saw you first? That he had you captured not just in a photo but in the next room.' Anger blazed in his eyes, though his voice stayed low, his body still.

Bo swallowed, the fear creeping over her like clammy hands. 'I can't help thinking, if that photo is his – then how many others are too?' she asked, a tremor creeping into her voice as she said the words out loud, as though putting voice to them made the threat real. 'I mean, it's obvious which photos have been posted by just random strangers we've actually met, all the selfies, they're fine – the girl today at the Christmas market, for example. But what about these ones . . . ?' she said, pointing to the grainier, blurrier covert shots taken at the airport, in the shop. 'Were they passers-by who just happened to see and recognize me out and about? Or are they from Him – following me?'

Anders reached forward, covering her hand with his, and the gesture was so startling, she almost shrank back in surprise. 'Bo, this is serious. You have to go to the police.'

His hand was warm upon hers. 'I already did but I told you before – technically he is committing no crime.' She gave a hopeless shrug and stared back at him, seeing the frustration bloom on his face.

'But this is different now. If he did take any more of these photos then he's not a troll, he's a stalker.' He sat back, lifting his hand from hers and she felt cold again. Vulnerable. A ripple of fear tiptoed up her spine at the word. Stalker. It felt unreal, hearing it being applied to *her*.

'You have got to be careful. You don't know what this guy looks like, where he's from, what he wants. You're right, he could well be following you. For all you know he was in the crowd at the Christmas market today.'

'Please don't say that,' she whispered, feeling a cold hand clutch her heart. Even the heat in his gaze couldn't warm her up.

He dropped his head lower, coming in closer, 'Look, I'm not saying it to frighten you. The odds are he isn't here. But I'm saying it because this threat is real. You cannot afford for Him to find out where you are.'

'And he won't,' she said firmly. 'Ever since he broke into my room, I've made sure *never* to post where I am at the time I'm posting.'

He looked at her blankly, as though not believing her. Wasn't that enough? She realized he was still holding her hand.

'Okay, so, say here – I just took a selfie, okay?' she said, explaining more fully. Perhaps he didn't understand the technology, he didn't see that she was untraceable. 'If I wanted, I could hit that tag there and it would show everyone that I took it at this coffee shop in Alesund. So then people following me on Instagram would know that I am sitting here, right now and anyone following me in the locality could come find me. But instead I keep the location setting switched off, right? Everyone following me knows I'm in Norway at the moment, but only because I've told them. And they have no idea where I am exactly. And if I ever do have to post exact details, I only release them after I've left.'

His eyes narrowed. 'And Zac and Lenny do the same?'

'Absolutely, they're really hot on the issue. None of us do it.'

'Well, that is something,' he conceded.

'Listen, it's sweet of you to worry but . . .' She took a deep breath. 'I'm fine. I am.'

'You didn't look fine when I walked in.'

'I'd just had a shock, that was all. Seeing that picture there . . .' Her voice faded out, the panicky voices in her head growing louder. She muted them out again, rallying. She knew how to fight fear: move on, find the light. 'But there's nothing to say those other pictures *are* by Him. I might be overreacting. They could be perfectly innocent.'

'Possibly.'

'I mean, that picture was posted *years* ago and I've only just seen it now, right? He may well not have posted anything since that.'

'Maybe.'

She looked at him, seeing how questions ran through his mind, his eyes serious and intense. 'You don't look convinced,' she mumbled.

He hesitated before replying. 'The thing that concerns me is why he has got in contact with you again after all these years.'

The question chilled her too. It was all she could think about in bed at night. Why? Why her? Why now? 'I don't know,' she said, her voice curled up and small.

'You said it only started up again when you got here? To Norway?'

She nodded.

'So then there must be something here you are doing that he does not like.'

She pulled a face, trying to think. '. . . Walking in snow a lot?'

In spite of the gravity of their conversation, he cracked a grin. 'That would be niche.'

She grinned too, thinking that if she didn't laugh, she might cry. His levity brightened her, gave her hope. 'It would, wouldn't it?'

They stared at each other, and for the hundredth time she wondered why it always felt so easy talking to him.

He looked away finally, inhaling sharply. 'Well, you will probably never know. There's no point in trying to second-guess Him or understand what's going on in his mind. There's no logic to people like that. But you need to stay extra-vigilant.'

'Yes.' Should she mention this morning's silent calls? She wanted to even though she knew she shouldn't. It was selfish, only adding to his concerns when he shouldn't be worrying about her at all; this wasn't his problem. She wasn't. But as their eyes locked again, she felt an irrational certainty that everything would be okay if she just stayed near him. That he was somehow her safety.

'. . . Eat up,' he said, pushing the plate towards her. 'You need the sugar.'

The moment had passed and she let it drift away. He had done more than enough.

'You're not being my nurse again, I hope,' she said, a teasing note in the words as she dared to reference their argument the other night. Could they laugh about it now? Was everything forgiven? Were they friends?

His eyes flashed up at her, the faintest trace of a new smile on his lips. 'Don't start that again.'

Chapter Twenty-One

They were supposed to meet at the car. Instead they received a text from Zac telling them to meet at a bar several streets away. Anders knew of it but though he walked her there, he left her at the door. 'I'll meet up with you in a few hours,' he said.

'But why? Come and have some drinks with us,' she implored. 'It's Christmas. It'd be so nice to have some fun together.' She looked at him, hands stuffed in his North Face jacket pockets, shoulders hunched. She wanted to say that it would be so nice for the others to get to see him in a social setting, to see him as she did, as he really was and not the prickly, reclusive guide he insisted on being during working hours. She wanted her friends to like him too, but she couldn't say that out loud and he wouldn't budge so, instead, a silence full of unspoken words ballooned between them, his eyes telling more than his mouth ever would.

'I'm going to visit a friend –'

What friend, Bo wondered? She was certain he was lying. Making an excuse.

'– I'll come back at eleven. That's the latest we can stay if we're going to drive back tonight.' He looked down at her extravagant collection of shopping bags, she was struggling to carry them all. 'Give me your bags. I'll put them in the car as I'm passing.'

She watched as he walked off, disappointment stalking through her as he disappeared up the street. Why did he have to be so elusive? She waited until he was out of sight, just in case he should change his mind after all, but he turned the corner without looking back. She just didn't understand him.

She pushed open the doors with a sigh. Purple neon lighting illuminated a stone wall in the lobby; a beautiful girl leaning against it as she texted furiously. The bar itself was in a contemporary all-glass building built out over the water, a rim of electric blue light shining directly into the sea below. It wasn't a large space but the intimate atmosphere was set off by tables and chairs set alongside the sea-view windows, with a selection of booths set on a raised, uplit platform in the centre of the room. Naturally, their group had the most prominent booth in the middle. Bo could see Zac and Lenny sitting with Anna between them and a group of three others opposite – two women and a man. They were all wearing coloured paper crowns.

'Baby!' Zac hollered, arms in the air, as he saw her standing by the door. It felt like every head turned as she made her way over, the music so loud it throbbed through her. 'Where've you *been*?' he crooned, pulling her down onto his lap and kissing her passionately. He always did this when they were in a crowd. And when he was drunk. It was almost like his signature move. But she couldn't pull away. There was nowhere else to sit.

'I did some shopping, then went for a coffee with Anders.' It was only just six o'clock but it had been dark for several hours now and it felt more like ten at night in here: the lights, the music, the booze . . .

'Coffee with Anders,' Zac echoed, wrinkling his nose as though he'd smelled something noxious. 'Poor you.'

348

'Why did you go for coffee with *him* when you could have been drinking here with us?' Lenny asked.

'Because I bumped into him in the cafe. And I had no idea you were in here till ten minutes ago,' she said, seeing the glimmer in his eyes that always came on when he and Zac drank. They were firm drinking buddies.

Bo smiled across at the assembled group, watching on with polite but rapt expressions, and she felt on the back foot that they should know her while she knew not one of them. 'Hi – I'm Bo.'

A big hand was extended across the table to her. 'Hey, Bo, I'm Trygve, CEO of Ridge Riders. And this is Anja, our CFO, and Ulla, our chief designer.'

The two women also shook her hand warmly.

'It is so lovely to meet you in person,' Anja said. 'It's so weird – I feel like I know you already.'

'You are even more lovely than your photographs suggest,' Ulla gushed, her eyes all over Bo as though she was a sketch come to life. 'Taller, too.'

'Oh, thank you,' Bo said, feeling embarrassed.

'We were just saying to Zac and Lenny what wonders you have done for our brand,' Trygve said. 'I take it Anna has told you the jacket and ski suit are completely sold out?'

Bo glanced back at Anna, who was somewhat squeezed between the guys. 'Yes, she did. That's such great news.'

'Better than great. We cannot keep up with the amount of enquiries we are receiving with suppliers wanting to stock us, editors wanting our clothes for shoots . . . And all because of you. You two free-spirited, inspiring people.'

'That deserves a toast!' Zac yelled, grabbing the bottle of aquavit in the centre of the table and splashily pouring schnapps into all their glasses. He held his glass aloft. 'To free spirits!'

'Free spirits!' they all cried, dispatching their drinks as one.

Bo, who didn't have a glass, watched on. How many had they had already?

'Here, you too, baby,' Zac said, hastily pouring her one too and handing it to her.

'Oh, no, I'm not really . . .' She felt out of the loop yet again, on the sidelines. Wasn't it always Zac and Lenny who were front and centre of their brand?

But Zac's expression silenced her. They were out with their sponsors, they were celebrating, it was Christmas . . . She took the drink from him and shot it back, trying not to splutter as it burned her throat but unable to refrain from pulling a face.

'It is an acquired taste!' Trygve laughed, along with the rest.

'So, Bo!' Lenny called over. 'Where is Anders, then?'

'He's visiting a friend. He said he'd collect us at eleven.'

'Yeah, right! Like we'll be done by then!' Zac laughed.

'Yeah, right, like he's got a friend, you mean!' Lenny guffawed, making Zac smack the table with hilarity.

Bo prickled at their taunts, but there was no point in upbraiding them; they were both drunk and steadily on their way to becoming plastered. Trollied.

'It's a two-hour trip back from here,' she said instead, although she couldn't see how any of them were going to cope with the trek up from the fjord in this state; not that she liked the idea of a post-midnight ride on the fjord herself. It was black as pitch out there at night and the snow-filled clouds made glimpsing even the moon a rarity, much less the stars or the fabled Aurora – Lenny was taking its sustained absence almost personally. Perhaps Anders would let them all sleep on his floor?

'Well why couldn't he be sociable and come in for a drink, at least?' Lenny asked, glassy-eyed.

'Because he's driving?' she shrugged. 'It's not much fun being sober when everyone else is drinking.'

'Yeah, right,' Lenny muttered sarcastically. 'He's just not much fun.'

'Who is this Anders?' Ulla asked, leaning forward on her elbows, a faintly dazed look on her face too, Bo could see. She wondered again how long they had all been in here; the bottle on the table was more than half empty.

'He's our guide. And a grumpy git with it,' Lenny said, not holding back. But then he always was a mouthy drunk.

'He looks *so* familiar to me,' Anna said, her voice comically sliding up an octave. 'But I just can't place him. Sometimes I think it's on the tip of my tongue – and then it goes again.' She looked baffled.

'School?' Anja asked.

'God no,' Anna scoffed. 'He's at least thirty.'

'Hey!' Trygve protested. He clearly looked to be in his mid-forties.

'Don't worry, Trygve,' Ulla laughed. 'You are still a very handsome man.'

'And now you are patronizing me.'

'Not at all!' she protested, placing her hand over his. For work colleagues, they seemed very close.

'There is a reason why I have a desk job and they –' he tossed his gaze towards Zac and Lenny – 'have a blog criss-crossing the world.'

Bo flinched. They? Zac and Lenny?

'Aw, but you can't compare yourself to them. You have

brains and they only have brawn,' Anna said, grabbing Zac's arm and squeezing the biceps.

'Hey!' the men all said collectively, seeing the compliment shrouding the insult.

'What?' she giggled. 'You know what I mean.' She shoulder-barged Zac playfully.

Bo watched them all, feeling as removed from the action as if she was still in the street with Anders.

'So what is next for you guys? Where do the Wanderlusters wander to now?' Trgyve asked, trying to draw her in. 'Whose will be the next company you transform?'

'We've not confirmed anything with anyone else yet—'

'Although I'm in talks with a number of people,' Lenny slurred, self-importantly.

Bo blinked. 'We try to only do one partnership per season; it gets a bit much for the fans otherwise if they feel like you're constantly trying to flog stuff to them. But we're going to stay on here for another couple of weeks after Christmas and do a little more relaxing than we have done so far.'

'Actually, babe, Lenny and I were discussing this earlier,' Zac said. 'We're up for moving on. Going to find the sun again. Whaddya think?'

'What?'

'I've managed to put a hold on a trip to the Exumas for Christmas and New Year. Fly out Christmas Eve, land Christmas morning, be swimming with the pigs by Christmas lunch,' Lenny grinned, looking over at Anja and Ulla.

'But . . .' Bo stammered. 'We've only been here two weeks. We're booked to stay for the month.' And that was to say nothing of her dislike of spending Christmas in hot climates. It was her one condition – they always had to have mountains for Zac, Cokes for breakfast for Lenny and be somewhere cold for Christmas for her.

'Yeah, but we can leave earlier if we want; we're all paid up so Anders and his grandmother won't care if we split early; frankly I think they'd be delighted to see the back of us,' Zac shrugged. 'And we've only got a couple more days' shooting for these guys and we're free to drift wherever the wind takes us.'

'Or a Boeing 787 anyway,' Lenny winked.

Ulla and Anja laughed again. Not Anna though; she appeared to be largely ignoring him.

Zac refilled everyone's glasses and Bo felt her stomach dive. She didn't want to get drunk.

'But what about Christmas here?' she asked him as he handed her the shot glass anyway. 'We've got the tree, the decorations—'

'Fuck! *Don't* mention the tree!' Lenny wailed dramatically as Zac reached over Anna and laughingly punched him on the arm.

'*Don't* mention the tree,' Zac said in his best don't-mess warning voice, pointing at everyone and making their hosts all look at one another in amused bewilderment, before shaking with laughter.

'. . . What about the tree?' Ulla asked, hands held out enquiringly.

'Nooo!' Lenny wailed, dropping his head on the table and banging it with his fist.

Everyone laughed at their histrionics.

'Fine, I'll tell you about the tree,' Zac said, playing to his crowd. 'But only after we've dispatched these.' And raising his glass, he waited for everyone else to do the same.

On the count of three, they necked the drinks, Bo several

beats later than everyone else. She didn't want to drink it, just like she didn't want to be in this bar, just like she didn't want to leave this country. But it seemed that what she wanted wasn't important. Apparently, she had become a bit part in her own life.

By eleven o'clock, everyone was looking significantly less pretty. Zac was slumped, Anja was asleep, Lenny was morose, and Ulla and Trygve were dancing together in the aisle. Bo was trying to get Anna to stop crying.

'. . . mustn't give up,' Bo said tiredly, feeling drunk and emotional herself. She had sung 'Merry Xmas Everybody' three times now and was beginning to lose her voice. 'It'll happen for you.'

'But I see you and Zac and I don't thin—' she hiccupped. 'I don't think it'll happen—'

A cheer from the corner of the room made them both look up. Two men were squaring off against each other, shoulders and elbows pulled back, chests out as they walked in slow circles, eyeball-to-eyeball. They looked like cockerels about to fight.

'What's going on?' Bo frowned as suddenly the music cut out too. Silence popped, and then a low rumble of voices began to jibe, swelling into a jeer, and was then replaced by – of all things – violin music. 'Jeez! Are they going to bow each other to death?'

'It is the fiddle, the Hardanger fiddle. Very famous for the *Halling*,' Anna sighed dismissively, wanting to get back to her problematic love life.

But Bo had stood up. 'The what?' she winced, watching as the crowd pushed back now, giving the men space. Unable to tear her eyes away, she wandered over to where Ulla and Trygve were standing. 'What's going on?'

'A dance-off,' Ulla shouted, looking excited. 'You have heard of the *Halling*, right? A traditional Norwegian folk dance? Argentina has the salsa; Italy has the tarantella; we have the *Halling*,' she shrugged.

'*This* is a dance-off?' Bo laughed, watching as the men began to move in step. Run-DMC it was not.

'Wait till you see!' Ulla grinned. 'It is a virtuoso display of power and strength.'

'Well, I guess I'd better capture it, then,' Bo said, surprising herself with a hiccup – she wasn't immune to the effects of five schnapps herself – as she got out her phone and automatically began recording.

Everybody began clapping in time, the men dancing opposite one another in a languid prowl, before suddenly pulling out some moves – dropping to their heels before springing up again like Russian dancers, beginning to leap and spin. The effect was slightly ruined by their being in suits, but she panned around the room, capturing the cheering crowd too, the lights on the water outside . . . It was another Norwegian party, albeit very different from the one she'd gone to with Anders.

She twisted to include Ulla and laughed in surprise to find Ulla doing exactly the same to her. Bo peeked out from behind her screen and playfully stuck out her tongue, Ulla did likewise, before they both turned back, laughing, to the dancers. The action was hitting a crescendo now. Someone had found a felt trilby in the cloakroom and was – bizarrely – hanging it off the end of a broom handle.

'Uh, *what*?' Bo asked, the screen shaking with her giggles. 'What's with the *hat*?'

'Hi.'

The voice in her ear was low. Sober. She whipped round.

'Hey!' She couldn't quite temper the happiness in her voice to see him.

Anders blinked back at her, taking in her drunkenness, before looking over to the action. 'So I see things are getting messy.'

'*So* messy,' Bo grinned, tipping her head behind her towards the others who were reclining in various states of consciousness. She was doing the best of the lot of them.

'Hmm,' Anders said, turning back with an arched eyebrow, just as one of the dancers did a high kick-flick and sent the hat flying off the broom. It spun through the air and Anders instinctively shot his hand out, catching it like it was a ball.

A huge cheer went up as he handed it back, and the hat was replaced on the stick. Bo cheered too, for she had caught it all on film! It would look great!

'They're doing it again?' she asked as the second man began to circle it too.

'Only one can win,' Ulla said. 'They are like stags, clashing antlers.'

'Oh.'

'Hey, I'm Ulla Hansen,' Ulla said, smiling up at Anders and holding out the wrong hand to shake (she was still recording with her other one). 'I'm part of the Ridge Riders team.'

'Anders,' he said, shaking it but not introducing himself further – not that he needed to.

'Oh, *you're* Anders,' she said, intrigue in her voice. 'Now, I keep hearing about you.'

Anders didn't reply.

Ulla's eyes narrowed as she took a better look, openly scrutinizing him. 'Yeah, come to think of it – you *do* look familiar, Anna's right.'

'I had never met her before last week,' he said tersely.

A huge cheer – the biggest yet – lifted the roof as the hat was kicked flying into the air again. But this time Anders made no attempt to catch it and it sailed past him. Bo glimpsed one of the men on the dancefloor holding the back of his trousers and guessed that they had split during his acrobatics.

'We need to go,' Anders said abruptly, looking straight at Bo. 'Either you all come with me now or I leave without you. You are very welcome to stay up here if you wish.'

'No, it's fine, of course we'll come,' she said, taken aback by a brusqueness that was unusual even by his standards.

He turned to leave and Bo went to stop recording. The dancing had stopped anyway, the music no longer playing—

'Oh, holy shit!' Ulla gasped, almost shrieked. 'You're Anders Jemtegard! The guy that was in the papers. There was that massive court case.' Her eyes widened, another expression coming into them as the alcohol-induced excitement dulled. '. . . You killed that guy!'

The entire bar fell silent.

What? Bo's jaw dropped open as she looked desperately from Ulla to Anders. No. That couldn't be true.

But one look at his face – furious, shocked, devastated – and she knew that it was.

'You killed someone?' she whispered, aghast.

Everyone seemed to be holding their breath, waiting for his reply, the attention that had been on the dancers now suddenly focused entirely upon them. But Anders didn't look back, not at a single person. Instead he stared only at her, making no move to reply. But she saw words – explanations, excuses – running behind his eyes and suddenly it all made sense: his aversion to company, the unnatural stillness, the sense of containment about him. He was keeping his violence boxed in.

She took a step back, just as he did the same. And then he

turned, pushing through the crowds that had begun to creep closer like he was an exotic breed in a zoo, everyone wanting to get a better look, to see, to hear . . .

Bo gave a horrified sob, the sound raw and wretched as she watched him leave, people jumping back from him as though afraid.

'What the actual *fuck*?' Zac demanded, staggering over to them, his eyes almost rolling around in his head independently of one another. 'Did I hear that right? He killed someone?'

Ulla nodded as the music started up again louder than ever, and the bar staff tried to get the party atmosphere back on track. But no one was listening to the music now; they were all huddled in horrified-delighted groups, trying to be heard over the Pogues and Kirsty MacColl. '. . . can't believe it's him!'

Anna was there too now. '. . . *knew* I . . . cognized hi—!' she said triumphantly – as though this was a good thing.

'What did he do?' Zac demanded.

'. . . killed this guy . . . with his girlfriend . . . locked up . . .'

Bo felt the room spin as she remembered the sudden stop of activity on his Instagram account, leaving his life in Oslo to come back here . . . It all made perfect sense. He had killed a man and gone to prison for it, losing his girlfriend, a woman he couldn't quite give up – keeping her clothes in a drawer, her picture by his bed, but that haunting portrait too lifelike, too painful to keep close.

She remembered the warmth of his hand on hers just a few hours earlier, the concern in her eyes. She had felt safe with him, drawn to him in ways she couldn't understand. But her instincts about him had been wrong, her faith misplaced. The others had been right about him all along. What the hell did she know?

Chapter Twenty-Two

'ImeanitBo! Dondothis!' Zac was jabbing a finger towards her, swaying as he did so, his words an unbroken slur. A single breath of wind would knock him over, he was so drunk.

'Where the fuck you going anyway?' Lenny sneered, seeing how she stood with her arm up, the orange light of the taxi getting closer. 'It'll be dawn before you get back there tonight!'

Bo's eyes slid sideways towards him, seeing how he stumbled over his own feet whilst standing still – but she didn't reply. She couldn't deal with this – them – right now. She was in a flat spin. Lenny always had been a mean drunk and Trygve and Ulla had already left, together, but Anja and Anna were watching from a polite distance outside the bar. The night breeze was freezing by the water and they were all shivering. The party was well and truly over.

'Lessjustgeddahotel,' Zac beseeched her, half hunched over as though he wanted to sleep in the street, standing up.

'You're welcome to come back with me,' she said, as the taxi drew up alongside her. She could scarcely think straight. She knew there were easier options: booking into a hotel was far easier than driving through the fjords in the dead of night but easy wasn't the priority right now. She couldn't stay here. She felt like she couldn't breathe. The world seemed to have collapsed in on itself. She had to . . . move. Go. Escape.

'Isstoofuckingfar,' Zac hollered, waving his arms up and down furiously. 'Lessjustgeddahotel!'

'No. I can't stay here, I told you.'

'Why?'

'I told you why.' It had been the final straw to her evening, seeing that Ulla had live-streamed the video, tagging up the location as clearly as a grid reference.

'Because Ulla fucking put that we're in Alesund?' he cried, throwing his arms out so wide he almost lost his own balance. 'So wha? Who *cares*? No one cares, that's who. I can promise you that out of 9.9 million people, not one of them cares that we are here.'

Bo blinked at him. It wasn't true. One of them did. The dangerous one.

'You're paranoid, Bo,' Lenny drawled. 'You're nuts.'

'Are you coming with me or not?' she asked Zac calmly, ignoring Lenny as she opened the door. It was bad enough dealing with one of them this drunk, much less two.

'Fuck, no, I'm not. And nor are you. I *forbid* it,' he spat. 'Get over here now. Stop pissing about.'

Bo stared at him in disbelief. She looked at him stabbing the air at her, Lenny's sneer of contempt as she took flight. They thought she was ridiculous, pathetic, hysterical – and maybe it was true; but neither of them knew about the battle she had been trying to deal with alone; they didn't know that the man who had chased her once before and invaded her room, was on her tail again. And now, standing there in the rain, watching them both sway and rail and curse, she didn't know how to tell them. Or even what good it would do if she did. They'd tell her to 'ignore' him, block him; that he was just a sad, harmless dweeb with nothing better to do with his time than pick on her. But she felt . . . no, she somehow *knew* this was more than that. It was real, a living breathing thing. She felt watched. Surveilled. Trailed. Hunted.

What was it Anders had said? He wasn't a troll but a stalker. That changed everything. Even just the imagery was different – taking the weak, hunched figure hiding behind a screen and switching it for a shadow across the street, a knock at her door, a breath on her neck . . .

A breath on her neck? A breath . . .

Her heart constricted tightly, forgetting to beat. Her body shuddered in disgust, just at the very thought. Or was it a memory? . . . It triggered a visceral response in her that she couldn't explain, but it was a fear that felt present. Right here. Right now.

She looked around at the revellers, some of them lighting up cigarettes, others still swigging from beer bottles or talking on their phones, most of them looking over and watching this. Her.

She couldn't stay here.

'Fine. I'll see you tomorrow then.' She slid into the back seat, shutting the door on them both, their ridiculousness seemingly amplified now that their voices were drowned out, both of them stumbling and swaying about. 'How much to Gerainger?' she asked the driver, her stare remaining pinned to the men outside.

'At this time of night?' the driver asked in disbelief. 'No, it is too far. The ferries are closed. It will take twice as long.'

'Then I'll pay you treble,' she said without hesitation, watching as Zac began to stagger his way towards her. She realized with a start that she didn't *want* him to come with her; the distance she had put between them suddenly made her want more.

'Treble?' the driver echoed. That appeared to change things. 'Then it'll be six thousand kroner.'

Bo calculated – that was, what, £600 or thereabouts? It was more than a flight home to England but flight from here was all she wanted right now. 'Fine. But go now,' she urged as Zac lurched over, within touching distance of the handle. 'Quickly.'

The driver pulled away and she saw how Zac spun as he leapt back, tumbling to the ground in a wretched heap. Lenny meandered over, trying to pick him up and falling over too. Anja and Anna ran over and tried to help but it was like the blind guiding the blind, all of them as incapacitated as each other.

Bo watched until they were out of sight, the four of them spotlit by the street lamps. But that wasn't what caught her eye in the darkness. It was the dozens of red lights flashing like tiny indicators in the shadows, strangers recording them, preparing to post these scenes of carnage and humiliation. This footage would tarnish their brand's illusion of perfection, she knew, revealing the underbelly of their aspirational lives as something a little bit tawdry and pathetic. People would see, finally, that she and Zac weren't anything special after all; they weren't different. For years, the camera had shown half-truths about them, glimpses of moments people wanted to believe were entire and whole, and they, the Wanderlusters, had simply caught that wave and ridden it. They had surfed across oceans, exploiting every opportunity that had come their way until finally, here, they had hit rocks below the surface that left them all thrashing in the water. Bo knew she ought to be devastated. She knew this could be the end.

But all she actually felt was relief.

*

She sat in the back of the taxi, the sleeping mountains walling either side of the road as she was driven through the night. She looked out into the fathomless darkness. With no light pollution, it was impossible to tell where the earth ended and the sky began; but then, she didn't think she could trace the outlines of anything real any more. She couldn't trust anything or anyone. In the quiet, on her own, she could finally think and she closed her eyes as the disbelief continued to spread over her like a stain, for it wasn't her fight on the street with Zac that was making her shake but that silence with Anders. Shock had her in its grip, the facts running at her before she pushed them away, unable to believe it, refusing to, and yet . . .

How could he have done it? Killed a man? On some levels, it somehow made perfect sense and yet she had seen his face as the revelation had ricocheted around the bar, as the weight of stares had amassed upon him, judgement passed in every set of eyes. Including hers.

She got out her phone and googled his name. Like her own, it was all that was needed. Far above the listing for the wholesome pursuits of cycling, hiking and kayaking in Geraingerfjord Guided Tours, were the less savoury headlines, so many of them: *'Double murder in Grunerlokka'; 'Brutal murder in hipster centre'; 'Star-cross'd lovers . . .'* It almost defied belief that they could pertain to him. Was this why he'd been so reserved with them all? Had he been waiting for one of them to check him out, knowing that when they did, his past would override everything? He would be exposed and then condemned?

Bo clicked on one of the links, feeling her breath snag as an image came up of Anders with his girlfriend, the girl she had seen at his house – in the photograph, in the portrait hidden in the shed . . . They were on a ferry, the wind blowing her hair around so that all that could really be seen was her beautiful wide laughing mouth and sparkling eyes, Anders grinning and so proud beside her. From the captions, Bo saw her name was Inger Pedersen, twenty-six.

Twenty-six when she died.

No. It made no sense, the words like rubber bullets bouncing off her. That stunning, luscious, vital woman – how could she be dead? And how could *he* have done it? How could his obvious love for her have turned into murderous rage? Bo read on, feeling sick, not wanting to know but not remotely able to stop.

. . . Police are continuing to interrogate the main suspect in the case, Anders Jemtegard, a twenty-seven-year-old former pilot, found covered in blood at the scene. Originally from Gerainger, he was living with Miss Pedersen at the time of her death. Neighbours describe them as a lively, happy couple, always out and very popular.

. . . It is alleged the second victim, Jans Bakken, had been visiting Miss Pedersen when Jemtegard returned home unexpectedly early. It remains unclear whether Bakken and Pedersen were in a romantic relationship.

Police recovered two large kitchen knives at the scene and forensics specialists are continuing their investigations at the Grunerlokka address. Jemtegard remains in custody, under constant guard, believed to be at suicide risk . . .

Bo looked away, feeling drained, overwhelmed. How? How had he done this? How had he been this person? She remembered the day he'd made her coffee in the cabin – their easy conversation; how he'd saved her at the waterfall, his kindness in bringing her back to his own home, his concern this very afternoon . . .

She clicked on another headline.

Grunerlokka killer pleads not guilty . . . Anders Jemtegard, the twenty-seven-year-old pilot from Oslo, has pleaded not guilty to the double murder of his girlfriend Inger Pedersen and Jans Bakken who were found with multiple stab wounds on the night of 17 August 2013. Jemtegard's defence team have put forward a plea of manslaughter on the grounds of diminished responsibility . . .

Jealousy.

'. . . *I know what beauty can do to a man. They need to possess it. It makes them crazy. Turns them inside out.*' Signy had said that; she had been referring to her beloved grandson, turned mad with jealousy over the woman he'd loved.

This newspaper had used a different photograph of the couple. It looked to have been taken at a university ball, the two of them full-cheeked and fresh-skinned, Inger in a peach dress, Anders in black tie. They had made a striking couple and Bo knew that had she seen an image of the two of them on Instagram, she'd have followed them in a shot. They weren't showy in their poses or outfits, yet they had a look of such togetherness, their bodies always angled in to one another even as they smiled or spoke to others . . . 'Forever' hung above them like a star, picking them out as special. Rare.

She clicked on a video link bringing up footage of a female news reporter standing outside a contemporary-looking building. She was wearing a camel coat and black scarf, trying not to shiver as sleet flashed past the camera screen like speeding bullets. '. . . *The trial continued at Oslo District Court*

*today, where in dramatic scenes, the defendant Anders Jemtegard
had to be removed from the dock when the prosecution tried to present photographic evidence showing the mortal wounds inflicted on
the victims. Becoming visibly agitated and verbally abusive, Jemtegard was warned he was in contempt of court. The magistrate was
forced to call a recess and Jemtegard was led back to the cells. Pro-
ceedings will resume tomorrow. Jemtegard is charged with double
murder and faces the statutory maximum of twenty-one years'
imprisonment if found guilty . . .'*

The footage cut to images of Anders being led out of the
court and into the back of a police van. His hands were cuffed
in front of him and he was wearing a suit. He looked gaunt,
haunted, his eyes pinned to the ground as flashbulbs and
jeers exploded around him, everyone watching, judging . . .

She clicked on another link, unable to stop looking. She
had to know it all – who he was, what he had done.

Jemtegard guilty!

Anders Jemtegard, the twenty-seven-year-old defendant in
the Grunerlokka murders, was today found guilty on both
charges and sentenced to nineteen years' imprisonment.
Jemtegard's defence counsel had argued not guilty to the
murder of Ingers Pedersen but guilty to manslaughter due
to diminished responsibility of Jans Bakken. The magistrate
sentencing Jemtegard, said the level of violence involved
made it one of the most disturbing cases he had dealt with
and Jemtegard's pleas had only added to the distress
already suffered by the victims' families.

Nineteen years. It was almost the maximum upper limit
allowed to the judge. It was one of the most disturbing cases
he had heard . . . So then why was Anders free? He had told

her he had come back here last year – she had assumed to look after Signy, but knowing all this now, how could he have returned to Oslo? His was one of the most notorious faces in Norway. In a country with a population of just over five million – half the number of people watching her – there was nowhere to hide. So he had gone to ground, come home to a town with just 240 residents and set up a company dealing specifically with tourists, people who would know nothing of his past – to them, he was just the guy leading the hike or driving the boat, his hood up, his beard wild. He could spend his days up a mountain or on the water, far away from all those people who knew and judged and condemned.

But what had changed? Why was he out?

She entered a different search – 'Anders Jemtegard freed' – seeing the links scroll down in perpetuity.

'Grunerlokka murderer appeals'; 'Killer Jemtegard appears before Courts of Appeal'; 'Grunerlokka killer freed!' –

She clicked on it, feeling her heartbeat spike at the sight of Anders standing outside a building flanked by a team of suits, his eyes blazing as he stared directly into the cameras – defiant. Furious. Vindicated. Broken.

Anders Jemtegard, the thirty-one-year-old former pilot convicted of double murder, today saw his sentence sensationally overturned as new evidence was submitted to the courts. At the original trial four years ago, Jemtegard pleaded not guilty to the murder of his girlfriend Inger Pedersen and guilty to manslaughter on grounds of diminished responsibility of Jans Bakken. His defence team had unsuccessfully argued that Jemtegard killed Bakken after returning home and finding the other man covered in blood and standing over Miss Pedersen's body on the floor

in the apartment they shared. The prosecution had success-
fully argued the case against him based on forensic evidence
taken from the injuries Pedersen sustained. However, in a
dramatic twist, fresh material has been submitted to the
courts proving Miss Pedersen had been stalked by Bakken
in the weeks preceding the attack and that she was in fact
attacked and killed by him. In light of the fresh develop-
ments, Jemtegard's guilty verdict was quashed in the case
of Pedersen and the murder charge against him for Bakken
commuted to involuntary manslaughter and suspended in
light of time already served. Jemtegard's legal counsel said
afterwards that his client was relieved the truth had been
revealed at last and asked for privacy in the coming months
that he might rebuild his life. It is understood the prosecution will not be appealing against the ruling and there are
already calls for an enquiry into what is being called a
'gross miscarriage of justice' . . .

Dear God. Bo leant her head back against the headrest, her
heart pounding erratically, trying to take it all in. So then he
had served four years in prison for killing the man who had
killed the woman he loved? She couldn't even begin to
imagine what he had endured, what he had seen . . .

She closed her eyes as the car continued to cut through the
night, tears streaming silently and unseen.

The solitary light glowed like a lone star as the taxi wound its
way down the Eagle Pass, taking the chicanes slowly, for the
rain in Alesund was falling as thick snow here, fat flakes spinning past the window and banking along the road. The rest
of the village was in darkness but for that one light. His.

It was almost three o'clock but he was home. He was up.

The Christmas Lights

She forgot all about the magnificent fjord carpeted before her as she kept her gaze upon it, as though worried she might lose sight of it – or worse, that it might switch off.

Four minutes later, the taxi driver wearily thanking her as she handed over the cash, she stood at the top of the narrow lane by the converted boatsheds, staring down at the single square of light pooling on the ground. She walked, listening to the profound silence that closed in once the sound of the car faded away. The unseen and invisible had presence here – the sea breeze that skinned the water, the face-aching cold that swept down from the arctic tundra, the past. It swelled and filled the air in the darkness in a way that would never be possible in the light or the warmth. There was something epic and majestic about its sense of desolation and she wondered whether this was what it sounded like in space – not the absence of sound but the pulsing presence of silence.

The snow creaked with every footstep and, too soon, she found herself outside the pretty white cottage, looking down the side path to the front door. She didn't even know why she had come. She had no words ready, no plan. Yes, the kayaks were moored by the jetty but it wasn't like she could paddle the fjord and hike that path at this time of night. Nor could she knock on anyone's door – even Annika and Harald's kindly patience would be tested by a middle-of-the-night social visit. In truth, she hadn't thought about what she would do when she arrived. She had simply known to follow her every instinct to leave Alesund and get back here.

And now she was, watching his shadow move in the twilight.

She knocked, bracing herself, trying to prepare what she should say. But what could she say, when he had seen in her eyes how quick she had been to judge and condemn, like the rest of them?

There was no reply and she knocked again, clutching the yellow jacket tighter, her gaze on her feet as she moved them about, trying to keep warm. After another minute of waiting, she looked up, scanning the upstairs windows. Had he seen her standing out here and refused to answer? Was that it? She dropped her head onto the door, her palms pressed flat against the wood as though not sure whether to knock, pound, beat it down.

But then she felt it, the weight of a stare upon her, and she turned. He was standing at the end of the path by the corner of the terrace, just watching her, a drink in his hand. He looked brooding, hostile and dangerous and she felt a frisson of fear because – justified though he had been – he had still killed a man, plunged a knife into another human body, over and over again.

'What are you doing here?' he asked, his voice low but unfriendly.

'I came . . . I came to see how you are.' She walked towards him but stopped short, seeing the rage in his eyes.

'Yeah, right.' He turned away and disappeared from sight around the corner.

'Anders, wait—' She followed after him. He was already at the back door, the fjord at the end of the terrace lapping the stones, as though listening in like a curious aunt.

'Go away, Bo.'

'Please. I know what happened to you. To her.'

His eyes flashed. 'She had a name.'

'I know,' she said quickly. 'Inger. Inger Pedersen. She was twenty-six and you . . . you loved her. Completely. You were going to marry her.'

'You don't know that.' The rebuttal was like the crack of a whip.

'Yes I do. I saw the photographs. It was all there to see, how you felt about each other. And I know you would never have hurt her. That you've suffered twice over.'

His head dropped then, a spasm of pain contorting his face and she automatically reached out, needing to comfort him. But he sprang back, not trusting her, not trusting anyone to help.

Her hand dropped.

'Just go.' His voice was raw, his eyes red-rimmed and appearing bluer than ever.

'But I want to help.'

'How?' he sneered, knocking the rest of his drink back. 'How can you help me?'

'The way you've helped me. By being a friend.'

He stormed over to her then, moving like a tornado – dizzying her, overwhelming her. 'We are not friends.'

'But—'

'This is not friendship,' he said, standing so close to her she felt she might fall back, his eyes boring into her. 'I don't need a *friend*.' She could feel his anger coming off him like heat and she sensed a shift, as though a pane of glass had shattered between them, bringing him into clearer focus. His control was slipping. He was loosened. Vulnerable. Just a man.

'So what, then? What do you need?'

He stared down at her then and she saw the answer perfectly spelled out in his eyes. And not for the first time. It had been flickering between them right from the start, from the first moment they'd met, but never quite brightly enough to grab or understand. It had been the acknowledgement she had been pushing for the night of the party, though she hadn't known it then. But she did now. Now she understood with sudden clarity that she hadn't left Alesund because of Ulla's footage, or Him, or Zac and Lenny's behaviour; she had left simply because *he* had; she had followed him here, her car chasing his through the night because even after what she'd been told he was, she hadn't felt it. She knew him. Just like he knew her. *Some people are like puzzle pieces – they just fit.*

'Say it,' she demanded, feeling her own anger rise as he let the silence simply swallow up all these unspoken words and carry them off into the night – just like he had the night of the party. He was going to let it go. Let her go. He knew what coursed between them; she could see it in his eyes, in the way his muscles were tensing – but he wouldn't act on it. He wouldn't let himself get caught again, he wouldn't be hurt.

He took a step back but she stepped into him, pushing his chest, goading him. She wouldn't let him turn her away this time. 'Say it! What do you need from me?'

Another moment contracted and tightened as if on a ratchet. 'More than I can have.'

'Which is what?' Her body was right up against his now, defiance in her eyes. He was a master of keeping people at arm's length – physically and emotionally. But she was in his face, in his space.

And then in his arms. He grabbed her coat and kissed her hard on the mouth, the bone-numbing cold dropping away as she felt only the heat in his lips. His stubble felt rough against her skin but she didn't care as she kissed him back. She didn't care about anything else at all. It was utterly unlike any kiss she had ever known and she would have lost herself in him, had he let her. But in the next moment, he pushed her away again.

'There's your answer. That's what I need – more than you

can give,' he said, his breath coming heavily, his eyes glittering angrily as though all this was her fault, as though she'd taken something from him, something more than a kiss. He turned away and strode back into the house.

But Bo was on his heels and she let the door close behind her with a slam.

He turned in surprise to find her already throwing off her jacket and pulling her jumper and T-shirt over her head in one swift movement. 'More than I can give?' She met his gaze, refusing to let him run again. 'I think I'll be the judge of that.'

Chapter Twenty-Three

'. . . He was left-handed, like me. Pretty much same height. Forensically, the wounds would have been inflicted similarly by us both in terms of angle and direction.' Anders' voice was flat as he spoke.

It still didn't feel real. Bo closed her eyes, feeling his heart thumping in his chest below her ear. 'Why was he there? Was it a burglary?'

There was a slight pause. 'He had helped her with a box she was carrying.'

'A *box*?'

She felt, as much as heard, the sharp intake of breath, as though he had a sudden stitch. 'A speaker I had ordered. It was bigger than I had realized and I had told Ing I would collect it at the weekend. But we were having friends round for dinner beforehand and she thought it would be fun if we had it for that, so she went to get it herself. As a surprise.' Bo heard the quaver in his voice, that sliding-doors decision that had changed everything. If she had just waited . . .

'A neighbour saw them walking down the street together; he was carrying the box for her. They were talking, Ing was smiling. He assumed they were friends – or perhaps more.'

'Which was why he wasn't seen as a suspect, just a victim,' Bo murmured.

'I don't know the rest for sure, no one does, but I assume he made a pass at her once they got to the apartment; that she turned him down and he . . . he snapped.' A heavy silence reverberated, filled with so much pain and anger, she could feel the heat in him rising. 'She was already down when I walked in. There was blood . . . everywhere. On her. On him. And he was –' His voice was diamond-hard. 'He was cleaning himself up when I walked in, getting ready to leave. And – I don't remember much after that. He tried to get past me and we fought. We fell over Inger lying on the floor –' His voice cleaved. 'And for just a moment, my eyes met hers, both of us lying there, in the blood. But she didn't see me, she had already gone. And that was when I felt something in me break. He couldn't match my rage then, my pain; I just killed him.'

'You avenged her,' Bo said quietly.

His eyes met hers momentarily and she saw in them the bottomless sorrow that he managed to hide day-to-day, his terse manner like a mirror reflecting away the curious gazes of strangers.

She had pushed herself up to sitting again, not caring that the duvet slipped off her shoulders, leaving her bare. They were beyond the physical now. Last night had seen to that, the passion between them swinging wildly between raging sorrow, despair and anger, to something calmer and more tender; something approaching peace. 'What happened to get you out again?' she asked, gently stroking his chest.

'A box of letters was found by the new tenants of our apartment. Ing had hidden them under a loose floorboard; they were only discovered when the new tenants decided to do some building works and replace the floors.'

'What kind of letters?'

'Similar to the messages you've been getting – they should

be together, she was a whore . . .' He flashed a look at her. 'Plus photos of her walking back to the apartment, at lunch with her colleagues . . .' A spasm of pain crossed his face again. 'If she'd just told me . . .'

But she hadn't wanted to worry him. He had been treated as a perpetrator and not a victim, his loss and the horror of what he found as he walked through his own front door a private hell he alone had to endure because a forensic coincidence and a well-intentioned secret cast him as guilty until proven innocent. She tried not to think about the terror Inger must have felt when she'd realized this friendly, helpful stranger was, in fact, Him.

He blinked up at her, one arm bent behind his head, his sabre-flash eyes now still pools, a Viking in repose. Her heart ached for his loss, her body yearned for his touch. She bent down to kiss him again, his lips so sweetly soft compared to the rest of him. He was muscle, sinew and bone, but in a different way to Zac. Zac worked out in order to climb in order to take photos to impress fans. Climbing was incidental to Anders, it simply got him to the top of the mountain and lifted him up to the view. He wasn't trying to live a life that was about looking good, but about feeling good. He didn't need an audience for validation. He actively didn't want eyes on him ever again, and who could blame him? He just wanted to be free – from iron bars, from bloodied memories, from pain.

He reached up as the kiss became longer, deeper, and he pulled her down to him, flesh on flesh, heart to heart, everything starting up again. She was a hunger he couldn't sate; he was a thirst she couldn't quench. And now that they had begun trying, she didn't know how they were ever supposed to stop.

*

They walked to the grocery store. It was all of four hundred yards from his house and they needed bread and wine and cheese. That was all. They could go that long, surely, without touching, without kissing, without needing to feel the other's skin beside their own and then they would be back in the house again, behind closed doors, and they wouldn't have to pretend to be something they weren't. Separate.

They pushed open the door, the small bell tinkling overhead as they walked in.

'*Hei-hei*,' the black-haired man behind the counter said, looking up and nodding as he saw Anders; a flicker of recognition passing over his face as he saw Bo too.

'*Hei*, Stale, how's it going?' Anders said in English, lightly skimming his hand over her backside whilst they were still obscured by the aisles, for the shelves came up to his shoulder height and up to her eyeline. 'How's it going?'

'Good. We got more Haandbryggeriet in if you want it.'

'Always. You know me.'

'What's that?' she whispered.

'My favourite beer.'

'Haandbryggeriet,' she murmured, trying to commit the word to memory.

They wandered down an aisle together, trying to hide from the shopkeeper's sight.

'Cheese?' she asked him, picking up a wrapped slab of cheese and trying to find any kind of identifying characteristics in English. Was it a cheddar?

'Butter,' Anders murmured, amusement in his voice as he came up behind her, his hands skimming her curves again and sending butterflies to take wing in her stomach again. 'Cheese is *ost*.'

'*Ost*,' she echoed, seeing how his eyes fell to her lips as she said it.

Anders glanced back at Stale to see if he was watching. He was. Anders cleared his throat and moved off. 'So did you catch the game last night? Was it good?'

'So-so,' Stale shrugged. 'Where were you?'

'Alesund. Running errands,' he shrugged, making no mention at all – either by word or action – of the behaviour he had endured there: the reckless judgements of a club full of strangers that carelessly overlooked that he had been both cleared of one murder and justified in the other. The stigma would stick, no matter what he did now. He was famous for being a killer. Not a pardoned one.

Bo watched him, swelling with pride that he was strong enough to keep putting one foot forward, to be the bigger man. She understood now why he had come home, and why his neighbours were so fiercely loyal to and protective of him. She found some *ost* and joined him over at the wine aisle. '*Ost*,' she said, showing him her prize.

A small smile hovered on his lips. 'Very good.'

'Shall I get the bread?' she asked, watching him watching her.

'*Can* you get the bread?'

'Depends. What's the word?'

'*Brod*.'

'*Brod*,' she echoed, pushing her lips together in a pout and eliciting a small groan from him. She smiled, taking her time. 'Then I shall go to get . . . *brod*.'

Unlike the cheese and butter, there was nothing else masquerading as bread and even without being armed with the correct vocabulary, she picked up a loaf.

They met again at the counter, amusement on their lips,

desire in their eyes; they needed to get back to the house and fast.

'How much?' Anders asked Stale, rummaging in his pocket for change.

'Two hundred and eleven kroner,' Stale replied, holding his hand out as he looked across at Bo.

Anders caught his stare. 'You know Bo, right?'

'Yeah, you came in the other day.'

'I did,' she nodded.

'I remember. Annika got you your medicine, right?'

'Yes.'

'Bo's a client,' Anders said. 'She's staying up at the farm at the moment.'

'Oh I wish I'd known that earlier. Did that guy catch up with you in the end?'

Bo felt her smile freeze in place. '. . . What guy?'

'He was in here this morning. A couple of hours ago. He showed me a picture of you and asked where you were staying. I didn't know you were one of Anders' clients or I'd have told him. Sorry.' He put the money in the till and handed Anders back some change.

But Anders didn't seem to notice. 'Did he leave a name?'

'No, I didn't ask.'

'Well, what did he look like?' he demanded.

'Uh, five eleven, I guess. Medium build. Greyish curly hair. Sort of Italian-looking. Glasses.'

'How old?'

'Mid-fifties?'

'Where's he staying?'

Stale looked taken aback by the interrogation. 'I don't know. He just came in, asked if I'd seen you and knew where you were staying. That was it.'

'And you told him—?' Anders pressed.

'That I'd seen you but I thought you'd gone already.' Stale looked between them. 'That's okay, isn't it?'

Anders' face had become rigid with tension; he was back to being the statue she had first met, a man set in concrete, shrouded in pain. 'If you see him again – you call me. Okay?'

'Sure.'

'*Immediately*.'

'Okay, man,' Stale said, looking bewildered.

Bo watched Anders, seeing the way his pupils had dilated, his cheeks flushed. Fight or flight. And he was a proven fighter.

'And don't – under any circumstances – tell him that you've seen her since, or where she's staying.'

'. . . Is everything okay?' Stale frowned.

'It's fine. But just don't tell him *anything*.'

'All right, all right, I won't.'

Anders looked across at her. 'Let's get out of here.' With a hand on her shoulder, he steered her to the door, looking outside left and right before he opened it, like a tracker scanning for clues.

'Hey, Anders, your change, man!' Stale called, holding out a twenty-kroner note.

But Anders didn't hear and the bell tinkled again as they walked back out into the snow, changed back into the people they had been before, the midnight spell already wearing off.

They stood in his kitchen, the curtains drawn even though it was light – one of the few hours of daylight today would enjoy.

'It could just be coincidence,' he said, pacing agitatedly as the kettle boiled.

She watched him, feeling a rock in her stomach at the sight of him. 'It's not.'

He glanced at her, their gazes tangling together in a web of pain and misery, before turning away again. They both knew there was an obvious solution, the only solution, one neither of them wanted to face. She watched as he heaped coffee into the pot before losing count, or interest, letting the spoon drop from his hand, granules scattering across the counter.

He dropped his head for a moment, taking a deep breath before he cleared his throat. 'Then you have to leave here. Get away as soon as possible.'

She stared at the ground. 'I know.'

The sound of the kettle filled their silence and she felt his eyes upon her for a moment before he turned and began rattling in the cupboard for cups. But he didn't want a coffee and nor did she. He was just trying to *do* something.

And that was the problem. He had already been through this – the woman he cared about under threat; that time he had been too late to save her, perhaps by only a few minutes, and he had almost lost his life and liberty in trying to do something about it. There were still conditions upon his parole, and affray or assault, anything to bring him in front of a judge again, would see him back behind bars. She couldn't expose him to that risk. She wouldn't let him fight this fight. It wasn't his problem. *She* wasn't his problem. Not yet. Not ever.

She cleared her throat, forcing herself to look at him, to say these words. 'I'll tell Zac. He'll know what to do.'

A frown crossed his face – hurt like a whipcrack through his eyes – and then his features hardened beneath the skin, the muscles becoming tight. 'Yes.'

'He's . . . he's good in a crisis.' She saw how his fist pulled into pulsing punches as he forced down the emotions rising in him. 'And he's been talking about us moving on anyway. He mentioned it last night.'

He frowned. 'Where?'

'The Caribbean.' Somewhere frivolous, photogenic. Far from here.

He was quiet for a long time, his words pushed back into silence again. 'Then I'd better take you back.'

Lodal, September 1936

First three lambs from the field and now, on her watch, two kids. Signy counted again but there was no disputing it. She even knew which ones had gone – the grey with the black face, and the black with the brown flash. She rang the bell harder, their mothers bleating and crying, but there was no sound of them coming over the rocks, back into sight. It had been forty minutes now since she had rung them back to her, shaking the seed box, seeing how they hungrily gathered back into a tight knot.

But not those two. They had wandered too far – chosen their moment when her back was turned as she picked the berries Brit had wanted; or was it when she'd counted the gyrfalcon chicks on their first flight? Either way, they weren't coming back. She picked up a rock and threw it in frustration, watching as it bounced off down the slope, making the other goats scatter. She had thought she was ready, she had thought she was prepared – the knife angled in her belt and grazing the herd closer to the *seter* too, knowing the wolf was tightening the loop, circling ever closer. But he had won by stealth and cunning. He wouldn't take on an open fight with her, with a knife. He didn't need to.

'Come on!' she snapped, beginning to stride out, jabbing her walking pole hard into the ground as she headed back for the farm. Looking for them wasn't an option – not on her own with the rest of the herd to corral.

The others were working in the field as she got back, marching up the grass, arms swinging madly. Kari and Ashi were lugging urns of churned butter between them over to the ground cellar, their backs hunched and arms stretched long as they lumbered across the uneven ground in an ungainly crab walk, both of them grunting with the effort.

'Two kids gone!' she cried as she stormed up to them, throwing down the basket of berries and feeling hot tears of frustration springing to her eyes. It felt like failure – her failure – to have lost them.

'Oh no, you are kidding,' Brit said, looking up from her stool. She was shoeing the horse, picking out mud from its hoof.

Signy shook her head woefully.

'You're sure they're not lost?'

'I'm telling you, it's a wolf, Brit. I've heard it.'

Brit suppressed a sigh. They had all been over this. 'But there's been no carcasses.'

'Yes! There was the deer carcass behind the forge,' Signy argued.

'That could have been natural causes. There's been no other sign of attack. And no one else has heard it. How do you know you didn't dream it?'

'I know what I heard,' Signy insisted, looking over at Sofie as she too turned to listen. She was pegging the washed clothes to the line strung up between the cabins, damp dresses, blouses, skirts and knickers fluttering above the path. 'Haven't you heard it, Sofie?' She knew full well she would have done. They had both been awake and outdoors when it had howled.

'No. Why would I have done?' Sofie said tartly, resting one hand on her hip.

Signy could only hold her gaze for a moment, certain the truth would shine in her eyes like a magical mirror. 'Well *I* have.'

She saw Margit come to the door of the storehouse and look down. 'What's going on?'

'We've lost two goats,' Brit called up.

'No!' Margit wiped her hands on her apron and began walking down the path.

'Signy's still convinced it's a wolf.'

'I know it is,' Signy insisted. 'I'm not making it up.'

The older girls exchanged looks.

'If it was, there would be evidence – blood; bones,' Margit said tactfully.

'And there will be – somewhere.'

Margit sighed. 'Well, if there was a wolf out there, that would mean *you* couldn't be up there alone. It's too dangerous.'

'No more dangerous for me than any of you,' Signy said defiantly. 'And, anyway, they're my flock. They listen to me.'

'Signy—' Brit said as Ashi and Kari came over, sinking into cross-legged heaps on the grass, elbows on their knees, cheeks flushed and hairlines damp.

'No. I can deal with it.'

Margit's eyes narrowed. 'What's that in your belt?' she asked, walking over to her and pulling out the threshing knife. 'What are you doing with this?'

'It's for if the wolf comes.'

'Signy!' Margit looked aghast.

'What? It's my protection if it attacks.'

'Signy, there is no wolf.' Her grip tightened around the knife. 'And I'm taking this. You are not to use it.'

'But it's my defence!' Signy protested, grabbing for it – but Margit stepped away.

'This isn't a game, Signy. You can't be arming yourself with weapons, roaming around the pastures with knives! What if you fell?'

'But I wouldn't. I never fall.'

Everyone's eyes pointedly fell to the scabs on her bare knees. 'Okay – *hardly* ever. And not when I'm carrying that. I'm extra careful.'

It was the wrong thing to have said as Margit's frown deepened. 'Exactly how long have you been carrying this around for?'

Signy bit her lip. 'For a few weeks – since I first heard the wolf.'

'Signy, enough! There is no wolf,' Margit cried, raising her voice. 'This has to stop. We don't have time for your stories here.'

'Why are you so sure I'm lying? The only person lying here is Sofie. She knows there's a wolf out there. She heard it, I know she did.'

Sofie gave a surprised splutter. 'Excuse me? Why are you so determined to think that *I* heard it?'

Signy stared at her, wanting to tell her – to tell them all – that she knew about her midnight assignations at the lake. But Margit intervened before she could summon the nerve. 'This stops now, Signy. The kids are lost because you were distracted.'

385

'Sleeping probably,' Sofie muttered. 'Or counting hawks.'

'I was not!' Signy said hotly, although she had pinpointed their nest after weeks of tracking and searching.

'Enough,' Margit said firmly. 'I'm taking this –' she held up the knife – 'and you are on your final warning. Of course the kids will stray. They're older and bolder now, you have to keep closer watch. Or these will be *very* expensive berries,' she said, picking up the basket. 'Lose any more of the flock and you'll have to swap chores with Kari.'

Kari looked as horrified as her. 'But—' Signy spluttered.

'No buts, Signy. That is my final word.' And she turned, walking back up to the *stabbur*.

Signy watched her go, her hands pulling into fists of rage. Brit went back to shoeing the mare. Kari held out her hand and pulled Ashi back to standing – another four urns needed to be moved.

'Signy, help me with this,' Sofie said, turning back to the washing.

Signy stood her ground for a moment, wanting to scream, to shout at them all. It wasn't fair that she should be taken off her post on account of her age or size. She was the best with the animals and they all knew it.

'Signy!' Sofie barked.

With a muffled cry of exasperation, Signy scuffed her way over.

'Peg that for me,' Sofie said, thrusting her favourite yellow dress at Signy.

'Why can't you do it?' Signy demanded, fed up with being pushed around by her, of her bare-faced lies. There was a wolf out there and Sofie knew it.

'Because I've asked *you* to,' Sofie snapped.

'But I've done my duties for the day.'

'Not well. You just cost your father two goats.'

'That's a lie!' Signy roared, letting the dress fall to the ground and feeling her self-control desert her. 'It wasn't my fault. There's a wolf out there and I know you know it,' she hissed, dropping her voice and advancing with a snarl. 'Because I know what you've been doing. And who with. And when.'

There was a short pause. '. . . Oh yes? And what have I been doing, then?' Sofie demanded, looking coldly furious. But if there was threat in her voice, there was fear too. Her coolness was a bluff.

'You've been sneaking around at night with Rag, behind Margit's back.'

The silence that followed was thunderous and Sofie's eyes glittered like black diamonds, boring into hers, before suddenly Signy saw a white flash – stars – her cheek stinging madly.

'You hit me!' Signy gasped in disbelief, her hand flying to her cheek and feeling the heat there. She looked to the others for help but no one was around. Brit had finished shoeing the horse and was leading her down to the bottom field, Kari and Ashi were up by the ground cellar, Margit was stocktaking in the *stabbur*.

'That's right and I'll do worse than that if you ever repeat such a filthy lie about me!'

Signy backed away from her, tears streaming down her cheeks now, fury and indignation a combustible mix in her blood. 'I don't need to,' she whispered viciously. 'Everyone's going to work it out for themselves soon enough anyway. I can already see it.' Her eyes fell pointedly to Sofie's belly – no longer flat but softly rounded below her skirt – and Sofie's arms automatically wrapped around herself, trying to shield her secret from Signy's laser gaze. 'You can't hide it for ever! Everyone's going to know what you are and what you've done.' A rictus smile twisted her mouth as the sobs and laughter heaved through her. 'I don't need to say a word.'

Chapter Twenty-Four

Bo stood in the cabin, looking around – at the ridiculous tree half hidden in the loft cavity, needles already dropping onto the floor; the coffee pot cold but still half full on the stove; Lenny and Zac's socks stiff from where they'd air-dried drooping over the backs of the chairs. Everything was exactly as they had left it and yet in the space of twenty-four hours, the world around them had changed. She had changed.

Anders was in the other cabin with his grandmother. From the air, as he had expertly brought the helicopter down to the ledge, Bo had taken in the sight of the remote homestead – the honeyed light glowing from its windows, the silhouetted tree, the puffing chimney – and she had felt a pang of homesickness that bordered on the violent. And standing here now, in this matching cabin that had all the same elements but none of the same feelings, tears streaming down her face, she felt it again.

She had never been more alone, more unrooted in this world. What was home, anyway? Anders had returned to it, here, after tragedy struck his life, but she had done precisely the opposite: when the car had come off the road, turning over seven times, and breaking her legs and rupturing Jamie's spleen, she had thought at first they would make it, that help would come. But there had been no witnesses. No phone reception. And the trees had screened them from the road. He had suffered slowly, haemorrhaging internally as she held his hand, trying to keep him awake; and when he had died, she had felt his hand become cool in hers, unable to move herself away. It was the horror of being stuck, of being in one place, that had stayed with her. It was why she had had to move, to run; it was why it had been four years since she had been home. But now, the thought of going another week without walking through her old front door and seeing her parents sitting at the kitchen table, felt unbearable. Suddenly she couldn't understand the drive, the determination that had enabled her to walk out the door and not look back, to think she could mask her pain with the studied pursuit of happiness.

Losing Jamie so young, she had felt almost like she had to live for the both of them. Life needed to be an adventure, didn't it? Working to pay the rent, a wage slave living for her annual holiday was a waste of time that she was lucky enough to have – and which Jamie wasn't. So she'd launched herself into a life of travel: new horizons, new adventures, new faces; and when she'd met Zac, he seemed to embody the heady, happy free-spiritedness she felt obliged to find on her brother's behalf. She was drawn to his zest, his happy-go-lucky easy manner. She *needed* it. He had shone light into her during her darkest moments and she realized now that at some level ever since, she had been afraid of falling back into the shadows without him.

But living in perpetual sunlight was exhausting too. Draining. It was true what she'd said to Signy: more people went mad under the midnight sun than the midday moon. And that was exactly how she had begun to feel. She had been slowly going crazy living in Zac's non-stop sunlight, the Wanderlusters' persistent spotlight, and it had taken a man who had retreated to the shadows to show her that.

The Christmas Lights

Trying to rub the tears away, she looked across the path and saw Anders moving past the window, bringing in more logs, talking to his grandmother. But he was going through the motions, doing what had to be done. He looked as desolate as she felt.

Already their night together felt like a dream. He had been quick to bring her back here, citing it as safer than staying at his house – the man asking after her wouldn't 'happen' upon this place, he wouldn't be lucky enough to catch a glimpse of her out here and he couldn't get to the farm without Anders' rib or skidoo. No one – apart from Stale – knew she was still here. It was the safest place for her to be right now.

She hadn't dared look in on Signy with him. Somehow, she feared the old woman would see what had changed between them. It was the same reason Anders had said he wouldn't look in on her here either: if the others were back, they couldn't trust their eyes not to betray them. But Zac wasn't around to wonder about anything. He was seemingly still in Alesund, in a sulk with her and no doubt hungover to hell.

It felt like a temporary reprieve, a chance for her to recollect herself. She wasn't ready to say hello again to Zac when it felt more than she could bear to say goodbye to Anders. She didn't want to deal with the inevitable confrontation when he got back, either, and she certainly didn't want an apology from him – for even if his and Lenny's behaviour last night hadn't been feral, what about her own? *She* had chased after Anders. *She* had forced things between them to a head. She was no injured party. She was no innocent. She wanted something Zac could no longer give her – what had once felt like freedom now felt like asylum and it was too big to wrap her mind around yet. She had sabotaged her own life and she wasn't even sure she was sorry about it.

She shivered, only now realizing how cold it was in the cabin, and she walked over to the stove and set it, crouching down on her haunches for a few minutes as she blankly watched the stripling yellow flames begin to dance. She washed out the coffee pot and made some fresh, looking in the cupboard for food. Pasta. Rice . . . She closed the cupboards again, her appetite utterly gone. Like Anders over the way, she was going through the motions.

The sound of footsteps outside made her look over to the window and she saw him walk past. But true to his word, his head didn't turn even fractionally in her direction and she too stayed where she was in the middle of the room, not daring to stand by the glass in case Signy should be watching.

She felt every sinew tighten and stretch as she braced for the sound of the rotors beginning to spin. The drone grew louder and louder, the timbers of the building vibrating gently and dislodging rivulets of snow from the roof, before whipping up a mini blizzard as the helicopter took flight. Bo felt her heart constrict as he rose higher, further and further away from her, before he slipped around the corner and out of range, leaving her and his grandmother alone on the snowy ridge.

'Anything?'
  'Nothing.'
  'Is he back?'
  'No.'
  '. . . Are you okay?'
  'Yes. Thanks.'
  'Sleep well.'

*

'There.'

Bo stepped back and admired her handiwork. The tree wasn't big – barely bigger than her, in fact but she had chopped it down using the axe she had found left on the log pile from where Zac *hadn't* chopped wood the other day, then dragged it back here all by herself. It had been exhilarating going up into the woods alone, cathartic – she had tied some orange nylon rope, found in the stables, around the trees as markers to help her find her way back and now she had decorated it, hand-tying red velvet bows on the ends of the delicate fronds and hanging the wooden decorations from the Christmas market at the windows and on random old nails knocked into the beams. The presents were wrapped and lay in a heap at its base; she'd forgotten to buy wrapping paper but had used old newspapers that were kept for setting the fire and leftover red ribbon for bows. It wasn't the grandest tree by any means, but its pine scent filled the cabin, wafting every time she walked past, and she kept looking over at it from her cosy spot on the sofa where she had curled up beside the fire.

Home? No. But it was something. A start.

After her strenuous activities, she had rewarded herself with a bath, boiling up the water and carrying it through in numerous pans to the bedroom until eventually it had been deep enough for her to soak, drift, wallow. Now she was scrolling again. There wasn't much else to do – the three books left by previous visitors, seemingly, were all in Norwegian – and though she hadn't posted a single thing all day, not even a picture of her toes or toast, she couldn't stop herself from clicking on the Wanderlusters' hashtag. The fact they'd lost two-hundred thousand followers overnight told her the videos from onlookers last night had been posted and – like the victim in any horror story, always walking towards the unlocked basement door – she had to look, to know what was out there. Because she knew He was.

She bit her thumbnail as she watched through slitted, grimacing eyes. Several people had recorded the fight, Zac and Lenny swaying and jeering like barbarians, her, shell-shocked and recalcitrant as she stood primly by the cab, hiding behind the door. She stared at her own face, looking in it for signs of what she was about to do – and finding none. She had been blind to her own heart.

The fans were decidedly unhappy with the scenes, scores of thumbs-down, split heart and crying-face emojis in the comments section. There was lots of 'disappointment': *'So sad to see this'*; *'Thought they were better than this'*; *'When your idols fall . . .'* He had weighed in of course, as she had known he would: *'You looked fuckable in those jeans tho.'*

As comments went, it was one of his more innocuous ones but the fear still lead-lined her stomach as it had since they had left the store. Was he still in Gerainger? Still looking for her? Had it just been coincidence he had asked for her there and he'd moved on already?

Shaking him from her thoughts and taking a deep breath, she found Ulla's account and clicked on her stories, seeing the live footage she had posted last night too – she felt a wave of nausea surge as the chaos in the club played back on a loop: the besuited *Halling* dancers squaring up to the quickening fiddles, the cheering rowdy crowd, her own face as she laughingly stuck out her tongue, the dancers beginning to show off and then . . . Anders. His angular, haunted face squarely in camera, blatantly uncomfortable as Ulla positioned her screen straight on him, the picture blurring slightly as they awkwardly shook hands . . . the cheers as he easily caught the hat . . . and then the music cutting out. '. . . *you killed that guy!* . . .' The deafening silence.

Bo closed her eyes, reliving it all. The horror. The shock. The judgement. People thinking they knew . . . This was what he had to live with, always—

She opened her eyes again, realizing suddenly something was wrong. Something didn't fit. It was like a tap on her heart, making her squirm, wriggle away.

But what . . . ?

Squinting, concentrating closely, she replayed the footage but she couldn't see . . . couldn't pinpoint what was niggling her. What was it? She went back to the Wanderlusters' hashtag and brought back the other videos – Zac jabbing the air, Lenny sneering, her behind the car door . . .

And then she saw it. Or rather, she *didn't*.

Only her upper body was visible in this film. And just her face in Ulla's.

She felt a shiver down the full length of her spine, the implication becoming clear. His comment hadn't been innocuous at all. It was another clue. A signal. A direct message hidden in plain sight – because none of that footage showed her in jeans. Which meant he had seen her himself. He had been there. Right there.

A sound outside made her startle. And now He was here.

Lodal, 13 September 1936

The sound woke her with a gasp. It had been close – right *here* – and she turned to wake Margit, to prove to her once and for all. But the bed was empty.

Signy stared at it, blinking hard several times, as though

she might still be dreaming. But the image remained unchanged and she threw off her covers, reaching across the narrow space between the beds, feeling the sheets. They were cold.

She would be in the outhouse, Signy knew, but with the wolf out there, the one that no one else believed was real . . . She got up, quickly pulling on a sweater and a pair of socks. One was scrunched up under Margit's bed from where Signy had kicked it off last night and as she reached under to get it, her fingertips brushed against something smooth on the sheets – something that wasn't cotton.

Frowning, she looked up. An edge of paper was peeking from beneath the pillow.

A letter?

Forgetting all about the wolf, she pushed the pillow aside but it wasn't a single letter she found; there were dozens, held together with ribbon, one of the flowers from the dried posy secured in the bow. Signy stared at the treasured package. Judging by the thickness of the bundle, Margit and her mystery lover had been writing all summer. But who was he, the one she'd dreamt about on Midsummer's Eve?

She heard the sound again but it wasn't the wolf howling; this was its prey, screaming. Without thought, she stuffed her feet into her boots and ran into the main room, scanning desperately for the threshing knife Margit had hidden. There was no sign of it, but no matter, there would be something she could use in the barns.

She flung open the door and was surprised by the relative darkness. Judging by how deeply she had slept, she had thought it was almost dawn, but the moon was still high in the sky, playing hide and seek behind tossed clouds. She pounded a fist on the other cabin windows as she passed; if the wolf was in the stables, she would need help, numbers, but there was no time to explain now. They would have to find her first, shout at her later. She ran up the path, her nightie bunched in one hand, her boots slapping against her skinny calves, but as she approached, she realized all was quiet with the animals. She slowed to a confused stop. There was the occasional lowing cow, a bad-tempered bleat, but none of the screaming cacophony she would expect from the goats if a predator was in with them.

But there was *something*. Movement in the haybarn. It might just be a fox hunting mice but if it wasn't, if it was the wolf . . . she needed something. A weapon. Was the pitchfork still in there? She tiptoed across the grass to the haybarn opposite, willing it to be the wolf. She needed the others to believe her. And God help her if she had just woken them all up on account of a fox.

The doors were closed, but not locked as they should have been (which was typical; it was Sofie's job). As quietly as she could, she pulled the doors ajar and peered round – and right then and there she grew up, her childhood dropping away like a too small dress. Margit was sprawled across a haybale, her legs splayed wide. A man was on top of her, jerking and thrusting, making the grunting sounds she had mistaken as coming from the animals. Signy couldn't see his face from here but she didn't need to. His white-blonde hair was a calling card.

He was the one. He was Margit's destiny.

For a second Signy couldn't react. She was paralysed with shock, watching the scene with horror, not understanding what she was seeing and yet still somehow *knowing*.

But then the details began to register, the minutiae she had initially missed now colouring in the framework of the scene.

She saw that Margit's eyes were bulging wide as she stared up at the rafters of the barn; that his hand was over her mouth and her tears were streaming over his fingers; that her dress was torn. And as Rag arched back, his face turning up to the sky like a wolf howling at the moon, she saw the man, face-down and unconscious on the ground; one eye was swollen shut, blood gushing from a split lip and seeping into the straw, staining it pink.

Signy felt her knees buckle as she screamed. It was an otherworldly sound, animalistic, something she couldn't recognize as coming from her and she staggered backwards, straight into the warmth of a soft body.

'No!' Sofie whispered, still warm from sleep but understanding immediately, the shawl slipping from her shoulders as she pushed Signy aside and lurched into the barn. Not seeing Mons, barely even Margit, her eyes were on him. Him alone. 'No!' she screamed out as Rag pulled himself off Margit, buttoning up his fly. A satisfied smile twisted his lips as he looked down at her spreadeagled before him, even though his face was badly scratched, blood drying at his nostrils.

Turning his attention to Sofie, he came down the haybales with almost a lope, pulling the braces of his trousers over his shoulders. He seemed not to have noticed Signy at all. She was too small, too young, too harmless.

Sofie flew at him. 'How could you? How could you?' she screamed, more wildcat than woman, her hair falling over her face as he grabbed her easily by the wrists, holding her in place as she flailed helplessly.

He tipped his head to the side, as though baffled by her curious response. 'What is this? You always knew Margit was to be mine.'

'You said you loved me!' she yelled.

He laughed at that. 'You're a pretty girl, Sofie. Of course I *wanted* you. But loved you?' A cruel smile spread. 'No.'

She began wrestling him again but he calmly stepped back and slapped her once, hard, across the face. The shock stunned her into silence, her hands flying to her cheek as she struggled to keep her balance. She stared back at him, tears blotching her face, her breath coming in heavy, clotted clumps.

'You're a cotter's daughter, Sofie,' he said simply. 'We both knew how it would end.' He wagged a finger at her. 'And besides, we both know you only wanted me because you knew I was tagged for Margit here. You always want what she's got.'

'That's not true!'

'Isn't it?'

He sighed, the action heavy and wearisome. 'Mons here has the same problem. He always wants what's mine – my father's attention; my future wife.' He kicked a lazy foot at Mons, groaning and still dazed on the ground. Sofie gasped as she finally caught sight of him, the truth of this situation beginning to dawn on her.

'You're a m-monster,' she stammered, his red handprint livid against her skin.

'No. He tried to take what was mine,' Rag sneered, looking down at Mons with a look of vicious contempt. 'I was simply protecting my rights. Droit de seigneur, I think they call it. He's been chasing her tail for quite a while by all accounts: secret love notes being carried up here every week, romantic walks together just the two of them . . . I was lucky to catch on when I did. It looks like we weren't the only ones—' and he suddenly threw his head back and howled. Like a wolf. Her wolf.

It had been him? Them? Their signal?

Signy felt a burst of rage explode through her. 'We'll tell my father!' she screamed, dancing her feet like a boxer, her hands pulling and releasing into panicky fists.

Rag's gaze settled upon her, noticing her for the first time. Something about her seemed to amuse him. 'And say what, little thing? That your sister is a slut, playing fast and loose up here with any passing stranger? What would he think, huh? How would he feel if the rest of the village were to hear that?'

'You leave her –' Behind him, Margit was trying to sit up, to gather her dress to her, bunching the skirt at the knees, trying to pin up the shoulder. Hay stuck out from her hair and she looked like she had the beginnings of a black eye too. Her face was blotchy and swollen and her breath came in rolling heaves that physically inflated and collapsed her. She tried to scoot forwards off the bale but a bolt of pain stopped her short, blood smearing her inner thighs, her face contorted in a grimace.

At the sight of her, Signy felt the fear switch – like blood marbling water, becoming pinker and redder, anger began to swirl in its place.

'As it is, your sister's *lucky*. I'll still marry her. As soon as you girls get back next week, in fact. I have to leave again—'

'I will *never* . . . marry you,' Margit panted, every word an effort, her voice low and split by pain.

'That isn't your choice to make now,' Rag said, watching as she pulled herself down the bales, scratched and bloodied, wounded and weak. 'You should be about ready to pop by the time I get back from training.'

Margit pulled herself to standing, her balance unsteady. 'I would kill it first,' she hissed, meeting his glare.

Rag took a step towards her, menace in his movements. 'Oh yeah?'

'Don't worry,' Sofie said from behind him, suddenly calm. 'We can always keep mine.'

He turned to find Sofie holding her arms around her stomach and pinning down the thin cotton of her nightdress. His mouth parted as he looked down at her gently swelling belly. A victorious glimmer sparkled in her eyes as she saw his shock.

Slowly, he looked back up at her. 'You stupid bitch!'

She snorted. '*I'm* stupi—?' But the word was smacked away from her as he slapped her hard with the back of his hand again. This time she did reel, spinning backwards and hitting the barn door before slumping to the floor.

'Sofie!' Margit cried, lunging forwards, but she was too slow to stop the backwards arc of his leg as it swung, kicking forward into Sofie's prone body with immense force. Sofie screamed out, curling around her stomach and trying to protect her unborn child – and for a moment, the valley rang with the sounds of their screams. Kari, Brit and Ashi had stumbled up to the barn just in time to see Margit launching herself at his back, fists flailing, but he swatted her away as easily as if she were a doll, his leg swinging back and forth at Sofie like a pendulum.

And then it stopped, the silence cracking like a gunshot as Rag fell still, his face a ghastly growing green. No one could speak as a few beads of blood crowned in his hair, before becoming a tide. His hand rose up, touching the warm, sticky substance as if in disbelief. Stumbling, he turned, lurching like a drunk man as he looked to see who had murdered him. And how.

Little Signy Reiten stared back at him, her chest rising and falling in breathless pants, her eyes as wide as his, and her arms still holding the old whetstone above her head, white-blonde hairs dangling down from it like mosquito legs.

Chapter Twenty-Five

The sound made her jump, her mouth frozen open in a perfect 'o' as her ears strained for another. It was so distinctive – the creak of snow underfoot . . .

There it was. Coming closer.

Feeling her heartrate spike, she looked around for something, anything, that could double as a weapon. He had the advantage. With the lights on, he could see straight in. He might be standing by the window, right now, staring in at her, his own face shrouded in the darkness. How long had he been there?

Her eyes fell onto the poker by the stove and she jumped up to grab it, knowing she couldn't get to the door in time to lock it, but she reached up for the light switch and cut the power, darkness drenching the room but for the glow of the fire. Crouching down by the side of the sofa, she waited. She felt the pound of her heart beat through her body as she tightened her fingers around the neck of the poker, bracing for the sound of the latch.

She heard the footsteps again, each one planted slowly, carefully. He was creeping his way closer. Did he know she knew he was there? He had to. He must have seen the lights, surely.

There it was – the click of the latch disengaging, a zip of

403

cold air nipping in before him. She felt the poker shake in her hand, an unstoppable hysteria rising up in her.

He was here.

He had found her.

'. . . Bo?' The whisper drifted in like a feather.

She clutched the poker tighter, willing herself not to drop it.

'Bo? It's me.'

What? The breath whistled from her like it was pulled on a string. 'Anders?' she gasped.

'It's me.'

The door closed behind him and she saw his already-familiar shape as her eyes adjusted to the darkness.

'What . . . oh my God, what are you doing here?' she whispered back, on the verge of tears, trying to stand again but not sure her legs would manage it.

'He's still not come back?'

'Who? Zac?' She wanted to cry with relief. 'No. No, he's . . . he's punishing me, I think.' He was in front of her now, the smell of him engulfing her. His hands on her arms.

'You're shaking.'

'. . . Just an overactive imagination,' she said, forcing a laugh. She couldn't tell him; she couldn't say that she'd thought he was Him – that he'd been at the club last night, that he had followed her back here as she had followed Anders, their cars snaking a daisy-chain through the night. 'What are you doing here?'

She felt his grip tighten on her arms, saw his head drop, and she didn't need an answer. They both thought it, both felt it. Separation was inevitable, yes, but there was still some sand left in the timer. There was still tonight.

She reached up and kissed him, feeling how quickly he

responded to her, the heat between them instantaneous. 'How did you get back?' she asked, eyes closed as she felt his hands on her.

'I took the skidoo . . . Parked it up the top and walked down so my grandmother wouldn't hear.'

'I thought you said . . . she's pretty deaf,' she gasped between kisses.

He gave her a wry look. 'She suffers from selective deafness.'

Bo laughed. 'And what if she sees you coming out of here in the morning?'

'Then I'll say I came in here first to go over the itinerary.'

They pulled back to look at one another again; it had felt like an impossible wish that they might have another night together, and his simmering look of intent made her stomach flip. She pulled back slightly as he pulled her top off. '. . . But what if Zac comes back?'

'He won't now. It's too dark.'

'But what if he gets here early?'

'Then we wake up early,' he said, his mouth back on hers, urgent now, walking her backwards into the bedroom. 'Or even better, we won't sleep at all.'

It was no stealth attack, but they were still in bed when she heard Lenny and Zac coming up the path the next morning. It was dark outside – Anders had kept the fjord-side curtains open especially, not wanting to sleep too deeply – and they looked at each other in a curious mix of wide-eyed alarm and resigned despair. They had both known this moment was coming. It was due payment for last night.

He planted another kiss on her lips and then threw back the covers, stepping into his clothes with brisk efficiency.

They heard the latch turn on the front door just as he shrugged on his sweater, but he didn't rush – his eyes never leaving her as she felt their goodbyes swim in the silence.

'What the hell?' Lenny's voice in the other room was muffled and Bo knew they were looking at the new, decorated, miniature tree. She had dragged the other one outside and left it propped against the wall. To hell with Zac's wounded ego.

Anders came back over to the bed, leaning over and kissing her lingeringly one last time. His eyes roamed hers, seeing everything but a solution there, and then he pulled back and walked over to the window. He flung it open and hoisted himself easily onto the frame, pulling up one leg, then the other. He looked back at her with an expression that made her feel like she was the one falling – and then he jumped.

It was a fair drop, even with thick snow to land in; the ground sloped sharply downhill there and the stables were accessible on that side. She jumped out of bed and looked out, seeing him run, crouched, around the side of the building. He was below the level of the windows in the main room – so long as no one was looking out of them, he would escape unseen. She quickly closed the window, climbed into her thermals and was knotting the belt of her cardigan just as the door opened and Zac looked in.

They stared at one another. He looked rough, unshaven and pale, puffy-eyed.

'Hey,' he mumbled.

'Hey,' she said simply, after a moment. 'You're back then.'

'Yes.' The word was short, his mouth a set line, and she couldn't quite tell if he was still angry or wanting forgiveness. Maybe both? Perhaps he was trying to gauge her reaction first.

She watched him glance around the room. Could he tell another man had been here? Did he sense his worst nightmare was in play? The bed was rumpled, chaotic, but she often spread herself across the bed when he got up, stretching up and outwards to sleep like a starfish.

Another silence bloomed, neither one of them sure how to fill it. The anger she felt at his behaviour in Alesund had diminished in the bright light of her realized feelings for Anders and she didn't want an apology from him – it didn't seem important; she didn't think she even cared.

'Would you like a coffee?' she asked, walking past him and registering his surprise at her calm manner. Had he been braced for a showdown? A catastrophic screaming match?

'. . . Sure.'

She went to the stove and scraped out the sludge from yesterday's coffee pot. She could feel him watching her as she busied herself with washing up and finding cups.

'What's this?'

'What?' She turned disinterestedly.

He was holding up Anders' distinctive North Face jacket. They both knew perfectly well to whom it belonged. 'Why's this here?' he frowned, looking back at her.

It had been lying on the ground beside the sofa where Anders had shrugged it off last night, concerned only with getting her into the bedroom. She had completely forgotten about it.

Her mouth parted but no words came. What could she say? Her eyes rose to his, panic clouding her brain, and she was sure she could see him begin to attach a narrative to it, to find a story that fitted perfectly. The only one.

The sound of feet being stamped on the mat made them both turn. Anders was walking in with a piled-high armful of logs. 'There, that should do it,' he huffed, before stopping at the sight of Zac. 'Oh. Hey. You're back.'

Zac's demeanour changed at the unexpected intrusion, Anders' uncharacteristic 'chattiness'.

'Yes – a load of snow dumped on Anders on the way over. He's drying it out before we all head off later,' Bo explained, walking over and taking the coat from Zac before he could process that it was bone-dry. She made a play of patting it down and positioning it in front of the stove.

But Zac couldn't take his gaze off Anders. 'What are you doing here?' he asked coldly, just as Lenny's booted feet sounded on the ladder and he emerged from his digs again. If Bo had thought Zac looked bad, Lenny had taken it to a whole other level – he didn't look like he'd slept in days. Had he lost weight?

Anders frowned at their frowns. 'We are still going out today, aren't we? I thought today was the big day?' And when Zac didn't – couldn't – reply, added: 'The last I heard we were doing the crevasse walk on Mount Åkernes?'

There was another silence and Bo knew exactly what Zac and Lenny were thinking – the last they had heard, Anders was a killer.

'Thought you weren't gonna do that?' Lenny said, hostility slicing through his words.

Anders shrugged. 'It's your last day with Ridge Riders and we know each other better now. I'm happy to go if you want.'

'Yeah,' Lenny murmured. 'We do know each other now.'

Bo swallowed. Were they going to confront him?

Anders' eyes narrowed as he pretended to care about their innuendo and insinuation. He opened his arms out, defiantly letting the logs drop to the ground where he stood. 'Okay, well why don't I leave you all to talk it over?' And he walked out, striding up to his grandmother's cabin in nine strides.

'What the actual fuck, Bo?' Zac exclaimed, as soon as she

408

was out of sight. 'Did you not hear what they said about him the other night?'

'And do you not *read*?' she spat back. 'If you took a few goddam minutes to find out the *whole* truth, you might discover the real story. His girlfriend was murdered! He walked in on it! He killed the guy whilst trying to protect her! Where's your fucking compassion?'

Zac's face changed at the sight of her white-hot fury, her bald facts, and he saw now the change in her, he sensed the distance. 'I'm sorry.' But it was an all-encompassing statement, not so much apologizing for rushing to judgement on Anders, she knew, as for his own behaviour. Like horses at the gate, they were off . . .

'Sorry doesn't interest me now.'

'Things got way out of hand. I was paralytic. Lenny too. I never should have . . . treated you like that.'

'I don't care, Zac.' She turned away to make the coffee but she was like Anders in his kitchen last night. She just needed to move, to do something.

'You don't *care*?' Zac asked, an edge of concern blading his voice now, his eyes weighty upon her as she kept her back turned.

'What are you saying?' Lenny asked too.

Bo glowered at him. Was he really going to inveigle his way into their domestics now too? 'Back off, Lenny,' she said flatly. 'This doesn't concern you.'

Lenny took a step back, stunned.

She looked back at Zac. A switch had been flicked in her. Suddenly she couldn't think or feel what it was that held them together, the magnetism between them had lost its charge. And yet, she couldn't leave him. If the chemistry had failed, fate was forcing them together anyway, pushing them back on the road and away from the only person who had briefly promised her a home. 'I'm saying I'm not interested in reasons or excuses.' She sighed. 'Let's just move on.'

There was another long pause as he watched her tip the packet of coffee into the pot and she could almost feel his relief that she wasn't pushing the red button, that she didn't want to make the fight bigger than it already was. 'Move on? Okay, yes, I agree. You're right—'

'I think we should leave here.' She stared at the counter as she said the words that had to be said. 'Let's go to the Exumas.'

'What? But I thought – I mean, you didn't seem keen –'

She turned her head fractionally, facing him and Lenny in profile. 'You reserved the flights, didn't you, Len?'

Lenny straightened up. 'Uh, yeah. Yeah I did.'

'Fine. So then let's go. Let's split.' Her voice was flat as she turned away again and stared out of the window, seeing Anders in the other cabin; he was leaning against the table, his head dropped, his shoulders hunched, his arms wrapped around his torso.

'The flight's tonight, you know that, right? We'd get there tomorrow morning: Christmas Day.' Zac placed a tentative hand on her shoulder. 'Are you really sure you want to go? I mean, it can wait a bit. It's Christmas Eve now and you've made this place look so pretty . . .' It was supposed to be a compliment, acknowledgement that he'd got it wrong with the tree and she'd made it right.

'I'm positive,' she said, feeling the tears press. 'I want to go as soon as possible.'

'Well, okay then. As soon as we've done the crevasse pass, we can head out of here.'

'What?' She turned to face him.

The Christmas Lights

'The crevasse pass? Anders has agreed to it; that's why he's here.'

'No, forget that. Let's just leave. Right now. I can't be here any more,' she said desperately.

'Bo, babe – today's our last day with Ridge Riders. We promised them a big send-off and contractually, we have to do it. We'll be in breach of contract otherwise and I don't want anything getting between us and that two hundred thou.'

She couldn't bear it. Another whole day – with Anders out of reach? With Him within arm's length? Abandoning the coffee, she walked past Zac, not wanting to look at him lest he should see it all written in her eyes, but he caught her by the elbow and swung her into him.

'Bo. Baby, look – I know it's been rough. But what they're saying about us? It's bullshit, you know that. Don't take it to heart—'

She stared at him in disbelief. Did he really think she cared about the noise on social media?

'But we'll show them what we're all about. *We* know what we've got. We're back on track, starting today.' He took her hand and kissed it, his eyes pinned on hers. 'It was one stupid night but I'm going to make everything up to you, just you wait.' He smiled, confidence coming back into his eyes now. 'This time tomorrow we'll be on a beach, swimming with pigs, and all this will be a distant memory. We got it wrong coming here, but that's how it is sometimes. Some you win. Some you lose.'

She closed her eyes as he kissed the tip of her nose, seeing Anders' face in her mind's eye: his sad eyes, his fragile heart.

Some you lose.

Lodal, 13 September 1936

The blood was forming a river, snaking slowly through the hay, the sweet metallic smell cloying as she sat slumped, watching it ooze. Margit was cradling Mons in her lap as Brit went down to saddle the horse; they had to get him to the doctor quickly. Ashi and Kari were trying to comfort Sofie where she lay curled on the ground, sobbing hysterically and refusing to stand.

But Signy had collapsed where she stood, shivering uncontrollably on her own and reliving the moment through open eyes. What had she done? Over and over the question ran through her mind on a loop. It had all been so fast, so terrifying. Too much. The reasons were numerous but the fact of it was simple: she had killed a man and damned her own soul.

She knew there was no escaping this. Rag was the *lensmann's* son, the village's heir apparent. He couldn't just *disappear*; this couldn't be explained away. His family had money, power, connections . . . No, she would be taken from her family, far from here. She would never again stride out over the fields, the goats butting her knees, the sun on her face, flowers under her palm, falcons in the sky. Her first summer of freedom was to be her only one. Her life would stop right here as surely as Rag's, her soul twisted around his in an eternal dance of death.

She felt her shakes increase – and it was a moment before she processed that the vibrations weren't coming from her. It was a growing feeling, a gathering sound – a monstrous moan like the earth was yawning open, distant and then suddenly *here*, the ground shaking violently beneath their feet. The girls gasped and cried out, throwing their arms protectively above their heads, lest the roof should fall along with the sky.

'What's happening?' Kari screamed.

Getting to her feet on wobbly, coltish legs, Signy staggered from the barn onto the grassy path. The animals were going berserk in their pens, the horse bucking in the field. Birds were shaking themselves from the trees and taking flight through the dawn sky.

What . . . ? The sound was apocalyptic, as though the heavens were falling to earth; it was bigger than anything they had ever heard and their gazes were automatically pulled to the far edge of the plateau where – from here – the ground seemed to drop away in a vertical slice. A great grey plume of smoke was filling the valley, barrelling through in roiling plumes, reaching up for the clouds.

'No!' Margit screamed, coming to stand by her, the torn dress hanging at the shoulder. 'It can't be. Not again.' Her hands flew to her mouth and she braced, as though expecting something else, something more – and a moment later, it came. *'No!'*

Signy began screaming too, panicking wildly now, trying to comprehend what her eyes were showing her: white froth topping and foaming as the wave built into a moving wall, hundreds of feet high. 'What is that?' she screamed as Margit clutched her, trembling violently herself, as helplessly they watched it surge towards the village. Their home. Their family. Nils. 'What is that? What is that?'

It broke, sinking from sight as suddenly as it had come and Margit too slumped to the ground, her head hanging like a broken-necked tulip, her skin scratched and bruised, silent tears streaming over her cheeks.

Signy stared into the void, her little body shaking violently in the new silence. It was minutes before she was able to move. 'W-what was that?' she whispered, balling herself up as small as she could and nestling against her sister, like one of the runt kids to its mother, her voice stripped thin and bleached white with terror upon terror. 'Margit?'

Margit slowly lifted her head to look at her, taking her hand in her own and squeezing it tight. 'I think it was an answer.'

Chapter Twenty-Six

'Signy?' Bo peered around the door, seeing the old woman sitting in her chair and looking out across the fjord. The log basket had been freshly stacked, golden light glowing through the stove-glass. 'We're about to go. I was just checking you're okay before we leave?'

'Where is Anders?'

'Loading the helicopter.'

Signy stared back outside again. 'Come in. You're letting in the cold.'

'Well we're just about to—'

'I said come in.'

With a sigh, Bo did as she was told. 'Do you need anything? Some water? A blanket?'

'Tell me where you're going today. My grandson is being evasive.'

Bo perched on the blue velvet settle beside the rocking chair. 'Have you heard about the crack that's developed along Mount Åkernes?'

'Heard about it?' she scoffed, folding her hands in her lap. 'Girl, my husband was one of the first to spot it.'

Bo's eyes widened. *'Really?'*

'Why should that surprise you? We know all the old farming families here. My husband hunted there every winter. He was with the farmer when they saw the first slip of the back scarp.'

'When was that?'

'1964.'

'Wow! Okay, well then, you'll know what I'm talking about when I say we're doing a walk through the crevasse.'

There was a short pause. '. . . Why?' Signy looked scornful.

It was a good question – why indeed? It wasn't an experience, it was a gimmick, just a dare – walking through the fatal chasm on the most monitored mountain in the world. 'Because no one's done it before and it will make for good footage,' she said honestly.

'But it could slip at any moment.'

That wasn't strictly true. Rather like an earthquake predictor, the sensors would register dramatic shifts in geological activity for at least seventy-two hours in advance. 'I know,' she said instead. If there was one thing she had learnt, it was that there was little point in arguing with the woman. 'But that's sort of the point – the thrill of it. Zac and Lenny are climbing up to it from the water right now – Anders took them up in the rib earlier and now he's come back for me and Anna and he's going to fly us up there to meet them. Apparently there's a research station where we can land.'

'Is he aware, this man, that this danger is real? That it is not a joke?'

Bo assumed 'this man' was Zac. 'Yes.'

'I don't think he can be. He does not understand the human cost. The mountain *will* fall.'

'One day, yes. My understanding is that it's a one-in-a-thousand-year event,' she said benignly.

'Oh, is it?' Signy asked, clearly rhetorically. 'So the fact that it happened twice in thirty years in my lifetime in the next fjord up from here counts for nothing, I suppose?'

'I – I didn't know that.'

'Why would you? You are tourists. But I have already lived through two and experienced one of them myself.' Her voice dimmed. 'It was what brought me here to this fjord in the first place.'

Bo was aghast. 'What happened?'

'Part of the mountain beside our village came away. Mount Ramnefjell, it is called. The rocks fell two and a half thousand feet into the lake. The force of it hitting the water created a wave three hundred feet high.'

'Oh my God,' she whispered.

'I was fourteen at the time. Seventy-four people died – and I knew every single one of them. My parents. My brother—'

'Oh my God,' Bo said again, the words more a moan.

'It happened at dawn when almost everyone was sleeping, still in their beds. All the farms in my village, Lodal, as well as the neighbouring village, Nesdal, were swept away by the wave.'

'So then, how did *you* survive?'

There was a pause. 'Because I wasn't there. I was further up the valley at the *seter* with my sister and some of the other girls from the village.' She glanced sideways at Bo, taking in her blank expression. 'The *seter* was our summer farm. It was where we took the animals to graze in the summer and where we could make hay for the winter stocks.'

'So then it was just sheer luck that you weren't there?'

'Luck? No. No one was lucky that night.' Signy's eyes became distant, fixing on a faraway point – further, Bo thought, than the waterfall on the other side of the fjord. 'Death was in the valley, both high and low.'

Bo looked at her, confused but not liking to press. They were quiet for a few moments, both lost in thought. 'You said it happened twice in thirty years?'

'Yes. This was 1936 but it had happened before that in 1905 on the same mountain, sending another giant wave over the villages. Twenty-four people perished that night too but only nine bodies were ever recovered. And then it happened again in 1934 at Tafjord just over the mountains from here – forty lives lost.' She looked at Bo with hard eyes. 'So when people like *him* behave as though these dangers are just a *joke* . . .' She gave a contemptuous shrug. 'Something to make him look brave . . . he does not know the meaning. Real bravery takes sacrifice.'

Bo knew then she was thinking of her grandson and what he had given up trying to protect Inger. 'Please don't be angry with Anders. He didn't want to take us. He's only doing it to help me.'

Signy looked at her, her shrewd eyes travelling over Bo, assessing her like she was a racehorse. 'I know. He does a lot for you.'

Bo stared at her hands, not sure what to say; this was becoming dangerous territory. Signy always seemed to see right to the heart of her. 'Did he tell you we're leaving tonight?'

The old woman looked alarmed, on the back foot for once. 'Tonight?' she frowned. 'But your booking runs into the New Year. Don't you like it here?'

'It's not that. I love it here.'

'Then what?'

Bo stalled. There was no way to possibly explain an online troll to her. 'We just have to move on. It's time for us to go.'

Signy stared again. '. . . Is it because of her? That girl? She has come between you?'

'Who?' And when Signy didn't reply. '. . . *Anna?*' Bo gave a small laugh. 'No. No . . .'

But as Signy continued to stare, her intimation loud and clear, the smile faded from Bo's lips. 'I saw her in the cabin that morning. Before you came back.'

'Yes. She was seeing Lenny briefly,' Bo explained calmly. But even as the words left her, she remembered that day, the morning after her 'fight' with Anders: how she'd seen Anna in the bath-towel through the window. Zac's overcompensating welcome. Lenny's . . . Lenny's photographs of that morning showing the two coffees on the tray, ready for breakfast in bed.

But Lenny never drank coffee.

Signy shook her head. 'They were in the bedroom together.'

Bo looked out of the window, feeling a cold wind whistle through her as she watched Anna standing with Anders down by the helicopter. She was looking down at her phone, ignoring him. Was she frightened of him now? Did she believe the hype, the headlines? It was a studied contrast to Bo's last image of her as she and Anja had run over delightedly helping Lenny and Zac off the ground. Where had Zac stayed that night and all yesterday – at a hotel? Or at Anna's?

Bo had thought her pale when she had emerged from packing up her things in the storehouse earlier, handing over today's kit – a white fur-trimmed belted jacket and matching stirrup trousers that seemed more St Moritz than Stranda – without a smile; but Bo had put it down to a lingering hangover, the cold . . . She'd not said much either, uncharacteristically standing by quietly as the men had run through their final checks of climbing equipment, Zac's studied purpose and intensity for this final expedition doing a great job of covering for the fact that he was actually . . . ignoring her.

Bo stared into space, trying to feel the hurt she knew must come with this news. But it wasn't emotion that was clamouring at her, so much as logic. Perhaps it was all too soon, too shocking to absorb yet, but as the truth settled into clarity, she knew it wasn't just Zac who had deceived her, it was Lenny too. Lenny had covered for him, she saw that now – his swagger out of the cabin deliberately leading her to assume Anna was his conquest; Anna and Zac's subdued mood as Lenny had taken it too far in the slope-side restaurant, kissing her intimately in front of them all; he had taken advantage of her knowing she couldn't resist or say no . . . that was why she'd been so angry with him afterwards. And if Lenny had helped Zac cover his tracks once, who was to say he hadn't done it countless other times as well?

The betrayal was two-fold. Both of them had been playing her for a fool, protecting each other's back. As she had long suspected, the primary relationship was between the two of them.

She felt her world shift off-axis again as the revelation settled; she had thought leaving here was the answer, that once this final assignment was done and the contract was fulfilled, that they would all go back to their own lives as before – Anna and Anders would disperse like seeds from a pod and the Wanderlusters would go back on the road. It had been naïve, perhaps, but she had told herself that with time, she would forget Anders and slip back into how things used to be with Zac. But it was all a delusion. How could she go with them now? How could they possibly carry on when everything was built on lies?

'Why have you told me this?' she asked, looking at Signy flatly.

'To help you, girl,' Signy said hotly, seeing her despair. 'You need to know that your worst moment can turn out to be your best. In every life, there is a defining moment of surrender where you must make a choice to let Destiny happen. You have to give yourself up to what must be.'

Bo was quiet for a long moment, trying to make sense of her words. 'I wouldn't have pegged you as a big believer in fate,' she finally muttered, staring at her hands.

'When you live for almost a century, you see patterns that are invisible close-up. But when I look back over the course of my life, I can see that the most pivotal moments were always the ones beyond my control.'

'That's not very encouraging.'

'It's not about what happens to you; it's about how you respond. Look at me.' She looked out across the fjord, the majesty of that view. 'Who has had a life richer than mine?' There wasn't a trace of irony in her voice. 'And yet when my worst moment came, I believed my life was over. I had killed a man and I could see no way out.'

Bo's head whipped up in stunned surprise.

'Yes, you heard me.' Signy stared at her for a very long time, seeing her but not, her jaw sliding side to side as she recounted the events in her mind. It seemed an age before she spoke again, settling her gaze upon Bo with studied exactitude. 'I've never spoken of this before – Anders knows nothing about it.'

'You don't have to tell me,' Bo said quietly.

'I know that.' She gave a heavy sigh. 'But I am old and everyone who was there is long since dead anyway. No, my time is coming and when it does, I want to be free of secrets.'

Bo stayed silent. There was nothing she could add to that.

'The man I killed was called Rag Omenas. He was supposed to marry my sister Margit, only Margit didn't love him. She loved another man, Mons, a newcomer to the village who worked for Rag's father. One day – and I don't know how exactly – Rag intercepted a letter from Margit asking her sweetheart to meet her at the *seter* that night. Rag followed him there and confronted them, before attacking them both. He fractured both Mons' cheeks and an eye-socket and left him with internal bleeding. Then he hurt Margit.' Her eyes misted, becoming rheumy, a chink in her armour. 'He was crazy. A madman. So I picked up a heavy stone and brought it down on his head.' Her eyes slid to Bo's. 'It was the only way to stop him, you see. It was us or him.'

Bo reached out and covered Signy's hands with her own. 'Yes, I see.'

'And it changed me, right in that instant. I was fourteen years old and I had killed a man. I couldn't stop shaking. But Margit was so brave, trying to think how to save me, when she – *she* had been hurt worst of all. I wanted to run away as far as I could get; Margit was insisting she would say it was she who had killed him – that Rag had attacked her and it was self-defence. But his father was powerful, he never would have accepted that. To lose his son and then have his reputation destroyed too?' She tutted. 'No.'

'So what did you do?'

'We didn't. The mountain did it for us.'

'The mountain?' Bo looked at her, confused.

'It fell.'

For a moment, Bo couldn't speak. 'That was the same night?'

Signy blanched. 'We saw the wave head to the shore.'

'But your family . . .' Bo whispered.

'Yes. We knew immediately what it meant. We had grown

up listening to the stories of 1905.' She closed her eyes for a long moment. '. . . Margit took charge. She knew in that instant we were orphans and that we were too far to save them, to do anything. But she also saw that it might save us.' She nodded solemnly, her pauses becoming longer as she remembered, thought back. '. . . So, in spite of everything, we managed to get the body on the back of the horse and we brought it down as fast as we could, dumping him in the debris down there.' She gave a small shrug. 'It looked like he had been killed by falling rocks. And I was saved.'

Bo had to force the words from her throat. 'That's . . . extraordinary,' she gasped.

'Life often is. It can be more tragic than we deserve, more punishing than we think we can bear.' Their eyes met. 'All you can ever be certain of is that it won't follow the path you envisage. It will force you down roads you don't want to walk, but you just have to trust. Look at me – it took a mountain falling down to save my life.'

Both women stared at one another, understanding each other more deeply than could be explained.

'– Bo?'

She looked back with a start. Anders was standing by the door, concern on his face as he looked over at her. 'Is everything okay?'

'Yes,' she said quickly. 'Your grandmother and I were just . . . talking.'

'We need to head off if we're going to do this. Time is tight.'

'Sure.' She went to stand up but Signy grabbed her hand, forcing her to stay crouched.

'Think about what I have told you,' Signy whispered urgently. 'Let. Destiny. Happen.'

Bo blinked back at her. 'I'll try,' she mumbled, before

making for the door – hoping to God a mountain wouldn't have to fall down in the process.

'Is everything all right?' he asked her, their legs moving in unison as they marched down the path towards Anna and the helicopter. 'You looked upset.'

'No, I'm fine,' she said, glancing up at him, wondering how it could be that he had only been gone an hour and a half for her to have missed him that much. '. . . Your grandmother's really incredible, you know.'

He glanced at her. 'She likes you too.'

'Right? Are we ready to go?' Anna asked, visibly inflating herself with a deep breath as they approached.

'Yes,' Anders nodded curtly.

Bo stared at her, wondering how Anna could stand there and just *act* to Bo's face, for there was no trace of her duplicity in her manner at all. No shame. No seeming regret. Only a sulky sorrow that Zac was giving her nothing more than a few drunken nights.

Not that Bo was standing in judgement of her. How could she after what had happened – was still happening – with Anders? But to cheat and then lie about it so casually . . . ?

He opened the door for them and Anna jumped in first, just as her phone rang. She looked over at them questioningly.

'You'd better take that,' Bo nodded. 'It might be your office.' No doubt they were wanting to add styling tips to her all-white snow-bunny outfit or give direction as to the pictures. After the damage of the last few days, they weren't going to hit ten million for Christmas, but it was still in everyone's interests to make sure today created a big splash.

'Hmm, no – it's an unidentified number,' Anna said, wrinkling her nose.

'Well take it anyway, just in case,' Anders muttered. 'We'll be out of reception over there.'

Anna shrugged and answered it. '. . . *Hei?*' she asked. Bo watched as a frown crumpled her brow before she silently held the phone out to her. 'It's for you.'

'For me?' Bo asked, taking it from her. So then it was Zac? 'Hello?' She frowned. '. . . Who is this?'

Anders took a step closer to her as she turned and looked up at him, open-mouthed.

'. . . Who?'

His arm reached out to her. 'Who is it?' he asked quietly.

'How did you get this number?' Bo stared back at him but she was pale, her attention on the voice in her ear. '. . . You want to do what?' she asked, pressing a hand to her ear. The reception was patchy. She couldn't hear very—

She fell silent again, listening to the voice but keeping her gaze on Anders all the while. His expression was concerned, focused. She was the only thing he could see. 'Where are you?'

Anders held his hand out. 'Give me the phone. I will deal with him.'

But she shook her head fractionally. '. . . Hello? Hello, are you there?' She took the phone from her ear, checking the screen before looking back at him. 'The signal's gone.'

'Who was it? Was it Him?'

She was silent for a moment, trying to absorb what had happened. 'I . . . I don't know.' She frowned, concentrating.

'Bo?'

'He said his name was Antonio Spandelli; he owns a small magazine here called *Northern Spirit*. He wants to interview me.'

'Interview you?' The word hung in the air like a pomander,

wariness drifting from it like a scent. 'That could just be a cover story. Something to bring you to him.' Like offering to help carry a heavy box . . .

Anders was standing close, his concern radiating from him like a white light and drawing Anna's attention. Bo felt her look between them both questioningly.

'I don't know,' she murmured, trying to examine her instincts. 'He didn't *sound* suspicious. He said his wife's from Eidesdal?'

'Yes, that's in the next valley.' He was watching her so intently, Bo wasn't sure he'd even blinked.

'He said they're over from Oslo to spend Christmas here. He follows us on Insta and recognized some of the locations in our posts. He wants to set something up whilst we're all in the area. He said he's been trying to track me down himself because he thought he'd have a better chance of success if he could pitch it to us in person, and that he'd enquired in the shop when he went in with his wife. When that failed, he contacted Ridge Riders, who gave him Anna's number.'

Anders looked down and a few seconds later held up the screen for her to see – he had googled Antonio Spandelli, proprietor of *Northern Spirit* magazine: salt-and-pepper hair, bespectacled, soulful brown eyes, a good head of hair for a man in his late fifties, early sixties. He certainly didn't look menacing. 'Did he sound like he looked like that?'

'Can you sound like a look?' she asked, a small laugh escaping her as relief began to take a hold, for in spite of it, he *had* sounded like he looked – bookish, considered, polite. And his wife had been with him – a small detail Stale had omitted but which made all the difference surely? 'But yes, I'd say so.'

'So you think Spandelli is not Him? *He's* not here?'

She heard the unspoken question – 'you don't have to leave?' – and she knew that if this was a reprieve, it was only a brief one. She had to tell him her latest discovery, before he began to believe, to hope . . . 'He may not be in Gerainger, no; but he's still somewhere close.'

'How can you know that?'

She swallowed, glancing over at Anna, and – not caring about being rude – pulled him by the arm, away from her so that they could speak more privately. The suspicion on Anna's face instantly magnified tenfold.

'I didn't want to tell you this, but He posted something again while we were in Alesund – it was about what I was wearing that night, something that couldn't be seen in the footage. It meant he had to have been there that night, that he was nearby.'

She watched the light go out in him again. 'But if he was that close to you and yet he still didn't do anything, he didn't try to talk to you . . . what does he *want*?' Anders asked in exasperation.

'He's watching me. Keeping me close. It's what he does.'

'But why? Why you?' His frustration had seeped out now and he dropped his head in his hands, tension like a harness across his back.

'I don't know,' she whispered, clutching his forearm, hating that she was putting him through this. He had been here before and suffered enough for four lifetimes. He deserved some happiness, some peace.

'Is everything okay?' Anna called over.

They ignored her. He took a deep breath, regaining focus. 'We need . . . we need to dial it back. If he's that close, then surely you'd begin to recognize if the same guy kept popping up wherever you went?'

'I'm vigilant to the point of paranoia,' she said quietly, remembering as she said it Lenny's slurred accusation outside the bar: *You're paranoid*.

'Then there has to be something. Something that tells us who he is.' Bo watched him, seeing his desperation to work it out, his need to help. 'You said he started up again when you got here. But when exactly?'

She thought back. '. . . It was the first or second night, I think . . . Yes, the second. He said he was back; had I missed him.' She shrugged helplessly.

'Like he was reintroducing himself then. Putting you on notice. Warning you.'

'Yes, exactly.'

'So why *then*? What happened that day?'

'Uh . . .' She frowned, thinking hard. 'Nothing spectacular. We were just here, getting set up, I think. The boys went into town to get food and supplies. Anna came back with them. Zac talked you into being our guide . . .' She shrugged. 'That was kind of it.'

He glanced across at Anna; she was sitting side-on on the helicopter bench, watching them intently. 'Could it be something to do with her, then? She was a new element to your lives.'

'Maybe,' Bo said consideringly. Before shaking her head. 'But why should she be a trigger for him? And besides, he wouldn't have known about her then. We didn't really *do* anything that day so I just posted throwbacks – you know, archive footage. He wouldn't have known she was with us.'

He looked at her through slitted eyes. 'Okay, so then not Anna. What was his next message?'

She gave a heavy sigh, hating that she had to think about

it, relive it all. 'Um . . . it was a few days later; the night of Annika and Harald's party.'

'And what did he say?'

She bit her lip, not wanting to say it. 'He called me a slut.'

'A *slut*?' He looked angry. Although he had seen some of the gossip and innuendo that night, she had managed to keep his message a secret, feeling ashamed somehow. 'Why?'

She shrugged. 'I don't know. I was hardly dancing on the tables. It was all carols and children and gingerbreads.' But they knew – she and he – that it had also been the first time she had let her guard down, the aquavit and antibiotics loosening her inhibitions and spurring her to act on her curious pull towards him: to find out what he really thought about her, to know more about his girlfriend.

She saw him remember it too, memories of the 'night that wasn't' as he'd done the gentlemanly thing flashing between them both and she felt the pull towards him increase, like a magnetic charge being turned up. She wanted to touch him, to reach out and feel his skin against hers. But Anna was in the helicopter, looking at them through the door with a puzzled expression.

He blinked back into focus. 'Exactly. So what did you post? . . . You ate the *risengrynsgrot* and got the scalded almond – I remember filming that . . .' He was thinking hard.

'Which reminds me. You owe me a marzipan pig.' But it was no time for jokes and the flash of his intense blue eyes, so stern and protective, made her stomach flip. '. . . I kept posting pictures of you,' she said hesitantly.

'Me? How? When?'

'When you were chatting to some of your neighbours. I'm sorry. Clearly I didn't know anything about your past or I wouldn't have done it. I thought you were just being . . . coy.'

'*Coy?*'

'You were getting a lot of comments from my female followers! They all wanted to know who you were. So I mucked around a bit, taking secret photos of you and uploading them. I did tag the website if that makes it any better? It was just a bit of fun, I thought. Although I guess I had had a few aquavits by then . . .'

But he wasn't listening to her excuses; his eyes had narrowed in thought. 'So – the night he called you a slut was the night you were mainly posting things about me?'

She hesitated. 'Well yeah, I guess. Maybe. Why?'

'Well that's it. If it all started up when you got here, hired me, came out to the party with me –' He looked at her with glittering eyes. 'The trigger is me.'

Chapter Twenty-Seven

The helicopter circled, an eye in the sky, looking down upon the snowy slopes that fell in almost vertical drapes here, the rock face pleating in on itself as the fjord meandered at its base. They were at Sunnylvsfjorden, a sixteen-mile-long, straightish channel which was the next fjord up from Geraingerfjord and led on to the greater Storfjord and the sea. The sky was clear, the light so blindingly pure that it felt to Bo that they were set within a brilliant-cut diamond – the world around them all hard angles and refracted light.

She had wanted to stay up there with him. It felt safe in the sky, all the dangers and threats on the ground reduced to mere specks. And as they had swooped above the fjord, their downdraught splaying concentric circles on the skin of the water, heading for the fabled Mount Åkernes, Anders had pointed out another shelf farm at the base of its slopes, telling her it had been unoccupied since the 1950s. Was that the farmer on whose land Signy's husband had hunted, she wondered, and who had first spotted the widening crevasse? The buildings, all turf-roofed and blackened timbers too, were set on a ledge much closer to the water than the Jemtegards' farm, but the land above it was so sheer, access from the ridge above would have been nigh-on impossible. They began to rise up the face of the cliff and she could see that when the crevasse did finally split and tear away, the farm would be in the direct run-off zone. It would be obliterated. Little wonder it had been abandoned.

The crevasse itself had been easy to spot from the air – a black scar against the white cliffs, but so much longer than she had anticipated at almost a kilometre long. All sense of scale was lost against these massive mountains when there was nothing to use for gauging perspective – not a house or car, dog or bike – and when she first spotted Zac and Lenny's neon orange rope, it had looked more like a thread, barely discernible against the vast terrain, like a single bright hair on a granite floor. It was almost impossible to fathom how they could be scaling it, and she tried to imagine both of them straining, bodies flexed, pitching themselves against gravity and the elements, seemingly fighting for something more than just a summit.

Beside her, Anders brought the chopper steadily down with customary focus, his eyes dead ahead as he made for the small concrete-cubed monitoring station, the only thing clinging to these slopes. They touched down lightly, the blades slowing into silence, and Bo looked out at the vast view. It took her breath away, as it always did, but this time she tried to memorize it, inhale it, taste it. In a few hours, she would be gone from here and she didn't know how she could capture it or take a slice of it with her. Not through a picture, that much she knew. She hadn't posted a single image since the selfie in the coffee house in Alesund and everything that had happened since with Anders: it was her secret, something rare and all the more special for being kept private. She didn't want to share any of it with the world. She wanted to protect it and keep it as her own, a pearl in her pocket.

'So the guys are going to approach from the west and we're

dropping in at the east end, is that right?' Anna asked as they jumped down, all of them pulling up their hoods and bracing against the chill. It was gusty at this altitude, the drop before them frighteningly steep. A short scramble down from where they stood was the opening to the crevasse.

Anders gave a baffled shrug. 'That's what they said, to meet them in the middle.'

'Do we have time for all that? Didn't you say the authorities would send in security?' Bo frowned, peering down at the great chasm. The walls were rippled with thick ice and the snowdrifts on the ground looked deep. 'I thought we were just getting the money shot and then going? Our flight's at seven.'

Anders went still at her words. It was eleven now.

'You're actually flying out tonight?' Anna asked her, dismay on her face too, the mask slipping.

Bo nodded. She didn't hate Anna for what she'd done; she felt sorry for her: Anna had been swept off her feet and then dropped from a height. Things had become personal and everyone was hurt. There were no winners in this sorry mess.

'How long have we got?' Bo asked, looking over at Anders. He was standing over the lip of the crevasse and staring into it, assessing the conditions.

'Forty minutes to an hour, maximum. There will be cameras everywhere so they'll see us. They're probably watching us now.' He scanned the desolate spot, taking in the steel towers supporting probes, sensors and boreholes. 'But hopefully by the time they can send anyone up here, we'll be gone . . .' He crouched down, carefully turning to face into the rock before lowering himself and dropping gently into the snow. He reached his arms up for the others. Anna went first, then Bo, his hands lingering ever so fractionally on her waist after she was set safely down.

'Follow me,' he said, leading from the front. 'It will be uneven underfoot. There are boulders and rocks under this snowpack, so tread carefully. You don't want your foot to go through. A broken ankle up here would be bad news.'

Bo rolled her eyes with a smile. 'I'm going to call you Mr Brightside,' she teased, prompting him to cast her an intimate glance – one which sent Anna looking between them both again.

It was like being in an ice cathedral, their voices amplifying in the narrow space. The crevasse was neither straight nor smooth and, in places, the ice was layered into thick, organic bulbous forms. They walked slowly and carefully, passing between the blue-white walls that stretched high above them, icicles hanging like two-metre daggers as thick as her arm. They staggered through in wondrous silence, only the occasional 'careful' coming from Anders every few minutes as he pointed out where they should tread.

'How will we know where to stop?' she asked after a while. It felt already like they had been walking for ages but the entire crevasse was only seven hundred metres long and if they were meeting halfway . . .

'I don't think we'll be able to miss them,' Anna said, a trace of sarcasm in her words.

They carried on, walking awkwardly along the mountain's icy corridor. It was slow going, especially because they kept looking around them. Bo had never been in anything like this before and a couple of times she had to remind herself to close her mouth – 'catching flies, darling?' her mother would say – as she caught the familiar red flash of Anna's camera recording her. It shouldn't have surprised her; this was their big finale, the dramatic denouement for Ridge Riders, and Bo had to admit that, in spite of her previous doubts about doing this, it made for a spectacular sign-off.

She looked up as often as she could, loving how the vast sky through which they had just glided was now a mere jagged slit above them, the occasional bird flitting across the frame in soaring silence. It was so cold her breath was coming in little clouds as she used her hands for balance against the ridged, rippled, swollen walls. They felt so solid and impermeable, older than time, it was almost impossible to conceive that they wouldn't always be here, that a day was coming when the pressure would become too great and a large part of this mountain would shear off with devastating, destructive power – just as it had that day in 1936, changing the course of Signy's life for ever.

'Damn.' Anders stopped in front of them; ahead was an area of snowed-over scree, from where a small rockfall had walled the pass. It had to be three metres high.

'Bugger,' Bo said, her hands on her hips as she saw the obstacle in their way, predicting no way through.

'It's fine.' Anders scrambled halfway up, using his hands as well as his feet – though the rocks were icy, there was just enough grip and he reached down to pull them both up in turn. Bo let Anna go first, knowing that his eyes would meet and remain locked on hers for another precious moment if Anna went ahead. These were their dying minutes together and she was greedy for as many as she could get.

But they didn't get the chance.

'Oh my God,' Anna gasped, standing on top of the snow-heap and looking down on the other side.

'What? What is it?' Bo asked, staggering up the last few steps herself.

Her jaw dropped down again – forgetting all about pro-
verbial flies – as she took in the extraordinary scene laid out
there. A couple of small benches had been cut from the snow
like igloo blocks and draped with reindeer hides; strings of
tiny white fairy lights were attached to the ice by climbing
nails; a bottle of champagne was plunged into a well of
snow. And Zac, he was standing there in his all-black layers,
looking as proud as a teenage boy who'd made his own bed.
Lenny was standing further back and taking photos, another
camera set up on a tripod beside him, its red light flashing.
Obviously.

'Oh my God . . .' she murmured as Zac stepped forward,
reaching up to help her down the other side. 'What is all this?
Are we having a picnic?' At ground level, it was even more
magical – so beautiful, so bizarre, so crazy and ridiculous. She
knew it would look great on camera, like a stage set from
Narnia.

'No, it's the beginning of our happy ever after,' Zac said,
reaching into his pocket and pulling out something. His hand
curled around it secretly – invitingly – and suddenly she
knew what it was.

The shock landed like a sucker-punch and she felt herself
tense; unbeknownst to him, she had the full picture, she knew
about both Anders and Anna. How could they possibly . . . ?

But then she saw what he was holding. 'A *pebble*?' she
asked, picking it off his palm. It was flat and bean-shaped, as
smooth as satin.

'Not just any. I've been looking for the perfect one since we
got here. Remember I climbed up the waterfall our first day
out here and you got annoyed with me for being a Boy
Scout?' He arched an eyebrow at the memory. 'Well, I needed
the smoothest, most rounded one, and I knew that water

436

pressure would do that for me. I've looked in every river, on every climb out here since.'

'But . . .' She looked up at him, a smile frozen on her lips. She sensed this was a grand romantic gesture but was damned if she knew why. In her peripheral vision, she could see Lenny had stepped forward, his camera trained on them both, intruding on the scene as ever. *'Why?'*

'As a token of love. Did you know Emperor penguins will select the very best pebble they can find and then give it to their mate, and she puts it in their nest? Penguins mate for life, Bo. Like us.'

She knew it was all for the camera, this: reinforcing their brand image, reassuring the fans. She was quiet for a moment, her finger rubbing over the polished stone. 'But penguins are also monogamous,' she said quietly, so quietly only he could hear.

'Huh?' He missed a beat, looking confused. But as she continued to look up at him, his smile faltered. '. . . I think you're missing the point, baby.' He laughed, but it sounded forced.

She stepped around him, wanting to see the set more closely. How had they carried these things up here on their backs – the hides, the champagne? And how long had it taken to carve out the benches? The snow shovels were lying on the ground further back, she could see. They must have been weighed down by it all.

From behind her, Zac spoke, looking flustered. 'Look, forget about the stone. And the penguins. What I'm trying to do here – what this is all about is . . .' She turned and saw that he had dropped down to one knee and was holding out a red box. 'Bo Loxley, will you marry me?'

'Oh God.' Her hands flew to her mouth and she stepped back as though in retreat. The shock was real. The bluff a second earlier had taken her off her guard and made her relax, but now she felt everyone's gaze on her, all of them – Anders, Anna, Lenny, Zac and nearly ten million strangers – wanting to see her reaction. She looked up and saw Anders, still at the top of the snow hill and keeping out of the shots. But his expression was open, more revealing than she had ever seen, sheer desolation barrelling through him as he watched the carefully staged scene unfold.

She had forgotten all about it, the dummy proposal, but she saw Zac must have been planning this since they got here. Him and Lenny. The champagne, these props, that ring. Had they bought it all in Alesund for her?

'Well . . . ?' Zac prompted her. 'Don't keep a guy hanging. It's cold down here.' He laughed but as her sorry gaze met his, she saw a flash of fear pass over his face. 'Just a straight yes or no would be good.'

She stared at him, tears swimming in her eyes and feeling the adrenaline coursing through her. She knew what she was supposed to say, do. Look surprised! Say yes! This was just a re-enactment, a public show of their private moment, giving the fans what they wanted; they were even dressed as bride and groom, she realized – him in black, her in all-white. Because this was damage limitation, an overblown romantic statement to make up for the messiness of their argument on the streets in Alesund.

She saw Lenny beginning to creep around them, finding the best angle, getting the best shot. 'That's not live recording is it?' she whispered, watching the red light flash.

'Huh?' Zac was looking openly panicked now.

She jerked her head towards the camera on the tripod. 'You're not doing a live video? Please say you're not.'

'Bo, what's going on?' Zac mumbled, trying not to move his lips, to keep his smile stitched on. 'Of course it's live.'

She closed her eyes. And there it was. *Of course.* 'Of course it is. Naturally. Why wouldn't it be?' She turned away, feeling her humiliation stretch around the world. Just say the words, she told herself. Play the part. Do what needs to be done and it'll be over. Say it. Say it!

SAY it!

She dropped her face in her hands and turned away.

'Bo?' Zac got up from his bended knee and stood before her. 'What's going on?' he asked in a low voice, angling himself away from the camera but still trying not to move his lips. 'We've already done this for real. You know what this is. You already said yes.'

She stared at him, tears beginning to shine in her eyes. 'And now I'm saying no,' she whispered.

'*What?*' His expression changed then and he whirled around, pointing at Lenny to stop filming. Bo saw Anna's hand drop too, Ridge Riders' dramatic moment falling flat on its face. 'What the actual fuck? You're saying no, after you already said yes?'

'Yes.'

He shook his head, looking confused, as though she was speaking in riddles.

'I can't marry you, Zac. I thought I could. I thought it was what I wanted. But . . . everything's different now.'

'In the space of three weeks?' he asked, incredulous.

She nodded. 'Everything you said to me in the cabin the other day – you were right. Bang on. I didn't want to face up to it but I have been running. This has all been an escape. What we've had has been *so* great up till now, it was what I

439

needed. And you too. But other people have come between us, which they couldn't have done if things were right –'

He paled, glancing at Anna.

'It's not about her. It's about us and what *isn't* there. I keep trying to set up a life with you, Zac, only it isn't a life – it's a feature. And we're not a couple, we're a brand. Something changed somewhere along the way for us – the tail started wagging the dog. I don't know when exactly but—'

'I do.'

They all whipped round to see Lenny standing with his arms hanging limply by his sides.

'Len, mate, this isn't the time,' Zac snapped.

But Lenny advanced, ignoring him, his focus pinned only on Bo. 'I know exactly when things changed. It was when we got here.'

'I've been unhappy for longer than that, Lenny,' she said dismissively.

'With *me* being around, hell yeah, I know, you always made your feelings very clear on that. But I'm talking about when your feelings for Zac changed.'

Bo frowned. 'How can you know that, if even *I* don't?'

'Because I saw it, Bo,' he sneered. 'I saw it happen.'

'Saw what?'

Lenny switched his attention back to Zac. 'You've seen it too, bud, I know you have. You've sensed what was happening; that's why you hate him so much. You knew he was *sniffing* around her.'

Slowly, Bo turned to look at Anders. Zac too. He was still on the top of the snow-pile, keeping out of shot, out of the way, but his expression had changed. Where before it had been open, showing her everything, now he was locked up and bolted shut, standing ominously still. Predator and prey all at once.

'Yeah, that's right. You know it,' Lenny snarled, seeing understanding dawn across Zac's features. 'Whilst she's pointing the finger at you for having a roll in the hay with her over there, she's been rutting like a bitch in heat with him.'

Bo gasped, feeling winded by his barely contained aggression, his coarse language. Their relationship had always been tricky – sometimes peaceable and benign, often fractious and low-grade irritable – but she saw now, it was more than that; bigger and far worse. He actually hated her.

'She was with him last night, man. I saw the tracks in the snow outside the bedroom window. He must've jumped when we got back.'

Bo's heart beat faster as she saw Zac's expression change, his lips twisting into a snarl. She saw Anders begin to come down the slope, ready to face him, but she stopped him with a hand. She wouldn't have him embroiled in this, risking his parole conditions.

'What the fuck, man?' Zac asked as he stared at Anders, wanting the details, not wanting them. 'What's going on?'

'You're being played for a fool, is what,' Lenny said, prodding, inciting him. 'I saw it all happen, right from the first moment when we were standing outside his house, waiting for him to fucking answer the door; I happened to look over at her just as he came out and I saw how her face changed.' He clicked his fingers. 'Just like that. Bam! Job done!'

'No . . .' Zac protested feebly.

'You *happened* to be looking at her?' Anders asked, his voice cool.

'Yeah.' Lenny turned to face him, a sneer twisting his mouth. 'And then the very next day, when we got back from town and there they were, cosying up in his cabin, talking intimately together like it was a first date—'

'His grandmother was there!' Bo interjected with a disbelieving laugh. He couldn't be serious!

But Lenny didn't hear – or care. His eyes were on Anders but he was talking to Zac. 'He was already making his first move – setting up his ducks. Then, of course, he got to play the hero – *saving* her in the waterfall, *marching* back for the boat, *flying* her back to safety. How you gonna compete with that, huh? You knew you couldn't. You knew – at some level you knew – what was happening down at his house, her all alone with him.'

'No—' Zac protested again, but his voice was clouded, confused, as Lenny led him on like a bull, waving the red flags around . . .

'Yes, mate,' Lenny insisted. 'It's why you copped off with her –' He jerked his head towards Anna again, not bothering to even grace her with a name. 'Getting her drunk.'

'*You* were the one refilling everyone's glasses!' Anna cried, her face blotchy with silent tears, anger and humiliation bursting from her in equal measure.

'Yeah, but you wanted it and so did he. I could read the signals. He knew what was going down and he needed to salvage a little pride. I get that!' He shrugged. 'And I'm always happy to play MC – whatever keeps these guys on track, I'm the wingman. Trust me, you're not the first indiscretion he's had, baby, not by a long shot.'

He looked over at Bo, expecting to see the hurt wash over her, but she was braced. This, at least, she already knew.

'Len, shut the fuck up!' Zac shouted as the secrets were spilled like a kicked bucket of milk. 'What the hell is wrong with you?'

'What's wrong with *me*? None of this is about me! I'm just calling it. I've been dragged from pillar to post, having to watch on as you both fuck up the best thing you ever had! It was obvious what was going on between them. If I could see it, why couldn't you?'

There was a sudden pause, the question hanging in the air like a chandelier.

'Because you're obsessed with her, that's why.' Anders' voice was suddenly very close and Bo turned to see he had come down the slope and was now level with them. Silently, as they had shouted and railed, he had brought himself into the frame. He was in shot. 'The reason *you* saw all this, and no one else did, is because you watch her all the time. If it's not your eyes on her, it's your camera. Always clicking. Always recording.'

'Yeah! Cos it's my fucking job!' Lenny spat.

'No.' The word was simple, clear. 'You *got* the job because it enabled you to watch her, it gave you a cover story. It got you close to her.'

What? Bo felt her heart forget to beat, the blood pooling at her feet as she looked in panic from Anders to Lenny to Zac. Was that true? Was that what he had been doing? All this time? Was he . . . was he Him?

She remembered all the photographs he had taken of her sleeping, in the bath . . . Inappropriate. Intrusive. All those times she had been unaware he was there, as well as the many, many times when she was. And that vague uneasiness she sometimes felt around him that she couldn't shake off or understand. '*Was* it just coincidence that day on the beach –' she whispered. 'When you got talking to Zac?'

He glanced across at her but didn't reply. He was watching Anders watching him, knowing he was a convicted killer, a man who had killed another in trying to protect the woman he loved. He knew full well Anders wasn't a man to test.

'Mate?' Zac asked, punching Lenny lightly on the shoulder – it was a brotherly gesture and yet also a warning – demanding his attention, wanting his denial.

The two men, old friends looked at each other then, the doubt creeping into Zac's eyes, and Lenny changed. He grew, like a snake shedding its skin and wriggling into a new guise, with fresher colours. Becoming its true self.

It was all the confirmation Bo needed and a sob escaped her, fright, disbelief and anger marbled into one strangled sound. Lenny was Him. He'd been right there, all this time.

'What?' Lenny shrugged, seeing the horror set in her features. 'You're my family, both of you.' He looked across at Zac, as if he'd understand it at least. 'She didn't want me but when she met you, you made her happy and I saw that. I accepted it. I found a way to make it work.'

'Make what work?'

'For us all to be together.'

There was a horrified pause.

'What do you mean I *didn't want you*?' Bo whispered.

Lenny looked back at her again and she felt that visceral retreat through her body she got whenever their eyes met. 'In Sri Lanka, when I asked you for a drink.'

'. . . But I never met you in Sri Lanka.'

'Sure you did. I was your waiter. I asked if you'd like to go for a drink when I finished my shift. But you said you had some fucking meeting you had to go to with sponsors.'

Bo looked at him blankly.

He gave a bitter laugh. 'And you don't even remember. The biggest fucking moment of my life – I felt like I was about to freaking ask you to marry me I was shaking so much, and you don't even remember it.' He shook his head. 'Of course you don't . . .'

Bo was trembling now. He was mad. Actually mad.

'Not that you went to any meeting. I followed you that night. You just went back to your room. You had lied to me. Rejected me.' He shrugged. 'But at least then I had your room number.'

Bo swallowed. 'You worked at the hotel I was staying in?' she whispered. That was how he had got into her room?

'Quit my job the very same day and just started . . . trailing around after you. It was so easy and I'd been saving up to travel anyway so I decided to just go wherever you did: Java, Sumatra . . . It seemed a simple enough plan and I thought something would happen, another way for us to meet again, only this time when I wasn't fucking serving you. I figured we just needed to meet as equals. But no.' He scoffed. 'No. Fate had other ideas. Six weeks later, you met our man Zac and that was that.'

Bo felt she might throw up. He had been trailing her, country to country? It was worse than she'd even imagined.

He slid his jaw to the side, looking at Zac with appraising eyes. 'God, I fucking hated you at first, man; I hated on you for a long time. I used to fantasize about what I'd do to you if I got you alone. I saw you eyeing up those other chicks every time her back was turned. You didn't know you were born, landing a girl like her . . .' His eyes glittered with repressed rage, his mouth drawn into a mean line. 'But then the weirdest damn thing went and happened: you noticed me, you *finally* noticed me and dragged me into that volleyball game that day. And when you turned your attention onto me, I saw what she saw. I couldn't hate you. I wanted to, but fuck! I think I even fell for you myself.' He gave a hollow laugh, the sound ringing through the ice tunnel. 'And that was when I had the idea. It was like this sudden epiphany: it could be the three of us. Not quite the way I wanted it –'

His eyes skimmed over Bo, raking up and down her like greedy fingers, and she gave a horrified sob as a memory suddenly burst through – not of him serving her in a waiter's uniform in Sri Lanka but the actual touch of him: his searching hands upon her cold skin, his hungry breath on her neck, as she had huddled deliriously against him by the waterfall that day. Everything had been so confused as the snow whirled around them dizzingly, her drifting in and out of consciousness as he kept talking to her all the while, his hands roaming under her clothes in the name of sharing body heat.

He saw her disgust and stepped closer, as though reading her fear as desire. 'No, it wasn't what I wanted but it was the next best thing – at least for the short term. It would do until I could get you to see what he was really like. We would become a family and I would keep us all together. I would let him get away with cheating on you, I would even cover for him; I would protect you from his lies and keep from you what he really was like and how little he truly loved you, until I had proved to you beyond doubt how much better *I* could look after you. That I was the better man.' He beat his chest with his fist. 'I did all that for you Bo, because you deserved more than someone like him. I kept you safe from his cheating ways.' He gave a snort of contempt, shaking his head slightly. 'Only it turns out, it wasn't *his* lies I should have been watching out for. He isn't the one who ruined it all. You are. You've destroyed us.'

A tear slid down her cheek as she saw what a lie, a twisted fantasy, this life they had all shared together had really been. And, yes, she had ruined it: she had fallen in love with someone else; she had said 'no' to him and 'no' to Zac; worst of all, she had said 'no' in front of ten million people, blowing up the brand for good – there would be no coming back from it now. They were all out of a job.

'You're sick, Lenny, you need help,' Bo whispered, stepping back.

She didn't see the punch coming and nor did he, as he flew backwards, his back slamming against the ice walls and sending him sprawling to the ground. Blood gushed onto the snow, seeping and spreading into its pristine purity – staining it and changing it forever, as he had done to them. They all stared, dispassionate. Calm. Disgusted.

'You – you broke my nose!' Lenny gasped, cupping his hands to his face as the blood poured.

'Yeah,' Zac murmured, shaking out his hand. 'Consider yourself lucky.'

Chapter Twenty-Eight

Hjelle, 27 miles away,
30 September 1936, two weeks later

Signy sat on the bed, their voices muffled behind the door. They were the grown-ups now, but she was still the child. Even after what she had done, she was the baby. Little Signy Reiten.

The men's voices were calm, Mons still talking with a slight lisp – his facial fractures would take a long time to heal but she wasn't sure his guilt ever would. Margit had told him over and over that he had nothing to feel guilty for, that she was fine; but it was Signy who still shared a bed with her here, Signy who was startled awake every night by her sister thrashing and flailing as she fought Rag in her dreams.

Signy thought it odd that she didn't have nightmares about him too and she wondered if she would ever dream again at all. Her nights were simply black oblivion. She didn't see his face or reimagine the sound of his skull caving against the whetstone. She simply closed her eyes – and fell.

Perhaps it would be different for Margit tonight, though. Mons would sleep beside her then and Signy – well, where would she be by then?

The Christmas Lights

The door opened and Mons looked in, just about able to smile. 'Come out, Signy.'

She rose and walked into the main room, Margit looking radiant in her borrowed dress. It was a little too big – they had all lost weight in recent weeks – but it was white, and she had a simple net veil pushed back, a posy of flowers in her hands just like the one he had given her at Midsummer's.

But as ever, it was to Nils that Signy's eyes strayed. He was wearing his uncle's suit, his blonde hair combed for once, and he was looking anxious, as though he might yet lose the mercurial woman he wanted for his bride. Sofie was sitting on a chair, her gaze on the floor as it so often was now; her dark hair still gleamed and the perfectly symmetrical arrangement of features still pleased, but something – a light – had gone out in her; the rose had lost its bloom. Her dress was a drop-waisted style that did little to flatter her figure, but it hid the bump that was fast becoming noticeable and Signy noted that she would have needed to be married quickly even without everything that had come after that dreadful night. Without a ring to accessorize that bump, her reputation and future would have been marked.

But Sofie was lucky as well as beautiful. She needed a father to legitimize this baby, she needed a husband to support them, and Nils loved her. In spite of his profound dismay on learning of her condition, he had rallied. Or perhaps he had known and understood that it was only the fact of the baby that would make her his and that was why he loved the child already. Sofie didn't know what she had won, only what she had lost. She cried and she railed, she threw things and screamed, but Nils wasn't deterred. He loved her enough for the both of them.

'Signy, we have decided that you will stay with us,' Mons

449

said, his voice dragging her attention off Nils. 'Although Sofie feels she will need help with the baby, she will be fine. She will manage. Women do it all the time.' He looked across at Sofie reassuringly but she kept her gaze down, bitterness and resentment setting her bones that the care of this baby should fall to her.

'I need you with me,' Margit said, coming over and clasping her by the hands. 'I know it's selfish of me, taking you to the city; you're such a country mouse, it's where you belong. But I need to keep you close; we're all the family we have now and I couldn't . . . I couldn't bear to be even a mile from you, much less fifty.'

A sob escaped Signy as she flung her arms around her sister's waist. 'I couldn't bear it either,' she cried, relief making her knees shake. The double wedding today was hard enough to bear but she would rather never see Nils again than have to live as a little sister with him and his wife, for life was grinding onwards – the endless deaths and funerals of the past few weeks making way for the new cycle of marriages and birth. They all needed to rebuild, to continue putting one foot in front of the other. Nils had bought a small shelf farm on Geraingerfjorden for his little family, Mons had found a job with a horologist in Alesund, and when the priest pronounced their two couples 'man and wife' this afternoon, they would be parted at last. For always.

'Our home is your home and you will live with us for as long as you want,' Margit said, clutching her tightly. 'All your life if that is what you wish.'

'Or at least until you are married,' Mons chuckled, looking a little nervous.

But Signy knew she would never marry. Margit was all she had left in the world. She had lost her parents, her brother and now, today, she was losing the only man she would ever love. She knew that fact in her bones as she stared at him from her sister's embrace as if for the last time. It was as indisputable as the sun in the sky. 'Deeds grow into Destiny', that was what her father had always said, and fate had played a cruel hand here – trapping Sofie who so desperately wanted to escape the life she was born to, whilst setting Signy free in the very fullest sense, for she would be always alone now, she would never belong to another.

A life for a life. It was the price she had to pay.

* * *

The landing skids touched the ground, the helicopter tipping slightly forwards, then backwards, settling lightly like a bee on a flower. Zac threw open the door and jumped down, pulling the rucksacks out behind him before reaching up his arm. Anna, closest to him, took it and jumped, landing awkwardly, and with her hands over her head, ran in a ducked position out of the downdraft.

'Bo!' Zac shouted up to her, his arm raised again.

Bo looked over at Anders, sitting in the pilot's seat in front of her. His head was angled back slightly, like a cab driver waiting for his passenger's instructions. He was wearing his ear defenders, his face set in the closed look he had worn the first time they met.

He had landed at the heliport for Alesund airport and she felt the panic rear up in her again that this was actually happening. She was really leaving him? It felt diabolical, against nature, against every instinct – and yet a chain of events had been set into motion and she couldn't seem to find a way to stop it now,

She wanted to reach out and touch him one last time, she wanted to feel his hand over hers, but it was impossible. Zac was right there, watching and waiting, and even though he knew about them, he didn't really know. He had no idea of the scale of what they had become.

'*Takk*,' she said in a quiet voice, her words carrying straight to him over the PA system. It was a small and inadequate word, but then what words could suffice? Not 'goodbye'. Not 'I'll miss you'. Not 'I'm sorry'. Nothing could fill this vacuum they were creating, this gaping hole in both their lives.

She saw the ball pulse in his jaw, emotions raging in him too. He gave the smallest nod, for what good were thanks to him? But it was the only word of his language available to her. Her Norwegian didn't extend much past this, apart from *Brod*. And *Ost*. And they had no context here beyond the memories to which they were now attached, that twenty-four-hour period in which the two of them had submitted fully, already but a dream.

'*Jeg elsker deg*,' he said back, his voice low and close in her ear. She didn't know what it meant but she heard the tenderness in it.

'Bo!' Zac shouted again.

She looked down at him, having forgotten he was standing there, braced against the punishing downdrafts, his arm still reaching out and up to her. She slipped the earphones off and let his hand grab hers, and in the next moment she was outside too.

'Thanks man – I guess!' Zac shouted with a hapless shrug. What else could he say? It hadn't been a conventional encounter between them but he could afford to be magnanimous in the end; he had got the girl.

Bo didn't want to move away from the chopper, she

wanted to stay there, to see Anders' face for one minute more, to let her gaze tangle with his for the last time, but the G-force was impossible to withstand, the noise an imperative to run, forcing her over to where Anna now stood. By the time she turned back, her hair flailing and whipping wildly, Zac was crouched and running over too, the helicopter already pulling up from the ground, Anders indistinguishable behind the reflection of the glass. She watched in teary silence as he rose up, up. Away. Putting air between them. Space. Soon it would be another city. And then another country. Another continent. And they would all go back to the lives they had carelessly dropped a few weeks earlier. They were all back on the right paths again. Regardless of how much it hurt.

Bo stood in the gift shop at the tiny airport, browsing blindly, her head turning every few seconds to check the departures screen outside. It was flashing green with 'boarding' for the flight to Oslo. She did another scan of the gate but it was deserted – Lenny hadn't made it back in time after all. She and Zac had agreed to delay boarding until the last minute, just to be sure. They wouldn't get on any plane he was on.

They had left him in the crevasse with the ropes and climbing equipment, Zac returning to the farm with her, Anna and Anders in the helicopter for a quick turnaround back at the farm before they made this dash for the airport. But still, there was a chance he might make it. Climbing down the other side of Mount Åkernes would have brought him not far from Stranda and if he hitch-hiked his way into town – which was an hour closer, up the road from Gerainger – he could still get a taxi to here. She wouldn't put it past him. None of them would put anything past him now.

How long had he stayed there after they'd left? Bo kept

imagining the scene that would await the scientists when they returned to work after the Christmas break – blood stains, a bottle of Dom and some reindeer hides halfway along a chasm. What would they think had happened there? They could never guess the truth – a fake wedding proposal, live-streamed globally and ending in a fist-fight.

No one had spoken on the helicopter flight back to the farm, all of them in shock, all out of words: Zac stunned; Anna ashamed; Bo horrified; Anders stoic, doing what had to be done. When they had reached the farm, he had watched in silence from his grandmother's cabin – Signy rocking agitatedly in her chair at the window beside him – as she and Zac had packed quickly, Bo rushing to make sure everything was left as beautifully as they had found it; Zac talking, explaining, pleading.

The truth about Lenny's actions seemed to have acted as a plaster for him, sticking the two of them back together again; for what Lenny had done, he had done to them both – they had each been exploited and manipulated by him and that must have changed everything, surely, having him at the beating heart of their lives? He had sucked away their intimacy, their joy; they would have been okay were it not for him. Zac was already blaming himself for having not listened to her concerns, for bringing him into the fold, even though blame didn't help anyone now. What was done was passed; didn't they owe it to themselves to at least try again, he kept asking. Forget the proposal, the weight of history was on their side; they had shared so much together. They could again be what they had been once before. Couldn't they?

Bo didn't know what to think. She couldn't think. She could only keep moving. That was what she always did – put distance between herself and trauma; it was distraction, perpetual motion. All she knew was she had to get away from Lenny once and for all. She had to leave here and go somewhere where he could never find her again. For three years she had been caught in a net and not even known it, thrashing without understanding why, her instincts vibrating, trying to tell her that something was wrong, but at too high a frequency to hear.

Escaping, travelling . . . it was all one and the same to her, it was what she knew, her path to safety. It had worked for her after Jamie died and it would work now. She was free again but there was no joy in it. She couldn't exult in the way Zac did because for her, somehow, this freedom always came at a cost: she had to lose someone close first, someone vital.

She closed her eyes, reliving the last moment with Anders, his face in profile, their final words mere formalities. *Takk*. The sheer inadequacy of it made her wince. But that goodbye had been as fake as Zac's proposal. The real farewell had happened earlier, out of sight. He had followed her after she'd given him and his grandmother their wrapped gifts, finding her by the log shed as she had gone to bring in a new load, ready for the next incumbents in the spring; and in those long, silent moments before their final desperate kiss, they had just stood looking at each other, knowing that words couldn't explain or save or change things. It was an impossible equation: he couldn't leave and she couldn't stay. He had to look after Signy and she had to shake Lenny off her tail once and for all. It was a cosmic push–pull they couldn't resolve and so she had left him standing by the logs, a requiem playing through his eyes even as her body still sang to his touch.

She looked down blankly at the card she was holding: a clutch of heart-shaped balloons floating from the collar of a puppy. She opened it. *Jeg elsker deg* was written inside.

Jeg elsker . . . ?

An announcement came over the tannoy. 'This is the final call for Flight 803 to Oslo.'

'Bo!'

She looked over and saw Zac standing by the gate, their tickets in his hands, their bags by his feet. He caught her eye and waved her over. Happy. Excited.

She replaced the card in the display and walked back over, but her throat had closed, blood rushing to her head, emotions pushing against her temples, trying to get out.

'It's all clear,' he said as she reached him. 'I've walked the hall three times already. Even checked the toilets. He's not here,' he said with an easy shrug.

'Right.'

Zac shot her a funny look. 'You okay?'

'Of course.'

'Sure? You look upset.'

She shook her head and he wrapped an arm around her. 'Stop worrying, it's all over now baby,' he murmured, kissing her forehead. 'You'll see.' He handed their tickets to the attendant.

They stood in silence for a moment as the woman tapped keys and read the computer screen. Bo felt she was only being kept upright by Zac's arm around her. Was it just her or was it incredibly hot in here?

'Ah, I see here you've been upgraded,' the woman smiled.

'Yes, result!' Zac laughed, giving a little air fist punch. 'Hear that, baby?'

Bo nodded but she wasn't really hearing him. Them. Her head was filled with other voices, other words.

'Speak to my colleague as you board and she'll take you to

456

your seats,' the woman said, handing back their boarding cards.

Zac picked up their bags and moved to go. 'Bo? You good?'

She looked up at him, feeling her heart beginning to jack-hammer against her ribs. '*Jeg elsker deg,*' she said.

'Huh?' he said, looking back at her blankly. But she couldn't say it again, she simply looked back at him, wiling him to know, to tell her, to confirm. She needed someone to say it.

The attendant leaned forward slightly and stage-whispered into the silence: 'She said, "I love you".'

'Aww, I love you too baby,' Zac grinned as he looked down at her, reaching for her hand. 'Now, let's do this!'

She watched as the disembarking passengers walked past on the other side of the glass, their faces shining with contained excitement. It was nine o'clock on Christmas Eve and they had made it home for the holidays – a feat she hadn't yet managed. She had been waiting on standby for several hours now. Zac's flight had left two hours earlier and she had seen three other Oslo flights, all full, take off without her. But they had confirmed a seat for her on this one. The last flight. She had been lucky: it would connect to a London flight that would arrive just before midnight, and although she had managed to book a car online, it would be too late to drive, so she had also booked to stay at an airport hotel for the night and would leave at first light tomorrow. It was a convoluted, expensive and exhausting plan but she had made it work, just.

She looked outside, watching as the plane was de-iced. It was a clear night, although the stars were hidden from view by the runway lights. But she only had to close her eyes to see the Gerainger sky – it felt pressed into her soul.

She wondered what Anders and Signy were doing right now. Well, Signy was probably sleeping, but Anders . . . she thought of him in the cabin; she knew he was staying up there for Christmas. She remembered their last moment again – their dummy goodbye painfully real—

The whine of the tannoy made her look up and she saw a member of the crew lean in to the microphone. They were ready to begin boarding. She picked up her rucksack and joined the queue. It was time to go home.

Christmas Day 2018

She stood at the door, willing herself to knock. Her heart was pounding so hard, it felt like it was going to jump clean out of her chest, but even though she had been over and over the words, reciting what she would say when the door was opened, her mind was blank, her body frozen. It was still so early that the sliver moon was hanging in the dark-tinted sky like a dainty earring, but she hadn't been able to wait another minute more, not for daylight, not for anything.

With a deep breath, she knocked on the door twice and waited. But there was nothing. No sounds from inside. She pulled the zip higher on her yellow jacket and knocked again, stamping her feet as she stood on the spot, her muscles tensing and relaxing with nerves and the cold.

And then she heard it, the sound of footsteps, slow and reluctant at this early hour. The door opened and she looked into the lined, loving face of the woman who knew her best.

She nodded as she looked back at Bo, her eyes shining, delight on her lips. 'I knew you would come.'

*

Bo picked her way across the ground, a light crackling sound reaching her ear intermittently, the smell of smoke twisting through the trees. The first flickers of brightness were reaching up from the horizon with the promise of a fiery dawn, but it was still hard-going in the crepuscular light. She moved slowly through the trees, ducking past the low branches, following the faint sizzling and snapping sounds that grew as she advanced until she came to a clearing where the trees parted in a semicircle, facing out to the water.

He was sitting on a log, elbows propped on his knees, a tin cup in his hands, a small fire dancing in front of him. He turned, rising in silence at the sight of her. She stepped forward, all her words deserting her too as he came over, disbelief written across his face as though she might be an apparition. 'You've come back.' It was a statement rather than a question, as though he was trying to convince himself.

'Yes. I got a taxi back from the airport last night.'

'Last night?' He looked concerned. 'So then where did you sleep?' Always so practical.

She bit her lip, feeling a smile creep into her eyes. 'At yours, before kayaking up the fjord this morning.'

'You broke into my house?' Anders looked bemused.

'Well I do know where you keep your keys.' She shrugged, her eyes greedy with the sight of him. Had it really only been a day?

His eyes narrowed with concern again. 'It would have been dark on the water. That climb up.'

'In case you hadn't noticed, I've become rather good at facing my fears lately,' she said, making light of the terror she had felt as she'd tied the kayak to the rail, balancing desperately over the black water.

He blinked at the reference to Lenny, remembering how

they had left things yesterday. 'I asked about in town when I returned last night. He didn't come back here. No one's seen him. He's gone.'

She felt her body deflate with relief. It was official then? She was off the grid? 'Thank god.'

His mouth flattened a little, his eyes never leaving her. 'And Zac? Where's he?'

'Also gone.' She swallowed. 'He should be landing in George Town right about now.'

'So then . . . ?' His reserve held, not daring to hope.

'I made him go without me. I told him it was over between us.'

'Because of Anna.'

She nodded. 'And Lenny. And Jamie.'

He frowned. 'Who's Jamie?'

She hesitated for a moment, not wanting to cry. 'My beautiful big brother. Who died four years ago.' She could only say the words in bite-size chunks. Having to swallow down the gulps that always followed them. 'In my arms. And was the reason I left home. And never looked back.'

'Bo.' Sadness suffused the word, blowing through it with love. He went to step closer but she put up a hand to stop him. For once, this wasn't about Jamie; his death had set her on the road but that wasn't why she was here.

'But the main reason I left Zac was because of you. Because I knew I couldn't live pretending I hadn't met you, or that you hadn't changed everything. And even if things could have somehow gone back to how they were before, I didn't want them to.' She realized she was trembling. '*Jeg elsker deg*. Too.' She gave a shy, uncertain laugh but a little sob escaped with it. She felt racked with emotions.

He came up to her then, kissing her with all the same

desperation of their kiss the day before in the log store, when time had been running out and the world was against them – even when he loved her and she loved him.

'I didn't think I would ever see you again,' he said, his true-blue eyes boring into the very soul of her.

'Me neither. It all felt so impossible.'

He kissed her again, staring down at her as though she was a fantastical creature of his imagination. He didn't look like he'd slept. 'Not to my grandmother. She said you would come back. She was certain of it.'

Bo gave a low laugh. 'She did look very unsurprised when she opened the door to me just now. What made her so certain, do you think?'

He gave her one of his wry looks. 'Don't ask me. She kept saying something about Destiny.'

Bo thought about it for a moment. 'Let Destiny happen', she had urged. 'Mmm, well maybe it was.'

'Not you too.'

'Well coming back here wasn't my original plan.'

'Thanks very much.'

'No I mean . . . when I ended things with Zac, I had intended to go home. I felt that was the right thing to do. I rebooked my flight and waited for hours at the airport. I really need to see my parents and spend some time with them. We've got a lot to talk about, things we've been avoiding for too long.' She looked away sadly. 'It would have been so perfect as well – turning up on their doorstep this morning, Christmas Day. The perfect reunion.'

'So what happened?'

She looked up at him with a cocked eyebrow. 'My flight was cancelled due to heavy snow in London – which will mean two or three centimetres.'

He chuckled, the sound reverberating through her.

'But that's enough to bring everything to a standstill over there.'

'You could ring them, explain what happened.'

'I already did. I've booked to fly back the day after tomorrow and we're going to have a Loxely family Christmas then.' She shrugged helplessly. 'I've been away four years. What's another three days?'

'So then that's all I've got you for? Today and tomorrow?' His eyes searched hers.

She reached up and kissed him, pressing her hand to his stubbled cheek, seeing the vulnerability in his eyes, loving him. 'I'll spend a few weeks with Mum and Dad, we all need it. But then I'll come back home.'

'Home? . . . You mean here?'

'Yes.' She pressed her hand to his heart. 'Here. My home is wherever you are.'

He squeezed her hand in his, looking at her intently. 'I have to stay here. For my grandmother.'

'I know.'

'But do you know how small life is here? It's not what you're used to. It's not exciting or glamorous.'

'That's where you're wrong. This –' she lifted her chin to indicate the vast view – 'is the biggest life.' And in that moment she caught sight of the sky and gasped – for there, above their very heads, it had begun to ripple and flicker, waving diaphanous pink and green banners like rhythmic ribbons. Like the mountains and the fjords that had stirred her soul on that first day here just a few weeks ago, so now the sky danced for her dressed in its finest robes. Her hands fluttered to her cheeks as she watched. The Aurora had come at last, Lenny's big dream arriving several hours too late –

perfectly timed. It was too beautiful to capture in a photograph anyway; the heart would remember what the eye could not.

She turned back to him, the colours of the sky reflected in her eyes, the love for this place settling in her like rocks coming to a stop after the mountain fell. 'Who has had a richer life than mine?' Signy had asked.

'This is the richest life I could ever have,' Bo said.

Something in Anders seemed to unblock at that; an inner release valve letting him go. 'Then I will give you something I should have given to you weeks ago.'

'What is it?' she asked, a tentative smile on her lips.

He reached into his coat pocket and pulled something out, turning over his hand. In his palm was a small marzipan pig.

She looked up at him with wide eyes, unable to speak for a moment. 'I really get a marzipan pig?' she finally asked in a half-whisper. It was the question she had asked the night of the party.

'Along with a husband, yes,' Anders replied, repeating his words too, but without irony now; his voice was thick with emotion. 'Harald gave it to me that night but I didn't dare show it to you.'

Her eyes flicked up to him. 'In case it made me stay?'

'In case it made you run.'

'You should be so lucky,' she murmured, stepping into his arms again and reaching for another kiss. 'I'm not going anywhere.'

Epilogue

Geraingerfjord, 22 August 1939

She climbed the path, feeling the unremitting sun on her face and the sea breeze at her back. The going was treacherous, the drop sheer in several places, but her bag was light and her body remembered what it was to climb in these mountains. It had stayed within her like a low-burning candle, never quite burning out.

With her breath coming hard, she stepped from the trees and stood on the ridge, looking up at the buildings. They were handsome and robust – two cabins and a *stabbur*, with long-stemmed wild flowers nodding on the roofs, a cow tethered to a tree and nosing the grass. The land was not quite level but for a shelf farm, on a ridge like this, it was flat enough and they were lucky to have the space they did. She calculated there was a couple of acres in all, enough room to plant some raspberry bushes, a small orchard . . .

The hayricks were already laden, the grassy bleached manes rustling in the breeze, and she heard a shriek come from behind them, a playful sound that made her turn. She walked over, setting down her bag as she reached them and peered around. A little girl in a white smock and red boots was sitting between two rows, playing with a toy as her father tossed the grass from a barrow onto the wires. His shirt lay on the ground, discarded in the heat. Sweat beaded his berry-brown back, his blonde hair uncombed and wild as he pitched and tossed.

She smiled at the sight of him. He hadn't changed a bit.

'*Hei!*'

The little girl's excited greeting made them both start, Nils turning around quickly, his mouth opening in surprise to find her there.

'*Signy?*'

She smiled, raising a hand in a shy wave.

He threw down the pitchfork and walked over, making no disguise of his scrutiny as he stopped in front of her, looking her up and down, and then up again. 'My God, you've changed.'

'Have I?'

He walked around her in a slow circle. 'Yes . . . y-your hair, your clothes . . .' He came back to face her again, looking at her searchingly as though trying to overwrite the vision of her in his memories with this new version before him. 'You're a real city girl now.'

'No,' she said simply.

He looked at her, their eyes meeting properly for the first time, and she felt what she always had: in spite of school and her typing job, her nylons and brassiere, nothing had changed for her. She was as constant as these mountains, and as strong.

But life had taken a bite out of him and as his gaze roamed over her face, she saw the sadness in his eyes, the hollow curve of his cheeks. They were both older than that last day in his aunt and uncle's house before they had all scattered like seeds to their new lives – but where she had grown up, he had aged. Having Sofie for a wife had been disheartening, draining and ultimately futile. She was a storm he had weathered and by the time she had left, he was just happy to have survived. Personally, Signy thought city life would suit her very well.

'It was good of you to come,' he said finally, hoisting up the little girl as she pulled on his trouser leg.

'I am pleased to.' She reached out a finger to the child, who grabbed it eagerly in her hand. She looked exactly as she had imagined she might – plump-cheeked and curious, with her mother's sparkling blue eyes and father's white-shock hair. She would one day be a fine beauty. 'Hello, Eva. I'm Signy.'

She smiled as the little girl reached her arms out, wanting to be held, and Signy pulled her in close, her eyes automatically closing as she smelled the clover on her hair. Overhead, a bird screeched and they all looked up. 'See that?' Signy pointed, her eyes beginning to shine. 'It's a gyrfalcon.'

'Grrfacon,' Eva repeated. She would be three next spring.

Nils raked a hand through his hair, watching her. '. . . I just didn't know who else to ask, you see.'

'Margit gave me your letter. I came as soon as I could.'

He looked down, suddenly catching sight of himself and reaching back quickly for his shirt. He shrugged it on. 'I'm sorry, I would have prepared things for you, only I wasn't expecting you so soon.'

Soon? Three years had passed since the chaos of that summer, since all their lives had been shattered by the events of one night. Things would never be exactly as they had been before, but his letter had been a cue that the world was resettling into position again, moving back to what always should have been, bringing them here. She shrugged. 'Why wait?'

He stared at her, before realizing he was staring at her. '. . . Come,' he said, collecting himself, picking up her bag as

466

she carried his little girl. 'Let me show you your cabin. It's just across the path from ours, so you can still have your space in the evenings but it is also close enough to share meals together – if you would like.'

They walked over the grass together, butterflies flitting at their knees, and she smiled as she looked across at him and felt the sun shine upon her once more. 'I think I would like that very much.'

Acknowledgements

If you've read *Christmas in the Snow*, based in Zermatt in the Swiss Alps, and *Christmas Under the Stars*, based in the Canadian Rockies, you'll know there's nothing I love more than a mountain and a rickety old hut, so here I am again, finding adventures in the hills. Only this time, I was greedy: I wanted to write about the humble beauty of the old shelf farms and the remote wildernesses of the *seters*. The only problem is the latter are, by definition, used in the summer months and this was for my Christmas book.

However, I already knew about nearby Mount Åkernes being the most monitored mountain in the world and I sensed that twinning the risk from the mountain now with the mountains then was a way to get the best of both these worlds. The mountains have indeed fallen in the past: Tafjord on 7 April 1934, and Lodal on 15 January 1905 and 13 September 1936, and whilst I have fictionalized elements within those scenes for the purposes of the plot, the bare facts remain true: innocent lives were lost, communities decimated. Mother Nature won then and she will win again. The risks and threats described in these pages are all too real.

When it comes to writing my books, I'm big on research and visiting the places I write about. However, I felt I had bitten off rather more than I could chew when I visited

Norway in the depths of winter and was unable to get on the water because the ferries don't run off-season and an access road was closed due to snow. It's difficult creating something from nothing at the best of times, but being stuck on the wrong side of a mountain in bad weather certainly doesn't help. Luckily, I had my husband with me to feed me cake and take me skiing; he bravely drives on the wrong side of the road for me, clocks where we can get good coffee and remembers to order foreign currency. He even let me buy the world's most expensive coffee-table book, despite being written entirely in Norwegian, because I said the photographs within were vital for research. They actually were – but he's more vital to me than anything.

Ollie, Will and Plum – just breathe and smile and this world is perfect.

Mum and Dad, you make being the best parents look so easy. I'm still trying to copy you, every day.

Vic and Lynne, thank you for being such amazing grandparents and stepping into the breach whilst we skipped off on our fjord adventure.

My agent, Amanda Preston, you always keep a steady hand on the tiller, helping me plough a straight path from original inspiration to final manuscript. Thank you so much, your advice and opinion is always crucial.

As for my Pan gang, we've been going a long time now. This is our fifteenth book together and it still feels as fresh and exciting as the first. Caroline Hogg, I know you're currently reading this from afar but you read this book when it was delivered in a jelly-like first draft and, as ever, knew how to chip and whittle it into shape. Come back soon! You are missed. The rest of the team – Jez Trevathan, Wayne Brookes, Anna Bond, Katie James, Jonathan Atkins, Stuart Dwyer,

The Christmas Lights

Charlotte Williams, Jade Tolley, Jayne Osborne, Natalie Young, Nicole Foster and Camilla Rockwood – you make hard work such fun; I always enjoy our meetings and the sight of chilled champagne on a conference table!

What larks! Thanks all.